HER RIGHTFUL INHERITANCE

*Also by Benita Brown
and available from Headline:*

A Dream Of Her Own
All Our Tomorrows

HER RIGHTFUL INHERITANCE

Benita Brown

headline

First published in 2002
by HEADLINE BOOK PUBLISHING

A Headline hardback

10 9 8 7 6 5 4 3 2 1

Cataloguing in Publication Data is available from the British Library

ISBN 0 7472 6987 4

Typeset in Times by Avon Dataset Ltd, Bidford-on-Avon, Warks

Printed and bound in Great Britain by
Mackays of Chatham plc, Chatham, Kent

HEADLINE BOOK PUBLISHING
A division of Hodder Headline
338 Euston Road
London NW1 3BH

www.headline.co.uk
www.hodderheadline.com

To Norman, who made all things possible.

Prologue

Newcastle, November 1893

'Look, Lorna, I've caught a leaf!'

Her mother smiled and Lorna thought how beautiful she was, with her pale face, and the wisps of red-gold hair escaping from her fur hat. Her father had said the hat made her mother look like a Russian princess. Now it was tipped forward so that silvery strands of fur trembled over her brow as she laughed. Her pearl drop earrings shone in the misty light.

'You take it,' her mother said. 'Keep it safe. Put it in your muff. You know it's good luck to catch a falling leaf; it means that you will have a long and happy life.'

Lorna took the leaf hesitantly. It was still soft and silky to touch, not like the faded crackling drifts blown up against the railings that marked out the boundary of Heaton Park. She held the leaf by the stem and looked at the streaks of colour spreading out across the green. Yellow and bright red. Sometimes her mother's cheeks burned red just as brightly, and Lorna had come to dread those days of high colour and the cough that left her breathless and frightened.

'But you caught the leaf,' she said. 'It's your luck.'

'I know. But I'm giving it to you.'

'But will it work? I mean, can you give luck to someone else?'

'I'm sure you can. If you love someone as much as I love you. Now, we must go. We've lingered long enough.'

Lorna tucked the leaf in the pocket in the lining of her black fur muff, which hung round her neck on a velvet ribbon. She gave her other hand to her mother. The smooth white kid of her mother's gloves was as soft as her skin. The two of them turned to look once more at the ivy-covered ruins. Two trees with silvery diamond-shaped patches on their trunks towered above the broken walls. A narrow archway led into a

1

forlorn courtyard open to the sky. Her mother had told Lorna that this was all that remained of an old castle.

'Did he really go away and never come back –' Lorna asked – 'Adam, the man who lived in the castle?'

'He went on a crusade to the Holy Land. And after the battle, some say he just stayed there.'

Lorna knew about the crusades. Her father had bought her *The Good Child's Book of History*. 'And did he sail from here?'

'What do you mean, sweetheart?'

'When he went to the crusades. Did his ship leave the river here – just like Father's?'

'I don't think so. I think they all sailed with the King from London.' Her mother placed both her hands on Lorna's shoulders and turned her so that she could look into her face. 'But unlike Adam, your father is coming home, I promise you. Now, let's leave these old ruins and collect your belongings.'

They walked back down a gentle slope to the path. The grass underfoot was crisp; the sun had not been warm enough to loosen the grip of the overnight frost. Mist hung in the branches of the trees, and once or twice her mother looked up at it and shivered. The sound of the carriages and delivery carts on Heaton Road seemed muffled, distant, as if coming from another world. There was no one else in sight. Lorna and her mother were alone here, and that's what they had wanted. For just a little while longer.

Lorna held on to her mother's arm as they climbed a steep set of steps to another level of the park. She pretended it was because she needed help but it was really because she was anxious about her mother; she didn't want her to walk too quickly.

At the top they followed a wide path round to the raised terrace and the pavilion where they had left the two suitcases. The park was deserted and their footsteps echoed eerily. They walked slowly, putting off the moment when they would resume their journey.

'Shall we have one more hot drink?' her mother asked as they passed the kiosk at one end of the pavilion.

'Yes, please.'

'And an iced bun? I'm sure you've got room for another one!'

Lorna looked up into her mother's eyes. They were bright with tears, as were her own. 'Yes, please, with a cherry on. And will you have one too?'

'Of course. Go and sit by your luggage. I'll bring a tray.'

All the other tables set out in the open-sided pavilion were empty, four chairs tipped up neatly around each one. When they had arrived her mother had put Lorna's two suitcases under one of the tables and pulled out two of the chairs. The walk uphill from Heaton station had left her mother out of breath.

To their delight the tea kiosk had been open and her mother had bought two cups of hot chocolate and an iced bun each. Lorna had eaten hers but after a while she'd noticed that her mother was crumbling her bun and throwing most of it to a lone sparrow, which dodged around the table legs.

'Poor thing,' she'd said when she'd seen Lorna watching her. 'He needs it more than I do.'

Now when she came back with the tray Lorna saw that she had only brought one bun. 'The last one,' she said as she placed the plate before Lorna. 'Weren't we lucky?'

Lorna's eyes widened. If that really was the last she wondered who could have bought all the others. The glass counter had been full when they'd first arrived and she certainly hadn't noticed any other customers.

Her mother sat down and sipped her chocolate. 'I used to play in this park when I was a child,' she said. 'With my brother, your Uncle Roger. Roger used to pretend he was king of that old castle – lord of the manor!'

Lorna stared at her mother. She didn't know what to say. She knew that her Uncle Roger had been a soldier who had died long ago before she was born, and that his wife had died too.

Her mother smiled at her. 'I'm sure you will come and play here with Roger's little girl, your cousin, Rose. That will be nice, won't it?'

'No.' To her dismay Lorna found that the back of her throat was hurting. 'I don't want to stay here in Heaton with my Grandmamma Cunningham and my cousin, Rose. I want to come home with you.'

Her mother put her cup down slowly, looking at it as she settled it in her saucer. 'You know why you must stay here,' she said without looking up. 'We've talked about it and you agreed that while . . . while I am ill like this, it's for the best.'

'No – I didn't. I didn't agree.' Lorna was sobbing now. 'I want to come home with you. Father will come back soon – he'll look after both of us.' Her mother was silent and Lorna swallowed her misery. Her throat hurt and her voice sounded strange to her when she asked, 'Why can't I stay with you until Father comes home?'

Her mother was so quiet that Lorna had to lean across the table to hear her. 'Because I'm not sure when exactly he will return,' she said. 'And because, while I'm ill I can't look after you properly.'

'But there's Hilda—'

'Lorna, stop this. You know that Hilda has to look after me and, besides, if I have to go into hospital I want you to be with my family. With my mother.'

Lorna might have said more but she noticed that the cup her mother gripped so tightly was shaking and that the hot chocolate had spilled over on to her gloves. The white kid was spotted with reddish-brown stains.

'Oh, look,' Lorna said, and she reached one hand across the table.

Her mother let go of the cup and took Lorna's hand. 'It doesn't matter,' she said. 'And, now, are you going to be a good girl and come with me to your grandmother's?'

'Yes. But . . .'

'What is it?'

'Bend down . . . your head . . . a little further . . .' As her mother did so Lorna reached up and took something that was caught in the fur of her hat. 'It's another leaf,' she said. 'It landed on your hat. So it doesn't matter that you gave your luck to me because you will have some too. You must keep this one – put it in your pocket.'

Lorna gave the leaf to her mother. She didn't know why but she felt that it was very important that her mother should keep it. The leaf was smaller than her own; it was pale green streaked with yellow. After looking at it solemnly for a moment her mother put it in the pocket of her coat as she was told.

Her mother took the larger case and Lorna the smaller, but neither of them was very big. Most of Lorna's clothes and toys would be sent on later. As they passed the kiosk Lorna noticed that the glass counter was still full of iced buns.

They stopped at the gate of the park and stared across the busy road at the avenue of tall town houses. Lorna had never seen anything quite like them. Instead of their front doors opening directly on to the street like those of the long rows of small narrow terraced houses they had passed on the way from the station, these houses had front gardens with walls and privet hedges. Some of them had trees in the gardens that had grown tall enough to hide all but the top storeys from view.

In spite of her misery Lorna imagined what it would be like to stand at one of those windows at the very top and look out over the road to the park and the bandstand and the ruined castle. In her room at home she could kneel on her bed and look out over the river . . .

4

'Hold my hand tight,' her mother said, and they started across the wide road as soon as there was a lull in the traffic.

Halfway across they realized that a hansom cab was speeding briskly towards them. The clip-clop of hoofs grew louder, and Lorna could hear the snorting sounds the horse made. They arrived, just in time it seemed, at the other side.

Her mother was panting. She moved away from the road and put down the case she was carrying on the pavement; she bade Lorna do the same. 'This road has grown so much busier since I lived here,' she said. 'I don't imagine your grandmother will let you and Rose go over to the park alone, do you?'

Lorna refused to respond. She didn't want to imagine doing anything with her cousin, Rose; the girl her mother had told her was nine years old, only two years older than Lorna herself. She'd never even seen her cousin, neither had she ever met her grandmother, never been to this house before, and suddenly she was supposed to be happy about coming here.

Instead of answering her mother, she turned to look at the road and wrinkled up her nose, 'Pooh,' she said. 'What's the smell?'

'Horse droppings,' her mother replied. 'I'm afraid it seems to be worse than ever.'

Lorna looked up and down the road at the offending piles of droppings. Some of them were steaming. 'It's disgusting. Don't they ever clear it up?'

'Of course they do. They clean the streets just as they do at home – it's only that this is a busy road and there's more of it. You'll get used to it. Now, pick up your case.'

Lorna frowned. She didn't want to get used to it. She wanted to go home to their house near the river where there was an entirely different set of sights and smells and sounds. The huddled old houses weren't so grand as these, but she had grown used to the spicy smells of cooking coming from the open doors, the tangy smell of the sea breeze blowing up river; used to the passing river traffic, the sailing ships, and the deep throb of the steam ships and the chug and splash, splash, splash of the paddle tugs and ferries.

When they reached her grandmother's house her mother paused with one gloved hand on the iron gate and stood and looked up at the house. Lorna stared at the bay windows and the grand front door. She wondered if her grandmother and cousin Rose had all this house to themselves or if they took lodgers like some of the neighbours did at home.

Then, as if suddenly making her mind up about something, her mother opened the gate and, reaching for Lorna's free hand, she led her along the stone-flagged path and up a flight of broad stone steps to the front door. The gate swung shut behind them. The metallic clang it made had hardly died away before her mother reached for the bell.

'I thought I told you in my letter to come to the back door, Esther.' The voice of the unseen person sounded angry.

'You did,' Lorna heard her mother reply.

And then the older voice said, 'Well?'

'My daughter will not enter this house by the back door, ever. She's a member of the family.'

There was a small silence and then the cross voice said, 'Well, I'd better have a look at her.'

'No, we'll talk first.'

'I want to see her.'

'And I know why. But there are things that must be said before you do.'

'Then for goodness' sake sit down.'

'Very well. Oh, wait a moment . . .'

And then, as if her mother had just realized that it was still open, the door across the hall closed with a soft thud.

Lorna's hands inside her muff were hot. She withdrew them and placed them on her lap. A young woman in a black dress and white pinafore had opened the door and then her mother had told Lorna to sit here before she walked across the hall and went through one of the doors.

Lorna shivered. The wood-panelled hall was cold, and the pale light coming through the fanlight above the front door only seemed to make it even more gloomy. The chair she sat on had a high wooden back and the seat was covered in dark green velvet. But it was not comfortable; and it was so high that her feet did not reach the floor.

She gazed down at her feet in her high-buttoned boots and began to swing them backwards and forwards. Her legs and feet cast moving shadows on the polished black and white tiles. Gradually the swaying motion made her feel strange. She realized she was tired.

It had been dark when Hilda had woken her that morning; she had taken her down to the kitchen and sat her at the table with a cup of sweet tea and a slice of toast. Then her mother's companion had gone back upstairs to help her mother dress.

6

The kitchen had been warm with the heat from the range, and the single gaslight over the oilcloth-covered table shed a cosy light. Lorna sat alone listening to the foghorns of the ships sailing on the morning tide, and the thin clanging of the bell on the buoy that guarded the Black Midden rocks at the river's mouth.

Later Hilda walked with them to the landing stage, insisting on carrying both suitcases. Before they boarded the ferry, she kneeled down and hugged Lorna tightly.

'Be a good lass for yer grandma, pet.' Then the tall, thin woman rose to her feet awkwardly and took her mother's hand. 'Take it slow and divven't tire yerself, Mrs Hassan,' she said. 'Just gan canny, now, promise me. I'll hev yer supper ready when you get back.'

Hilda hurried away and they boarded the ferry.

All the way across the river from South Shields to North Shields Lorna thought about that supper that Hilda was going to have ready for her mother, and she was as angry as the herring gulls seemed to be as they wheeled screeching overhead. The screeching grew louder and angrier when a solitary trawler returned from a night's fishing and the large seabirds swooped and fought in its wake, following the boat to the fish quay.

Lorna turned on the bench and she gripped the rail as she leaned over to watch them. She loved the river – the River Tyne, it was called. She had lived in South Shields all her life. As the ferry docked on the north shore and the passengers stepped out on to the swaying ferry staging she wondered how long it would be before she would come home again.

She and her mother hardly spoke as they walked up the steep streets in North Shields towards the station. Her mother had to stop now and then to catch her breath. The train was crowded; the people were going to work in Newcastle, her mother told her. They got off at Heaton, and again it was an uphill walk but not quite so steep. When they reached a park, her mother said, 'We can cut through here – and, I know, let's stop a while. There's a refreshment kiosk. We'll have iced buns and hot chocolate for our lunch. It will be like a picnic!'

Lorna had been happy to agree. No matter how cold, she would have stayed in that park for ever, she thought, or at least until her mother changed her mind and took her home again. But her mother had not changed her mind. And, now, here she was, sitting in this gloomy big house while her mother and the grandmother she still hadn't met seemed to be having some sort of argument.

She could hear their voices but not what they were saying. Suddenly, from much closer than the room across the hall, she heard the words, 'My goodness me, you must be the little heathen!'

Startled, Lorna looked up and all around. The stained-glass door that led into the porch was still closed. The long passage that led away to the back of the house was empty. Where had the voice come from? Was someone hiding behind one of the large potted plants that were taller than she was?

From the corner of her eye she caught a quick movement, a flash of colour, and she turned her head quickly but it was only to see herself, in her red coat, reflected in the mirror of a tall coat stand standing at one side of the door of the room her mother had entered.

'I didn't know little heathens had smart velvet coats with fur-lined hoods and muffs.' The voice spoke again. And this time Lorna placed it.

Across the hall, someone was sitting on the stairs staring at her through the carved wooden banisters. She stared back. It was a girl with hair so fair that it was almost white. Two blue ribbons held back her ringlets and her eyes were the same colour as the ribbons and her blue shiny dress. She looked like a beautiful princess in a storybook, except that, at the moment, she was a cross princess. Lorna had never seen anyone scowl quite like that.

The girl saw that Lorna had noticed her and her scowl cleared. But she still didn't look friendly.

'Are you my cousin, Rose?' Lorna asked.

'My, my, the little heathen can speak English.'

'Of course I can.' The older girl hadn't answered her question but Lorna supposed she couldn't be anyone but her cousin, and the knowledge filled her with dread. Rose obviously didn't like her. 'Why do you call me a heathen?' she asked.

'Because that's what you are. Or at least your father is a heathen. Grandmamma told me that it broke her heart when your mother ran off and married him. So it serves you both right that he has run off and abandoned you now that your mother is so ill. That's what Grandmamma says!'

Lorna slid off the chair and stood with clenched fists. 'He hasn't abandoned us! My father has gone away on business. And when he went he didn't know my mother was so ill. But he is coming back.'

'When?'

'I – I don't know . . . My mother says there must have been some problem . . . but he will come back.'

8

Lorna watched as the other girl rose to her feet and walked the rest of the way downstairs. At the bottom she turned and came towards Lorna. She stared at her for a moment and then she said, 'Well, I suppose your mother would tell you that. Grandmamma says that she probably believes it herself.'

Lorna hated the way that Rose was looking at her – half scornful, half pitying. She also hated the idea that her grandmother and this spiteful girl had been talking about her mother and her – and in such a manner.

'Well, I believe it too, and when he returns he will take me away from here. And you must never call me a heathen!' Lorna knew she was shouting and she could feel her face flushing with anger. 'I think you're hateful.'

Rose's eyes widened. 'Do be quiet,' she said. 'Grandmamma won't put up with that caterwauling.' She glanced over her shoulder towards the door of the room where Lorna's mother and grandmother were still talking, then she looked back and smiled. 'I think we should be friends.'

Her smile was sweet but Lorna sensed that it was false, and she knew instinctively that her cousin, Rose, had no intention of being her friend.

The door across the hall opened and Rose turned quickly. 'Hello, you must be my Aunt Esther,' she said.

'And you must be Rose.'

Lorna's mother smiled and Lorna hated the way her face had softened with pleasure. She wanted to warn her that no matter how much this other girl smiled she wasn't to be trusted.

Before her mother could respond, another figure appeared in the doorway behind her and Lorna saw her grandmother for the first time. She stared at her in surprise. She had been expecting to see an old woman like the grandmothers in fairy tales; dressed in black with some kind of shawl, and perhaps stooped.

But the woman standing behind her mother was tall and straight and, although her gown was black, it was like one of the gowns in her mother's fashion magazines, and, far from being old and wrinkled she looked young and beautiful. Neither was her hair white; it was the same red-gold as her mother's hair, perhaps a shade lighter, and it was thick and glossy.

'Don't stare, Lorna,' her mother whispered, and the older woman's lips drew back in a tight smile.

'We are looking at each other,' she said. 'Come, child, let's move into the light.'

9

She walked back into the room and they all followed. 'Over here,' she said, and motioned Lorna to stand beside her in the window bay.

'Mother . . . don't . . .' her mother said, but Grandmamma Cunningham ignored her.

She continued to stare at Lorna and then she said, 'Come here, Rose, stand beside your cousin.'

'Mother . . . please . . .'

'Be quiet, Esther. It's all right.'

Lorna had been growing more and more puzzled. When they had arrived she had heard her grandmother asking to see her but her mother had said they should talk first. It must be something to do with what she looked like. But why was it so important?

'Why are you looking at me?' she asked.

Suddenly Rose came to stand beside her. She took her hand and held it out. 'This is what Grandmamma is looking at,' she said.

'What do you mean? My hands?'

'Not just your hands, silly. Look.' Rose took Lorna's hand and laid it in her own larger one. 'Look at us both together.'

Lorna looked down at Rose's smooth white hands – as white as her mother's kid gloves – and her own smaller, more delicate, hand which her mother had told her was the colour of honey. Suddenly she realized that somehow it mattered that she and Rose were different.

She heard her mother begin to cough. She pulled her hand free from Rose's grasp and started towards her, but her mother shook her head and gasped, 'It's all right, sweetheart.'

The coughing stopped and her mother dabbed at her mouth with a clean white handkerchief. She put it in her pocket quickly but not before Lorna had seen the spots of red.

'I should go now,' her mother told her and they stared at each other miserably.

'Let me send the girl for a cab,' Grandmamma Cunningham said, 'to take you as far as the station.'

'No, I'll walk.'

'For God's sake, Esther—'

'No. You've agreed to take my daughter, your granddaughter, and I'm grateful. But I won't take anything for myself. Not from someone who refuses to accept my husband.'

The two women stared at each other. 'Very well,' the elder woman said, 'but you must write – or send word somehow when – when the time is near.'

10

'I will. Now, if Lorna will come with me to the door I'd like to say goodbye.'

They didn't speak until they reached the front door. Then, before opening it, her mother said, 'You know I wouldn't leave you here unless I had to, don't you?'

'Yes.'

'And you know how much I love you?'

Lorna stared up into her mother's face. She thought she had never looked so beautiful – or so sad. 'How long will I have to stay here?' she asked.

'Until your father comes home.'

'Will he know I'm here? Will he find me?' Even as she asked Lorna realized that she did not expect her mother would be there to tell him where their only child was living.

'Don't worry, sweetheart. I'll make sure that he knows where to find you.'

As they looked at each other Lorna knew that they were both thinking of her father, the dark, handsome and loving man that they both loved so much. And she also finally acknowledged that, while she hoped with all her heart that she would see him again, her mother never would.

'Lorna, you're so young' her mother said. The tears were streaming down her face.

'Don't worry. I'll be all right.'

Sobbing, she hurled herself against her mother's slim body and her mother caught her and held her tightly.

'Darling – I'm not allowed to kiss you,' her mother said. 'You know what the doctor said – you understand?'

'Yes.'

Her mother took hold of Lorna's shoulders and pushed her gently away. Then she kept hold of her as she kneeled down to look into her face. 'Let me look at you,' she said. 'Do you think you could smile?'

Lorna did her best and somehow they were both smiling before her mother got swiftly to her feet.

'No!' Lorna began to protest, but her mother opened the door and stepped out.

'Close the door now, Lorna,' she said. 'It's cold out here.' She turned and walked swiftly down the steps.

Lorna did not do as she was told. She held on to the door and watched as her mother opened the gate and walked out into the street. Only when she was lost to view at the other side of the busy road did Lorna begin to close the door. Then something caught her eye.

11

Something glinting on the doormat. She picked it up. It was one of her mother's pearl earrings.

Lorna ran out of the house and down the path as far as the gate but something made her stop. She would keep the earring. Her mother would have one and she would have the other. She would keep it for ever. She turned to go back into her grandmother's house but before she did she placed the earring carefully in the pocket inside her black fur muff. Along with the leaf.

Chapter One

December 1903

Lorna stood at the window of her bedroom on the top floor of the house. The streetlamps illuminated Heaton Road, still busy with horse traffic, electric trams and the occasional motorcar. Beyond was the park, shadowy in the moonlight. She could see the glimmering outline of the old castle through the bare branches of the trees. Lorna thought it looked romantic.

The crowds gathering for the festive band concert were dark silhouettes, which, in her imagination, seemed to be moving in time to the music – *The Skaters' Waltz*. They flowed towards the bandstand, an island of warm light. Very few lingered by the trees. That was just as well.

Made nervous by anticipation of what she planned to do later, she closed her eyes and tried to control her ragged breathing. When she opened them again she caught sight of her reflection in the windowpane. It looked as though she were standing out there amongst the stars in the cold winter sky.

'What are you doing, Lorna?'

She spun round at the sound of her cousin's voice. Rose stood in the doorway. She wore a pale blue silk robe and her hair was tied up in curling rags. The rags did nothing to detract from her beauty but they did make her look younger than her nineteen years. She looks like a child, Lorna thought, a petulant child.

'I'm looking out of the window. Can't you see?'

'Oh, clever. I mean, why haven't you come to help me dress for dinner? I told you I wanted you to do my hair.'

'*Told*?'

Rose moved into the room impatiently, pushing the door shut behind her. 'Oh, very well, I *asked* you to help me.'

13

'And did I agree?'

Rose scowled. 'You're just being awkward because you're jealous.'

'Why should I be jealous?'

'Because you're not allowed to join us at dinner tonight.'

'Why on earth should I be jealous, suddenly? Why is tonight any different? I've never been invited to meet Grandmamma's guests, either when we go visiting or here in our own home.'

Rose's eyes widened and Lorna realized that she had shown more emotion than she usually did. Over the years, pride had taught her not to reveal how wounded she had been by the different way their grandmother treated them. Rose was the favoured child, indulged and loved, whereas she, Lorna, although not neglected in any material sense, had simply been tolerated.

Suddenly Rose said, 'God, it's cold in here. Why don't you build up the fire? Here, let me.' She strode across the room and reached for the bell pull on the wall at the side of the fireplace.

'Don't,' Lorna said. 'I'm perfectly capable of doing it myself. There's no need to bring Molly all the way up from the kitchen. They'll be busy enough preparing for Grandmamma's dinner party.'

Rose stood over her and pushed her hands up into the opposite sleeves of her robe, shivering exaggeratedly. Lorna ignored her and kneeled down to build up the fire. When she stood up she found her cousin staring at her as if she had just noticed something. 'What is it?' she asked.

'Why are you all dressed up?'

'I don't know what you mean.'

'If you're going to stay up here reading as you usually do, why are you wearing one of your best dresses?'

Lorna turned away and glanced involuntarily into the mirror above the hearth. She was glad the glow from the fire disguised the telltale heat that had risen to suffuse her face. She flinched slightly when Rose reached out and stroked the sleeve of her crushed-velvet dress.

'You look good in that dark red, you know,' her cousin said grudgingly, 'in spite of the coppery tints in your hair.'

Lorna continued to look in the mirror and saw what a contrast they made. Rose so fair and herself so dark, and yet there was a distinct family resemblance.

'But I don't know why on earth you should wear a dress like that to sit up here with your book and your tray.'

Rose raised her head and looked at Lorna's reflection. She frowned and Lorna felt a knot of unease begin to tighten as she recalled the old

14

superstition. If someone looked over your shoulder into a mirror it was supposed to bring you bad luck – or at least it meant that the two of you would quarrel. Well, that would be nothing new.

'And your hair's nice too,' Rose said. She shook her head. 'What a funny girl you are.'

Lorna moved away. 'That's right, I'm strange. Your strange cousin, the "little heathen". Remember you called me that the first day I came to this house?'

Suddenly Rose shrugged. 'Oh, Lorna, do stop this. I just wanted you to do my hair.' Her smile was placating. 'You have such good taste – such an idea of style.'

Lorna shook her head. 'It's no use, Rose. You can't persuade me.'

'Oh, very well. But I can't understand why you won't help me. You really are ungrateful.'

'Ungrateful? What do you mean?'

'Well, Grandmamma has fed and clothed you all these years—'

'As she has you!'

'That's different.'

'Why? We're both her granddaughters.'

'That's as may be, but my father was her only son.'

'And my mother was her only daughter.'

'But my father was a hero and . . . and . . .' Rose faltered, then she drew herself up and went on, 'and, furthermore, he was respectably married.'

'So was my mother.'

Rose sniffed. 'Respectably? My father married a lady from a good English family, whereas your mother ran off with an Arab – a common deck hand from an old tramp steamer that fetched up in the Tyne!'

Lorna stared at her cousin, all the old hurts rising up to choke her. She could feel the bitterness at the back of her throat.

Rose sensed the advantage and drew herself up to declare dramatically, 'Your mother broke Grandmamma's heart!'

'Yes,' Lorna said, and her words were barely audible, 'and I have been made to pay for it.' To her dismay she felt her eyes brim with scalding tears. She turned away before Rose could see them. 'You'd better go and get ready,' she said.

'Lorna—'

'Just go.'

She stood with clenched fists, not moving until she heard the door close behind her cousin. The fire was blazing now and she moved away from the hearth. She would have to put the cinder guard up before she went.

Restlessly she walked over to her bookcase and chose a book, but she didn't even glance at it before replacing it and returning to the window. She would have to wait until Molly came up with her supper tray before she could go. And she would have to remember to tell the young maid not to bother to come back for it tonight. She could say that she knew how busy they would be.

She pressed her forehead against the cold glass and tried to control her emotions. The argument with Rose had been no different from many that had raged between them over the years, but her cousin was quite wrong if she thought Lorna had refused to do her hair because she was jealous of Rose's favoured position in this house and in their grandmother's affections.

With so much to occupy her thoughts she had simply forgotten. And, then, when Rose had stormed into her room just now, she had realized that, for one very good reason, she would not be able to concentrate on helping her to dress for dinner.

For Lorna had no need to be jealous. Not now. And Rose would have known that if Lorna had only dared to tell her whom she was slipping out to meet in the park tonight.

'I'm here . . . behind you.'

Lorna heard the whispered command above the sound of the band and the carol singing. She caught her breath and the cold seared the back of her throat. He must be close. She turned to peer through the darkness. At first all she saw was the stark shapes of the trees, but then one of the shapes moved, reached for her hand and pulled her into the shadows.

'Maurice,' she breathed as she felt the shock of her body meeting his.

Her breath frosted on the air and the cloth of his coat was cold against her face as he pressed her close. She moved her head back a little and looked up. As her eyes became accustomed to the dimness underneath the leafless branches she saw that he was frowning.

'What is it?' she asked.

'Did anyone see you leave the house?'

'No, I crept down the back stairs like a thief.'

'The servants?'

'Too busy with Grandmamma's dinner party.'

16

His frown deepened. 'Have you passed any friends or acquaint-ances?'

'I have no idea. I pulled up my hood, kept my head down and made for this grove just as you told me.' She knew her voice had grown sharp but she was not so much annoyed with Maurice as frustrated that they had to keep their meetings secret like this.

'And where does your grandmother think you are?'

'In my room. Look . . .' She took his hand and drew him out a little. Then turning, she pointed to the row of houses that overlooked the park. One of them, larger than the rest, had a turret at the very top above the jutting bay windows. 'There, that's where they keep me,' she said. 'Up in the tower . . . see . . . There's a gap in the curtains . . . The light is on. They think I'm there reading while Grandmamma and Rose entertain their guests.'

'Rapunzel,' Maurice whispered.

'Mm?'

'My princess in the tower. When are you going to let down your hair?' He pulled her back into the dark space beneath the trees and pushed the hood away from her face. It fell back and his fingers pushed through her hair, loosening the pins until it fell about her shoulders.

'Maurice . . . no . . .'

Lorna caught her breath and she felt her pulse quicken as he parted her cloak and moved one arm around her body to hold her even closer. His other hand cradled her head as he brought his mouth down on hers. His breath was warm and sweet but his lips were cold, and Lorna gave herself to the delicious sensations that they aroused deep within her.

I should be feeling guilty, she thought, guilty to be here with Maurice, even though I know very well that Rose hopes to marry him. But how can I feel guilty when I love him so much? When at last I have found someone who holds me dear? Maurice loves me, not Rose.

She felt Maurice's breathing grow more urgent and his mouth move more forcefully. Suddenly he pulled away.

'Lorna,' he said roughly, 'I can't go on like this. We must be together. You want that, don't you?'

Before she could answer a voice rang out behind them. 'Haldane, is that you?'

Maurice straightened up swiftly and drew Lorna's cloak across her body. He thrust her aside, pushing her behind a tree, then he stepped out of the shadows.

'It is you!' the voice said.

'Bertram,' Maurice said. 'How did you recognize me?'

17

'You can't disguise that bright thatch of yours,' the voice said. 'Shines like silver in the moonlight and, as well as that, old chum, there's no one I know who is quite as tall as you are.'

'What are you doing here?'

'Same as you, I suppose. I've come to join in the fun.'

'The fun?'

'The concert – the carols.' The other man laughed. 'And to tell the truth I had pretty much the same intentions as you. But I haven't seen anything that takes my fancy. The rougher sort are here tonight.'

'Yes . . . well . . .'

'You want me to go? Did I interrupt just at the wrong moment? Tell you what, Haldane, I'll wait over by the refreshment kiosk until you've finished your business and then we'll go into town together. What do you say to that?'

'Very well.'

Lorna's cheeks were burning when Maurice returned to her. She couldn't look at him. She understood very well what his friend had been saying – what kind of woman he thought Maurice was with – and she was distressed that Maurice had not contradicted him. She held herself stiff when he tried to take her into his arms.

'What's the matter?' Maurice asked.

'Why did you let him say those things? Why didn't you tell him?'

Maurice sighed. 'Tell him what?' He placed a finger under her chin and gently brought her face up until she had to look at him. 'Tell him who you are and that you had sneaked out of the house to meet me secretly? That we were engaged in a passionate embrace in a public park?'

Lorna gasped. 'Stop it – don't say such things. You make it sound so . . . so sordid.'

'I didn't mean to. But, Lorna, you know I can't let it be known that we are seeing each other. Not yet. Can I?'

'No, I suppose not.'

Maurice drew her close but this time he simply kissed her brow. 'I'll have to go,' he said. 'Look, I'm sorry I can't see you home but we simply can't—'

'Be seen together,' she interrupted him. 'I know.'

'Don't linger. The crowd is good-natured now, but soon the dangerous element will arrive, full of drink and eager for the free food at the end of the concert. Wait here until I've had time to collect Bertram and get a cab, then you must go straight home. Promise?'

'Yes.'

18

Lorna watched him walk away. He was soon lost among the crowd and she hoped that he would find his friend soon and leave the park, because she didn't intend to stay here much longer. She was cold and unhappy. What had promised to be a delicious escapade, a chance for Maurice and her to be alone together for an hour or two, had been frustrated by this chance meeting with his friend.

The excitement and romance of a secret tryst with Maurice had somehow become tarnished and, instead of exhilaration, her feelings now were very close to shame. But that was because of the way Maurice's friend had spoken. He'd believed that she was some . . . some loose woman that Maurice had picked up in the park. If only Maurice had been able to tell the truth perhaps she wouldn't feel so humiliated.

And yet . . .

Maurice was right: the truth would not have helped. For what respectable young woman would have behaved in such a way in a public place? She felt a hot rush of embarrassment as she remembered how eagerly she had given herself to his embrace, how she had not protested when he had held her so closely.

She swallowed a lump of misery that was almost choking her. She was confused, confused by the fact that her feelings had led her into such unknown territory. If only she had a mother to advise her but she was quite alone. Maurice's parents wanted him to make a good match. They approved of Rose – but he didn't love her. And as for Rose . . . did she really love Maurice or was it his wealth and position that attracted her?

Maurice was a good son. He didn't want to upset his father – that's why he hadn't said anything so far. But this was the twentieth century, wasn't it? People were allowed to marry for love, no matter how rich and important they were. Maurice had told her that he hated the deception as much as she did. He'd promised her that they would be together as soon as he could work out some way of achieving it. Lorna hoped with all her heart that would be soon.

She pulled her cloak tightly round her body and began to make her way back across the park. The moon sailed high in the clear sky, draining the world of colour and highlighting the scene in sharp contrasts of black and white.

Over the heads of the crowd she could see the bandstand and the moving brass instruments catching and reflecting the warmer light of the naphtha flares. The audience grouped round the stand were still singing carols, but the sound became ragged as some of them began to drift away. Perhaps the cold was too much for them, or perhaps they

19

were tempted by the appetising smells coming from the baked potato and roast chestnut stalls.

'Hey! You canna just barge in like that – there's a queue! What do you think you're doing?'

'I beg your pardon!' Lorna stopped and stared at her interrogator in fright. The girl was young, probably only about fifteen, but she was taller that Lorna and sturdy. She was scowling fiercely.

'Oh, la-de-da!' the girl mocked. 'I said there's a queue for the baked tatties. And get yersel to the back of it.'

'But I didn't want—I mean, I didn't know . . .'

Realizing at last that the angry girl thought she had been queue jumping, Lorna stumbled backwards, only to come up against an obstruction.

'Hevin' trouble, Jess? Is this lass trying to push in?'

Lorna felt her shoulders seized and, panicking, she pulled away and twisted round to face her new tormentor. It was a man. He was tall and well built, and surprisingly well dressed in a good overcoat with a white silk scarf tucked at the neck. Surprisingly because his speech and his manner were coarse. He stared at Lorna, his eyes widening.

'My, my, here's a bonny one,' he said. He reached forward and lifted a lock of Lorna's hair. 'Like silk,' he said, rubbing it through his fingers, 'tawny silk.'

'Let go of me,' she gasped.

'Not until you tell me what you're doing here.'

He leaned closer and Lorna gagged at the mingled odours of cheap pomade, sweat, and beery breath. She pulled away and he grinned at her.

'Doing here?' she asked.

'Aye. Here in the park,' he said. 'All on your own by the look of it.' His grin turned into a frown as if she puzzled him.

'Oh, let the lass alone, Mr Brady,' Lorna was surprised to hear her first tormentor say. 'I reckon she's only some bit lady's maid from one of them big houses over there. Probably came to meet her sweetheart and got lost.'

'Jealous are you, Jess?' the man called Brady asked the girl.

'Divven't be daft. There's nowt on her. Wouldn't suit your purposes. Not like me.'

Suddenly the younger girl stepped forward and gave Lorna a vicious shove. 'Haddaway, yem,' she hissed, 'afore you start something you can't finish.'

20

The girl began to laugh and so did other members of the queue. Lorna's face burned. Her heart was thumping so violently that she thought it was going to rise up and choke her. She turned and sped away, losing all sense of direction, and when she found herself tripping over a clod of frozen earth she realised that she'd left the path and stumbled on to one of the flowerbeds.

She stopped, took a deep painful breath and tried to find her bearings. She looked back the way she had come. There was a steady stream of people walking in one direction. She watched them for a moment and saw that they were making for a long, low open-fronted building with lights inside. The pavilion. Not far beyond the pavilion lay the gates that opened on to Heaton Road. That was the way to go.

Soon she saw the reason why the crowd was gathering. The refreshment kiosk was being used to distribute the free Christmas parcels that had been promised at the end of the carol concert. Tickets had been doled out to the needy, and the food had been provided by local businessmen.

Lorna began to breathe more easily. Now she could see the lamp standards on Heaton Road and hear the rattle and rumble of the trams interspersed with the staccato sound of the cab horses' hoofs on the cobbles. She'd soon be home.

'Lorna . . . Miss Hassan . . . is that you?'

She stopped when a familiar voice called her name. 'Edwin Randall?' she asked hesitantly.

A young man emerged from the queue of people waiting for the food parcels.

'Are you all right?' he asked.

'Of course, why shouldn't I be?'

His gaze was concerned and she realized how she must look with her hair tumbling untidily about her face. She clutched her cloak about her body in a defensive gesture.

'I thought you looked distressed,' Edwin said.

'Well, I'm not,' she retorted sharply. Edwin said nothing but he frowned. 'I came to listen to the concert,' she went on, 'but I got jostled in the crowd. Some great lump of a girl thought I was stealing her place in the queue for baked potatoes. She – she told me to go home in no uncertain terms!'

She had managed to inject some humour into her voice and she was relieved to see him smile. 'Then perhaps you should. It's getting late and the crowd may get rowdy.'

21

Lorna could have smiled and said good night and left him, but curiosity got the better of her. 'But what about you? Why are you here? Are you queuing for a Christmas bundle? I never imagined your uncle to be like Mr Scrooge.'

Edwin laughed. 'He isn't. In fact he pays me more than I'm worth, considering I probably spend more time reading the books in his shop than selling them.'

Lorna laughed too. 'Then what are you doing here?'

'Helping to distribute the parcels. Making sure that they don't fall into the wrong hands.'

'Wrong hands?'

Edwin frowned again. 'There are always some who will try to get more than their share – who will threaten and bully ticket holders into parting with them – even steal them.'

'And you would know such people?'

'Some of them.'

'Of course.'

Lorna remembered that Edwin worked in his uncle's bookshop in order to earn a living while he studied medicine. She did not know how many more years he had to go before he qualified, but she knew that he was already passionate about the living conditions of some of the people he saw at the infirmary. He believed that disease was actually spread by the way they were forced to live. His research took him into the slums regularly. And he did what he could to help.

'But, if you don't mind the impertinence,' he told her now, 'I'd like to see you home safely.'

'Oh, that's not necessary.'

'Isn't it?' He raised his eyebrows and cocked his head. 'Listen – or rather listen but not too closely.' He smiled. 'Those aren't carols that the crowd are singing now. The respectable folk have gone. And so should you before the gathering becomes too disorderly.'

'Very well.'

Edwin was not much taller than she was, but he was strongly built and she supposed he was good-looking in an intense, intelligent sort of way. But compared to Maurice he was ordinary. Anybody would be.

Maurice was well over six foot, had eyes that were violet rather than blue and silvery blond hair. His features were beautiful and yet in no way effeminate. Maurice resembled one of the illustrations in a picture book her father had given her when she was a child. The book was called *Gods and Heroes* and it was all about the people who had lived in Ancient Greece thousands of years ago.

22

Edwin walked her as far as the front gate. 'Thank you,' she said. 'You'd better go back to your duties.

'Good night, Lorna. Oh, that book you wanted has arrived, the book about Persia.'

'Good. I'll try to come in before Christmas, then I'll have something to read while my grandmother and my cousin are visiting and entertaining.' He looked at her askance. 'I'm sorry,' she said. 'Did I sound resentful? I'm not a bit resentful; I should hate to have to dress up and chatter brightly about things of no consequence all the time.'

'Nevertheless, it must hurt that you are part of the family and yet not included in their social life.'

'It used to.'

'But now?'

'I'm not sure. When I was a little girl I used to cry when Rose was invited to parties and I was not – I wasn't even allowed to attend my cousin's own birthday parties in the house I live in. But, as we grew older, I began to wonder if, even if they wanted me, I could ever be part of Rose's circle. Except I would dearly have liked to join the tennis club!'

She'd surprised herself by that outburst and she saw Edwin's eyes widen.

'Why?' he asked.

'Because I'm good at tennis. I learned at school where Grandmamma was paying the fees so they had to include me. I suppose I saw myself, all in white, winning every trophy and being reported in the newspapers.'

'You're serious?'

'Half serious, I suppose. Don't we all have dreams like that at that age?' She smiled at him but to her dismay she felt her lip begin to tremble. 'But, in any case, as I grew up a little I became less certain that I wanted to be part of their world . . .' Her words tailed away.

'Forgive me, Lorna,' Edwin said. 'It is none of my business. But now I'll see you to the door.'

'No, that's all right. Good night and thank you.'

Lorna opened the gate and walked slowly up the path. She was aware that Edwin was still standing there and she took her time as she climbed the steps. At the top she turned and waved. She didn't want him to guess that she'd sneaked out of the house without permission. She realized that it was important what Edwin thought of her. She was relieved when he returned her wave and then set off back across the road towards the park.

23

She watched for a moment and, when she was sure he had gone, she went back down the path and out into the street. The frost sparkled on the pavement and she had to take care as she hurried along to the end of the block to turn into the side street that led to the back lane.

The door into the back garden and yard area had not been bolted. The extra help taken on for the dinner party would not be leaving until after midnight. Lorna had not left by the back door – that led straight into the scullery and then into the kitchen. She had left by the French windows in the conservatory.

Taking the key from her pocket she let herself in and, locking the door behind her, she replaced the key in its customary place in a brass pot containing a leafy aspidistra. The conservatory, heated by a large green enamelled oil stove, was warm and moist. Pools of water lay on the tiled floor and the air smelled slightly musty. Lorna, her senses heightened by the risks she had already taken tonight, stood by the door, something stopping her from going forward. There was another smell. Tobacco smoke.

Had one of her grandmother's guests come in here to enjoy a cigar or cigarette? If so, why was he sitting in the dark? Why hadn't he lit the lamps? Outside the moon was still riding high and bright, and, as her eyes adjusted to the dimness, she saw a pinpoint of glowing light, a faint plume of smoke and a puzzlingly pale shape sitting in one of the high-backed cane chairs.

Slowly the shape rose, tall and ghostly white from head to toe. Lorna stepped backwards in fright and came up sharp against the glass door.

'Well, well,' the shape said, and Lorna caught her breath. It was her cousin, Rose.

'What are you doing here?' they said in unison, and then Rose laughed softly.

'I'll answer first, because it's plain to see that I came to have a cigarette and to escape from Grandmamma's dull guests for a while. But your presence is harder to explain, isn't it? What on earth are you doing sneaking in like this?'

'Sneaking?'

'Don't dissemble, little cousin. You look positively furtive. I wonder what on earth you have been doing.'

Lorna felt her cheeks flaming. She was glad of the darkness. She knew it was fanciful but she imagined that, if Rose could see her properly, look into her eyes, she would know exactly what she had been doing. That she had gone to the park to meet Maurice Haldane.

'Why are you sitting here in the dark?' she countered.

24

There was a pause and then Rose laughed. 'So my refuge won't be discovered. You've no idea how boring it is to have to be pleasant to Grandmamma's guests. Well, to the sort of person she has invited tonight,' she qualified.

'Sort of person?'

'The tradesmen, the small builders, the plumbers, the joiners – all the worthy folk she needs to keep her property in order – all those rows of neat little artisans' dwellings. And not to mention the other guests, shiny-elbowed little officials from the Town Hall. Honestly, Lorna, you should be grateful instead of resentful that you never have to be present at these occasions.'

'I'm not in the least resentful. And Grandmamma doesn't approve of your smoking.'

'She just doesn't like me to smoke in public. There's a difference.'

'Well, good night, Rose.'

'Wait a moment.' Her cousin bent swiftly to stub out her cigarette in an ashtray on a low table and then she straightened and moved just enough to block Lorna's way to the door. 'You still haven't told me where you've been.'

'To the park – to hear the band.'

'Really?' Rose sounded incredulous. 'Why would you want to do that?'

'I could hear the music from my room – the carol singing. I – I wanted to join in.'

Her cousin shook her head. Her tone when she spoke was a mixture of pity and incredulity. 'Poor Lorna. I realize that you must be lonely up in your room sometimes – especially when you imagine that I'm enjoying myself downstairs – but to go to the park alone at night! Don't you know how dangerous it is? Especially now.'

'Now? I don't understand. Because it's nearly Christmas?'

'Don't be silly; of course not – although the band concert and the free food parcels will undoubtedly have attracted more riffraff than usual. No, I meant because of the murders.'

'The murders.' It wasn't a question. Lorna knew what her cousin meant. 'But the victims . . . those women . . . were all prostitutes.'

'I know. But where do they meet the man who kills them? According to the newspapers the police think it is the same man.'

'But the park is crowded with people and, furthermore, I am not a prostitute!'

Rose remained maddeningly dispassionate. 'No, but you went there alone. A young woman going unchaperoned to a public park after dark.

And a young woman who looks so . . . so different. Any man could be forgiven for thinking you were not respectable.'

Lorna gasped and would have spoken but Rose hurried on, 'And as for the park being crowded, that means nothing. Once the bargain had been struck such a woman would take her – her clients away; to the old ruin, for example, or simply under the trees.'

Lorna caught her breath. Having come in from the cold her face was now burning in the humid heat of the conservatory. She felt a trickle of sweat run down between her breasts as she tried to suppress the memory of herself and Maurice embracing under the twisted branches. What had his friend said? *'Did I interrupt at the wrong moment? I'll wait until you've finished your business . . .'*

She closed her eyes but the picture remained with her. And what had Maurice said when he left her? He had told her not to linger, had made her promise to go straight home. He had known of the danger . . . but it was not his fault that he had not been able to escort her out of the park.

She felt her shoulders grasped and was enveloped by Rose's favourite gardenia perfume. 'I can see I've upset you,' her cousin said.

Lorna opened her eyes and looked up into Rose's beautiful face. Her cousin was regarding her through narrowed eyes. 'I'm sorry, Lorna, but you shouldn't have gone to the park alone at night, should you? It doesn't bear thinking about – what might have happened.'

'Because of the scandal you mean?'

'Why do you say that, Lorna? Why are you always so defensive?'

Lorna began to edge past Rose and make her way to the door.

'Look – I won't tell Grandmamma,' Rose said, 'if that's what you're worried about.'

'Worried?'

'Well, I know I've frightened you, and I'm sorry. But there's something else, isn't there? You're nervous about something – uneasy.'

Lorna paused in the doorway and forced a grateful smile. 'Thank you. I'd be grateful if you didn't tell.'

'Of course I won't. After all, I've relied on you to keep secrets for me. Look, I'd better get back to Grandmamma's guests. I'll have to keep her sweet so that she'll go along with my wedding plans.'

Lorna found herself gripping the door. 'Has he asked you?'

'Not yet. But he will. I'm sure of it.'

Lorna sped upstairs to the attic floor, her emotions churning. She was sure that Rose didn't actually love Maurice. He was simply a good catch: tall, handsome and very wealthy.

But facing Rose tonight – thank goodness her cousin hadn't lit the lamps in the conservatory – facing her when she had just come home from a secret meeting with the man Rose planned to marry – the man Rose imagined was going to propose to her any minute – Lorna had suddenly had brought home to her the enormity of what she and Maurice planned to do.

And now, ironically, in promising not to tell their grandmother that Lorna had been out tonight, Rose had become an accomplice.

Ever since they had been children Rose had been pleasant only when it suited her. Both of them had lost their parents and they should have been drawn together. But Mildred Cunningham's disapproval of Lorna's very existence and her blatant adoration of Rose had destroyed any chance of real friendship.

Rose had needed a friend as much as Lorna had, but her nature was shallow and she had been unable to resist taking advantage of her position as the favourite. And this had led to many petty cruelties; sometimes merely thoughtless but often deliberate.

If Rose had been her true friend Lorna knew she would never have been able to betray her by stealing the man she hoped to marry. No matter how much she loved him.

Once in her room Lorna slammed the door shut and leaned back against it, seeking support until she regained her composure. Whatever Maurice's plan was, he would have to act soon for she didn't know how much longer she could live in this house without betraying their secret.

Chapter Two

'It's beautiful,' Lorna said.

Edwin smiled at her. 'You haven't opened it yet.'

'I know, but don't you just love the feel of new books – the smell of them?' She ran her hands over the leather-bound book where it lay on the counter and then she picked it up, opened it and buried her face in its pages.

'You look as though you're going to devour it,' Edwin told her. 'Are you hungry?'

She laughed. 'Yes – for knowledge, and for stories. You've no idea of the people I've met and the places I've been without even leaving my room. And now I'm going to Persia!'

'Again?' She didn't answer, she only smiled and he said, 'Well, that's all very well but I wasn't joking about being hungry. It's time for my lunch and I'm going to close the shop for a while. I can either put you out in the snow or you can come through into the den and share my meal with me.'

'Oh . . . that's kind of you . . . but I don't know . . .'

'Whether you are already tired of my company or whether you think it would be unkind to take part of my meagre portion?'

'You're teasing. Of course I'm not tired of your company, but—'

'If you think I shall starve if I share my lunch with you don't worry. My aunt has no sons of her own and she demonstrates her love for me with food. Usually I can only eat about half of what she prepares for what she calls "a little snack" to keep me going until I get home for what she deems a "proper meal". Will you stay? You'd be doing me a favour.'

Lorna thought of the big house in Heaton where she would eat a solitary lunch because her grandmother and her cousin were out for the day. They had gone to the dressmaker's for the final fitting of the gowns they were to wear at a party at the Haldanes' house that evening. A party to which, as usual, she had not been invited. They planned to come back for a sandwich and then rest until it was time to get ready. Rose must look her best tonight. She had told Lorna that Maurice would not be able to resist her.

'Well, I can see from your troubled expression that you would rather go,' Edwin said. He reached for the brown paper and began making a parcel of the book she'd just bought.

'No, I'm sorry, I was thinking of something else. I should like to stay.'

'Good. Then you go and lock the door while I finish this.'

Lorna went to the half-glassed shop door and looked out. It was only midday and yet it was quite dark, for here, in the Groat Market, the winter light barely filtered down through the tall buildings at either side of the narrow street. Edwin had not been joking about the snow, although the large plashy flakes were too wet to have much chance of lying.

'Turn the card over, will you?' he asked.

'The card? Oh, I see.' A piece of pasteboard hung down with the word 'OPEN' on one side and 'CLOSED' on the other. She turned it over to indicate the shop was closed, then turned round to face Edwin. 'Do you know, I should love to work in a shop,' she said.

'Really? Why?'

'I can't explain . . . but I should love to handle nice things, like books or fine fabrics or luxury food – flowers – hats – anything!'

She laughed and for a moment Edwin smiled. 'But what about working in a corner shop; a sparsely stocked general store where most of your customers can hardly afford enough provisions to see them through a week, if that. And some of them have to ask you to put it on the slate? That means they ask you for credit. And sometimes you have to decide whether to give them any more credit or let them starve.'

'Don't, Edwin. I'm sorry.'

'Why are you sorry?'

'I know about your work. I must sound frivolous.'

'No, Lorna, *I'm* sorry. None of it is your fault.'

Leaving her parcel on the counter, Edwin led the way past the crowded bookshelves and through the stockroom to the small back room. A tiny barred window looked out into a yard with high walls, and hardly let in any light. But a fire glowed in a small hearth and Edwin reached up and lit the gaslamp.

29

'How cosy this is,' Lorna exclaimed. 'How I should love to hide away here and read by the fire.'

Edwin smiled. 'Look – over there – the table.'

Lorna looked where he was pointing and saw a table at the back of the room. Its red chenille cover was almost completely covered with books and notepaper. She walked over to examine one of the open books.

'These are your medical books,' she said. 'You do your work here.'

'My uncle is kind enough to let me have this room when he is on duty in the shop – and even sometimes after closing hours. It's more convenient than trying to study at home.'

'You live with your aunt and uncle, don't you?'

'I have ever since my parents died. They've been marvellous, but I have five cousins, all girls, aged from six to sixteen and the house is full of chatter and music practice and the comings and goings of all their friends. Sometimes my uncle comes to join me here and he sits quietly reading while I work. Then we go home together when we judge the girls to be in bed.'

'It must be wonderful.'

'What? The noise?'

'No, I meant to have a home like that.'

She looked at him and smiled, not wanting to say more, terrified of being judged self-pitying.

'It is, and I wouldn't have it any different. Now, come and sit down by the fire.'

They sat at each side of the hearth in comfortable old leather armchairs. Edwin insisted that Lorna rest her feet on a small footstool to avoid the draught that whistled in under the back door. The heat given off by the fire was so intense that she soon had to remove her coat.

Edwin had pulled forward a small table and set out the food. Lorna smiled when she saw the 'little snack'. There was a home-made pie the size of a dinner plate, sausage rolls, a slab of fruit cake, bread rolls and cheese, and a bag of apples.

Edwin took down a tea caddy from a shelf at the back of the room and made a pot of tea using water from the kettle that was already steaming on the small hob.

'Hold on to your hat!' he said suddenly, and grinned as he opened the back door. A blast of cold air caught her unawares but he was back in a moment, holding a bottle of milk. 'We keep it in the yard,' he said.

'It's as good as an icebox, although we have to stand it in a bowl of cold water in the summer months.'

Edwin poured the tea and, with a large clean napkin each spread across their knees, they ate in companionable silence. When they had eaten as much as they could, they leaned back in their chairs and sipped the hot sweet beverage and gazed into the fire. At least Lorna did. She stared at the glowing coals, playing the nursery game of trying to visualize castles and mountains. At one point she looked up, to ask Edwin if he played that game too, but she caught her breath when she found that he was staring at her solemnly.

'What is it?' she asked.

The glow of the fire made it impossible to tell whether he had flushed but he looked discomforted when he answered, 'I'm sorry, I know it's rude to stare.'

'But what's the matter? Why were you staring?'

'I was just thinking that all the years we've known each other we've never been as close as this – as intimate.'

Either the intensity of his gaze or his choice of words unsettled her. She laughed nervously. 'And are you enjoying the experience?' she asked.

'Yes.'

And then, abruptly, Edwin rose to his feet and carried their plates over to the small sink. Lorna busied herself tidying up the uneaten food.

Next he kneeled on the hearthrug and began to bank up the fire. 'Just so that the place is welcoming for my uncle,' he explained. 'I'll be going as soon as he arrives.' He sat back on his heels and smiled up at Lorna. 'I don't work in the shop all the time, you know. I do have lectures to attend and visits to make,' he said.

'Visits?'

'Yes.' Edwin began to make small parcels of the remaining food, wrapping it up in greaseproof paper. He put the parcels into a leather bag. 'I have theories about some of the diseases that are rife in the poorer parts of the city. I need to carry out research to prove my point – although it should be self-evident.'

'What do you mean?'

'The crowded living conditions with sometimes four to a bed, the insanitary housing, the damp, the vermin, the bedbugs, and then the starvation wages – no wonder diphtheria and consumption are rampant. I'm sorry – I shouldn't be shouting at you; none of this is your fault.'

31

'No, it's all right. You weren't shouting. But you did sound angry.'

'I do get angry. I love this city; I wouldn't live anywhere else. But how can I rest easy when alongside the wealth and ease there is such misery?'

Lorna remembered the reason Edwin had been in the park the night before; he had been helping distribute the food parcels. 'So you do what you can,' she said.

'I beg your pardon?'

Lorna nodded towards the bag. 'You're taking that food to people who need it.'

Edwin's smile was thin. 'This is nothing. And as for the soup kitchens, the free handouts, the poor children's holidays – they're all worthy causes, but more than that will have to be done.'

Then, as if he didn't want to say any more he gathered up the cups and plates they had used and took them over to the sink.

'Let me do that,' Lorna said.

'No, sit by the fire a moment longer. I like to think of you warm and safe in my domain.'

She watched him wash and dry the dishes. His movements were neat and precise. What an odd thing he had just said, she thought. Why should Edwin Randall think of her? And why should he want her to be warm and safe? Did he think she needed a protector?

She thought back over the years she had known him. She had met him here, in his uncle's bookshop, the very first time she had ventured into town herself to spend her allowance on books. From the start he had allowed her to roam the shelves, pulling books out, looking at them, replacing them, choosing others until she was satisfied.

Soon he was helping her to decide what to buy and, when he got to know her preferences, he would show her the publishers' catalogues and order anything she especially wanted. She supposed they had become friends – and yet they had never met outside the bookshop until last night in Heaton Park. All the stranger, she supposed, that she could be sitting here so comfortably with him now.

She examined her feelings and realized that she felt easy and at peace. Which was not how she felt when she was alone with Maurice . . .

'What are you thinking?'

Lorna looked up and found that Edwin had come close. He was looking at her curiously.

'Nothing special.'

'You looked troubled for a moment. I hope it's not because of anything I've said.'

32

'Oh, no. I was thinking that I've enjoyed our meal together.'

'Really?' Edwin laughed. 'Then from the expression I saw on your face perhaps there is something you need to tell me about my aunt's cooking.'

'No, of course not. Every bite was delicious.' Lorna joined in the laughter and was pleased that Edwin let the subject of what had troubled her drop.

'So what will you be doing this afternoon?' he asked. 'Let me guess; you'll be sitting curled up in a armchair devouring your new book?'

'I will.'

'About Persia.'

'Mm.'

'You like books about that part of the world?'

'I do.'

Edwin looked at her as though he would have liked to question her further but he had sensed that she didn't want that. Instead he smiled and went to the hearth to place a cinder guard in front of the fire.

'Uncle Humphrey will be alone here this afternoon; he's a little absent-minded. We don't want the place to burn down if a coal falls out while he's serving a customer. Now – it's time to open up again.'

Edwin left her and went into the shop. She heard him withdraw the bolts and then she heard the bell over the door tinkle as it opened. There was a murmur of voices; he must have a customer. Lorna pulled on her coat and began to button it up. She looked around the small room and realized that she felt slightly regretful to be leaving it.

In the shop Edwin was busy serving two threadbare young men who might have been students. He looked up as she picked up her own purchase from the counter and excused himself to his customers. He came around the counter and followed her to the door.

'My uncle will be here at any moment,' he said. 'If you wait, I'll run and get you a cab.'

'No, thank you. It's not far to the tram stop.'

Lorna opened the door and stepped out into the swirling snow. She hoped that she had not sounded too abrupt, but as soon as she had glimpsed the outside world through the window in the door, she had begun to wonder at the fact that she had been so completely relaxed and happy in Edwin's company.

She hurried up the Groat Market towards the Bigg Market and the junction with Grainger Street. She didn't have to turn round to know that Edwin was standing on the narrow pavement watching her go.

* * *

33

Lorna glanced at the long queue waiting at the tram stop and hurried by. She guessed that the trams would be full of cold, damp and irritable people, and she was glad to delay her journey to Heaton a little longer. For she'd had no intention of going straight home.

Maurice had said that he would try . . .

When she'd asked him last night whether he would be there today, she had meant would he be going to the café in the Grainger Market where they had first met by chance last summer. The tearoom had become their secret meeting place. It was unlikely that anyone either of them knew would ever see them there.

That warm summer day Lorna had gone to the large covered market in the centre of town in order to browse in the second-hand bookstalls. The market was crowded. Eventually the smells from the goods on the stalls, the fish, the meat, the cheeses, mingling with the sharper aromas of coffee and fruit and vegetables, and all intensified by the heat, had become too much for her. Carrying the book she'd bought she made her way towards the nearest exit.

But all the aisles were crowded and tempers were short. She was jostled from side to side. She couldn't see where she was going and she began to imagine that, somehow, she had turned back on herself and was being carried along the way she had come. Then, suddenly, a red-faced, unkempt-looking woman shoved her viciously aside and she began to fall.

She had visions of hitting the ground hard and then being trampled underfoot. She was just about to scream in terror when someone caught her and hauled her to her feet.

'Why, it's Lorna Cunningham, Rose's cousin, isn't it?' Lorna looked up to find Maurice Haldane smiling down at her. Before she could answer he continued, 'Yes, it is. I met you when I escorted Rose home from the tennis club just last month.'

'Hassan,' Lorna said.

'I beg your pardon?'

'My real name's Hassan, not Cunningham. But, yes, I'm Rose's cousin.'

'Ah.'

Lorna had no idea what Maurice was thinking. His look was thoughtful – speculative – but he continued to smile. He began to say something: 'So you're—' but he never finished the sentence because a man with a sack of potatoes over his shoulder suddenly shouted, 'Move yerself, you pair of daft puddin-heads! I canna get by!'

Maurice turned swiftly and glared down at the man. Lorna couldn't

34

imagine Maurice Haldane ever having to look up to anyone – he was so very tall. He didn't say anything; he didn't need to. His look was so cold, with just a hint of menace, that the poor man actually apologized.

'Sorry, sir,' he mumbled, and waited until Maurice took Lorna's elbow and guided her out of the way.

'Come along,' Maurice said to her. 'You look in need of refreshment.'

Still holding her arm, Maurice strode through the crowd, which seemed to melt away before him. Lorna realized that they were indeed going back the way she had come and she soon found herself being ushered through the doorway into a small tearoom with blue-and-white-gingham-covered tables.

'I would have gone to the café on the balcony,' Maurice said. 'It's amusing to look down on the central hall, but as you know, heat rises, and on a day like this that means the perfume of the populace rises too.'

'Perfume of the populace?'

'The crowd – the general public – the proletariat – whatever you call them. Let's face it, most of them stink.'

'Oh.'

'Have I been vulgar? I'm sorry.'

'No, it's just that, I mean . . .'

Lorna was at a loss. She was always uneasy when Rose and her friends talked like that about people less well off than themselves. She thought it wrong, but she didn't want to say so to the man who'd just rescued her from disaster; a disaster brought about by the action of the same kind of person he had just disparaged.

'I know I shouldn't talk like that,' Maurice said as he settled her at a table at the back of the room, 'but I suppose I was still angry with that man and his potatoes.'

Lorna looked at him quickly, trying to decide whether he'd said that because he'd guessed at her disapproval but, at that very moment, he smiled at her so engagingly that it took her breath away.

She'd thought about that moment often in the months since that meeting and she still couldn't explain to herself exactly what had happened. She supposed that whatever it was, it must have happened to Maurice too, for, since then, they had sought every possible moment when they could be together.

That first time, without asking her, Maurice had ordered a pot of tea and toasted teacakes. 'They do them well here,' he'd said.

'You've been here before?' Lorna asked.

She must have looked surprised because he smiled as he responded,

'Yes. But tell, me, I'm curious, why did you come to the market today?'

'I sometimes come to see what they have on the second-hand bookstalls.'

'Ah, yes.' Maurice glanced down at the neatly wrapped brown-paper parcel. 'I see.' But he didn't ask her what she had bought.

Perhaps she didn't give him a chance because she asked immediately, 'And why do you come to the market?'

'The gunsmiths. Today I'd been in to order some spare sights.'

Lorna frowned. 'Sights?'

'For a hunting rifle. But I can sense you wouldn't want to hear about that.'

He smiled at her again and, without warning, he reached across the table and gently pushed her hat further back on her head. 'That's better,' he said, 'it must have been knocked when you nearly fell and, charming as the effect was, it gave a slightly tipsy effect to your otherwise perfect appearance.'

Lorna shrank back in her chair. 'Don't tease,' she said.

'I'm not teasing. You're lovely.'

After that he had called for the bill and told her that he would have to go but he would see her to the tram stop. Just before they left the tearoom he'd asked when she would be visiting the bookstalls again.

'Next week,' she'd said. 'But . . .'

She almost asked why he wanted to know. She opened her mouth to form the words but he caught her hand. Her white lace glove was no protection against the warmth of his flesh. It was as if an electric current passed between them.

'Oh,' she breathed, and she saw his eyes widen in surprise as if he had been taken unawares.

He bent his head and she saw the gleaming brightness of his hair. Unable to move she watched as he raised her hand to his lips. But, instead of brushing the backs of her fingers politely, he turned her hand over and placed his lips on her palm. She caught her breath as she felt heat flood through her body.

She had no idea how much time had passed before he straightened up and, still holding her hand, murmured, 'At the same time?'

'Mm.'

'I'll be here.'

And that had been the start of it.

But now the overripe smells of summer had given way to the scent of evergreen and the tang of oranges. The only unpleasant odours were those rising from the damp, musty clothes of tired shoppers, but, fortunately, the worsening weather had driven many of them home and the market aisles were not too crowded.

Lorna barely noticed the seasonal decorations, the garlands and the Christmas trees. The nearer she got to the tearooms the more anxious she became.

Maurice had said he would try to be here today.

She knew it would be difficult for him for he had told her so. His parents were giving a grand dinner in their house in Jesmond. House? It was more like a baronial hall, according to Rose. Although, no doubt, there were plenty of servants to prepare for such an event, Maurice had told her that his formidable mother liked to keep him at her beck and call on such days in case there were any last-minute arrangements that only a member of the family could make.

Her grandmother and Rose had been invited to the dinner and Lorna knew this was significant. Normally, although rich, Grandmamma Cunningham did not move in quite the same social circles as the Haldanes. When she had been widowed relatively young, Mildred Cunningham had been left to run her husband's small building firm. George Cunningham had already moved on from simply building rows of neat artisans' houses to being a landlord as well, and his widow expanded the business by buying up existing housing in other parts of the city. The rent this brought in enabled the Cunninghams to live very well indeed.

The Haldanes, on the other hand, starting with one department store in Newcastle, now had stores in most major cities, even one in London, and had built up a retailing empire. They were able to live the life of landed gentry.

Rose said that Maurice's father, although he had a keen business brain, was completely dominated by his wife in domestic matters. And Mrs Haldane liked to forget that her way of life was made possible by trade. She would have preferred Maurice to marry into an aristocratic family.

But unfortunately those families thought the Haldanes' wealth too new and were not ready to accept Maurice for one of their daughters. So, in that case, a bride wealthy in her own right would be the next best match for him.

Lorna knew that Maurice was prepared to please his family in his choice of wife; he'd told her so. He knew that they would be happy if he chose Rose Cunningham and he was aware that Rose would accept him. But from the moment he'd met Lorna he'd been procrastinating.

Lorna felt uneasy when she thought of all the times Rose had confided in her about her hopes of marrying Maurice. Whenever she'd speculated on why on earth he hadn't declared himself yet, it took all Lorna's willpower not to flee whichever room they were in.

And now it was the day of the Haldanes' party, and her cousin was convinced that he would propose tonight. It would be betraying Rose to tell Maurice that, and yet perhaps she should warn him, drop some kind of hint. He'd said that he would work something out soon – some way for them to be together. She had no idea what that would be. She could not imagine his parents giving their consent for him to marry Rose's cousin, the poor relation who depended on her grandmother's generosity. And, more importantly, the Haldanes would not welcome into their family a bride of mixed race.

As she drew nearer to the tearooms Lorna allowed herself to examine the idea that had been growing in her mind. Maurice had been so eager for them to be together, had declared so passionately that he must find a way . . . could he possibly mean that he intended them to elope? To Gretna perhaps? And would he tell her today?

Chapter Three

Edwin was on his way to see Irene Lawson and her baby sister, Ruth. He got off the tram at the bottom of Shields Road and crossed over to walk down Byker Bank. A cold damp wind blew up from the river. The snow was still too wet to lie, but the large soft flakes looked pretty as they fell, making even the view down to the Ouseburn Valley look attractive.

The Ouseburn, which hundreds of years ago must have been a pretty stream, was now little more than an open sewer. The small industries, such as the lead works, the flint mills and potteries that had established themselves in the valley, had long been in the custom of dumping their waste in the burn. The inhabitants of the decaying dwellings followed suit with their household waste and ordure.

All this was carried the short distance to the River Tyne. On hot days the stench could be unbearable and even now, in December, there was no escape from the ever-present stink of the tannery.

The people who lived here made a hard living on their own doorstep but there was also an ever-changing population of transients, the sailors who brought their custom to the cheap pubs and lodging houses.

Irene Lawson's father had been one of these sailors, although he'd started off as a local lad. His grandfather had filled his head full of tales about how the Lawsons had once been an important family in Byker, owning much land in the area. But that was hundreds of years ago, and now they were as poor as the rest of the population. Perhaps these tales were to blame for the fact that young Jim could never settle and, at twelve, he'd run away to sea.

Not very far at first. He'd started working on the colliers that took the coal from Newcastle to London. Then, as he'd grown older, the call

39

of the deep sea had got him and he'd started sailing on longer and longer voyages to foreign ports.

But he'd always returned. Once he'd been home long enough to marry a local girl, Alice Sims, and he'd fathered a daughter, Irene. After that his visits home had been sporadic. Irene was fourteen and her mother a worn out thirty-two when he stayed long enough to father another child, Ruth, the baby girl Edwin was on his way to visit now.

Jim Lawson had not come home in time for the birth of his second child eighteen months ago, and he hadn't come home yet. So he had no idea that his wife had died not long after the baby was born and that his older daughter, not much more than a child herself, was struggling to bring up her sister.

She must have been watching out for him for, as soon as Edwin had passed the window, the front door opened and Irene welcomed him with a finger to her lips. 'Whisht, the bairn's sleeping,' she whispered, before turning to lead him along the stone-flagged passage to the door that led into the room where they lived.

When her mother had been alive, with both of them working, and helped by the largesse Jim sometimes brought home, the Lawsons had been able to afford both the downstairs rooms in the house, although they shared the back scullery with the tenants upstairs and also the back-yard privy.

Now, Irene and the baby lived in this one room, and in it was everything they owned. Which wasn't much. Edwin glanced round at the scrubbed floorboards, the bare table, the bed and the one comfortable chair. He noticed that the rug that used to cover the floor near the hearth had gone. Sold or pawned, he thought.

At least the fire was adequate, probably because one of Irene's daily cleaning jobs was in the offices of the coal yard and they allowed her to bring a scuttle full of coal home. But still the room was cold. Baby Ruth was sleeping in her pram near the window which Edwin now noticed was open enough to let the draught howl in, spotting the clean pram blankets with soot.

Irene saw his frown. 'You said she needed fresh air,' she said. 'I divven't like leaving the bairn in the pram at the door like the others do, not on this steep bank.'

'I know, and you're right, but if you can manage to take her up to the park each day, that would do. There's no need to keep the room as chilly as this. You've got to think of your own comfort too.'

'Well?' Irene asked as he leaned over the pram and looked down at the sleeping child. 'What do you think?'

Edwin placed one hand on Ruth's brow and then, using both hands, very gently felt each side of her neck under the fat little chin. The child hardly stirred. Her complexion was clear and her long dark golden lashes lay like half-moons on her skin of milk and roses.

'Gan on – get her out of the pram – wake her up if you hev to,' Irene said.

Edwin straightened up and smiled. 'There's no need. I can see she's fine.'

'But the cough—'

'Is she still coughing?'

'No – just a snuffle or two. But her cheeks get red, and I thought—'

'I know what you thought, Irene. And because your mother died of consumption you'll always have that worry. But you are clear of the disease and baby Ruth is lucky to have you to look after her, to keep her clean and well fed.'

'But—'

Edwin turned to look at the sleeping child once more. 'I don't want to waken her but if I did I could show you the cause of her troubles by simply opening her mouth.'

Irene joined him and looked down at her sister. 'You mean the new teeth?'

'I do.'

Irene sighed and shook her head. 'I worry too much, divven't I?'

'You're doing your best to be a mother to her, Irene. Ruth's lucky.'

'Lucky? Is that what you think? Her mam's dead and her dad doesn't even know of her existence. Poor bairn – I'd hardly call that lucky.'

Edwin stared at Irene. Her young face was tired and drawn. Not quite haggard – she still had youth on her side and, of course, she was beautiful. She was small and her womanly figure was no doubt kept trim by sheer physical labour; for Irene, who was certainly intelligent enough to have found better employment, had settled for various cleaning jobs for whoever would allow her to take the baby with her.

She was naturally fastidious and she kept herself clean. Her dark blonde hair was smooth and shining. She tied it back into a severe knot on the base of her neck, an old-fashioned style, but it kept the heavy locks out of the way and the severity of it, instead of making her look plain, enhanced her fine-boned features.

She gazed at him now from dark blue, almost violet, eyes and he was surprised by the faint stirrings of attraction. But, immediately, the image of another young woman filled his vision. That of Lorna Hassan.

41

Lorna was not much older than Irene but she was slightly taller and much slimmer. Her eyes were deep brown instead of blue and her skin was darker, almost like that of a gypsy woman, except that instead of being weather-roughened it was smooth and supple.

Why should he think of Lorna now, he wondered. Lorna, who lived less than a mile away from Irene and yet whose world was so different.

Lorna's grandmother, Mildred Cunningham, lived in one of the grand houses looking over Heaton Park, there were servants to look after the family's every need and Lorna had been sent to one of the new independent girls' day schools. She had good, even fashionable, clothes and she had certainly never gone hungry. From the few facts he knew about her, Edwin believed that she owed her good fortune to her grandmother's generosity in taking her in when her mother had died, leaving her penniless.

Irene Lawson, too, had lost her mother. In her childhood her sailor father provided for them whenever he could, and Alice had augmented their income by temporary daily skivvying jobs in the big houses at the other side of Shields Road as well as some 'waiting on' in the various pubs and hotels nearby that provided a restaurant service. It was in one of these establishments that she had met Jim Lawson in the first place.

When Alice had died shortly after giving birth to baby Ruth, succumbing to the consumption that was rampant in the poorer parts of the city, Irene's life had changed just as Lorna's had when her mother had died. But Irene had no wealthy relatives to look after her. Beautiful and brave, she was doing the best she could and surviving by sheer hard work.

So why should she make him think of Lorna?

Because Lorna was struggling to survive too, he imagined. Not in any material sense – she would never go hungry – but he sensed that she was more alone even than Irene. Irene at least had her sister to love and care for. Who was Lorna close to?

He could picture her now, a dark curl escaping from restraint and falling over her brow as she examined a new book, the pleasure that suffused her face when she found a book she wanted. All that passion going into her love of printed words on a page.

And today . . . sitting by the fire in the back room of his uncle's shop sharing his meal and talking as if they were old friends. Were they friends? He supposed they were. Some kind of relationship had developed over the years. And yet he might never have asked her to stay and eat with him if he had not met her in Heaton Park the night before.

What on earth had she been doing there on her own in the dark? Why

42

had her grandmother allowed it? Perhaps she didn't care what happened to Lorna. Or perhaps she did not know that she was there. And if that were the case, why had Lorna deceived her grandmother? A schoolgirlish prank? Edwin didn't think so. Intense and serious-minded as she was, Lorna had surely outgrown such escapades.

The only explanation that he could think of was that she had gone to meet someone . . . a man. Edwin frowned as he realized how much the idea disturbed him.

'Will you take a cup of tea, Mr Randall? You look fair done in.' Irene laid a hand on his arm and looked up into his face anxiously.

'No, it's kind of you but I have some more visits to make.'

Baby Ruth stirred and whimpered as she woke up. Immediately Irene left him and leaned over the pram. 'Now then, me bairn,' she murmured, 'what's the fuss about?'

The child opened her eyes and, seeing her sister, she smiled.

'Isn't she bonny?' Irene asked. 'Isn't she going to be just like our mam? The spitting image of her, in fact.'

'And like her sister too,' Edwin said, and wished he hadn't when he saw the surprise in Irene's eyes. 'I'll have to go now,' he added quickly. 'Are you managing all right? Not working too hard? You won't be much good to Ruth, you know, if you tire yourself out.'

Irene laughed as she picked her sister up. 'I work as much as I hev to. And I'm lucky I can take the bairn along with me. Don't worry, Mr Randall, and forget what I said before – Ruth and me's lucky to hev each other. I know that.'

Edwin took some of the food he had brought and left it on the table. Irene, absorbed in her baby sister, hardly noticed as he took his leave.

He had to walk carefully; the snow had stopped but the pavement was damp and slippery. Edwin thought the air had turned colder. If there was a frost tonight these steep streets would be treacherous and broken bones would be added to the miseries of the local inhabitants.

With no money to go to a doctor, many would try to set the bones themselves and this could lead to misshapen limbs and permanent disabilities. In old people it could lead to death. Edwin wasn't a qualified doctor of medicine yet, but at least he could help in these cases if they asked him.

As for the other scourges of this community, the diseases brought about and encouraged by poverty, he had no magic potions, no cures. All he could do was offer common sense advice. Keep clean, eat the right food, and separate the sick from the healthy.

And even these measures were just about impossible for some of the people he visited. How do you keep clean if you can't afford to buy soap or to heat your water? How do you afford nourishing food on starvation wages? And most worrying of all, how can you isolate one sick family member from the rest if up to twelve people could be living in two rooms?

Irene and her baby sister might be motherless and lonely but at least, as long as Irene could work to support them, they would have a better quality of life than many of their neighbours.

Edwin turned up the collar of his overcoat and set off down the bank. He would be spending another hour or two here before going home to the comfort of his uncle's house and another good meal prepared by his aunt. Then he would work late into the night, writing up his notes and also doing the reading necessary before he attended the next lecture at the medical school.

Lorna would be reading now, he thought, and he smiled as he pictured her curled up in a chair by the fire in her room. The sky was darkening and, as the shadows lengthened, the glow of the firelight would encircle her. She would be lost to the world as she read her book, absorbing the facts, looking at the pictures, with her fingers tracing the maps of a faraway land.

Edwin caught his breath, taken aback by the intensity of the image and the emotion it aroused in him.

The three women at the next table gathered up their brightly wrapped parcels and, still laughing and gossiping animatedly, prepared to leave the café. The youngest of the waitresses opened the door for them and smiled a thank you as she pocketed the tip.

Lorna glanced round. The other tables were empty. She was the last customer remaining. She picked up the little china teapot. Its shiny surface was cold. Nevertheless she tipped it up and watched as a brown sludge of water and tea leaves dribbled from the spout into her cup. The matching rose-patterned milk jug was empty.

She glanced towards each of the two waitresses – she knew them to be mother and daughter – but they kept their heads turned away from her as they hurried round with trays, taking everything from the tables, even the cruets and the little flower vases. The younger woman began to remove the tablecloths.

Lorna decided not to ask for milk and risk being told that the café was closing – which it obviously was. Instead she took her time measuring two spoons of sugar into her cup and stirring it deliberately.

The liquid in the cup was too cold to dissolve anything and she felt her spoon going round and round in the sludge of sugar and tea leaves.

The result was disgusting but she forced herself to sip it slowly with an expression of enjoyment. However, she knew that she couldn't keep up this charade much longer.

Maurice hadn't come to meet her. He had promised that he would try. He knew she would be waiting here . . .

Her hand shook as she put her cup down; it caught the spoon and nearly tipped over. She saved it from falling and sat holding it with both hands. Her eyes filled with tears.

'Excuse me, miss . . .'

She heard the girl's voice but she didn't look up. She knew what the waitress was going to say.

'Yes, I know, you're closing and you'd like me to go,' Lorna said. Her voice was unsteady and she was glad that the girl stood back and didn't say anything as she opened her purse and put the correct number of coins on the table. She hesitated before adding a tip. She hoped it was enough. Maurice usually dealt with the bill.

But he hadn't come.

She suddenly realized that both women would know what had happened. They would have recognized her and would know that she usually met Maurice here. Would they laugh at her when she left? Would they talk about her and speculate why her handsome companion hadn't turned up? Would they think he had abandoned her?

Lorna snapped her purse shut and rose to her feet. The movement was too abrupt and she stumbled.

'Whoops-a-daisy!' The younger waitress smiled and looked as if she were about to come forward and steady her.

'I'm all right . . . really,' Laura said, and she turned to walk away.

She felt the movement of the cloth before she heard the crash. She knew what had happened before she turned back to see the table bare and the cruet, teapot, milk jug and sugar lying in a jumble on the floor. The cut-glass vase was lying on its side with the posy of winter roses still in place but the water was streaming out and soaking into the spilled sugar.

Lorna was appalled. 'I'm sorry,' she began, and then backed away, startled, when the young waitress stepped towards her. The girl had her hand raised and, for a wild moment, Lorna thought she was going to hit her.

'Don't!' she cried.

45

'Now then, whatever did you think I was going to do?' The girl reached forward slowly and took Lorna's purse from her hand. 'See?'

Lorna looked at the girl's outstretched hand and saw the reason for the disaster. She felt the colour rising in her face.

'You caught the tablecloth when you closed it,' the girl explained as if to a child. 'See?' She opened the purse, releasing the cloth, and handed the purse back to Lorna.

'But it's dreadful,' Lorna began. 'I mean, I've wasted all that sugar . . . I must pay for it.'

'For goodness' sake, divven't fret yourself over a bit sugar.' The older woman came forward. 'There's no harm done. Now, let's hev a look at you – no, nothing spilled on your coat, so if you don't mind, hinny, you'd better be gannin' yem. Me and wor lass hev to clean up and lock up.'

Lorna fled from the café. She didn't think she would ever be able to go there again. Maurice would have to find some other place for them to meet.

Maurice . . .

After what he had done today she wondered if he even wanted to meet her again.

Some of the stalls were closed. The weather had driven the customers home so it wasn't worth staying open. Lorna hurried out on to Grainger Street and turned automatically to head for the nearest tram stop.

'Lorna! Thank goodness!'

'Maurice?'

She turned to see him hurrying after her, the light from the shop windows catching his bright hair, illuminating his smile.

'Oh, Maurice . . .' She fought to control the tears.

'Did you think I wouldn't come?' He had taken her shoulders and was looking at her with concern.

She didn't trust herself to answer. She just stared up at him, allowing herself to believe again that he loved her.

'Come, we can't stand here in the cold.' He took her hand and began to pull her in the opposite direction to the way she'd been going.

'But where? I was going for the tram . . .'

'We'll go to the station, to the cab stand. I'm going to carry you off in a hansom!'

At home, later, she still felt perturbed when she remembered what she had imagined. Had she really thought that they were going to elope then and there when he'd laughingly proclaimed that he was going to carry her off in a hansom cab?

As they'd hurried down Grainger Street her imagination had them halfway to Gretna. The light had been poor and in her agitated state the people they passed seemed unreal – dark insubstantial shadows.

Maurice didn't speak. He held her hand as they almost ran to the cab stand. The horses stood patiently, gently steaming as they waited. The cab drivers stood in a group, talking, their long waterproof capes, all the same, making them look anonymous. It crossed Lorna's mind that no one ever thought of them as individual people with lives of their own. Their purpose was simply to convey their passengers about the city. All they needed to know was where they were going. They never asked why. She wondered if they were ever curious about the people who travelled in their hansom cabs.

One of the drivers detached himself from the group as Maurice pushed her up ahead of him into the first cab and then turned to speak to the coachman. She didn't hear what he said. Only then did it occur to her that if they were going to Gretna perhaps they might have taken a train. Were they going to travel all the way to Scotland in a hansom?

And what of clothes? Was she to go to her wedding simply in the clothes she was wearing? Maurice took his seat beside her and she turned towards him, panicking, but before she could ask him anything he took her in his arms and pulled her towards him. He didn't speak; he simply kissed her long and passionately, arousing such feelings within her that, for the moment, all else was forgotten.

She had no idea how long it was before she tried to pull away. 'Maurice . . .' she sighed.

She could feel her heart pounding. She breathed deeply and could smell the leather upholstery, the lingering aroma of a previous traveller's cigar, and the sweet, sharp tang of bay rum in Maurice's hair dressing. She heard her own breathing, the sound of the harness jangling, the steady clip-clop of hoofs and the rattle of the wheels.

'Don't waste these moments,' Maurice said urgently, and again his mouth closed on hers.

His embrace became fiercer. He pulled her tightly against his body and then, for a moment, his grip slackened, but it was only to allow his hand to start unbuttoning her coat and then her blouse. When she felt his fingers on her bare flesh she thought she would swoon with the sheer delight of the sensations he aroused.

This time it was Maurice who broke away. She reached for his face and tried to pull him back but he took her hands and gripped them. He laughed softly. 'No, Lorna, no more, not now. But we'll be together soon. I promise you.'

'Soon? But . . .?'

Lorna freed her hands and began to fasten the buttons of her blouse. She kept her head down. She didn't want to betray by any look or gesture what wild speculation had been going through her mind when they got into the cab together.

'That's right,' Maurice said, 'make yourself look respectable. Here, let me fasten your coat.'

She sat still and allowed him to do so. He leaned over towards her and she glanced beyond him to the view of the passing street. She saw that he was taking her back to Heaton. She didn't look at him when he pulled her into his arms again, and she sat with her head resting against his body for the rest of the journey.

'I won't get out,' he had said when the cab came to stop. 'Do you mind?'

'No.'

She made to get up and he pulled her down on to his knee. 'Don't sulk,' he said.

'I'm not sulking.'

'Yes, you are.' He put one finger under her chin and forced her to raise her head and look at him. 'You know we can't be seen together,' he said, 'not yet.'

With those last two words her heart lifted. 'Not yet, Maurice?'

'It won't be long. Do you trust me?'

She nodded mutely and got down from the cab.

'Lorna!'

'Yes?' She looked back hopefully.

'Don't forget your parcel. Another book, is it?'

'Yes. Thank you.'

They had stopped some distance away from the house. That was just as well, for the short walk home had given her just enough time to compose herself.

Chapter Four

Mildred Cunningham dismissed her maid when she was satisfied that the girl had done the best she could with her hair. Mildred had fine bones and she suited the upswept style, although she acknowledged that she needed the softening effect of the delicate tendrils Violet had teased and twisted to fall at each side of her face.

Her hair was still thick and glossy, but it was so white that in certain lights it looked blonde – like Rose's. Her maroon silk and chiffon evening dress with the embroidered darker red bugle beads around the low neckline had fashionable tiny puff sleeves. She examined her upper arms critically in the dressing-table mirror.

Not bad for a woman of my age, she thought, but she was still glad to be able to pull the black lace and feather boa around her shoulders. Violet had fastened her collar of garnets around her neck; they glinted in the light from the dressing-table candles. Almost like rubies, she thought. Rose will have rubies and emeralds and diamonds and anything she wants if Maurice proposes tonight . . .

Mildred reached for a small oak box with a spring lid and opened it to reveal neat rows of imported Egyptian cigarettes, her one indulgence. When her poor son's effects had been sent home to her, among them had been a tin of gold-tipped cigarettes manufactured by Hadges Nessim in Alexandria. She had opened the tin and fingered them, knowing that Roger had probably been the last one to touch them. That's when she had started smoking. Had she imagined that it would bring her closer to him?

Roger, her only son and her heart's darling. Roger, so tall and handsome, who would have made his tradesman father so proud by simply gaining his commission, let alone fighting so bravely with General Gordon in the Sudan against the Mahdi, that madman whose

49

followers claimed he was some kind of Muslim messiah. Roger's poor wife, Emily, had been six months pregnant when she heard the news of his death; no wonder she'd died in premature childbirth – and the baby hadn't stood a chance. The baby had been a boy. Roger's son.

So Rose had come to live with her, a bewildered little girl, just a year old, who had lost both her father and her mother. Mildred had determined that, henceforth, the child's life would be as easy as possible.

And it would be even easier if she married Maurice Haldane.

Mildred struck a match and frowned through the smoke as she lit a cigarette. The usual light-headed sensation came as she first inhaled, but her enjoyment was marred by the worrying thought that Maurice might not do what was expected of him. Rose was more than beautiful, her looks and figure were sensational; she was as well educated as most girls of her class, and she was heir to a respectable business fortune.

A few months ago Mildred had been sure that Maurice was on the point of proposing. What had happened to make him delay?

Had he heard something? No, he couldn't have done. No one of consequence knew anything, did they?

Mildred stubbed out her cigarette in a cut-glass ashtray and reached for her packet of Parma violet cachous. She must sweeten her breath before going to the party at the Haldanes'. It still wasn't considered quite proper for a well-brought-up lady to smoke, although many did, including Rose. Mildred sighed. She would have to talk to her granddaughter about that. She would tell her that if she couldn't give up the habit then she must be discreet. Keep it secret from her husband, if need be.

There was no need for Maurice to know everything.

When Mildred went to see if her granddaughter was ready she found that Rose had persuaded Lorna to help her dress.

'You could have had Violet,' Mildred said. 'I've been ready for some time.'

'But Lorna is better at arranging hair than Violet and I reminded her that last time I asked her to help she went . . . . I mean, she forgot all about it.'

Lorna let the comb drop on the dressing table with a clatter and Rose examined her reflection in the cheval glass. She turned and smiled brilliantly, and Mildred couldn't help responding. But she saw how Lorna stepped back into the shadows, averting her face. However, Mildred had seen her expression, the look of hurt – and was it longing?

50

Did her other granddaughter want to come to the party too? Did she resent being left at home like Cinderella?

She had never seemed to mind until now, but lately Mildred had noticed a change in Lorna's disposition. She had been brought up to accept that her life would be different from Rose's; that she would never be accepted into the same level of society. But perhaps she had never realized before exactly what that meant. Now that Rose was about to make a brilliant marriage perhaps Lorna was suffering the pangs of jealousy.

Smiling, pretending to admire Rose, Mildred took the opportunity to observe them, one so fair and the other so dark. The contrast was all the more noticeable because they had exactly the same fine-boned features. If it wasn't for the colour of their eyes, hair and skin, and for the fact that Lorna was slimmer than Rose, they could have been sisters rather than cousins.

Looking at the girls together always aroused in Mildred the same feelings of angry regret. They were so beautiful – and so different. And she didn't think she would ever be able to accept that difference. Why hadn't she been aware all those years ago of what Esther was up to? Sneaking off to meet that man – that heathen.

She said she'd met him at the library – offered to teach him to read English. That was just the kind of thing Esther would do; it was one of the consequences of her church school education. But to fall in love with him! A dark-skinned seaman! Oh, she knew very well that respectable Englishwomen had married Eastern princes and potentates, and men like that were even presented at court. But Said Hassan was a lowly deck hand who'd jumped ship in South Shields and claimed he had every right to live here because he'd been born in the Yemen. Claimed that made him a British citizen!

A British citizen who couldn't read English when he'd arrived and who wasn't even a Christian. And, wherever he was born, he was still an Arab – a member of the same benighted race that had killed Esther's brother, Roger. How could she?

'What is it, Grandmamma?' It was Lorna who asked when Mildred turned away, clutching her side with both hands.

Mildred had to wait until she caught her breath before she answered, 'Nothing, a slight pain. Indigestion, I think.'

'Can I get you anything?'

'No, it's passed.'

'Oh, good,' Rose said, 'now what do you think of me? Will I pass inspection?'

'Perfect,' Mildred said. 'Just perfect.'

Rose had chosen pale blue satin embroidered with slightly darker blue bugle beads, the colour of her eyes. The neckline was low and revealed her smooth white shoulders. The boned bodice emphasized her small waist and her flaring hips; a womanly shape which, thankfully, was fashionable, for Mildred couldn't imagine Rose staying with any kind of reducing regime. The tiny dropped sleeves were covered with dyed blue swansdown, and the delicate strands trembled as she moved. Surely Maurice wouldn't be able to resist her.

For jewellery she had wisely chosen a single strand of pearls. Would Maurice want to fasten something more exotic round that smooth white throat? Mildred noticed Rose's self-satisfied smile as she fastened on her earrings, which were simple pearl drops on diamanté clips.

'Well, Lorna,' Rose said, 'you haven't said anything. Will I do?'

'You look lovelier than you've ever looked before,' her cousin said, and her voice seemed to tremble.

Rose looked at her in surprise. 'Why, Lorna, are you crying?'

'No, of course not.'

'Well, your eyes look suspiciously moist. You *are* crying. You're happy for me, aren't you? You want me to succeed.'

'Succeed?'

'In bringing Maurice Haldane to heel. Oh, Lorna, I would hug you except that I might disarrange my hair!'

At that moment Violet knocked and entered. 'The carriage is waiting, Mrs Cunningham,' she said.

'Carriage?' Rose exclaimed. 'We don't own a carriage.'

'The Haldanes have sent theirs to collect us,' Mildred told her.

'Ah,' Rose said. 'That's significant, don't you think, Lorna?'

'Maybe. Now, if you don't mind, I'll go back to my room.'

Lorna left them and Violet helped both Mildred and Rose on with their evening cloaks. As they went downstairs, Mildred could see that her elder granddaughter was already dreaming of her triumph.

But what of Lorna? She couldn't believe that her younger granddaughter's emotion had been prompted by her hopes for Rose. No, her tears had been for herself. But why? Mildred had an uneasy suspicion that there was more to it than resentment at being left at home.

The old woman from the rooms upstairs had offered to sit with baby Ruth but Irene could never have left her at home. She'd thought about it. Mrs Flanagan was clean and respectable, and she wouldn't have wanted payment. She would simply have welcomed the opportunity to get away from her family for a while and sit by Irene's fire in peace and quiet.

Mrs Flanagan was a widow who had been forced to live with her daughter and son-in-law, and Seth MacAndrew resented what he regarded as an extra burden. He saw to it that her life was made a misery. And when he got drunk he became completely unreasonable and his wife's mother was the first to suffer his rage. That's what Irene was frightened of: not that the old woman would neglect Ruth, but that Seth might barge in and cause trouble.

So when the request had come for her to help out on a busy night at the Commercial Hotel she'd agreed to come only if she could bring Ruth with her. Mrs Hepburn, the housekeeper, had known Irene's mother. In fact Alice Sims had been working at the hotel as a waitress when she'd met Jim Lawson. He'd come home with a pocketful of money and wandered into the hotel dining room one night, determined to treat his pals to a slap-up meal. Alice had caught his eye and that had been that.

Now, Irene worked at the hotel on a casual basis, cleaning mostly, although tonight she was helping in the kitchen. Mrs Hepburn had told her that if only she would find someone to mind the bairn she would be happy to train her up as a waitress, but Irene wouldn't do that. So now Ruth was sleeping in her pram, which had been pushed into one of the large store cupboards, and every so often Irene slipped away from the sink to check up on her.

It seemed to her that she had been washing dishes for hours. Every now and then she was allowed to change the water but not often enough. Mostly she seemed to have her hands and arms immersed in a greasy lukewarm swill and she had to scrub extra hard to get the plates clean.

During a brief break while she sat at the table and drank a mug of tea she looked at her hands in despair. The skin was wrinkled like the shell of a walnut. She knew this would fade but, worse than that, her hands were becoming red and roughened, from not just the dishwashing but the cleaning and scrubbing jobs she did as well.

'You'll hev to get yerself some hand cream.'

Irene looked up to see Betty, one of the waitresses, smiling at her. The woman had just poured herself a mug of tea and she sat down opposite to her looking exhausted.

'Hand cream's pricey,' Irene said.

'Well, then, rub a bit of dripping in before you gan yem. That's what I would to do. It'll stop your hands getting cracked and sore in this cold weather.'

'And it'll stink as well.'

'Beggars can't be choosers. But seriously, I divven't know what a clever bit lass like you is doing cleaning jobs for. Mrs Hepburn's said she'd be willing to take you on as a waitress.'

'So's I could ruin me feet and ankles instead of me hands,' Irene said, and she grinned.

Betty laughed. 'Aye, there is that. But in a place like this, a lass with your advantages could do well.'

'My advantages?'

'Divven't pretend you divven't know how bonny you are.' Betty looked sour for a moment. 'Someone like me has to smile and act oh, so obliging no matter how they order you about and insult you. But you would just hev to be yerself and the gentlemen guests would tip you way over the odds.'

'And the lady guests?'

'Aye, well, you'd hev a problem with a bit jealousy there,' Betty conceded, 'but there's not many of them in a hotel like this. It's mostly business gentlemen, commercial travellers and the like. And tonight the place is full of them – you'd make a fortune!'

'What *is* the occasion tonight?' Irene was curious. It seemed to her, from the scraps left on the plates so far – the roast meats, the stuffings and sauces – that tonight's dinner was something special.

'Wilkinson's annual dinner,' Ivy said. 'And I'd better be getting back in there.'

'Wilkinson's?'

'The wholesale drapers. Every year, just before Christmas, old Wilkinson gives a dinner for his staff; all the people in the warehouse as well as the salesmen. The senior fellows bring their wives along. It starts off very proper, like, but by the end of the evening most of them are rolling along to the cab stand singing carols and shaking hands with anyone they meet!'

'He must be nice, Mr Wilkinson, to give them a treat like that.'

'Aye, and he arranges summer holidays too, for the children. It's a pity there aren't more like him.'

For the rest of the evening Irene wondered what it would be like to have a job in Wilkinson's, handling the fabrics and the silks and the cottons. She would like that. She might even meet a nice young man, one of the travelling salesmen. He would have to be presentable and speak nice, wouldn't he? After a while he would ask her to marry him and they would set up home in a neat little house, perhaps at the coast, perhaps in the country – she didn't mind where so long it was as far away as possible from where she lived now.

It was late when at last Mrs Hepburn bustled into the kitchen, cast an eye round the work still to be done, and judged that Irene could go home. She thanked her, paid her well, and insisted that she take the remains of a boiled ham wrapped up in a clean tea towel.

Irene tucked the ham under the mattress in the pram. Something like this made the work worthwhile, this and the scuttle of coal she got when she cleaned the coal office. She'd learned to go to the butcher's just when he was parcelling up the waste for the bone yard and he often gave her a few bones with enough meat on them to make a nice bit stew.

Most of the time she could do without the leftovers that Edwin Randall brought but she didn't like to hurt his feelings. And anyway, nothing went to waste. Poor old Mrs Flanagan was kept on starvation diet by that ruffian of a son-in-law and her daughter couldn't do anything about it. If anyone stood up to Seth they risked serious harm.

So when the old lady crept downstairs and into Irene's room to keep herself out of the way, she was often greeted with a nice little snack and a good fire to sit by for an hour or two.

Irene's choice of jobs would be far wider when the bairn was at school, of course. But that was years away. And meanwhile, Irene thought, I'm ruining me hands and probably losing me looks.

She winced when she did up the buttons of her coat. The skin of her fingers was sore and cracked. Perhaps she should rub in some dripping, like Betty suggested. But would she be able to bide the smell? She decided she wouldn't. She smiled to herself; she smelled bad enough already, what with the smell of the cooking – the roasting and the frying. The greasy odour of hot fat would linger in her clothes for days after a job like this unless she gave them a good possing. It was no good simply hanging them out in the back yard to let the breeze freshen them up. The stink from the tannery was worse than the smell of cooking.

Mrs Hepburn herself helped Irene lift the pram down the back steps and told her to get home quickly. 'I know it's not your sort of lass he's after but I don't like to think of you going home alone.'

Irene knew she was referring to the recent murders of lone women. 'Divven't fret,' she said. 'There's plenty of light on the main road and once I get over Byker Bridge I'm nearly home.'

But Mrs Hepburn was troubled. 'I'd send the pot boy with you if I could, but Gordon'll be busy for hours yet.'

'I know. But there's no need. Like you say, it's not my sort he's after and the poor lasses have been found in the parks or the alleys, not the main streets.'

'All right, pet. You've worked hard tonight and I'm grateful. But remember, there's a better job for you in the dining room whenever you say the word.'

Irene crossed the yard, taking care to manoeuvre the pram round the rows of rubbish bins. In doing so she startled a cat. It hissed at her and leaped from the top of one of the bins on to the wall. She didn't know whether the resulting clatter of bin lids frightened the cat or herself the more. She glanced into the pram but Ruth didn't stir.

On the wall the cat arched into a black silhouette against the moonlight. It turned to look back at her, its eyes glinting; then it dropped out of sight at the other side.

There was no sign of it when Irene let herself out into the lane. No doubt it would be back to forage in the bins as soon as it thought it safe. In spite of the fright it had given her Irene bore it no malice; in fact she realized that the army of stray cats that patrolled the alleys was a good thing – they kept the mice, and worse, the rats, at bay.

Turning the corner at the end of the lane Irene began to push the pram up the slight incline towards the main road. She thought about what Mrs Hepburn had said about a job in the dining room, and about her daydreams earlier of working in Wilkinson's. She had no false pride, she knew there were many better ways for her to earn a living. It wasn't just her looks, although she realized that helped, but she also had a good brain. She knew she was capable of taking on a job with prospects.

She had been good at spelling at school and quick with her numbers. She always came top in the mental arithmetic tests and Miss Davis had even said she might be capable of staying on to be a pupil teacher. But with her dad being so unreliable, her mam had needed her to leave school and start earning. And then her mam had died, and that had changed everything.

She peered into the pram at the sleeping baby. Did she mind? Of course she did. But it wasn't Ruth's fault, poor little bairn. She hadn't asked to be born and then made motherless before she knew what the world was about. Irene sighed. At least she had her health and her strength, and could earn enough money to keep them both from the workhouse. And for now, that would have to do.

Irene stopped before she got to the top of the side street. She could see three people standing on the corner and they were talking with raised voices. Were they arguing? Were they drunk? Could she be in danger? She moved into the shadows and peered ahead.

Two of the figures were women, one tall and well made, the other smaller and thinner. The third figure towered above both of them, a powerfully built man. Irene strained to hear what they were saying.

'What did you expect, Mr Brady? That Hepburn wife took one look at the little trollop and threw us out.'

Irene recognized the coarse tones of Jess Green, a girl who lived down Byker Bank in Quality Row. She supposed the 'little trollop' she was referring to would be Jess's sister, Sarah. Sarah was a year younger than Jess and much prettier. And in Irene's opinion they were both too young to be doing what they were doing, earning their living by prostitution. Not that any woman in her right mind would do that at any age.

'Eeh, our Jess, I'm not a trollop!' The younger girl sounded indignant.

'Yes, you are. Just look at you, got up like that with that daft hat and that mangy feathery thing round yer neck! Cheap, that's what you look. No respectable man would want to gan with you!'

Irene smothered a laugh. For indeed no respectable man would want to have truck with either of them. Suddenly she stiffened when the man turned, stepped apart from the two girls and seemed to stare down the street towards her. But the next moment his attention was taken by Jess again.

'Huh!' the girl continued. 'That wife had the cheek to tell me that the Commercial was a high-class establishment and the likes of us weren't welcome!'

'I know, I know,' the man called Brady soothed. 'Divven't get upset, now. It was my mistake to send you in there but I didn't think old Ma Hepburn would notice with the place full like that.'

'Well, it wasn't very nice, you know, being treated like muck.'

'I know, Jess, pet, but I was only thinking of your comfort on a cold night. I thought if you went into the saloon bar you might have a nice little sit-down in the warm. And perhaps be treated to a drink or two before getting down to business.'

The older girl sighed. 'So what'll we do now?'

'I judge the party will be over soon,' he said. 'The guests'll be coming out and most of them'll be making for the nearest cab stand. If the pair of you saunter along in that direction, looking as fetching as you can, you'll soon pick up a customer or two.'

Poor bairns, Irene thought. For the Green sisters were little more than children. They'd been left alone in the world just as she had been and, somehow, they'd been drawn into the sordid world of prostitution. So here they were, on a winter's night, dressed up in their tawdry finery to attract 'customers'.

And where were they going to take these customers? A cheap lodging house that let rooms by the hour? Or more likely some back lane where their business would be transacted as quickly as possible in the dark and the cold, and to the accompaniment of squalling alley cats. And worse than that, with the recent murders in mind, they were risking their lives.

Irene wondered if they thought of that when they handed over their pitiful earnings to their protector, Brady, before he sent them on their way to find another customer.

She could no longer see the little group; they must have moved on. After waiting for a moment or two, she judged the coast to be clear. She knew the Green sisters from school but there was no love lost between them. Jess Green, who'd used her size to advantage in playground squabbles, had always accused Irene of having 'airs and graces'; of thinking she was better than the other bairns, as indeed she had. But she had always done her best to avoid confrontation. And tonight, particularly, she hadn't wanted any caterwauling that might wake up her sleeping baby sister.

She hurried along Newbridge Street to Byker Bridge. The bridge, which soared high over the Ouse Valley, was wide and well lit but, once there, she was exposed to the wind blowing up from the River Tyne. She quickened her step, but then she saw the figure of a man coming towards her.

Something was wrong. Instead of hurrying as she was, to get across the bridge quickly and get out of the wind, the man was slowing down. And instead of moving to the side, out of the path she was taking, he seemed to be coming deliberately to meet her head on.

What should she do? Turn on her heel and run back into the busier streets of the town? Swerve and run past him because she wasn't far from home? Before she could make up her mind, she saw, to her horror, that he had speeded up and was running towards her.

He began to shout. At first she couldn't make out what he was saying but as he got closer his words grew more distinct.

'Wharrer yer got there? Wha's in the pram?' he yelled. 'Hawway, tell us, what yer've got?'

He's mad, she thought, and before she could dodge round him he was upon her. His eyes were glinting, like the cat's, in his filthy face. He was big and wild-looking, with long unkempt hair, ragged stinking clothes and foul breath. It was his breath that told her that rather than mad he was drunk. Or perhaps he was both, his brain raddled by cheap liquor and rough living.

He seized the handle of the pram and began to tug it away from her. 'Give us it – give us it!' he screeched.

Irene hung on desperately. If he ran off with the pram she might never see her baby sister again, for whatever he imagined he had taken, when he discovered it was a child, he might simply throw her into the river.

'Whaddya got in here?' he yelled. 'Coal? Firewood? Been pinchin' the silver where yer work? Give us it or I'll tell the polis on yer!'

'Go away! Irene shouted at him. 'I haven't stolen anything! It's a baby— There – you've woken her up. Can't you hear – it's a baby!'

Ruth had indeed woken up and the violent shaking of the pram must have terrified her for she started crying. The sound must have penetrated his fuddled brain for the wild man loosened his grip on the handle of the pram just enough for Irene to tug it free.

What would he have done next? Would the crying of the baby have been enough to send him away, or would he have attacked her in a fit of drunken rage? Irene would never know for, at the same time as she pulled the pram out of his grasp, someone came from behind her and seized her attacker.

The drunk was big but her rescuer was bigger. Irene watched the brief struggle as each man fought to gain ascendancy. One man fought in a controlled way – his stance reminded her of the pictures of the boxers on the posters outside St James's Hall – the other was driven by drink and rage and eventually terror, and his limbs flailed wildly as he was forced near the parapet of the bridge.

Then, with a heave of his right shoulder, the bigger man lifted the drunken wretch off his feet and propelled him backwards on to the barrier. He balanced there for a moment, desperately trying to save himself, but then he fell the wrong way and disappeared.

Irene had never heard anything as blood-chilling as the scream that echoed away into the darkness below.

Chapter Five

Ruth was still crying but Irene couldn't tear herself away from the parapet of the bridge. She leaned against the iron rail and stared down. Far below she could see light catching on the narrow Ouseburn as it made its sluggish way to join the wider river. Moonlight reflected off the rooftops of the buildings huddled along the valley bottom. Smoke rose from the chimneys.

Where had he landed? In one of the cobbled streets? Did he lie sprawled there, his body broken and his soul departed, or had the poor man gone straight into the water to float like so much rubbish until the tide carried him down to the Tyne and then on to the North Sea?

She became aware of the man standing beside her. He too stared down silently. 'You've killed him,' she whispered.

'I saved you.'

'Did you?'

'How can you ask?'

'He knew it was just a baby – he would hev gone away.'

'You're sure of that, are you?'

She tried to recall what had happened. The drunk had heard Ruth begin to cry and he had faltered. In that moment she had wrested the pram away from him. But then she had barely had time to look at his face and see his confused expression before the other man had seized him from behind.

Would her tormentor have gone away, or would his poor frazzled mind have driven him to witless aggression? Irene shook her head. 'I divven't know,' she whispered.

'Me neither,' the man said, 'but I had to get him away from you and what happened after that was an accident.'

'Accident?'

'I didn't mean him to gan over.'

He sounded so subdued that, at last, Irene nerved herself to turn and look at him. He was staring down at the scene below just as she had been. Sensing her scrutiny he turned towards her and she recognized him.

'Mr Brady?' she said.

'Do you know me?'

'No . . . but I heard someone say your name.'

'On the corner by the hotel.'

'Yes, how did you know?'

'I saw you watching us.'

She remembered the moment just after she had suppressed a laugh when he had seemed to stare down the street towards her. She looked up at him now, studying his expression. After all, he had just sent another human being to his death. Would his face betray any emotion? Horror? Guilt?

The gaslamps revealed a broad-featured face. He looked grave but somehow composed, confident in the rightness of what he had done. He looked back at her, studying her in turn.

It was Irene who turned away first. She looked down into the valley again. 'What should we do?' she asked.

'Nowt. Just gan yem.'

'But shouldn't we tell someone?'

'Who?'

'The polis, of course.'

'The police? Are you mad? Do you want to go looking for trouble?'

'Trouble?'

'Lissen to me – but first you'd better quiet that poor bairn before we draw attention to ourselves.'

Realizing that he was right, and feeling guilty that she had left Ruth to cry for so long, Irene moved away from the parapet and, taking the handle of the pram, began to rock it gently.

Her rescuer also turned but kept his distance. Irene was aware of him standing with his hands in his pockets of his good overcoat, waiting quite calmly. It was only when Ruth's crying lessened into indignant whimpering and then ceased altogether that he spoke again.

'The less said about this the better,' he said. 'The poor beggar was drunk; he toppled over the bridge. If they ever find him, that's what they'll think. And isn't it best that they should? Do you really want them poking into your life? Do you want to risk this getting into the newspapers? Do you want some la-di-dah, do-gooding wife from

61

Jesmond asking why you had the bairn out at this time of night and mebbes taking it away from you?'

'No!' Irene gasped.

'And it could get worse than that. The way things get twisted round you could be accused of murder. You could end up swinging from the end of a rope.'

'But I didn't push him over!'

'Who did then?'

'You. I mean I know you were helping me – but it was you.'

'So you want me to swing for it, do you?'

She was frightened by the change in his expression. 'Of course I don't,' she said, 'but—' She broke off as she saw him shaking his head.

'Lissen, pet, I wasn't even here. If you insist on telling such a pack of lies, I've got plenty of friends who would swear I was miles away.'

Ruth had gone back to sleep and in the silence Irene stared at the big man uncertainly. She was relieved to see his features relax again.

'You've had a fright,' he said. 'Nothing that happened was your fault. And what happened next wasn't my fault, was it?'

'N-no . . .'

'That's right. Now we've got to make the best of it. This will be our secret. No one will know except you and me. And now, I'd best see that you get home safe. Where do you live? Far from here, is it?'

'Wait!' Irene said. She was by no means sure that she wanted this man walking home with her.

'What is it?'

'How is it that you arrived just when . . . just when . . .'

'Just when you needed me?'

Irene didn't like the way he put it but she nodded agreement.

'I was following you.'

She realized that she wasn't surprised by his answer but she needed an explanation. 'And why was that?'

'I was curious,' he said. 'Just like that poor wretch I wondered why you were out so late with a pram. I thought you might hev stolen goods of some kind.'

'Why should that concern you?'

'You're a young woman. I wanted to get a look at you. And now that I've seen you I know that you're too bonny to have to resort to thieving to feed you and your bairn.'

'Ruth's me sister,' she retorted quickly.

Instead of a quick glance at her ringless wedding finger and the usual mocking laugh, he simply raised his eyebrows and then smiled

62

sympathetically. 'Poor little lass,' he said. 'Are the pair of you alone in the world?'

There was something about the way he asked it that made her want to tell him no, and that her mother and father and a pair of big strong brothers were waiting at home, but she knew that he wouldn't believe her. So instead, she just kept silent.

'Hawway, bonny lass. Jack Brady'll see you to your door and then leave you in peace.'

'Why should you?'

'Why should I what? Leave you in peace? That's what you want, isn't it?'

'I didn't mean that. I meant why should you help me any further?'

He sighed as if hurt at her suspicious tone. 'I can't leave you here after what's just happened. I feel responsible for you in some way. I can see you're upset and I want to see you home safe. That's all.'

Irene set off, pushing the pram, and didn't say anything when he fell in step beside her. As they moved between the gaslamps their shadows walked behind them, caught up and walked with them for a while, before racing ahead, only to start the game all over again.

Jack Brady's shadow, she noticed, was broad and powerful-looking, almost as if it had a life of its own as it moved along beside hers, which was mostly obscured by the pram with its spoked wheels spinning. They made a comical pair, she thought, the shadows like puppets in the shadow plays she'd seen in the school hall.

Without realizing it she'd speeded up. The big man didn't say anything, he simply kept pace. But then, when they reached Byker Bank she was forced to slow down and almost lean backwards, pulling on the pram, to stop it accelerating down the frosty slope and dragging her with it, willy-nilly to disaster.

'Here, let me.'

Unwillingly she allowed Brady to take the pram from her and they went the rest of the way at a more dignified pace. He stood back while she opened her front door and then handed the pram over, making no attempt to follow her in. She pushed the pram ahead of her into the stone passage and then turned to face him from the doorstep. He was still standing there, waiting. Waiting for what, she wondered.

'Good night,' she said. He nodded but didn't move. She knew something else was expected of her. 'And . . . thank you.'

Then he stepped forward so quickly that she was taken by surprise. He stood so close that she could smell his cologne, and his breath, which was slightly beery. 'Remember, say nowt about what happened tonight,' he said, 'or it'll be the worse for you.'

Was he threatening her? Or was he simply giving advice? She couldn't be sure. She felt herself begin to shake.

From the look he gave her she guessed that he knew perfectly well that he had frightened her but he chose to say, 'You're cold, get yerself in.' Then he turned and walked swiftly up the bank.

Irene stayed in the shadow of the doorway. When she could no longer hear his echoing footsteps she glanced up and down the road fearfully. There was no one in sight. And nothing to be seen lying on the road. She shuddered and shut the door, not wanting to admit to herself what she'd been looking for.

Once in their room, Ruth didn't stir; she would probably sleep till morning. Irene eased the cooked ham out of the pram gently and put it in the cupboard on the window wall. It would be cool enough to keep it there for a day or two. Then she built up the fire and pulled a chair close. She sat there hunched and miserable. She didn't even take off her coat. She was still sitting there when it was time to get ready to go to one of her cleaning jobs the next morning.

The maps in the book had been drawn by the author, Sir Charles Blackwell, and he had marked his journeys across Arabia and Persia with dashed and dotted lines of varying sizes. Lorna sat propped up amongst her pillows, tracing those journeys with her finger. The purpose of his journeying was to discover the old trade routes, and Lorna would close her eyes and try to imagine the caravan of camels, crossing the deserts with cargoes of brassware, rugs, leather goods and spices.

Some of the routes were so old that they had been established hundreds, perhaps thousands of years ago, and in his writing Sir Charles had tried to convey how little had changed for the traveller in all that time. How once you set off, leaving the world you knew behind, you could have been a man of any century facing the age-old problems of carrying the right amount of water and provisions to get you from one stopping place to the next. And then finding a comfortable place to sleep.

Long ago her mother had told her that her father had gone back to this part of the world. He had been born there. That he would be travelling, finding the right sort of things to bring home with him, goods that the people in England would want to fill their houses with. That like the merchants in the fairy tales he would load his ship with

64

these magical cargoes and sail home to his family, and they would become rich.

But Lorna hadn't cared about being rich. She had just wanted her father to come home to them. And in the long years since her mother had died, she had gone on hoping and praying that he would. That he had not forgotten all about her like her grandmother said.

So, when she was feeling most bereft, she would take refuge in the world of books. Not just travel books; she read voraciously – history, myths, and all the latest novels. She spent most of her allowance at Edwin's uncle's shop and at the bookstalls in the Grainger market. But, in any case, Heaton public library was just a short walk away so she never had to do without reading matter.

Here in her room at the top of the house, no one would disturb her. In fact they were probably pleased that she was keeping out of the way. Often she would build up the fire in the small hearth and, by the light of the oil lamp on her bedside table, read long into the night.

Tonight, however, it had been difficult to concentrate. She tried very hard to forget that her cousin, Rose, looking more beautiful than she had ever looked before, was at Maurice's house, no doubt winning the approval of Maurice's parents and maybe, at this very moment being held in his arms as they danced, delighting all who saw them.

She found herself reading the same paragraphs over and over again. The lines showing Sir Charles's journeys seemed to merge and become a maze leading nowhere. Lorna tried to conjure up the glare of the sun on the sand, the jangle of the harnesses as the camels swayed along the paths they knew so well they could have followed them in their sleep, the welcome coolness of an unexpected breeze.

But instead she was aware of the cold darkness outside her window, the chimes of the church clock striking midnight, then one o'clock, then two, and the hot flush of envy and rage when she realized that Rose had still not come home.

Eventually she closed her book and laid it on the bedside table, but, unable to settle, she got up, pulled on her robe, went over to her bookcase where she took out another book. She went to sit by the fire. She threw some cushions on the hearth rug and sat with her back against the armchair and her knees drawn up into the circle of her arms. She put her head down and closed her eyes. For the moment the book lay on the rug beside her.

Outside the wind must have risen, for the windowpane began to rattle. The wet snow had turned to rain and it spattered against the glass. Some drops came down the chimney to hiss in the coals. All these sounds she heard but they did not drown out the relentless tick of the clock on the mantelpiece.

She opened her eyes and raised her head wearily to glance up at it. Half-past two. Surely the Haldanes' party was over by now? Or perhaps it was over but her grandmother and Rose had been invited to stay the night. That would signify something, wouldn't it?

She picked up the book that she had brought from the bookcase: *Caravan Tales*. It was not another travel book; it was a collection of stories based on the Arabian tales told by a princess called Scheherazade. She had married a king and when she learned that the king had his wives put to death when he tired of them, she saved her life by telling him stories, always interrupting them at some interesting point and saying that she would continue the next night.

By the time she had finished her thousand-and-one stories, Scheherazade had borne the king three sons and for the sake of the three young princes, even though she had no more stories to tell, the king spared her life.

In *Caravan Tales* the stories had been adapted for children and there were wonderful illustrations of flying carpets, fishermen and genies, thieves hiding in giant wine jars, and Sinbad the sailor setting off on his many voyages. Sinbad had set out to make his fortune . . . just as her father had done.

Lorna's father had bought the book for her before he had left them and it had come with her in her little case on the day that she had come to live here. She opened it now to look for something that she had placed inside it on that very first night in this house.

It was still there, preserved between two pages – the leaf that her mother had caught in the park. The green colour had faded to browny-yellow, shot across with red. Her mother had said it would bring her luck, but if that were so, she imagined the luck had long since run out. With a sigh, she closed the book.

What was she hoping for, she wondered. That Maurice would defy his parents openly and declare his love for her tonight in front of all their important guests? He would say, 'Actually, Mother and Father, no matter how lovely Rose Cunningham is, it is her cousin, Lorna, that I love.'

There would be horrified gasps and exclamations from the guests.

'Yes,' he would continue, 'Lorna Hassan. And it is Lorna that I intend to marry!'

In spite of her misery Lorna smiled. That would be too much like a fairy story. But what *would* Maurice do? He had told her to trust him, that they would be together soon, and he had hinted that he had some kind of plan. If only he would put it into action soon. She could hardly wait for the day when there would be no more deception, no more hiding their love, when she and Maurice could be together openly and she would never be excluded from her rightful place in his life again!

Then, just before three o'clock, she heard the carriage pull up outside the house. Lorna put the guard in front of the fire and hurriedly went back to bed. She turned off the reading lamp. Having spent the whole evening feeling jealous of Rose, she now felt guilty because she knew Rose's hopes would have been dashed. Even if he had not declared his true intentions, and that was most unlikely, Maurice would not have asked her to marry him.

And no matter how Rose has behaved in the past, Lorna thought, with little regard for my feelings, no woman deserves such heartbreak.

Rose would be disappointed and fretful, and she might want to come and talk to Lorna about her frustrations. Better to pretend to be asleep, Lorna thought, and she pulled the bedclothes up so that her face was almost covered.

She knew that Violet had stayed up to let her grandmother and Rose into the house and help them into bed. She could hear voices as they ascended the stairs. Then the voices stopped. The house was quiet and Lorna began to relax. Thank goodness Rose must be too tired to come to talk, she thought. She always needs an audience to play to, and I am all she has. No doubt I will have to face her over breakfast but at least I will get some hours' sleep.

It must have been half an hour later when the door opening roused her from her half-sleeping state.

'Lorna, are you awake?' Rose whispered.

She didn't move. If she pretended to be asleep Rose might go away. She listened for the door closing again but, instead, she heard a soft swishing and she half opened her eyes to see a shadow moving across the wall in front of her. When it stopped she judged Rose to be standing directly over the bed.

'Lorna!' Not quite a whisper now. Rose sounded tense. 'For goodness' sake, Lorna, do wake up! But you *are* awake, aren't you? Please stop pretending. I want to talk to you!'

Lorna sighed and stirred as if she were just waking. She turned and tried to look surprised then she sat up and yawned. 'What is it?'

Violet must have helped Rose to undress before she came up, for now she had on her pale blue silk robe. The robe clung to her body, revealing its womanly shape. Her hair had been combed out and it fell down on to her shoulders and beyond. Even in this state of undress – or perhaps more so – she looked ravishing.

She sat at the bottom of the bed and drew up her feet. But instead of saying anything she dropped her head into her hands. Her hair fell forward, hiding her face completely.

Imagining Rose to be unhappy and thinking she knew why, Lorna's feelings of guilt probably made her sound brusquer than she intended to be when she asked, 'So what do you want to tell me?'

Rose looked up and snapped, 'For goodness' sake, don't be so crabby. I thought you would want to hear about the party at the Haldanes'.'

Lorna stared at her cousin's indignant face. She felt the ground shifting. She remained silent.

'Well, do you? Do you want to hear what happened?' Rose asked.

'I suppose so.'

'Honestly, Lorna, I don't understand you. You were so sweet earlier tonight when you helped me get ready. You can't deny there were tears in your eyes when you saw how lovely I looked and when you knew how much I was hoping for, can you?'

'No, I can't deny it.'

'Well, then.'

Rose got off the bed and walked towards the fire. She stood with her back to Lorna, gazing down into the flames. Lorna slipped out of bed and began to walk towards her. 'Rose,' she began, 'I'm sorry.'

'That's all right,' Rose said. She turned to face Lorna. She was smiling. 'I know I'm selfish sometimes. You don't have to apologize for being cross when I come and wake you up at this ungodly hour.'

'No, I meant . . .' She faltered. How could she explain that Rose had been disappointed because of her. Because her own cousin was the reason she had lost Maurice?

But the ground was shifting further. Rose's smile was radiant. Lorna stared at her in disbelief when she said, 'But ungodly hour or not, I had to tell you the wonderful news.'

'Wonderful?'

'Yes, Lorna. Wonderful, wonderful news. Maurice has proposed to me at last!'

Chapter Six

In spite of coming home so late from the Haldanes', Mildred had instructed that breakfast should be at the usual time; she did not believe in making life difficult for the domestic staff. She could remember a time when she had been grateful to have one little maid-of-all-work so, although she was an exacting mistress, she was always fair.

She expected the hearths to be cleaned and the fires to be lit each morning before she even got out of bed. And she expected the breakfast to be ready and waiting for her. The house must be kept dust free and the windows sparkling, and the laundering of bedding and her and her granddaughters' clothes should be accomplished without her even having to think about it.

And the advantage that Mildred Cunningham had over most other middle-class women was that there wasn't a single one of those household tasks, even lighting the range in the kitchen, that she couldn't have done herself.

Her granddaughters had managed to appear at the table by nine o'clock, which was late by Mildred's standards, and, unusually, it was Lorna who had arrived last. Mildred observed them silently as she sipped her second cup of coffee. Dr Gibson had told her that she was drinking too much strong coffee and that she only had herself to blame for the occasional debilitating palpitations, but, try as she might, she found she couldn't do without it.

Rose looked tired, Mildred thought. Her usual creamy complexion was drained and pallid. Her eyes were puffy. She would have to take care not to let Maurice see her looking like that. Mildred guessed that Maurice Haldane, like other men of his class, would expect certain standards in the woman he married. Rose must learn to be ornamental, not just in public but in the boudoir also.

Her elder granddaughter had not bothered to dress. She had simply pulled on her robe and tied her hair back with a blue velvet ribbon. Mildred disapproved of this. She considered it a sloppy lowering of standards, but this morning she was prepared to be indulgent. After all, she was as pleased as Rose herself that Maurice had finally proposed.

Rose looked strangely young, like a contented child, Mildred mused; a child who had just got her own way. She watched as her elder granddaughter went back to the sideboard to choose more food from the various hotplates.

Rose helped herself to poached eggs, venison sausages, grilled bacon and tomatoes. She had already had a plateful of sprats fried in batter. Mildred had always encouraged both her granddaughters to eat well. One of the joys of having money was to be able to provide a good table. She herself had had a good appetite until recently and, like Lorna, she was lucky that she seemed to be able to indulge herself without putting on weight.

But poor Rose was different. Over the last two or three years, her physical make-up seemed to have changed. If she did not want to end up as portly as Maurice's mother, she would have to start practising a little discipline at the table. And Mildred would have to tell her so. But not today. Let her enjoy her triumph, dream her dreams.

Rose sat down and began to eat. Something made Mildred glance across at her other granddaughter. Just like Mildred herself, Lorna was watching her cousin surreptitiously over the rim of her coffee cup. What was she thinking as she sat there so silently toying with a slice of toast? Her dark eyes were narrowed, the pupils almost concealed by her long black lashes. Lorna, too, looked tired, Mildred thought, her skin unusually sallow.

Mildred had heard Rose go up to Lorna's room last night, or rather in the early hours of this morning, even though she had told her not to. Mildred had been aware of Lorna's strange mood yesterday and had thought it was because her younger granddaughter was beginning to realize how very different her life was going to be from Rose's.

But Rose, no doubt wanting to share her good news immediately, had gone anyway. Mildred had expected Lorna to be out of sorts, this morning, even to sulk a little, but she had not been prepared for this strange air of detachment. It was as if Lorna, some time during the night, had withdrawn herself from her family.

Who can blame her? Mildred thought. She's young, she's lovely and she's intelligent, and yet she must know that no man from the right sort of family will want to marry her. Her mother never thought of that, of the consequences of marrying a man such as Said Hassan.

Suddenly Rose looked up and stared at Lorna. 'Why are you watching me like that?'

'I'm not watching you.' Lorna drank from her cup, put it down and made a play of putting more apricot preserve on her toast.

Rose frowned. 'But you were.'

Lorna bit into her toast and Rose, realizing that her cousin was not going to answer her, sighed. 'Ah, well, I expect you're still cross with me for waking you up when I came home, and I suppose I don't blame you.' She spooned sugar into her coffee and began to drink it.

Was that all it was, Mildred wondered. Did that explain the strange look she had seen on Lorna's face just before she glanced away from her cousin? She wished she could have observed her longer and determined whether it was simply resentment. But she was sure that there had been a flash of some other emotion in those dark eyes before Lorna glanced away from Rose and concentrated on her coffee.

Had it been a look of contempt? No, that was too strong a word. It was almost as if Lorna, rather than envying her, felt that Rose wasn't worth bothering about. Mildred closed her eyes. I must be wrong, she thought. I'm tired and perhaps I had too much wine last night. And, whatever Lorna feels, she will cause no trouble. She never does. At least I've made a better job of her upbringing than I did of her mother's.

Rose had finished her breakfast and she dabbed at her mouth with her napkin. Mildred noticed a dribble of egg yolk on the collar of her robe. She dropped the crumpled napkin on the table and yawned, remembering to mask her mouth with her hand when she saw Mildred's frown.

'So,' she said. 'I'm to be a June bride.' She smiled at Lorna, expecting some response but her cousin simply reached for another piece of toast.

Mildred was amused. She was fairly sure that Lorna did not want any more toast. She had watched her play with the first piece and only begin to eat it in order to avoid talking to Rose.

'My gown will be white, of course,' Rose said. 'I thought heavy silk, no, that might crease too much. Perhaps, satin then, what do you think?'

For answer Lorna gave an almost imperceptible nod as she took a bite of toast.

Rose looked irritated at this lack of interest but she continued, 'And the veil will be full length. Shall I have lace or tulle? What do you think?' She didn't even pause for an answer this time before she continued, 'And I'll have a chaplet of orange blossom to secure the veil

71

– just simple flowers – more effective than diamond headdresses, don't you think?'

Mildred suppressed a wry smile. She knew very well that even if Rose did choose to have a headdress of orange blossoms – a symbol of chastity, incidentally – she would no doubt demand that a few pearl and diamond decorations were scattered artfully in amongst the flowers.

As Rose watched Lorna spread butter on the toast her smile became strained but she continued, 'I shall have a long train, fitted from the waist, I think – from the shoulders is too regal – but it will be long enough for the six little attendants to have to carry properly.'

Lorna still didn't speak and Rose paused and leaned back in her chair. Then she smiled.

'By the way, I suppose I'll have to have Maurice's sisters as my bridesmaids . . .' Rose left her words hanging in the air as she watched Lorna.

Had it been a question, Mildred wondered. Or had Rose already made up her mind? In any case it was the only option. Maurice's mother had already hinted as much. She had also let Mildred know that her husband's nephews and nieces could muster enough small children between them to make the most darlingly cherubic little attendants.

'Charlotte and Geraldine are not as tall as Maurice,' Rose went on. 'I would hate to have them towering over me. But they are just as fair. As I am, of course. We will look so . . . so picturesque.'

Lorna put down her toast, sat back a little, and looked at her cousin as though she were trying to conjure up a picture of Rose and her bridesmaids. Rose, satisfied at last that she was getting some attention, looked gratified. But Mildred saw that Lorna wasn't smiling. She also noticed that Lorna's hand now rested on the envelope that lay on the table beside her plate as though she was prepared to listen patiently to Rose but would rather be dealing with her morning's correspondence.

Notification of another book she has ordered, no doubt, Mildred thought. Most young women spend their allowance on clothes, but I suppose I ought to be grateful that Lorna has something to interest her.

'You do understand, don't you?' Rose asked.

'Understand?' Lorna's voice was low.

'Why you can't be a bridesmaid?'

Oh, no, Mildred thought. Don't go on, Rose. Of course she understands. 'Rose,' she said aloud, 'I'm sure Lorna doesn't expect to be—'

'No, I'm not sure,' Lorna interrupted before her grandmother could go any further. 'Do tell me, Rose.'

'Well, er . . .' Rose suddenly didn't look so confident. 'I mean, it's the look of it. I mean, Maurice and I and his sisters and all his little cousins are all so fair and it would look strange to have someone so . . . so different, wouldn't it?'

Once more Lorna leaned back and gave Rose that considering look. Mildred noticed that her elder granddaughter was distinctly uneasy.

'Don't worry, Rose,' Lorna said at last. 'I understand exactly what you mean. Now, if you don't mind, may I leave the table?'

Lorna had directed the question to her grandmother and, expecting Mildred to agree, she began to rise from her chair. But Mildred held up a hand to stay her.

'Wait, Lorna. I have to talk to both of you.'

'About the wedding?' Rose asked.

'No.' Mildred smiled. 'Not the wedding. We'll start with the wedding plans when I get back.'

'Get back?' Rose's eyes widened. 'But where are you going? It's nearly Christmas.'

Mildred sighed. 'Exactly. And I have to visit Hannah, so you two must manage the house while I'm away.'

'Oh,' Rose said, 'your cousin Hannah.'

'Yes,' Mildred replied, 'I must take the usual hamper. Would you like to come with me?'

The moment the words left her lips she realized her mistake. She wasn't surprised to see Rose's eyes widen and to hear the astonishment in her voice when she asked, 'Why should I want to come with you?'

Mildred saw that her question had shaken Lorna out of her strange detached mood. She was looking at her curiously.

'Oh . . . no reason,' Mildred said to Rose. 'I was . . . I was just being selfish. Wanting your company. But forget it. Of course you don't want to come.'

Lorna was frowning as if considering what had just been said. Mildred hoped her explanation had sounded convincing. 'So,' she said, 'I'll leave for Corbridge in the morning but I'll be going shopping today. The hamper is already ordered at Haldane's but I must get something personal for Hannah and . . . and her family.'

'Couldn't you have everything delivered?' Rose asked. 'You'll be away for days – you always are when you go there – and we've so much to do.'

'Delivered? From Haldane's?'

'Why not?' Rose smiled. 'And if you tell them you are about to become one of the family – through marriage, that is – they might give you a discount.'

'Don't be stupid, Rose.' Mildred's voice was sharp and Rose flushed. Lorna's frown deepened. Mildred forced herself to smile. 'So, I shall have to leave you two alone for a day or two. Our own preparations for Christmas Day are well under way. There's nothing for you to do except I must ask you not to make life difficult for the servants.'

'I won't, I promise,' Rose said. She made a soft *moue* of pretended pique. 'Maurice has promised to visit some friends in the country, it seems, so there won't be much for me to do except rest and make up on hours of lost beauty sleep. In fact, if it's all right with you, Grandmamma dearest, I might just go back to bed now and stay there until lunch is ready.'

'I suppose so,' Mildred said. 'You know I don't approve of healthy young women wasting the daylight hours in bed, but today I suppose I must indulge you.'

'Thank you.' Rose got up from the table and walked over to the door where she paused and smiled at Lorna. 'We'll talk later, shall we?'

'Why?'

Mildred thought that Lorna looked genuinely surprised.

'Well . . .' Rose was taken aback. 'I mean, you'll want to hear about my wedding plans . . . where Maurice and I will go for our wedding journey . . . where we are going to live . . . won't you?'

Lorna's only answer was to stare at her cousin, and, again, Mildred saw an expression in her dark eyes that she couldn't define. But it made her uneasy.

When Rose had gone Mildred hesitated before she spoke to Lorna. 'You'll be all right here while I'm away?'

'Why shouldn't I be?'

Mildred caught her breath. Lorna's response was so brusque that it was almost rude. 'Very well, I'll say it,' she snapped. 'I don't want you upsetting Rose, not at this happy time in her life.'

Lorna looked down at her plate. Her lips moved and Mildred thought she heard her say, 'happy time . . .' Then she looked up and said, 'Is that why you asked her to go with you to cousin Hannah's?'

'What do you mean?'

'To take her with you so that I couldn't upset her?'

'No, it wasn't that. I felt like some company . . . I told you.'

'But you must have known that she wouldn't want to go. She hated staying on the farm that summer when you banished her.'

'It was for her own good,' Mildred said hurriedly. 'I had to get her away from that man. She was becoming too fond. Too involved.'

'Were you frightened that she would elope? That there would be another disgrace?'

'Disgrace?'

'Another unsuitable marriage?'

'Don't look at me like that, Lorna.' Mildred was vexed. She had never known her younger granddaughter to talk to her like this. She had never allowed it. 'That fellow was hardly a good marriage prospect. A travelling actor! And don't think I absolve you from any blame. You knew very well what was going on. You accompanied her to the coast, to the theatre all those times. What were you doing when they were sneaking off to be alone together?'

'I was sitting alone in the floral gardens, mostly,' Lorna said, and Mildred was shocked by her almost flippant tone. 'You know what Rose is like,' she continued, 'nothing will stop her when she wants something.'

'I know.' Although it pained her Mildred tried to be conciliatory. She wanted to end this conversation. 'But you could have told me instead of leaving me to find out when . . . when it was almost too late.'

Lorna looked at her coolly. 'Do you know I never did understand how you did discover Rose's secret. Had somebody seen them? A friend of yours?'

'It doesn't matter now,' Mildred said. 'It's over. Just be thankful that I found out in time.'

'So you could save her for better things. A respectable marriage.'

Mildred rose from the table. She was angry but she could feel herself getting short of breath and she had much to do. 'I don't know what makes you think you can talk to me like this, Lorna, and I suggest you reflect on your position here. If I hadn't taken you in all those years ago you might have ended up in the workhouse. Instead you have had a comfortable home, a good education and I believe I've given you a generous allowance. Is it too much to expect a little gratitude?'

Lorna also rose to her feet. Her cheeks were flushed and her dark eyes were blazing with emotion.

'Well?' Mildred asked.

'I'm your granddaughter.'

'What does that mean?'

'I'm not just some orphaned child you rescued from the streets.'

'No, but what difference—'

75

'What difference does that make?' Lorna asked. 'All the difference in the world. Yes, I'm grateful, but remember, I didn't want to come here. I had no choice. My mother brought me to you, her own mother, when she knew she was dying.'

'Lorna—'

'She thought my father would be coming back for me. So did I. I'm sorry that I've been such a burden to you.'

'I didn't say that.'

'But I've always been made aware of my position. The granddaughter that you wish had never been born.'

'No.'

'No? You opposed my parents' marriage.'

'Of course I did.'

'You see?'

'What do you mean?'

'You opposed the marriage because my father was of a different race.'

'He was also an illiterate deck hand.'

'Not illiterate!'

'He couldn't speak English.'

'Yes he could.'

'Your mother had to teach him.'

'To *read* English. But, in any case, if you thought him so unsuitable you could hardly have welcomed the outcome.'

'Outcome?'

'My birth.'

Mildred felt a band of pain tighten round her head. The fire had been burning brightly since early in the morning. The heavy crimson velvet curtains helped to keep the dining room warm in spite of its proportions. She took hold of the chair back with both hands and stared at her granddaughter.

'No, I didn't welcome it,' she said, ignoring the dangerous gleam in Lorna's eyes. 'I thought they had been selfish to bring you into the world. You would belong to neither one race nor the other. But that doesn't mean that I wasn't prepared to do my duty.'

'Your duty. And for that I acknowledge you have the right to expect my gratitude. But has it never occurred to you that I might have had the right to expect your love?'

Lorna didn't wait for an answer; she didn't seem to expect one. Mildred held on to the chair and watched as her granddaughter walked from the room without looking at her.

76

The house was quiet as Lorna ascended the stairs to her room on the top floor. She had not slept at all last night after Rose's announcement and, like her cousin, she would like to have gone back to bed now. But that would be pointless. For, no matter how tired she was, she knew sleep would elude her.

She had to be alone; she had so much to think about. She raced up the last flight of stairs and flung herself into her room, almost slamming the door behind her. But once there, she couldn't settle, either in the armchair near the fire nor on the bed, which had been neatly made for her since she'd gone down for breakfast.

For a while she paced about, going to look out of the window at the view of the park with the leafless branches of the trees stark against the winter sky, then returning to the hearth to gaze into the flames.

Rose had stood here just a few hours ago when she had told her that Maurice had proposed to her. Lorna had backed away from her, had sat on her bed, shrinking back into the shadows.

'I can tell you are surprised,' Rose had said. 'But you shouldn't be. After all, it was the perfect occasion, wasn't it?'

'Why?' Lorna whispered.

'Oh, the party, his parents were able to tell the family. And now Maurice says they'll be so happy that they won't raise objections to his going away for a few days just before Christmas.'

'He's going away?'

'Yes,' Rose sighed as if she were already an indulgent wife. 'Apparently he's promised a friend of his to visit some little house he's bought in the country. A bachelor affair, you know. Maurice gave me the impression that his parents might not altogether approve of this friend, but now his mother will be so pleased about the wedding that she will raise no objections.'

'I see.'

'And now I suppose I must let you go back to sleep.' Rose yawned and, smiling, pleased with herself, she had left the room.

But Lorna had not been able to sleep. Her initial shock had been so severe that her heart was still pounding. Maurice to marry Rose after all he had said? But after the first moment of anguish her spirit had begun to rally. No matter what Rose said, Lorna couldn't believe that it was true.

Oh, she hadn't thought that Rose was lying. Maurice must have asked her and Lorna wished that he hadn't, for, of course, he could have no intention of going through with it. How could he have after everything he had said to her?

No, Rose had said it herself. He was keeping his parents happy, wasn't he? He was allowing them to believe he would go along with their wishes while all the while he was making his own plans. Rose had said that he planned to go away . . .

But if what she hoped was true then Maurice had been very cruel. But he must have been desperate to have acted so dishonourably. Would his parents ever forgive him? Would Rose ever forgive *her*?

By the time morning came and she dressed and went down for breakfast, Lorna no longer knew what to believe. She had paused before entering the dining room. She could hear her grandmother and Rose talking and she knew she must control her emotions before she faced them.

And then she had seen the letters on the hall table. She walked towards the table slowly but she already knew – was convinced – that one of the letters would be for her. She had opened it and read it before going in for breakfast.

Now, in the safety of her room, she took it from her pocket and read it once more. It was unsigned and there were only two words written in a hand that she had never had cause to see before.

'Trust me,' it said.

Chapter Seven

It was bitterly cold and Edwin's hands ached as they gripped the ladder. The ladder was old and splintered, but it had been all that they could find when they had asked him to take a look at what was on the roof of one of the riverside cottages. All but the most elderly and unfit of the local men were at work, so the small crowd gathered on the cobbles below was mostly composed of women and children too young to be at school.

Edwin stared through the top rungs at the face lying just a few inches away from him. The man's eyes were wide open; it looked as if he was staring up in the direction of Byker Bridge far above them. But, in truth, he couldn't actually see anything. He must have died some hours ago, during the night, Edwin judged, almost as soon as he'd landed here.

He looked like a puppet who had fallen when its strings had snapped – or had been cut unexpectedly and swiftly, Edwin thought, for he couldn't shake from his mind the image more suited to a sudden and horrifying death. The man's arms were stretched out at each side of him, the fingers of each hand curved into claws as if he'd grabbed frantically at the very air on the way down. Or had tensed like that in his death agony. His legs were out of sight on the other side of the ridge, and it was those broken limbs that the children playing on the banks of the burn had seen that morning.

The poor wretch's back must have snapped with the impact and Edwin could only imagine the pain. He hoped the end had been quick. He sighed and his breath frosted in the air. He suppressed a fit of shivering brought on by horror as much as the cold.

'Who is it, Mr Randall?' The woman's voice wavered up from below. 'For pity's sake, tell me it's not wor Billy!'

Edwin looked down. Jane Potts stood clutching her shawl around her old bones, her lined face pale as whey as she stared fearfully up at him. Edwin glanced at the woman standing behind her. She had her arms folded across her body as she clutched at her shawl and she was shaking her head as if she still couldn't believe what had happened. What had landed on her roof.

'Will you take Mrs Potts into your house, Mrs Charlton?' Edwin asked. 'It might be better if she waited inside by the fire.'

'What fire!' Bella Charlton said, and the lines of her face hardened. But she took hold of Jane Potts' shoulders and began to guide her towards her front door.

The old woman resisted. 'Billy didn't come yem last night,' she said. 'He might be a bit simple but he's a good lad, even with drink inside him. He wouldn't worry his poor mother by not coming yem.'

'Hawway in, Jane,' Bella said. 'It's bitter cold and you don't want to stand here with all these nebby beggars gawpin' at yer, do yer?' Bella nodded contemptuously at the silent crowd that had gathered in the narrow lane to watch the drama.

The two women went into the cottage and those who had so far watched silently, now began to talk amongst themselves. Edwin caught some of the words.

'. . . never could hold his drink . . . poor Billy . . . what a way to die . . . must've come off the bridge . . . poor Jane . . . what'll she do without that daft son of hers . . .'

Edwin turned his attention back to the man lying on the roof in front of him. The clothes were old and dirty but, at some time, an attempt had been made to mend and patch them. His hair was long and unkempt, his face unshaven, and there was an undeniable smell of drink mingled with the odours of old sweat and urine.

He was pretty sure that it was Billy Potts. Billy had never had the wits to keep a proper job but, when sober, he'd had enough gumption to earn a little by running simple errands and, when he only had a little drink in him, he danced a crazy jig on street corners, and was amusing enough for folk to toss coins at him. When he had too much to drink, he acted wild and crazy and frightened people, although he had never been known to hurt anyone.

'What do you say, Mr Randall? Is it Billy Potts, then?' The voice was authoritative and Edwin glanced down to see that the constable had arrived.

'Yes, I think it is.'

'Dead, is he?'

'Yes.'

'Ah, well. Now if you'll come down now, Mr Randall, you'd better leave the rest to me.'

The constable turned to one of the eager lads clustered round behind him and murmured a command. The boy took off up the hill, followed by a string of smaller lads. No doubt the constable had sent them off to the police station in Headlam Street.

Edwin climbed down carefully. As well as being splintered, the rungs of the ladder were slippery with frost. When he reached the bottom the constable offered a hand to steady him. Edwin was glad of the support.

'Do you think he came off the bridge?' the constable asked, and he craned his neck to look up at the modern structure far above them.

'That's the way it looks,' Edwin replied.

'Drunk?'

'Maybe.'

'What other explanation could there be?'

'A fight?' Edwin ventured.

The other man frowned as he considered the possibility, then shook his head. 'I don't see how we could ever know, do you?'

'No.'

'Has anyone told his mother?'

'Not yet, but I think she's guessed. She's in there with Mrs Charlton.'

'Aye, Bella's a good soul,' the man said. 'Then I wonder if you'd mind telling Mrs Potts? I mean the folk round here know you, they respect you. No doubt that's why they asked you to go up and take a look when you arrived.'

'I'll tell her.' Edwin dreaded the task. 'But Billy?'

'I'll see he gets down safe. But keep his mother inside, will you? I'll have to ask her to identify him up at the morgue, but we'll try to make him look decent before she sees him. It's only right.'

Edwin nodded and, as he knocked and entered Bella Charlton's cottage, he heard the constable begin to tell the crowd to move off. He also heard the heavy tread of reinforcements arriving from the police station. His part in the drama was over.

As his eyes became accustomed to the gloom inside he saw the women sitting by the hearth. There was no fire and it could only have been habit that made them huddle there as if seeking any lingering warmth.

The older woman looked round at him. 'It is me son, isn't it? I can see by yer face.'

81

'I'm sorry, Mrs Potts, I think it is.' Edwin felt inadequate. He was expecting her to cry out but, instead, she just seemed to shrivel into herself in the dimness.

Very little light came through the window, not sufficient to make out the expression on Bella Charlton's face but there was no mistaking the compassion in her rough voice when she said, 'There, there, Jane, hinny. Weep if yer want to.'

If the old woman wept she did so silently. The room was not only cold, it had an air of dampness. Edwin supposed that was because it was so near the Ouseburn.

'Have you no coal?' he asked Mrs Charlton quietly.

'Not till pay day,' came the brusque reply.

'How do you manage? How do you cook?' Edwin knew that the only means of cooking in most of these old cottages was the fire, but he saw that Mrs Charlton, whose husband was a casual labourer in the yards and could earn a fair wage, was also lucky enough to have a round-doored oven to the side and he guessed a water boiler at the back. The kettle was in its usual place on the hob, the hearth was empty. There would be no warmth, no hot food and no hot water.

'It'll be bread and dripping when me man comes home tonight. There's nowt else and it's his own fault for gambling his pay away.'

'I've got some coal,' Jane Potts said unexpectedly. 'You can hev some if yer like, Bella.'

'I'll not take yer coal, hinny.'

'Just enough to see you through. I've got plenty. Mr Randall will come with me to help me carry some over, won't you, sir?'

The old woman got to her feet and she shuffled over and plucked at his sleeve. Edwin sensed that she wanted to speak to him privately. But before he could answer her there was a sound above them that made them all look up fearfully. A dragging sound, a pause and then a shout, 'Ha'ad on a minute!'

Silence while they waited and then the same voice said, 'That's right, lads, now gan canny and let's get this job done properly. And show some respect, will you?'

Mrs Potts tugged at his sleeve again. 'Let's gan out the back door,' she said.

'I beg your pardon?' Edwin dragged his mind back from visualizing what must be happening on the roof above them.

'To fetch some coal.'

'That's right,' Bella Charlton said suddenly, 'fetch some coal back and I'll make us a cup of tea. We could all do with one.'

82

As Jane Potts led the way out of the room and along the short stone-flagged passage to the back door, Bella Charlton motioned to Edwin to hang back. 'Take your time,' she whispered. 'Try to judge how long it'll take them to get him down and away. Get my meaning?'

Edwin nodded and followed the old woman out of the cottage.

The back door opened into a small yard with room for an earth closet and a coalhouse, then a further door opened on to a stone- and litter-strewn bank that fell away quite sharply into the Ouseburn.

Glancing neither back nor upwards, Jane turned downstream and picked her way along the rough ground until they drew nearer the point where the burn emptied its sluggish waters into the Tyne.

Edwin couldn't imagine where they were going. Up the bank to their left was a huddle of old houses and industrial buildings. At the other side of the burn lay the tannery, a pottery, more houses and a few inns and drinking houses. But ahead of them lay nothing except a row of old stone boathouses, long since deserted.

Finally he realized that Jane was making for one of these structures, perhaps less ruinous than the others. There were large double doors at the back. They were padlocked and barred with rusting chains, but a smaller door was cut into one side and it was this that the old woman opened, fiddling with a padlock that looked as if it had been fitted fairly recently.

'Wait there, hinny,' Jane told him as she vanished into the dimness. He heard a scrape of a match and saw a wavering light before she called, 'Hawway in, and push the door to behind you.'

Edwin entered to find the old lady waiting with two lighted candles. She gave one of the candle holders to him. 'Divven't want yer falling over.' She moved away from him, expecting him to follow but, before he did, Edwin waited for his eyes to accustom themselves to the murky light. He glanced round to get his bearings.

There was an area of level floor before it began its slope towards the water. About ten feet away, perhaps more, he could see the Ouseburn and hear it lapping against the stone slope. At this point the Tyne, and therefore the Ouseburn, were tidal. He guessed the tide was out now, but, when full, Jane must lose at least half of this shelter floor space.

Not that there was any sign of her habitation in the space in front of him. He turned to see where she had gone and peered through the leaping shadows into the back corner of the building. By now his eyes had adjusted, but all he could see at first was what appeared to be a wall of packing cases. He moved towards them carefully and stopped when he saw Jane waiting for him in a gap in the wooden wall. She was holding back a ragged blanket that acted as a door.

'Hawway in,' she said.

The living area was larger than he expected, and an attempt at dividing it into more than one room had been made with more packing cases and planks of wood. But there was such a jumble that he barely made sense of it. He saw bits of old furniture, blankets hanging, a collection of household pots and pans on makeshift shelves.

The place was unexpectedly warm, and Edwin traced the heat to a makeshift hearth put together with bricks and bits of metal. The hearth was set against the side wall where an attempt had been made above it to knock out some of the old stones to let the smoke escape. However, it looked as if the smoke, perhaps influenced by the direction of the prevailing wind, found its way out wherever it could. There were soot stains on the wall all the way up to the rafters.

The fire had been left burning low, and a dented old cinder guard had been fixed to a pair of hooks, one at each side. Jane saw him glancing at it. 'Divven't want to come yem and find me place up in flames,' she said. She nodded towards an old bucket full of coal. 'And I've got more than that. I wasn't romancing when I telt Bella Charlton that I had plenty. Look yonder.' She nodded back the way they had come. 'Take yer candle and fill any buckets you find there, if you don't mind, Mr Randall.'

Edwin retraced his steps, pushing aside the greasy blanket that served as a door and crossed over to the other back corner. Now he saw that some wooden planks confined a heap of coal. A shovel lay on top of the coal, as did four rusting old buckets.

'That's how Billy brings it yem.' Edwin turned to see Jane standing in the doorway of her makeshift residence. 'He gans ower the wall at the coal yard at night, just like I did when I was a bairn. Billy won't let his mam catch ca'ad.'

Edwin knew that old as she was, her wits were sharp. She hadn't forgotten what had happened, it was just too soon to talk about Billy in the past tense.

Jane let the curtain fall again and he could hear her rummaging around as he set to to fill the buckets with coal. He wasn't a bit shocked that Billy had been stealing coal. In fact he knew that many of the poor people he visited in the course of his research 'sent the bairns ower the wall at night' to do likewise. And he didn't condemn them. How could he?

Here in Newcastle there were coal pits at the end of almost every street, or that's how it seemed, and networks of wagonways from these pits crisscrossed their way down to the river where for hundreds of years, coals from Newcastle had kept the fires of London burning, and had made fortunes for the pit owners.

The hundreds of colliers, or coal ships, weren't the only traffic on the Tyne. Newcastle was an important seaport, with hundreds of ships arriving on every tide. But it wasn't just the wealth of trade the river brought. Nearly half of all the world's shipping was built in the yards on the Tyne.

Just a couple of miles upriver from here at Elswick, Lord Armstrong's twenty thousand workers manufactured guns and warships for the armies and navies of the world, while engineers from the North East forged railways across continents.

There was no doubt that men like Armstrong, Swann and Stephenson had brought employment and prosperity to Tyneside, and yet, alongside the wealth there were people living in utmost squalor.

Jane Potts and her poor son were like characters in the novels of Charles Dickens. Edwin could only hope that now the world had entered the twentieth century things would change.

When he had filled all four buckets he went back to see what Jane was doing. He found her standing by an upturned packing case that served as a table. On the table were a shopping basket and some provisions. He saw a jam jar full of tea-leaves, another that looked as if it contained sugar, a tin of Fry's cocoa, a lump of sweaty-looking cheese and a large but stale-looking loaf of bread.

'Got the bread just last night,' she said. 'They sell it off cheap at the end of the day.'

She began to wrap each item in newspaper before putting it in the basket. The cocoa tin she thrust into a pocket in her skirt and as she did so it rattled. Edwin guessed it contained not cocoa but coins, perhaps all her worldly wealth. Then she turned to look up at one of the makeshift shelves.

'I couldn't reach that tin at the back' she said. 'Would you get it down for me? Billy usually puts everything away for me. We hev to keep it up a height if we don't want the rats to get it. It's bad enough sharing me bed with them.'

Jane laughed but Edwin was appalled. She looked up, saw his face and said, 'Divven't fret, Mr Randall. If the little beggars get worrisome, Billy fights them off with a hot poker— Oh . . .'

They stared at each other for a moment, the candle flames wavering

85

in the draught, making the shadows dance wildly all around them. 'Jane . . . Mrs Potts, what will you do?'

'Do?'

'You can't stay here alone.'

'Well, I'm not, am I? We're taking this lot back to Bella – and the coal – she'll keep me company for an hour or two until her man gets yem.'

'But then?'

'I'll come back and gan to bed.'

'But that's what I mean, you can't stay here alone.'

'Where else should I gan?'

Suddenly she couldn't meet his gaze and she sank on to a chair. She clasped her arms around her body, pulling her shawl tighter in a characteristic gesture.

'I know what you're thinking and I'm not gannin' in there,' she said finally. 'After all, I'm not a vagrant, I've got me own place.'

'But how—'

'How will I manage without Billy to bring a bit money yem? Is that what you mean?'

'Yes.'

'I've got a bit put by. It'll see me through for a while, buy me bread and that.'

'And how will you get more coal?'

'You can see I've got enough to see the winter out. Then I'll start burning firewood. There's always plenty of that – driftwood and the like.'

'But when the money runs out?'

She looked up at him, her eyes flashing with sudden vexation. 'Will yer ha'ad yer gob, man! I'll find somat to do. I'm not too old to scrub steps, mind bairns, run errands. And divven't worry, I'll not gan beggin' because there's no way I'm going to let 'em put me in the workhouse!'

'Why?'

'Why? Why! Are yer crazy?' She was almost speechless with rage and fright. 'If I gans in there I'll never come out again. Do yer think they're going to waste good victuals on an old wife like me?'

Risking her wrath Edwin felt that he had to continue. 'Look, I know they're strict—'

'Strict!'

'But they're not murderers.'

'But they treat yer like dirt!'

'You'd have clean clothes, a clean bed and no worries about where the next meal is coming from.'

'I divven't hev those worries now. And here I can come and gan as I please. Look around you, Mr Randall – I've got everything I need here. I'd be out of me mind to give me own home up for a bed in the workhouse. Now, if you don't mind, there's something else I want to ask you.'

Edwin knew that it was pointless to press his argument and, although he could not admit it to her, he sympathized entirely with her desire to be in her own home. If she survived this winter, the summer months wouldn't be so bad, and then, with the next winter to face and no coal and perhaps no money left, he would have to think of something else. But perhaps it would be better if, in the end, she died here in her own bed, he thought, than live a few more miserable years in the institution she feared so much.

'Mr Randall?' Jane had calmed down and now she was looking up at him with a different kind of worry in her eyes. 'Pull up a chair, will yer? There's something I want to ask before we gan back to Bella's.'

'Of course.' Edwin sat opposite her. 'What is it?'

'What'll happen to Billy?'

'Well, first you'll have to go to the mortuary and identify him.'

'And then?'

Edwin frowned. 'I'm not sure what you mean.'

'I can't afford to bury him. Even if I emptied me cocoa tin.'

'The parish will pay for the funeral,' Edwin told her.

'A pauper's grave.'

'There's no shame in that.'

Jane shook her head. 'It's not the shame I'm worried about. It's whether they'll let his poor body rest in peace. You know what I mean?'

Edwin stared at her but there was nothing he could say.

'I can see you do. Well, of course you do. You're one of them, aren't you?'

'One of them?'

'You're studying to be a doctor. You hev to hev bodies to cut up to find out what's going on inside. And where do you get them poor bodies? Where else but from the paupers' graves.'

'Jane – it isn't like that – not now.'

'Isn't it?'

'I wouldn't lie to you.'

She peered at him through rheumy eyes and then she smiled sadly. 'Aye, bonny lad,' she said, 'I know you wouldn't.'

They looked at each other for a moment longer and then she sighed. 'Hawway then,' she said. 'Let's gan back to Bella's. You'll hev to make more than one trip with the coal. Do you mind?'

'No, Jane. I don't mind.'

By the time Edwin left Bella Charlton's she had got a fire going and the kettle was steaming gently. Jane was sitting by the fire while Bella made doorstep sandwiches with the bread and cheese. Her innate good manners made her offer him a sandwich but, equally, she knew that his good manners would make him refuse.

He made his way up Byker Bank, abandoning any thought of what he had come to do that morning, that was to carry on with his survey of where the communal fresh water supplies were and how many families shared one tap. These facts, along with the number of shared privies, were all part of a larger piece of research into the causes of the epidemics of typhoid fever.

But Edwin's morning had been taken up with the drama of Billy Potts' brutal death and now he had to make his way back to his uncle's shop where he would be on duty until it was time for him to attend an evening lecture at the Newcastle College of Medicine.

He knew how lucky he had been. When he was a small child his parents had died of influenza and his father's brother had taken him in. Both he and his wife had made him welcome. Edwin himself had been quite poorly and his kindly aunt had loved and nourished him like one of her own.

His father had been a country doctor and his mother had had no money of her own. So Edwin's inheritance had been modest. His uncle had insisted that it should be used for Edwin's education, and he had clothed and housed his nephew at his own expense. That was why Edwin was more than willing to help out in the bookshop. Of course, he'd have loved the job, anyway – all those books to peruse at his leisure, and the opportunity to hide away in the back room and get on with his studies whenever he could.

'Mr Randall.'

He heard someone call his name and stopped to look behind him. At first he couldn't see anyone but then the voice called out again and he saw a movement in one of the doorways. Irene Lawson's door.

'What is it, Irene?'

Edwin retraced his steps. Irene didn't say anything, she opened the door wider and stepped back, beckoning him in, then closing the door behind him. Edwin followed her into her room. The fire was blazing and baby Ruth was propped up amongst the cushions in the old armchair, frowning and smiling alternately as she played with a wooden clothes peg.

The room, in spite of its lack of luxuries, was clean, and the warmth of the fire should have made it cosy, but Irene was pale and shivering.

'Are you ill?' Edwin asked, and he reached for her wrist to take her pulse. He found it to be racing and he looked into her face worriedly. There were dark smudges under her eyes.

'No, I'm fine,' she said, and she snatched her hand away and wrapped both arms around her body.

'Are you in pain?'

'No.'

'Then, what is it?'

'I just heard,' she said at last, 'the man on the roof . . . you went up to look at him, didn't you?'

'Yes, I did.'

'They're all talking about it – all the neighbours – dreadful, isn't it?'

'Yes, it's very sad.'

Edwin stared at her wonderingly. He knew her to be hardworking and loving. Loving towards her baby sister, that is. He had never suspected that her sensibilities were such that she could be so visibly moved by the death of a stranger, no matter how tragic.

Irene's eyes were huge as she looked at him. 'And it's Billy Potts, is it?'

'Yes. His mother will identify him, but I'm pretty sure it's him.'

'I didn't know.'

Edwin frowned. He wasn't sure what she meant. 'Nobody knew,' he said. 'Although his mother suspected it because he didn't come home last night. That's why they asked me to go up and have a look. The police were taking their time and the poor woman was standing in the street below—'

He broke off when he saw her drop her face into her hands. 'I didn't know it was Billy,' she said. 'Poor harmless Billy.'

Edwin thought he was beginning to understand. Irene was touched because the man had been simple, like a child – given to strange behaviour at times but, on the whole, he'd been harmless. Even the toughest of working men had treated him kindly.

He stared at her perplexed. He didn't know what to do. She obviously needed comforting but what could he say? And then, when he saw that her shoulders were shaking and he heard muffled sobs, instinct took over. He reached out and drew her towards him. Perhaps he was expecting her to resist. After all, they were hardly even friends, but instead she came willingly into his arms and he began to soothe her as if she were a child.

'Don't fret,' he said. 'It's natural that you should be shocked and saddened by what has happened, natural that you should shed a tear for Billy, but try to take comfort from the fact that the tragedy won't touch your life. Your life here with Ruth.'

Gradually the sobbing subsided and she became still. Ruth had gone to sleep sucking on the clothes peg, and the only sound in the room came from the hearth as the coals burned and shifted in the grate.

Suddenly, instead of another human being that needed comfort, Edwin became aware of Irene as a woman, her small body soft and compliant in his arms, her clean-smelling hair brushing against the skin of his face. Perhaps she too was aware of the change, for she moved away just as he controlled the impulse to hold her even more closely.

I cannot be alone with her again, he thought. For in spite of the strength of the sensations that had momentarily surged through him, he knew his response to be purely physical. He liked and admired Irene; he sensed she had a keen and complex intelligence that had not been allowed to develop and flourish, but he was not drawn to her in any romantic sense.

No, it was not Irene who had begun to haunt his dreams and his waking moments too. Wonderingly he acknowledged to himself that there was another woman that he desired in every way – a woman whom he longed to share his life with.

That woman was Lorna Hassan.

Chapter Eight

Mildred Cunningham had left for Corbridge the day before and the atmosphere in the house had changed subtly. Her grandmother was not a severe mistress, Lorna mused, but she expected everyone to do their best at all times. There was no excuse for sloppy work; not even minor coughs and sneezes in the winter months.

The staff respected her, and as they had better-than-average wages and good food provided, they knew that they had nothing to complain about. And, yet, when she was absent, Lorna noticed everyone smiled more.

Also, they seemed to have decided that she, Lorna, was in charge in Mildred's absence. Mrs Hobson, the cook, had already consulted her about the menus for the next day or two, and now Violet stood before her, hesitantly asking if she would ascertain whether Miss Rose intended to leave her bedroom today or whether she wanted all her meals served up there.

In spite of her worries about when Maurice would get in touch with her, Lorna couldn't suppress her wry amusement. She turned to gaze out of the dining-room window to hide a smile. Rose was taking full advantage of their grandmother's absence. She had ordered her breakfast to be taken to her room, and then her lunch. Lorna doubted if she had even bothered to get out of bed and get dressed.

The day was dismal and Lorna could see the neatly dressed parlour-maid reflected in the net-free upper half of the window as she waited patiently for an answer. Behind Violet, Molly, the young general help, was clearing Lorna's luncheon plates from the table.

Violet coughed discreetly and Lorna turned to her and said, 'I'll try to persuade my cousin to come down for dinner tonight. I know it makes it easier for you.'

'Miss Lorna, please don't think that—'

'Don't worry, I know you weren't complaining. But I also know that it must be very trying for whoever has to run up and downstairs.'

'Molly,' Violet told her.

'For Molly. I know how hard to please my cousin can be and no doubt she's been ringing the bell and giving orders all morning.'

Lorna stopped abruptly. She realized how indiscreet she'd been when she saw the embarrassed expression on Violet's face. Violet was a superior sort of parlourmaid, for Mildred Cunningham often excused her other household duties in order for Violet to act almost as a lady's maid to Mildred herself. But she was still a member of the household staff and Lorna should not have said anything that might be implied as a criticism of a member of the family.

Violet suddenly shot her a warm smile. 'If you don't mind my saying so, Miss Lorna, you can encourage Miss Rose to stay up there all day if you like.'

'Why should I do that?'

'Well, that might make it easier for you. I mean, you could have your meals in peace and not have to listen to her going on about the wedding. Oh, I shouldn't have— I mean—'

'Don't worry. It's a kind thought but we don't want to annoy Mrs Hobson nor make life harder for Molly. I'll go up and see her now. But, in any case, I was going to ask Cook to simply leave a cold buffet tonight, then Rose and I can eat when we please without having anybody to wait on.'

Lorna, against her will, went up to Rose's room. As she'd suspected, she found her still in her robe. Her cousin was lying on top of her bedclothes, propped up amongst her pillows, seemingly sorting out her correspondence.

Lorna had knocked before she entered and Rose had called for her to enter but she didn't look up. 'There's nothing much here,' she said. 'Just letters from old school friends and postcards and the like. Nothing I have any sentimental attachment to.'

'Does that mean you're going to dispose of them?' Lorna asked.

'I might as well. I don't want to take too much clutter with me to my new home.'

'But you're not getting married until June. Surely there's no need to do this now?'

'Why on earth shouldn't I? And why are you so concerned about letters from my school friends? Most of them wouldn't even speak to you.'

Lorna felt herself flushing but she controlled her anger. 'I'm not a bit concerned. I simply thought it was premature. Much could happen between now and June.'

Rose stared at her, her eyes widening. 'What are you suggesting?'

'Nothing. For goodness' sake, I wish I hadn't said anything.'

'But you did. And you meant that the wedding might be called off, didn't you?'

'Rose, I'm sorry—'

'So you should be. You're just being jealous and spiteful. And let me assure you that this wedding will certainly not be called off. Maurice is desperate to marry me!'

Lorna longed to ask Rose what made her so sure of that, for she couldn't believe that Maurice had asked her with any real enthusiasm. She believed he had proposed to Rose, as his parents wanted him to, only to allay their suspicions and to give him time to arrange his elopement with Lorna herself.

'Now don't just stand there looking thunderous,' Rose continued. 'Pass the wastepaper basket, will you?'

Lorna did so and held it while Rose gathered up the letters and cards and dropped them in.

'There,' Rose said when the basket was filled almost to overflowing, 'take them away.'

'You've missed one.'

'Where?'

'That lavender-coloured envelope near your pillow.'

'Oh, no, I'm keeping this one.'

Rose picked up the envelope and held it tightly with both hands. She stared across the room towards the fire dancing in the hearth but Lorna knew that her cousin wasn't really seeing anything. Lorna knew who the letter was from. She had delivered it into Rose's hands herself because Harry had not been able to post it to her.

How long ago was it now? Almost a year and a half? Rose, weeping, more with rage than with sorrow, had asked Lorna to take a letter to Harry at the theatre in Whitley Bay where he was part of the summer troupe of entertainers, telling him that she was being banished to the country and that her grandmother had forbidden her to see him ever again.

Lorna had taken the letter, mainly because she had felt sorry for Harry, and he had begged her to wait while he wrote a reply. Lorna had no idea what he had written. Rose never told her. She had gone to Cousin Hannah's smallholding in the Tyne valley, taking her secrets with her and she had not been allowed to return until the following spring.

Lorna had thought it severe of their grandmother not to allow Rose, who after all was her favourite, not to return for Christmas – she had even plucked up the courage to say so – but her grandmother had said that Rose must stay away until she was satisfied that she had got Harry Desmond completely out of her system.

The punishment must have worked, because once she had returned, Rose had never mentioned Harry again. So what was Lorna to make of this behaviour now? She watched, wonderingly, as Rose opened the envelope and took out a bit of pasteboard – a photograph. She looked up at Lorna and smiled.

'You know who it is, don't you?' she asked.

'Yes.'

'Here, I've never shown you this.' She passed the photograph over. 'He's very handsome, isn't he?'

Lorna took the photograph. It was a publicity postcard, the sort they sold in theatre foyers. It was signed with a great flourish across the bottom: 'Harry Desmond'. The signature looked as if it was part of the printing process but, above it, in a slightly different colour, there were the words: 'To My Darling Rose'.

Harry looked very debonair. He wore a striped blazer, bow tie, flannel trousers and a straw boater. His pose was both elegant and cheerful as he shouldered his walking cane and turned his head towards the camera in half-profile. Behind him there was a backdrop depicting the hint of a view of a promenade by the sea.

And he *was* handsome, Lorna thought, in a romantic sort of way. A hero from a light-hearted novel or a froth of a stage entertainment. For, of course, Harry was an actor, and she and Rose had first met him when they had gone for a day trip to Whitley Bay and then taken shelter from a sudden rain storm at the afternoon matinée in the theatre on the lower promenade.

Harry was top of the bill. His light tenor voice had enchanted Rose and she had insisted on waiting at the stage door after the show to ask him to autograph her programme.

Lorna handed the postcard back to Rose, who replaced it in the envelope. 'I know it's foolishly sentimental,' she said, 'but I can't bear to part with it. You mustn't tell him that, of course.'

'Tell him?' Lorna stared at her in puzzlement. 'What on earth are you talking about?' She thought that Rose must have become confused, that her mind had slipped back to the days when Lorna had been forced into the role of an unwilling go-between. But Rose suddenly said, 'Sit down, Lorna, here on the bed beside me. Look at this.'

'Look at what? That newspaper?'

'Yes.' Rose picked up the newspaper that was lying on the bed, the *Daily Journal*. It had been opened and folded over to show the page advertising the Christmas entertainments and pantomimes at the theatres in Newcastle and the nearby towns.

'The Grand,' Rose said. 'Byker. Just a twenty-minute walk away. Look at the cast list.'

'I see. Are you telling me that you want me to go and see him?'

'Yes. You must.'

'Must?'

'I want you to give him this letter.' Rose picked up an envelope from her bedside table.

'But why, Rose? It's all over between you, isn't it?'

'Of course it is. Grandmamma saw to that. So much so that poor Harry fled to London and said he would never set foot in the north of England again. But he has. And that worries me.'

'Why?' Lorna tried but couldn't conceal a flash of scorn. 'Do you think poor lovesick Harry will try to see you again?'

Rose looked away. 'I know you think I'm vain and frivolous, Lorna.'

'No I don't.'

Rose's smile was without malice and Lorna felt momentarily ashamed of her reaction. 'Yes you do, you're so much cleverer than I am. The answer to your question is that I don't know if Harry wants to see me again. And now that I am to be married there are things that need to be said, that's all.'

Lorna frowned. She had immediately assumed that Rose had written the letter because of her unwillingness to let go, a desire to keep the poor man in thrall, but, looking at her now, she could see that her cousin looked genuinely sad.

'Do I have to take the letter?' she asked. 'Why can't you just post it? I'll take it to the post office now, if you like.'

'No, I don't know where Harry is staying, and if I send it to the theatre he may not get it. They might assume it's a letter from one of his followers and just toss it aside, mightn't they?'

'I suppose so.'

'I don't know *why* Harry has come back to the North East,' Rose said. 'He may have no intention of contacting me, but I can't take the risk. Nothing must come in the way of my marriage to Maurice.'

Lorna had already taken the letter when Rose uttered those last words and she gripped it tightly. 'So that's it.'

Rose looked surprised. 'Of course. What did you think?'

Lorna had begun to imagine that Rose still had tender feelings for Harry Desmond, that the letter was an outpouring of regret and affection. But if it was not, wouldn't it be hypocritical of her to help Rose – when she herself was going to be the reason why the marriage would never take place?

'What's the matter with you?' Rose asked. 'Why are you scowling like that?'

'Am I? Perhaps I just don't want to go out on such a cold miserable day.' Even as she spoke, Lorna knew that she would have to. Until Maurice let her know what his plans were she would have to go on pretending that nothing was wrong. And besides, she doubted if she could stay here with Rose for one moment longer. Her feelings of guilt were driving her crazy.

Neither would she be able to settle in her own room with her books. Whenever she was alone she was tormented by the constant worry of Maurice's silence, his failure to get in touch again since he'd sent the letter. No, it would be better for her to get out.

'I'll take it,' she said.

'Oh, good.' Rose smiled up at her as she turned to leave. 'And, Lorna, before you go would you just pull the bell cord? I think I'll ask Cook to send up a pot of tea and some iced fancies.'

But Lorna, pretending that she hadn't heard, hurried out of the room and closed the door briskly behind her.

'I'd like you to leave straight away, miss.'

'But—'

'No buts, if you please. You shouldn't have come in here.'

Lorna stared at the old man and tried to control her irritation. She'd got as far as this, just inside the stage door, by attaching herself to a lively group of young women, probably chorus girls, as they hurried in out of the cold, but then had been confronted immediately by the cross features of the stage doorkeeper.

He was incredibly wrinkled. He sat in his glass-fronted cubicle and leaned forward across the wooden counter to point the way to the door. Lorna was sure that she got a whiff of mothballs. The man wore knitted half-gloves on his claw-like hands and a woollen muffler round his neck. There was a look and a sound of the previous century about him and Lorna wondered how long he'd worked here, how many troupes of actors he'd seen come and go – and how many unfortunate stage-struck girls he'd sent packing.

But she wasn't a stage-struck girl. She'd been sent here on an errand and, having come this far, she was determined to carry it out successfully. She knew she would get nowhere if she wasn't polite. The door behind her opened as another two girls hurried in, bringing with them a blast of cold air. The doorkeeper was distracted for a moment as he peered at them over the top of his rimless spectacles, nodded, ticked off some names in a ledger, and then turned his attention back to Lorna.

'Still here?' he wheezed.

She smiled as sweetly as she could. 'I have a letter for Mr Desmond,' she said.

'Why didn't you say so?'

'You didn't give me a chance. I mean, I was just going to.'

'Give it to me. I'll see that he gets it.'

He leaned right out of his kiosk and stretched a hand towards the envelope that Lorna was holding. She thought he was going to take it and she moved back quickly. Her movement caught the old man off balance and he fell forward on to the counter; Lorna heard the legs of his stool scrape across the floor under him. When he righted himself he glared at her crossly.

'I have to give it to him personally,' she said.

The doorkeeper cackled, 'In love with him, are you?'

'Of course not.'

Lorna raised her chin and they glared at each other. She wished she hadn't agreed to do this, and right at this moment she was tempted simply to hand the letter over and walk out. But she had promised Rose that she would deliver it personally. When she got home her cousin would no doubt ask her exactly what had happened and she couldn't face having to tell any lies. Her conscience was bad enough already.

'I understand,' the doorkeeper said, and he leered knowingly. 'You're delivering it for your mistress, some society lady who wants to invite Mr Desmond home for a cosy little supper after the show, and you'll get what for if you don't do as you're told. Is that it?'

He thinks I'm a lady's maid, Lorna thought. Well I don't care; if that's what it takes to see Harry I'll go along with it. The old man was staring at her speculatively. 'You're a bonny, brave lass,' he said eventually, 'and I wouldn't want to cause trouble for you. Look here, if you tell me who the letter's from, I could ask Mr Desmond if he'll see you.'

'I can't do that.'

He shrugged and looked exasperated. 'Well, that's that, then. You'd better go and stop wasting my time.'

'I'll give you *my* name, that will do.'

The old man looked surprised but he nodded, and as soon as Lorna had informed him who she was he turned to a telephone mounted on the wall, wound a handle and dialled a number. He turned away from Lorna when he began to speak. It didn't take long. When he replaced the receiver he simply said, 'He's coming.'

She had to wait only a minute. She heard a movement in the dimly lit womb of the building and then footsteps hurrying towards her. 'Lorna,' a pleasingly resonant voice called, 'are you alone?'

'Yes, Harry.' She smiled up at the tall handsome man who appeared beside her. 'It's just me, I'm afraid.'

In spite of the disappointment she guessed him to be feeling, he managed a brilliant smile. 'Well, then, come along to my dressing room. We can talk while I get ready for the rehearsal.'

She heard the stage-doorkeeper sniff with disapproval as she followed Harry along the narrow corridor. He strode ahead, the wall-mounted gaslamps glinting on his fair head and on the shining brightly coloured satins of his theatrical costume.

'What do you think?' he asked, smiling as he stood in the middle of the cramped dressing room and took up a commanding pose.

'Impressive,' Lorna said. 'What are you meant to be? The prince – oh, no, there isn't a prince – it's Aladdin, isn't it?'

'Ah, no,' Harry smiled ruefully, 'I'm getting a little long in the tooth for that part. And, even if I wasn't, Aladdin became a breeches role nearly a hundred years ago.'

'Breeches?'

'Played by a young actress with good legs. Many of the principal boys are played by women now.'

'So you . . .?'

'I'm Abanazar, the scheming magician who claims to be the poor lad's uncle and tempts him with the magic lamp. But have you never seen Aladdin? Is that why you came? To ask for tickets for you and . . . and . . .'

Suddenly Harry looked so miserable that Lorna felt his anguish more keenly than her own. She at least was confident that Maurice would be sending for her soon; he'd told her to trust him, hadn't he? But Harry must be wondering what on earth was going on.

'No,' she said quickly. 'It's kind of you but I don't want tickets. I've brought a letter from Rose. I don't know what's in it but don't . . . I mean, please don't hope for anything . . . I'm sorry.'

Harry took the letter and she turned to go. 'No wait,' he said. 'Maybe she wants an answer.'

Lorna wasn't sure about that but she took the seat he indicated. Harry sat at his dressing table, a bench against the wall. There was a mirror mounted above it with a gaslamp at each side. The room was small and Lorna felt that she was far too close to him at such an intimate moment.

She looked all around, examining the colourful costumes hanging on rails and the alarming set of pipes running up and down the walls and around the room which seemed to be some sort of heating system, judging from the warmth that emanated from them. There was a strange sweet smell, not unpleasant, and Lorna thought it must come from the jars and pots of what she took to be stage make-up on the dressing table.

Harry had turned away from her as he read Rose's letter. She tried not to look at him but it was hard not to. Although he had his back to her his face was reflected in the mirror.

He'd made a joke just now about being long in the tooth, and she realized that he was older than she had thought him to be when she and Rose had first met him. He had looked so young and dashing then as part of the troupe of entertainers at the Sea Front Theatre in Whitley Bay two summers ago. But, of course, he was an actor and he'd probably been hanging on to the parts given to young men, not wanting to be consigned to the roles of comic buffers and nice old gents in the comedies that were the usual fare.

Now Lorna saw that, although he was still a good-looking man, he would probably never play the young hero again. She wondered if he minded. She saw him sigh and return the letter to its envelope. He smiled at her sadly.

'There isn't an answer,' he said. 'At least she doesn't want me to write one. Just tell Rose that I'm pleased that she's going to be married and I wouldn't dream of causing any trouble.' For a moment he looked angry. 'As if I would.'

'I'm sorry,' Lorna said.

He looked surprised, 'Why should you be sorry?'

'Well . . . whatever Rose has said, it's upset you.'

'Rose was worried that I had come back to Newcastle in order to be near her again.'

'You don't have to tell me anything.' Lorna rose to go.

'Obviously I thought of her – in fact, even now, there's not a day goes by when I don't.'

'Please don't.'

'But she made it quite clear in the last letter she sent – you brought it – that she never wanted to see me again.'

'Did she?' Lorna was startled. She had thought that Rose had been unwilling to end the romance and that she had had to be forced to go to Corbridge.

'Oh, yes.' Harry smiled sadly. 'And I tried very hard to keep away. But work is harder to find when you've never quite made it to the top of the bill and you've turned— I mean, you're pushing forty. It was the chance of a good part that brought me back, that's all.'

'I'd better go.'

'Of course.' Harry dragged a warm smile from somewhere. 'But, remember, if you change your mind about coming to see the show just leave a note with the doorkeeper and I'll arrange tickets. We open on Boxing Day. And now, do you think you could find your own way out? I've got to get my make-up on.'

Lorna nodded but as she got to the door he called out, 'Lorna, forgive me, I never asked about you.'

'Me?'

'Don't look so surprised. I mean, is life going well for you? Are you happy?'

Lorna considered the word and wondered if it went anywhere near describing the turmoil of emotion that being in love with Maurice had caused. Did the shame of having to be deceitful about their meetings taint the bliss of simply being with him, and threaten her dreams about their future together?

'I'm not sure,' she told Harry at last, and she smiled when she saw his frown. 'But I know that I'm going to be.'

Chapter Nine

The wind from the river was keen, and Lorna pulled her fur collar up around her ears as she waited to cross Shields Road. Horse-drawn delivery carts, hansom cabs, and the occasional motorcar rumbled by. Lorna began to despair of ever reaching the tram stop at the other side.

She stepped back from the edge of the pavement as a tram from the city clanked to a stop just a short way away from her a little further up the hill. A few passengers alighted but she didn't take much notice. So she was startled when, a moment later, someone took her arm.

'I'll see you across,' a familiar voice said. She turned her head to find Edwin Randall smiling at her.

Together they dodged across as far as the tram poles in the centre of the road; then they had to wait while a tram going towards the city approached and passed them.

'Oh, no,' Lorna said, and she moved forward instinctively.

'Don't!' Edwin pulled her back just as a grocer's delivery boy on a bicycle sped by. 'There'll be another tram along soon.'

Ironically, when they reached the other side of the road, there was a lull in the traffic. They looked at each other and laughed.

'What a nice surprise to meet you here,' Edwin said.

Lorna smiled and then there was an awkward silence. She was aware that Edwin wanted to know what she was doing in this part of town. And, of course she couldn't tell him.

'I thought I'd walk down and get the tram to the town centre from here. More direct.'

'I see.' It was obvious that he didn't believe her but he was far too polite to say so. 'Going shopping?' he asked.

Now there was an awkwardness between them and, for some reason, this made Lorna feel guilty. She decided to tell him the truth in so far as it didn't affect Rose; that at least she could do.

'I just wanted to stay out of the house for a while. Grandmamma is visiting her family in Corbridge and Rose is – Rose is being insufferable.' She smiled and was pleased to see his expression lighten.

'I see,' he said. 'Discretion being the better part of valour.' She frowned and he continued, 'Being a sensible young woman you thought it better to walk about in the cold rather than stay in an overheated atmosphere and risk quarrelling with your cousin. Is that it?'

'Something like that.'

'Miss Hassan—'

'Lorna.'

'Lorna, come with me.'

'Where to?'

'I'm going to visit an old woman. She's just lost her son. He died in a ghastly accident. I want to see if she's all right.'

Lorna couldn't disguise her surprise and, for a moment she didn't know what to say, even though she sensed Edwin's growing embarrassment.

'I'm sorry,' he said. 'I don't know what made me ask you. Of course you don't want to come with me when you could be looking at the Christmas windows in Northumberland Street.'

'Oh, but I'd like to come,' Lorna said at last.

'Would you? Would you really?'

'Yes, I've been thinking about the people you visit, the work that you do.'

And it was only when she'd spoken that Lorna realized that that was true. Her mind hadn't been entirely taken up with her own problems over the last few days. Seeking distraction from her uncertainty about her future, her thoughts had occasionally taken refuge with Edwin Randall. She had remembered the safe intimate feeling of sitting with him by the fire in the back room of his uncle's bookshop, and her interest in and admiration for the work he was doing amongst the poor.

She had only been going into town to avoid being in the house with Rose. She had no real interest in the Christmas displays in the shop windows on Northumberland Street. She might as well go with Edwin. At least she would have someone interesting to talk to.

She realized that Edwin was looking at her with an expression of surprise and pleasure. Such intense pleasure that she immediately felt uneasy. 'Should we go?' she asked awkwardly. 'I'm getting chilled to the bone standing here.'

'Of course,' he said. 'I'm sorry.'

He took her arm once more and they set off to walk down Byker Bank.

'Take care,' he said. 'The pavement's slippery. In fact I think you'd better link arms and hang on tight.'

Although she lived so near, Lorna had never ventured into this area at the other side of Shields Road. She glanced with interest as they passed the ends of the streets of terraced houses rising steeply back up the hill to their left. The front doors opened directly on to the pavement but most of the steps were scrubbed and soapstoned, and the few inhabitants who had ventured out on this bitterly cold day were adequately dressed.

But as they went further down the bank towards the valley bottom, the houses grew older and more dilapidated and, to her dismay she began to see signs of real poverty. Peeling paintwork, torn curtains at the windows or even bits of sacking, and the children playing on the cobblestones wore ill-fitting, ragged clothes; some of them were even without shoes.

Edwin must have sensed her horror at these sights, but he didn't say anything. He simply reached for her gloved hand and squeezed it. Instinctively she found herself drawing closer to him as they ventured further and further into a world she had barely known existed.

The nearer they got to the bottom of the bank, the worse was the smell. Lorna could only guess at its origin. She thought it might be a mixture of the refuse thrown into the Ouseburn and the smoke belching from the chimneys of the various small factories along the banks.

She had only ever viewed this area from above before, from the tops of trams going over Byker Bridge. From that vantage point this small industrial area looked interesting but now she began to guess what it must be like actually to live here.

Finally Edwin stopped and said, 'The woman I've come to see may be in this house.'

As he knocked on the door Lorna glanced around her. The row of old dwellings that she faced was actually a little better kept than the others along the waterside. The windows were clean and the door brasses shining. She watched with interest as a tall, raw-boned but respectable-looking woman opened the door. From the smile she gave Edwin, Lorna realized that he was welcome here.

'Is Jane with you?' he asked.

'No, I tried to make her stay with us for a bit, till after the funeral at least – we've a spare room now that Joseph's joined the army – but she wanted to be amongst her own things. You can understand that.' All the time she spoke she shot quick curious glances over Edwin's shoulder. Lorna smiled at her hesitantly. 'But divven't stand out in the cold like this, Mr Randall. Do you want to bring your young lady in?'

Edwin turned and took Lorna's arm. 'Miss Hassan isn't my young lady, Bella. She's just a friend.'

'I see.' The woman looked her up and down as if trying to make up her mind why this well-dressed young woman would want to accompany Edwin on a visit to this part of town. But her gaze wasn't unfriendly and she smiled when she said, 'Well, anyways, do you want to come in? You could sit by the fire and I'll send the bairn next door to fetch Jane.'

'Thank you, Bella, but we won't bother you. I had hoped Jane would stay with you for a while but the fact that she hasn't gives me all the more reason to go and see if she's all right.'

After Mrs Charlton had closed her door, Edwin guided Lorna down to the bottom of the street to where the houses gave way to a patch of litter-strewn waste ground. She couldn't imagine where the woman called Jane Potts might live until she saw they were headed towards some old stone boathouses on the bank of the burn.

She watched incredulously as Edwin knocked on the door of one of them and when she heard shuffling sounds within and saw the door open to reveal an old woman bundled up in an odd assortment of old clothes she shook her head and murmured, 'I had no idea . . .'

'Mr Randall,' the woman said. 'Hawway in. Wait, I'll light you a candle – and one for the lass as well. I divven't want you falling down and spoiling yer bonny clothes.'

Lorna gripped the candle holder tightly and she was grateful for Edwin's hand as they followed Jane Potts into the shadowy depths of the boathouse to an area marked out by packing cases. Edwin introduced her briefly but, after that, he didn't seem to expect her to take part in the conversation.

She sat on a rickety old chair at the table seemingly made from an upturned packing case and listened as Edwin asked the old woman how she was coping and whether she had enough to eat.

'Folk've been very kind,' she told him. 'Divven't worry, I'll not want for food and drink.'

While they talked Lorna could hear the crackle of the fire in the makeshift hearth, the more distant sound of water slapping against the entrance to the boathouse and, more disturbingly, strange darting rustling sounds that she imagined betrayed the presence of rats.

'Remember, Jane,' Edwin said when he rose to go, 'if things get too difficult for you, you only have to tell me and I can find you a place in—'

'In the workhouse? Nivver. Hell will freeze over before I gan in there!'

Lorna remained silent when they took their leave. She didn't know what to say. She admired Edwin all the more for the way he seemed really to care what happened to these people. The old woman, although she obviously respected him, had not been in any way overawed by him. They had sat at her table and talked like equals.

An uneasy memory stirred of the day she had first met Maurice in the Grainger Market, of the way he had spoken so scathingly to the man who had bumped into them with his sack of potatoes. And what had he said about those he called the proletariat? *'Let's face it, most of them stink.'*

When he'd seen her expression of dismay he'd apologized. He'd said that he'd spoken like that because he'd been angry. But now she tried to imagine how Maurice would have spoken to the woman she had just visited. What he would have made of the dirt and the squalor and the ever-present smell of poverty?

'What is it, Lorna? What are you thinking?' Edwin asked and, uneasily, she dismissed all thoughts of Maurice.

'I was wondering why Mrs Potts prefers to stay there on her own,' she replied, and that was half of the truth.

'It's her home,' Edwin said. 'She lived there with her son. Once she leaves there she will feel that her life is over.'

'What happened to her son?'

'A tragic accident. He fell from the bridge.'

'Did he drown in the burn?'

Lorna stopped to look back at the two stone bridges that crossed the Ouseburn at its mouth. A public house lay between the two. In her mind's eye she saw the poor man stumbling home over the smaller and older of the bridges. Perhaps he'd been drunk and unsteady on his feet, the cobbles slippery with frost or wet with rain.

'No, he didn't fall from either of the Glasshouse bridges,' Edwin said. He took hold of Lorna's shoulders. 'Look.' He turned her so that she was looking up the bank again. With horror she realized where he was directing her gaze.

'Byker Bridge?' she whispered as she gazed at the newest of the bridges soaring high across the Ouseburn Valley.

105

'Yes. He landed on the roof of Mrs Charlton's house, where I called first to ask after Jane.'

'But how dreadful. Was he . . . was he drunk?'

'Perhaps.'

'You're not sure?'

'Well, when I examined the body—'

'You?'

'Yes,' he smiled ruefully, 'I happened to be here not long after the children had seen something on the roof. Anyway, when I first saw Billy I thought there was the smell of drink about him but that doesn't mean he was incapable.'

'But if he didn't stumble and fall?'

'Look,' Edwin pointed towards the bridge. 'The parapet is too high for it to have been an accidental fall. One possibility is that he was leaning over in order to vomit.'

'Oh.'

'I'm sorry,' he said when he saw her expression.

'No, it's all right. I know you're trying to explain.'

'But if that were the case, surely he'd have tumbled straight down. He would have landed a little further upstream, I think, although I can't be sure.'

'Why not?'

'Well . . . if there was a wind, for example. Oh, I just don't know. I'm not a meteorologist.' He sighed. 'But the more I think about it, the more I think that Billy wasn't alone when he died.'

'You mean he was pushed?'

'Or thrown over with some force.'

'But who would do such a thing?'

'Some other drunk – we're supposing that Billy was drunk. Someone he'd annoyed. Whoever it was, was probably some other poor unfortunate, so perhaps I'm glad that we might never find out what really happened.'

'But if you're right, unfortunate or not, it was a wicked thing to do.'

'Mr Randall,' someone said.

The voice startled her and Lorna tore her gaze from the bridge to see a young woman standing before them. She was a little smaller than Lorna, and very fair. She had large blue eyes and she would have been very pretty except that now she looked strained and anxious. She stood clasping the ends of a knitted shawl, pulling it tightly round her body. But there was something in her stance that made Lorna think she was frightened rather than simply cold.

'Irene,' Edwin said. 'What's the matter? Is it Ruth?'

'No, the bairn's fine. I've left Mrs Flanagan minding her for a moment. I saw you come down, I guessed where you were going and I wanted to ask you . . . ask you if she's all right . . . bearing up . . . Billy's poor mam.'

'She's unhappy, of course,' Edwin replied, 'but she seems to be managing.'

'Does she want for owt? Is there anything I can do?'

'I don't think so. People seem to have been very kind. It's good of you to ask. But did you know her?'

'No. Does that make a difference?'

Lorna was puzzled by an undertone in the girl's voice. At first she'd thought it was defiance but then she realized, puzzlingly, that it was more like fear.

'No, of course it doesn't make a difference,' Edwin said. 'But come along, it's cold standing here. Let's walk back up the bank together. This is my friend, Miss Hassan, by the way. Lorna, this is Irene Lawson.'

The girl barely glanced at her before they began to walk back up the bank.

'I heard what you were talking about,' Irene Lawson said. Edwin glanced at her and she continued, 'Just now, you and Miss Hassan, about Billy Potts falling from the bridge. Do you really think someone might have pushed him?'

'As I said, I don't really know.'

'What if he jumped?'

'Why would he do that?'

'Well, everyone knows he was a bit simple in the head, poor man. And if he was drunk – I mean, he might have been acting daft, walking along the parapet, then he jumped down. The wrong way.'

Lorna glanced at Edwin; he was frowning thoughtfully. 'It's as likely as any other theory,' he said. 'And, do you know, I imagine the people who live here will speculate about it for years to come.'

Irene's expression seemed to become more pinched as she said, 'No, they won't forget it.' Then she stopped walking and, with her hand on a front door, she asked, 'Would you like to come in?'

'We-ell,' Edwin hesitated.

'The old lady, Mrs Flanagan, I'd like you to look at her ankle. I think she's broken it.'

Lorna followed Edwin into Irene Lawson's home. She was surprised to see how clean and well kept the room was. An old woman sat by the fire and on a rug at her feet a beautiful child sat concentrating hard as

107

she pushed wooden clothes pegs one after the other through a hole cut into an upturned cardboard box.

'How ingenious,' Edwin said.

'I remember me mam making a box like that for me,' Irene said. 'It used to keep me occupied while she did her bit housework. All she had to do was fish them out again when I'd pushed the pegs all through.'

'She was a good mother,' Edwin said.

'Aye, and I'll do me best to bring Ruth up as she would hev wanted.'

Lorna seemed to have been forgotten about so she took a seat at the table and sat quietly listening to the conversation.

'I know it's hard for you, Irene,' Edwin said, 'and it must make it all the more difficult not knowing if you'll ever hear from your father.'

'That's not likely.'

'Why do you say that?'

'Well, he didn't just abandon us, you know. He made an allotment before he sailed, and me mam used to collect her portion at the shipping office. When she was too ill to leave the house, I used to go. And then the money stopped. He'd jumped ship, they said. In America. But it's my belief he died.'

'Died? How?' Edwin asked.

'Got sick or went overboard in some scrap. They wouldn't let on. They never want trouble.'

'I see.'

'I didn't tell me mam. She was too ill by then to know what was happening. And I couldn't face charity if it meant the workhouse. So, ever since then, I've managed somehow.'

Lorna sat very still. She was startled by the similarity of Irene's personal circumstances to her own. Not in any material sense, of course – there was no way this Spartan room could be compared with Mildred Cunningham's comfortable house overlooking Heaton Park. And, as the granddaughter of a relatively rich woman, Lorna had never had to work to provide for herself. And also Irene had to care for her baby sister.

But both of their mothers had died while their fathers had been away at sea. Lorna's own father had gone to seek their fortune. He had worked and saved and set off with a definite purpose in mind. He had always intended to come back to his wife and daughter when he had established some kind of business. As far as Lorna could understand from what her mother had told her when she'd been a child, he was going to bring home fine carpets, leather goods and brassware that people would like to buy to make their homes beautiful.

Irene's father had made his living as a sailor. He had travelled the world but he had always come home to his family in between voyages – until the last time he had sailed away, apparently not knowing that his wife was expecting another baby. It seemed that Irene was now convinced that he would never return; that she would be responsible for bringing up her baby sister.

And what do I think? Lorna wondered. Do I still believe that after all these years my father is going to return for me as my mother promised?

She could hear the murmur of voices as Irene explained to the old woman – what was she called? To Mrs Flanagan – that Mr Randall was going to look at her ankle. But she closed her eyes and tried to discover what she really believed. Her father had loved her and, even to a small child it had been obvious that he adored her mother. So why hadn't he returned?

She opened her mind to the memory of the day that Hilda had come to her grandmother's house. It was just after the most miserable Christmas she had ever spent, the first Christmas she had been apart from her mother. Her grandmother had allowed Hilda to be the one to tell her that her mother was dead.

She seemed to remember that her grandmother had been unable to speak for a while but she had mentioned that she would write a letter to Lorna's father. Hilda should post it that very day.

So why hadn't he come back for her?

As the years went by her grandmother had told her that her father had forgotten about her. That he had no intention of returning, that he had probably never intended to come home to her and her mother and it had all just been some grand pretence, an excuse to return to his homeland. Lorna had never believed that.

But now, hearing Irene Lawson's stark appraisal of her own situation, she was forced to consider the possibility that her own father might be dead. In fact, he most probably was; she just hadn't wanted to admit it to herself.

'Drink this, you look as if you need it.'

Lorna opened her eyes to see that a cup of tea had been placed on the table before her. She looked up to find Irene looking down at her.

'Thank you,' Lorna said, and smiled, but the girl's response was guarded.

'Are you all right?' she asked. 'You looked a bit femmer just now.'

'No, I'm not ill, perhaps a little tired,' Lorna said.

'I'll sit by you while you drink your tea. Mr Randall's seeing to her ankle.'

Irene turned her head and nodded towards the hearth where the old woman now had one foot resting on a wooden stool while Edwin kneeled beside her to bind it with a clean strip of rag.

'Is it broken?' Lorna asked.

'No, just sprained, thank goodness. I doubt her old bones would set properly, the life she leads.'

Lorna looked at Irene questioningly and the girl explained: 'Mrs Flanagan is a widow. She lives in the rooms upstairs with her daughter and her family. They give her no peace. That's why she likes to come down to my room.'

'Does she help you with your sister?'

'Yes, she's good with Ruth, and I'd let her help more if it weren't for her son-in-law. He resents having to keep her and he's a violent man when he's had a drink. I wouldn't trust him not to come in here looking for her. She says she went over on that ankle when she tripped on the stairs, you know. I'm not so sure Seth MacAndrew didn't push her.'

'But that's appalling.'

Irene gave her a cool look and said, 'Yes, isn't it?'

Lorna was aware of the hint of scorn in the girl's voice and she looked down at her tea. Perhaps Irene thought of her as one of the middle-class do-gooders who visited the poor out of some shallow sense of duty and then went home to regale each other with tales of the simply dreadful behaviour of the slum dwellers.

She had sensed a certain antagonism from the moment Edwin had introduced them and she supposed she couldn't blame her. But just now, when Irene had brought her the cup of tea, she had seemed to be genuinely sympathetic. For a fleeting moment Lorna had wanted to talk to her as a friend, to tell her that they had so much in common with one another.

That was impossible now, she realized. Not only had the moment passed but she suspected that Irene didn't like her. She wished that wasn't so but she didn't know what she could do about it.

Irene stood up again. 'Drink your tea,' she said. 'Mr Randall asked me to make it for you.'

Edwin rose to his feet and she heard Mrs Flanagan murmur her thanks. 'Are you going to work, tonight?' he asked Irene.

'Aye, just to the coal office. I'll not be long.'

'Good. It's a night for staying in by the fire.'

They took their leave soon after that and when they reached the top of the street Edwin asked, 'Do you still want to go into town?'

'No, I think I'll go home now,' she replied.

'I'll walk with you, if I may?'

'No, it's all right. I can cut along by Beavan's and then go through the park.'

'Then I'll definitely walk with you. It's getting quite dark and you shouldn't go that way alone, it's dangerous.'

Lorna knew he was referring to the murders of young women. Still no one had been arrested and charged with the crimes. She simply nodded and they set off together.

'You were very thoughtful when we were at Irene's,' he said.

'Yes.' Lorna didn't feel like telling him where her thoughts had taken her. She was always worried that people would think she felt sorry for herself. And she didn't. Especially when she compared Irene's living conditions with her own. 'Life must be very hard for her,' she said.

'Of course. And even worse for many other people that I visit.'

They walked in silence for a while and then Edwin asked, 'Would you like to help me?'

'How?'

'Well, I've been thinking of starting a small class. A reading class. Some of the older women, like Mrs Flanagan, never learned to read properly. Not because they weren't capable. There were various reasons. Perhaps when they were girls childhood illnesses kept them away from school, or their mothers kept them at home deliberately to help with the smaller children.'

'Just the girls?'

Edwin smiled. 'Well, there were boys who missed school too, but the girls seemed to suffer most because there are still people who think education isn't important for a woman.'

'I've been lucky in that respect,' Lorna said.

'Yes. And that's why I thought you might like to help.'

'Would they want to learn? People like Mrs Flanagan?'

'You mean because she's old?'

'I suppose I do.'

'No matter how old she is, life would be easier for her if she could read the instructions on a bottle of cough mixture, say, or a recipe sheet provided by the good women at the soup kitchen.'

'Of course. I didn't think.'

'And then there's the sheer pleasure of reading. Imagine how good it would be to sit by the fire and escape into a better world for a while.'

'Just as I do.'

111

They had reached the corner where Beavan's department store stood. The lights from the shop's windows fell across Lorna's face and Edwin looked at her keenly.

'Just as you do,' he said. 'I knew you would be the right person to ask. So, once Christmas is over, will you help me to organize a reading group?'

'Yes – oh . . .'

Lorna had just been about to agree when she remembered that after Christmas she might not be here. In fact, she hoped with all her heart that she would not be. For any day now Maurice would be getting in touch with her; any day now they would be eloping together. And, once she was his wife, they might not even be living here in Newcastle. And suppose they were, she suspected that Maurice might not agree to her spending so much time with Edwin Randall.

'Well, I'm not sure,' she said, and she saw the look of keen disappointment that he tried to hide.

'Of course, I shouldn't have asked you.'

'No! You have every right to ask. It's just that I might not be— Oh, I'm sorry.'

Lorna felt dreadful. She felt that Edwin deserved an explanation but she couldn't give him one without betraying her secret. And, somehow, even though their friendship seemed to have grown closer suddenly, she could not confide in him about Maurice.

Or was it because the nature of their friendship had changed? Over the years she had enjoyed talking to him whenever she had gone to his uncle's bookshop. She thought it had been because only he understood her love of reading. But they had never grown close enough for her to confide in him why she had ordered certain volumes. Books about Arabia.

But since the night she had met him in the park something had changed between them. It was not simply that their friendship had grown deeper. She realized that Edwin might now be hoping for something more than friendship. But that could never be possible. And, puzzlingly, she acknowledged that that filled her with feelings of regret.

'Well,' he said now, 'at least think about it, and if you change your mind, let me know.'

'I will.'

'I suppose I could ask Irene,' Edwin said.

'Irene? You mean the young woman I've just met?'

'You sound surprised. You shouldn't be. Irene is intelligent, much too intelligent for the life she chooses to lead in order to care for her sister.' Edwin's tone was cool and Lorna felt herself flush.

'No, I'm not surprised, really. I suppose I wondered whether she would have time.'

Edwin nodded. 'There is that. But if I could find some money from somewhere, some charitable organization that would be prepared to provide the funds, I could even pay her a small wage. Then she might be able to drop one of her cleaning jobs. Yes, that's an idea.'

He sounded pleased and Lorna supposed that she should be pleased too. She was confused to find that she wasn't. It wasn't because she begrudged Irene Lawson the chance to be paid for doing something useful, it was because Edwin already seemed to have given up the hope of persuading Lorna herself to help. And he actually seemed to be happy with the thought of working with Irene.

What on earth's the matter with me? she thought in exasperation. I can't help with the reading group, I won't even be here. So why does it bother me that Edwin will be able to manage without me?

She was glad when they entered the park. It was dusk and the lamps were lit. But in between the gaslamps there were pools of shadow so deep that even if they wanted to they would not have been able to see each other's expression clearly.

When the path began to descend steeply into a little valley Edwin said, 'Take my arm.'

'No, it's all right,' she said, and moved a little apart from him. She felt rather than saw his hurt bewilderment.

A little later Edwin stood at the gate and watched as Lorna entered her grandmother's house. They had hardly spoken since the moment she had refused to take his arm. He had asked if she would be coming into town, and maybe visit the bookshop before Christmas, which wasn't far away now, but she had said probably not. Now, she turned briefly and waved, and then the door closed behind her.

He crossed the road, then began to walk to the nearest tram stop and thought about the time he had just spent with her.

He wasn't sure why he had suddenly asked her to come with him to visit old Jane Potts. He certainly hadn't intended to. But he had been thinking about Lorna so much lately that when he had seen her waiting to cross the road, he had imagined for a fleeting moment that it was his own desire that had conjured her up.

And then she had behaved so naturally in Jane's makeshift dwelling – oh, she had been taken aback, who wouldn't be? But, allowing for her nervousness at finding herself in such strange surroundings, her interest and concern had been genuine.

Then, in Irene's house, she'd sat and waited patiently and, although he had been busy binding up Mrs Flanagan's sprained ankle, he'd been aware that she had smiled and tried to talk to Irene. Strangely, it was Irene who'd been standoffish and even resentful, although he couldn't imagine why.

But Lorna, although showing signs of tiredness, had acted naturally. So why had she refused to help him? He knew it had been a refusal, even though she was supposed to be considering his request. Perhaps she had been plunged too suddenly into a world she had only guessed at before. Perhaps it was not fatigue but disorientation at finding herself in such a different world she had been experiencing when she sat at Irene's table. Now that he thought about it he should have realized that she was distressed, not tired.

Just before he boarded the tram that would take him into town, Edwin glanced across at the house once more and saw a light go on in a room on the top floor. Was it Lorna's room? Was she in there now, perhaps changing her clothes and washing the smell of poverty away before she took her evening meal?

He wished he knew what she was thinking.

Later that night Irene Lawson poured hot water from the kettle into a bowl and stripped off her clothes to wash before the fire. She'd turned off the lamp and Ruth was already sleeping in the bed they shared, and with any luck she would sleep through until morning. She was usually a contented child but her recent teething troubles had caused some broken nights, which was bad for both of them.

In places like the coal office it didn't matter if the child was fractious because Irene worked there alone. The watchman did his rounds and only complained if the baby cried when he was trying to snatch a few moments by the fire with a mug of tea.

But it was more difficult if Ruth made a fuss when Irene went to scrub out the corner shop in the mornings or had occasional jobs at the Commercial. Luckily that hadn't happened often. However, once her sister grew too big to sleep in the pram Irene didn't know what she would do.

Earlier tonight Mrs Flanagan had offered once more to mind the bairn while Irene went to work and she'd been very tempted to accept. Perhaps she was wrong to fear that Seth MacAndrew would cause trouble. Perhaps he would be glad to get rid of his mother-in-law for hours at a time.

The old woman was good with Ruth and she'd reminded Irene that she didn't want payment. Just a chance to sit in peace and perhaps have a bite to eat. Irene would have to think about that, perhaps have a word with the old woman's daughter, Seth's poor downtrodden wife, and ask her what she thought about it.

When she was ready for bed she warmed the milk that Ruth had left and poured it into a mug. She would sit by the fire while she drank it and try to relax. But no sooner had she settled back in the chair than her mind flew back to that dreadful moment when poor Billy Potts had gone hurtling to his death from the bridge.

She hadn't known it was Billy. She hadn't recognized him. She had been so frightened when he had come charging towards her like that that she hadn't looked properly. But would any one believe that?

The best she could hope for was that no one would ever discover what had really happened. The gossip round here was that he had been acting daft and fallen over in a drunken stupor.

But Edwin Randall didn't think so.

Irene remembered his words earlier today when he'd been talking to that girl, when they hadn't realized that she was listening. Even though he'd admitted it could never be proven it was obvious he believed that Billy had been thrown over the bridge.

She stirred uncomfortably as she remembered what the girl had said: '*But if you're right, unfortunate or not, it was a wicked thing to do.*'

Irene's thoughts took a new direction. Lorna, her name was, Lorna Hassan. The name Hassan and the girl's dark skin . . . more than likely her father was a darkie like the sailors who came in on some of the ships. Now and then one of them would marry a local lass, and the children growing up in the houses round the quayside looked a bit like Lorna Hassan.

But what about her clothes and the way she spoke? It was obvious she didn't belong in this part of town. Her father had done well for himself then.

Irene sighed. She was tired and she didn't really care to puzzle out the answers that would explain Lorna Hassan. Except for one thing. She would dearly like to know what she was doing with Edwin Randall.

Chapter Ten

February 1904

Dear Grandmamma,

Please do not worry about me. I am quite safe. I know you will be angry when I tell you this but I am going to be married. I am sorry it has happened this way, but you will understand why when I tell you that my husband-to-be is Maurice Haldane.

Maurice did not want me to tell you yet, I suppose because he is worried that you will try to find me and attempt to bring me home. I hope you won't do that because I wouldn't come. And there would be no point, for Maurice is in love with me, not Rose, and we would simply wait until I am twenty-one and we could marry without your permission.

However, I did not think it fair to leave without telling you. For me to go into town and not come back would have been irresponsible, particularly when they still have not caught the man who preys on lone women. I believe you care enough for me to have worried at my absence.

Also I have to ask you to break the news to Rose. I know I have behaved badly by taking her sweetheart, but I'm sure in my heart that she does not love him as I do. Maurice will have to face the task of telling his family.

I do not know when I will see you again, or if you will want to see me, ever. I hope so. For I am grateful to you for taking me in when my mother died, and providing for me when you believed that my father had abandoned me. I still don't think that this is true, you know.

My father loved me and he would have returned for me if at all possible. I have come to believe that he must be dead. And that has made me all the more determined to make a happy life for myself. Maurice wants us to be together and an elopement seems to be the only way to achieve this.

Perhaps you will expect me to beg forgiveness? I can not do that. I am sorry for any distress this will cause Rose but, in the long run, she would never have been happy with a man who did not truly love her.

It is too much, I suppose, to ask for your blessing, but I hope, at least once the shock is over, you will understand that this had nothing to do with Maurice's wealth or position in the world. It is simply that I love him.

Lorna

The train rattled through the frozen countryside. Lorna looked out at the winter landscape. It was a bright day and the sunlight glanced off the rushing streams and sparkled along the ploughed furrows rimmed with frost. After the smoky gloom of the city she took this as a good omen. She did not allow the outlines of the leafless trees, rising stark against the sky, to cast any shadow on her happiness.

She was pleased to have the carriage to herself. She wouldn't have been able to make sensible conversation with anyone – she was so excited. And, besides, she wanted to savour this moment alone. To revel in the sense of freedom – of destiny. She had never felt so alive, so exhilarated. She had taken her life into her own hands. Now, at last, she was rushing headlong towards her future, her happy future with Maurice.

The last few weeks had been miserable. When her grandmother returned from Corbridge, just before Christmas, Lorna had had to listen to her and Rose endlessly discussing plans for the wedding.

Believing as she did that the wedding would never take place, she hadn't been able to eat or sleep. Her grandmother had noticed the state she was in and, although she hadn't said as much, Mildred Cunningham had obviously believed that Lorna was being eaten away by jealousy and spite.

And then there'd been the torture of not knowing when Maurice would get in touch. 'Trust me,' his first letter had said . . .

Lorna and her grandmother had spent Christmas Day alone together. Rose had been invited to the Haldanes' country house in Yorkshire. She stayed there until after New Year, and that must have been the worst week of Lorna's life, knowing that Rose and Maurice were under the same roof.

She had not even been able to escape the house because her grandmother had been ill. A slight indisposition she'd said but,

117

nevertheless, it kept her confined to her room. She had asked Lorna to see to the running of the household.

Her grandmother had forced herself, it seemed to Lorna, to be up and about again by the time Rose returned full of talk about Maurice's family and how they had made her *so-oo* welcome. And how large and impressive and full of luxury the house was.

Perhaps that had been the darkest moment of all. But she should have trusted Maurice for, when the letter came at last, it was everything she'd hoped for. At first she had been puzzled. The envelope bore the name of a city bookshop in the top left-hand corner. Once she'd opened it, Lorna smiled as she wondered how Maurice had acquired it – and thought how clever he was.

How many times had she read it? She took it out of her small travelling bag now and read it yet again. It wasn't a long letter. The instructions were simple. On a certain day she must leave the house straight after lunch and catch a certain train to Brampton. She mustn't bring a great portmanteau full of clothes, that would arouse suspicion. Maurice would provide her with everything she needed from now on. And he had stressed that she must tell no one. Leave no word. They would find out soon enough, his letter said, and there must be no hint, no clue that would make it easy for anyone to come after her.

Lorna put the letter back in its envelope and put it back in her bag. She would have to confess to Maurice that her conscience had forced her to leave a letter for her grandmother. When she explained why she was sure that he would understand. And she'd probably brought more with her than she should have done. But no one had seen her leave the house.

It wasn't her clothes that filled the travelling bag, although she'd brought her nightclothes and a change of underwear at least, it was some of her books, especially the ones her father had bought for her when she was a child. And also the muff she'd had with her when she'd arrived at her grandmother's house. And tucked away inside it, one pearl earring.

Lorna closed the bag and her smile faded. What would her mother have thought of her actions now? Her mother had married for love. She had not eloped, for she'd already had her twenty-first birthday and she hadn't needed her mother's permission. She had simply left home one day, just as Lorna had done now, married Said Hassan at the register office and never returned to her mother's house. Not until she was dying and needed to leave Lorna there.

Yes, surely her mother would have approved. Lorna frowned and tried to push thoughts of her parents aside, for it had just occurred to her that if they had still been alive and she, Lorna, was living at home with them, she might never have met Maurice.

When the train pulled into the station Lorna was waiting at the door, ready to get out. Only one other person alighted, a middle-aged woman, who, judging by the number of parcels she carried, had been to the January sales in Newcastle. A man, some years older than she was, hurried forward to greet her and relieve her of the parcels.

Lorna was surprised by the warmth of his greeting and the smiles they exchanged. They were obviously a married couple and still in love – at their age. Lorna took this to be a good omen.

She looked around. There was no one else on the platform. Had she caught the correct train? Or had it arrived early? Why wasn't Maurice waiting for her as he said he would be? As the train behind her gathered steam and began to pull out of the station, she walked towards the exit and surrendered her ticket to the attendant. A single ticket. There had been no need to buy a return.

Hesitantly she walked out of the station building into the street. As she did so a small trap drew up and the coachman leaped down and hurried towards her. No, it wasn't a coachman, it was Maurice!

'Lorna,' he said. 'At last.'

And there, in full view of anyone who might have braved the frosty air, he took her in his arms and held her close.

In no time at all, it seemed, they had left the streets of the small town behind them and were bowling through the countryside at a cracking pace. The cold air burned her cheeks and the horse's hoofs struck sparks on the frost-bound road.

They travelled in silence, neither seeming to want to break the spell. The road was empty of other traffic; the hedges at each side wound away into the distance, the only sign of life a few black-winged rooks high in the leafless trees.

It could so easily have been the landscape of a ghost story, a tale told by the fire on a winter's night. But to Lorna it was a land of enchantment. She knew she would remember this journey for ever.

After a short while Maurice turned to her and asked, 'Are you warm enough?' He held the reins with one hand as he leaned over and adjusted the blanket round her knees.

'I'm fine,' she said, and the wind snatched her words away. 'But where are we going?'

'Wait and see. It's a surprise. A marvellous surprise.'

She glanced sideways at his face and saw that he seemed to be as exhilarated as she was. But she wished that he would tell her what his

119

plans were. She had not been surprised when his letter had instructed her to go to Brampton. More than forty miles west of Newcastle, Brampton was within striking distance of both the Lake District and the Scottish Border. And just over the border lay Gretna Green.

Lorna lifted her arms and pretended to feel for her hatpin and made a show of securing it. While she did so she moved her head so that she could glance behind her into the well of the trap. Only her own travelling bag lay on the floor between the bench seats. Surely, if they were going straight to Gretna, Maurice would have brought some clothes.

Or perhaps he had already been there to arrange the accommodation. Lorna knew that they would have to reside in Scotland for three weeks before they could get married. She had heard all the stories about runaway couples finding lodgings with farmers' wives. Sometimes furious parents sent the police after them and they would hide in specially furnished farm buildings which were often little better than hen huts.

She almost laughed out loud at the idea of Maurice in a hen hut. He was so tall. And, also he was used to luxury. No, she didn't imagine that they would be living in a farm outbuilding for the next few weeks. The wealthier runaways sometimes rented more substantial cottages along deserted tracks, hard to find unless you knew the area. Surely that would be the plan.

A sudden coil of tension knotted within her when she realized the implications of this. She would be living alone with Maurice in a remote cottage. Would he expect them to live as husband and wife? She glanced sideways. Even in profile she could tell he was happy, but she realized that she had no idea what he was thinking. She loved him, she was physically attracted to him, and yet she really didn't know him at all.

'What is it?' He had sensed her gaze.

'How much longer before— How much longer are we going to travel?' she asked.

'Be patient, sweetheart,' Maurice said. 'I told you, I have the most wonderful surprise in store.' And then, almost immediately, he said, 'Look!'

The house took her by surprise. They had just passed a group of cottages with small gardens bound by grey stone walls. There were enough dwellings to earn the place the title of village, she supposed. But then they reached a more substantial house, set back from the road and approached, through tall wrought-iron gates, along a short gravelled drive.

A groom hurried out from a small stable block set to the side, and took the reins.

'Are we staying here?' Lorna asked. She was puzzled for she had believed they would have to find lodgings in Scotland.

Maurice had already descended. He went round and reached up to lift her down bodily. She looked up at the stone façade of the house while Maurice got her bag from the trap. He didn't answer her question; he simply took her arm and guided her up the wide stone steps to the front door.

'Maurice, what is this place? Is it a hotel?'

'No, my darling, it's not a hotel. This is our home.'

Before she could question this statement the front door was opened by a fresh-faced young servant girl. She stood aside and then closed the door after them as they entered the large entrance hall. The girl smiled and curtsied before she took the travelling bag from Maurice and hurried away with it up the well-proportioned staircase.

'Home?' Lorna looked up at him in surprise. 'What do you mean?'

She looked around her. A fire blazed in a stone fireplace. The parquet floor was well polished. Richly coloured oriental rugs covered its surface. There was a small door tucked away behind the staircase which she guessed led to the domestic quarter but wide doorways at each side of her gave glimpses into well-proportioned and luxuriously furnished rooms.

'Do you like it?' Maurice asked. 'I wanted it to be just right.'

'But what do you mean, it is our home?' Lorna asked him. 'Are we staying here until we get married? Have you rented it?'

'No, I haven't rented it. I've bought this house. And when I told my parents and Rose I was staying with friends, I was making sure the house was ready for you. This is where you're going to live.'

'*I'm* going to live here? Don't you mean *we* are going to live here?'

'Of course. Now take off your outdoor things.' Maurice began to divest himself of his travelling coat. 'Here's Hetty – that's your name, isn't it?'

The girl, who had just come back downstairs, bobbed and smiled.

'Take our coats, Hetty, and tell Cook to be ready with a tray of tea and cakes for you to bring to the sitting room. I'll ring for it when we're ready. You're not to disturb us until then. Do you understand?'

'Yes, sir.'

The girl did her bob of a curtsy again and Maurice smiled.

'And Hetty . . .' he said.

'Yes, sir?'

121

'You needn't curtsy all the time. You can do it now and then if it makes you happy, but don't bob up and down like this all the time or you'll make me dizzy.'

His smile was warm and Lorna saw how the girl responded to it with shy delight. Her rosy cheeks flushed even further and she burst out giggling as she hurried away with their outdoor clothes. Lorna just had time to notice her opening a cleverly concealed door set in the panelling at the back of the hall before Maurice led her into the room on the right and closed the door behind him.

'Look around you,' Maurice said. 'Everything in here is the very best that Haldane's has to offer.'

Lorna's glance was perfunctory. Indeed, the room was well furnished. The curtains, the carpet, the comfortable chairs by the fire, a writing desk and occasional tables, all smelled as well as looked new. A vase on each of the two deep, low windowsills held arrangements of evergreen leaves.

There were pictures on the walls – delicate watercolours of pastoral scenes, the kind that could be bought by the dozen in the better department stores. The overall effect was light and airy and very up-to-date.

'I didn't want to spoil the surprise by telling you,' Maurice said, 'so I had to guess what you would like. But, of course, you can change anything – everything if you want to. I'll have the latest illustrated catalogues of household goods sent here for you. You must order anything you like!'

'But, Maurice, I don't understand . . .'

Maurice caught at her hands and said, 'In a moment we will sit down and I will explain everything. But first, come over here. Look, new books. See how much I've thought of what will make you happy.'

Lorna looked at the bookcase. In spite of her bewilderment the books caught her attention and she examined their spines.

'All the latest novels,' Maurice said. 'I've opened an account for you at a bookshop in Edinburgh. They will send you their latest listings and you can have whatever you want, my darling. I don't want you to be too lonely when I can't be here.'

'Maurice, listen to me.' Lorna turned and faced him. 'What are you telling me? Is this house to be our home?'

'Yes.'

'But why? I mean it's charming – and you've gone to so much trouble – but why are we to live here, in a village in the country? I thought that after we were married we would return to Newcastle and—'

Maurice's smile and mood of animation vanished. He drew her into his arms and, cradling her head with one hand, he held it close to his chest so that she could not turn her face to look up at him.

'Do you love me, Lorna?' he asked.

'You know I do.'

'And do you want to be with me, for always?'

'Yes.'

'And that's what I want. In fact I want you so much that I cannot imagine life without you. We have to be together. I had to find a way. Don't you understand?'

'No, I don't understand. What are you saying?'

Lorna broke free from his embrace but he caught her hands and led her over to the hearth. 'Sit down, sweetheart,' he said. Unwillingly she did, and he sat down beside her. 'Now, before we talk, perhaps you'd like some tea to revive you after the journey.'

He reached for the bell pull and Lorna caught at his arm. 'No, I don't want anything until you explain things to me.'

'Very well.' Maurice sighed and there was a worrying pause. Suddenly he looked so grave that Lorna was frightened. When he spoke he could not look her in the eyes. 'Sweetheart,' he said, 'I can't marry you.'

She thought she had never received such a shock in her entire life. She stared at him, hoping that it was a joke, that in a moment he would smile and apologize. But he remained silent.

'Can't marry me?' she asked at last. 'Then why have you brought me here?'

'Because married or not, I want you to be mine. I want to be able to come to you whenever I can.'

'You mean you want me to be your mistress?'

'Yes, but you won't suffer, I promise you.'

'Suffer?'

'I mean in any material sense. This house – it will be yours. I'll make it over to you. You will have your own accounts at any shop you wish – perhaps not Haldane's – but any other. You can order whatever clothes, books, household goods you want. I won't question anything. I won't be mean.'

Lorna tried to stand and found she couldn't. Sometimes in romantic novels, when the heroine has received a shock, she had seen the words: 'she felt as if the room was spinning round her'. Well, that was a pretty good description of what was happening to her now.

123

The ticking of the clock on the mantelpiece seemed to be coming from a long way away. She could feel her heart pounding and she imagined that the discomfort she felt was because it was rising up in her throat to choke her. She leaned back against the cushions and tried to swallow the pain.

'But why here?' she breathed at last. 'Why so near to the border and to . . . to Gretna?'

Maurice turned his head away from her and seemed to be staring into the fire. There was a long silence before he said, 'I'm sorry. I know that seems deliberately cruel, but I could see no other way.'

'Cruel?'

'Yes.' He turned to look at her at last and he took her hands. She tried to snatch them away but he held on tightly. 'I knew that you would assume that we were going to elope to Gretna to be married and therefore you would come unquestioningly.'

'I see.' She heard the break in her voice. 'So that means you knew I wouldn't agree to this – to this other arrangement.'

'Yes.'

'So what makes you think that I will agree now? That I won't go straight back to my grandmother's house?'

'Because once I had you here, I was sure I could persuade you to stay.'

'Bribe me with material things, you mean? With houses and furnishings, with books and clothes?'

'No, of course not. What do you take me for?'

'What do you take *me* for?' At last indignation gave her the energy to rise to her feet.

'Lorna – sweetheart – listen to me!' Maurice rose and took her shoulders. She tried to twist free but he caught at her and pulled her closer. 'I know you love me,' he said. 'And every time we've discussed this you made me believe that you want us to be together too.'

'Yes, but I thought—'

'Like all romantic girls you thought the only way to achieve that was to be married.'

'But you said that you would find a way.'

'A way to what? Think carefully, Lorna. I never actually mentioned marriage, did I?

'No . . . but I assumed—'

'I know, and I'm sorry. You thought I would tell my parents and try to persuade them to agree that I should marry you. I thought about it, believe me, I did. I thought long and hard, but I decided that it would be hopeless.'

124

'Because . . . because my father is of a different race?'

Maurice's paused before he answered. 'Not entirely. If your father was an Indian prince or a rich plantation owner I'm sure they would have got used to the idea. But—'

'I'm poor. It's money that's important to people like your parents, isn't it? Well, Rose is no great heiress. My grandmother's little property company surely doesn't compare with Haldane's commercial empire!'

She knew she'd sounded spiteful, but instead of admonishing her Maurice looked surprised.

'You obviously don't know the extent of your grandmother's business interests. As well as the flats that your late grandfather built, she has bought property all over Newcastle. It will all belong to Rose one day.'

Lorna frowned. She didn't know what to say. Her grandmother never talked about her business interests at home but, from the way they lived, she supposed it should have been obvious that they were more than just comfortable.

She was confused to find herself thinking of Irene Lawson, and worse, of old Mrs Potts, who had lost her son so tragically. While she, Lorna, had been living so comfortably in her grandmother's large house, those poor people lived on the very edge of a bearable existence.

'Are you listening to me, Lorna?'

She dragged her mind back to the immediate present and her own predicament. Maurice was looking at her keenly.

'Yes,' she said. 'Please go on. I think you were saying that you knew your parents wouldn't approve of me as a wife for you.'

Maurice missed the edge of sarcasm and continued, 'That's right. I knew I had to find another way.'

'Another way!'

'Lorna, I'm sorry. Please sit down again.'

'No, I don't want to.'

Lorna knew that she sounded like a petulant child and the tender smile her angry response drew from Maurice made her want to cry.

'I think you should. You're trembling.'

She allowed him to lower her on to the sofa but only because she was afraid she would fall if he didn't.

'Thank you.' Then, 'Don't!' she said, when he sat beside her and attempted to hold on to her hand.

'So your parents know nothing of this . . . this plan?' she said.

'Of course not.'

'They would disapprove?'

125

'In theory my father wouldn't disapprove of this kind of arrangement. My mother would simply prefer not to know about it. But in this particular case, yes, they would.'

'This case?'

'You are Rose's cousin. If she ever found out it would be very – very uncomfortable.'

'Found out? You mean you intended to keep this secret?'

'Yes. Why not?'

'But my grandmother . . . she would have to know.'

'All your grandmother needs to know is that you've left home.'

'But she would worry . . .'

'Would she? Admit it, Lorna. You have not been happy in her house. Oh, she fed you, clothed you, educated you, but how does your life compare with that of your cousin?'

Lorna stared miserably beyond Maurice into the fire crackling in the hearth. 'I don't think she ever forgave my mother for marrying my father. She found it hard to accept me.'

'Whatever the reason, she hasn't loved you. I love you and we will be happy here together. I searched for a long time for somewhere suitable.'

'Suitable? You mean hidden away?'

'I would rather say discreet! And I can get here so quickly from town. I will be able to be with you as often as I can get away.'

'And what am I supposed to do when you are not here?'

'I've told you – you can have anything you like. Books . . . do you want to take up embroidery? Sketching?'

'In other words I am to wait patiently until you appear. I am to be a prisoner here, hidden away from the world.'

'Not all the time. We can travel – we can go abroad together.'

'But not as man and wife.'

'No, darling, I've told you.'

'And of course I would never see my family again.'

'Would you care?'

Lorna thought hard before she answered. 'Probably not. In fact I'd already thought about that. I had faced the possibility that my grandmother would never want to see me again if I married you.'

'There you are!'

'And if I stay here— No, don't.' Maurice had moved towards her and tried to take her in his arms. 'Answer me. If I were to stay here what am I supposed to tell my grandmother?'

'I've thought of that. You can write a letter. Tell her that you have been unhappy and you are leaving home. Running away. I can have the

126

letter posted in London, Manchester, Liverpool, anywhere you like. You can make up some story of seeking employment. She knows that you are intelligent enough to fend for yourself.'

'She might believe that,' Lorna said softly, as though she were considering it. 'Heaven knows she has been aware that I have been miserable lately. I think she believes that I'm jealous of Rose, so it might not surprise her if I chose to leave Newcastle.'

'There, you see? It will be easy.'

'But it would be all lies. And, in any case, it's too late.'

Lorna got up swiftly and walked across to one of the windows. She stared out at the neat front garden. The day was bright but the lawn was silvered with frost. The water in an ornamental stone birdbath was skimmed with ice. Some buds on the rose bushes had never opened during the summer months and now they never would.

'What do you mean, it's too late?' she heard Maurice say as he crossed the floor to join her.

'I've already written to my grandmother.'

'You've what?'

'I know you told me not to but I couldn't let her worry about me. And neither could I lie. I didn't realize that you would expect me to lie.' She couldn't keep the note of accusation out of her voice. Neither could she turn to look at him.

When he spoke he sounded furious. 'What did you tell her?'

'That we are – were to be married. And that she shouldn't come after me and try to prevent it because we wouldn't be dissuaded. I thought that was the truth.'

Maurice had stopped close behind her. He was very still. He asked, 'Did you post this letter today?'

Lorna knew what he meant. If she had posted it before she left town her grandmother would get the letter in the morning. 'No,' she told him.

'You still have it?' It was hateful to hear how hopeful he sounded.

'No, I left it in my room. Don't worry, she won't have read it yet.'

'How can you be sure?'

'My grandmother and Rose are going to the theatre with your mother, remember? And then they are going, with some other ladies, back to your house for supper.'

'Oh, yes. How grateful I was that husbands and sons were not required to be present. So they will be late home?'

Lorna sighed. 'I imagined that my grandmother wouldn't notice my absence until I failed to appear at the breakfast table in the morning. Then she would send someone up to my room—'

'And they would find you gone.'

'And the letter on my pillow.'

'So we have until tomorrow to retrieve the letter?'

'Probably . . .' Lorna frowned.

'What do you mean, probably? Lorna, don't play with me!'

'Rose. There was always the possibility that Rose would go to my room tonight to tell me how much she'd enjoyed herself. The letter is addressed to my grandmother but what if Rose opened it? Oh, Maurice, she would be the first to know. I didn't think of that!'

'You little fool!' Maurice took hold of her arms and spun her round. 'You've ruined everything for us. We could have been together—'

'When you weren't with Rose!'

'Be quiet! It wouldn't have mattered that I was married to Rose. It's *you* I love, *you* I would have spent as much time as possible with. But now, you'll have to go back. You'll have to go up to your room and get the letter and destroy it.' He pulled his watch from his fob pocket and studied it. 'If you catch the next train back to Newcastle and then get a cab,' he said, 'you ought to get home before your grandmother.' He frowned. 'But if the train is delayed for some reason, you might not.' He put his watch away and, still frowning, asked, 'Have you a friend in the house?'

'A friend?'

'One of the servants that you trust?'

'Well . . . I suppose there's Violet.'

'Good. You must telephone her now and ask her to remove the letter. Tell her that you're on your way home.'

'But won't she think it strange?'

'She's a servant. She'll do as she's told. Tell her that as soon as she has handed the letter over to you – unopened – she'll be rewarded.'

'Rewarded?'

'I haven't yet come across a servant who would refuse a few extra coins for a service rendered.'

'I see.'

Suddenly Maurice looked beyond her. He narrowed his eyes and spoke slowly as if he were thinking things through. 'Then . . .' he said, 'then dismiss her . . . that's it – tell her that you're going to bed. Listen at your door and, as soon as the house is quiet, slip out again. You'll have told the cab driver to wait, of course.'

'But why?'

'Because, my darling,' he looked into her eyes and smiled brilliantly, 'you must come back here.'

'Come back?'

'Of course. We can still be together as soon as you have retrieved the letter!'

Maurice took her in his arms but she held herself stiffly. He mistook the reason. 'Lorna,' he said, 'I'm sorry I was angry with you. This muddle is my fault and it wouldn't have happened if only . . .' he faltered. 'If only I had been honest with you. But you understand why I couldn't be, don't you?'

She didn't answer. Instead she asked, 'And if I come back here, where is my grandmother supposed to think I have gone?'

'What?' Maurice frowned. 'Oh, I see. Lorna, Mildred Cunningham doesn't deserve your concern. But if you must leave some sort of word for her, write another letter. Write it on the train on the way back to Newcastle – I'll give you some notepaper and an envelope. Have it all ready to substitute for the first letter.'

'And what do you think I should tell her?'

'What do I think? Oh, for goodness' sake,' not noticing how coolly Lorna was regarding him he began to smile, 'tell her anything. Tell her you've gone to London . . . to Mandalay . . . to Timbuktu. Tell her you've run off with the circus!' His eyes were shining and he began to laugh in earnest.

'Stop it, Maurice, stop it!' Lorna wrenched herself free and stepped back.

'What's the matter? Why are you looking at me like that?'

She hid her clenched fists in the fold of her skirt. 'I'll telephone Violet as you suggested,' she said. 'I'll ask her to remove the letter from my room and keep it for me. Then I shall drop it in the fire. But that is all. I'm not coming back to you.'

He stared at her as if he didn't believe what he had heard. 'Not coming back? Why? Why are you denying us this chance of happiness?'

'If you need to be told the answer to that then you don't know me very well.'

'Know you? I thought you loved me!'

'I . . . I do . . . but I . . .' Lorna was overcome with a mixture of rage and anguish. She stared at him wildly, not knowing what to say.

'But not enough, it seems,' he said at last. 'If you loved me the way I hoped you did, you'd come and live with me.'

'Hidden away,' Lorna said, her voice strengthening as she regained her composure, 'in a sort of half-world.'

'What are you talking about?'

'Never to meet your family or friends, never to be acknowledged as your wife. No, Maurice, if you loved me sufficiently you wouldn't ask this of me. I'm leaving here now and I'm not coming back.'

The telephone was in a small room at the other side of the hall. It was furnished as a study. 'This was to be your office,' Maurice said, 'where you could sit and order the household, do the accounts, the servants' wages and so on. You see, I intended you to be independent.'

Lorna refrained from questioning an independence that would depend on Maurice's bounty and got on with her phone call. It was Violet who answered as Lorna thought she would. She was the only servant her grandmother trusted to take messages accurately. Violet sounded uneasy and to begin with she was hesitant but she agreed to do as she was asked. Lorna felt embarrassed to mention a reward but, as Maurice was standing over her, she did so.

'So, no one will ever know,' she said as she replaced the receiver.

'That's right. Unless you tell anyone. And you won't.'

'You seem so sure.'

'Of course. What would you say? That I persuaded you to run away with me and you were stupid enough to think that I wanted to marry you? That I simply wanted to make you my mistress, would you tell anyone that?'

'No.' She barely whispered the word.

She knew that Maurice was right. Her pride would never allow her to reveal what had happened.

Maurice left her standing there while he summoned Hetty to fetch her outdoor clothes and her travelling bag. No sooner had Lorna buttoned up her coat and secured her hat, than the trap appeared outside the front door. Maurice helped her in. This time she sat in the back with her bag, rather than on the driver's bench with the groom.

'I won't come with you,' Maurice said. 'There are things I have to do so I'll follow by the later train. But take this.' He pressed two sovereigns into her hand.

Lorna flushed. 'I don't need your money.'

'Don't be silly. You will have to buy a ticket for the train, and also pay the cab fare from the Central Station back to Heaton. And then you must judge how much to give Violet.'

Before she could return the coins, he stepped back and gave the order to the groom to be on his way. As they set off down the drive, Lorna raised her arm and flung the sovereigns at Maurice's feet. She heard them land amongst the gravel but she had already turned her head away to prevent him seeing the tears in her eyes.

130

Maurice stood very still, holding his temper in check. He waited until the trap had turned into the road and was out of sight before kicking at the gravel and scattering the coins she had thrown at him. How dare she!

He had seen the anger in her eyes and the contemptuous way she'd turned her head the moment before the coins fell. But it was he who should be angry. She'd ruined everything. She could have had this house, clothes, books, foreign travel, and his devotion, and she'd spurned it all for the want of a wedding ring.

He was all the more angry because he'd suspected as much. That was why he'd wanted to get her here before explaining that, much as he loved her, he simply couldn't marry her. And he did love her; he loved her with a passion that he would never be able to experience with Rose.

And he knew that her feelings for him were equally passionate. That was what he'd been counting on. That once here he would have been able to seduce her, rouse her to heights of passion that, once experienced, she would never be able to give up willingly.

The moment he'd seen Lorna in the market that day he'd known that he must have her. Not just because of her beauty, but because he'd sensed a vulnerability about her. Her miserable upbringing had left her susceptible. Whether she knew it or not, she'd been looking for love.

He'd believed that once he had won her heart, once she had succumbed to his lovemaking, she would be easy to control, and the idea of having power over such a woman had excited him, had fuelled his passion.

And he'd been so sure that once he got her here, shown her the house and the way she could live in comparative ease – luxury, even – she would have agreed to anything. But he'd been wrong. She had surprised him with a spirit of independence and a resolution that would have done justice to his diamond-hard mother; that domestic tyrant who ruled his father's life and who sought to rule his.

Now his feelings of rage and sexual frustration seethed within him; they were almost unbearable. He would go back to Newcastle later tonight. But he wouldn't be going straight home to his parents' house in Jesmond. He had imagined he would be spending this night with Lorna. Instead, he would have to find relief the usual way, with the sort of woman whose submission could be bought. It sickened him all the more to contemplate what Lorna could have rescued him from.

131

Chapter Eleven

'You don't have to do that, Irene.' Edwin smiled as he took the broom from her hands. 'Mrs Collins is paid to keep the room clean and warm. It's part of the rental arrangement. Now have you time to drink this tea she's brought us?'

Irene watched as he put the broom back in the cupboard and then she joined him at the table, which also served as a desk during the reading classes. 'I've just about time,' she said. 'But I'll hev – have to get back home and check on Ruth before I—' She broke off and looked uneasily at Edwin.

'Before what? He looked at her questioningly. 'Oh, no. You're not going out to a cleaning job, are you? Not tonight? I thought that now I'd got you this small salary for helping with the classes that you would be able to give up all the night work except the coal office.'

'Well, I have. I hardly ever gans – go out at night now. It's just that tonight's special. There's to be a party at the dancing school on Heaton Road and they need a bit extra help. But I'll be finished by half-past eleven. They've promised that.' She looked at him anxiously, hoping that he wouldn't be vexed with her.

Mrs Hepburn from the Commercial Hotel had put her in the way of this job. There was to be a buffet at the party and they needed a smart lass to carry trays round and see that everybody had something to eat or drink. She wouldn't have to do any washing up.

It sounded interesting but, all the same, she wished she'd been able to refuse. She hated going out at night and leaving her baby sister. But Ruth was growing fast and she needed new clothes – and shoes. Now that she was walking properly Irene had no intention of letting her go barefoot like most of the neighbours' bairns.

She was glad that Edwin seemed to have decided to let the matter drop. He smiled as he poured her tea and then took something out of his briefcase. 'My aunt's best raisin cake,' he said as he opened up a clean white napkin to reveal two slices of rich, dark cake. 'We'll use our saucers as plates, shall we?'

'Thank you.'

After a few moments, when only the crackling of the fire in the hearth behind them broke the silence, and they ate the cake and sipped their tea, Edwin asked, 'Are you enjoying this work, Irene?'

'Oh, yes.'

'Even though some of your pupils can be difficult about the way words are spelled.'

They both smiled as they remembered Mrs Haggerty's latest outburst. 'Lissen, bonny lass,' she'd said to Irene, 'I divven't understand why they puts "go" when they means "gan" or "have" when they means "hev".'

'Yes, you do,' Irene had retorted, knowing that the old lady was teasing her. 'And I'll make you wear a dunce's cap and stand in the corner if you go on causing trouble.'

Irene had wagged her finger like a strict schoolmarm and the class of women had burst out laughing, enjoying the fun. Edwin had long ago explained that you could say the word in any way that pleased you, so long as you understood the proper way of spelling it.

'And what's "proper" when it's at home?' had been Mrs Haggerty's sharp retort, so Edwin had gone on to explain that it was all one language and you couldn't have different ways of spelling words in different parts of the British Isles, or nobody would understand what anybody else meant.

Irene knew very well that Mrs Haggerty and the rest of the reading class grasped exactly what Edwin meant but they did like to tease him. Irene, unconsciously at first, had started to try to improve her speech. To speak more like Edwin.

The class was held in the front room of what had once been the comfortable home of a sea captain. But that was long ago, and when the captain's family had moved away from the quay and further up the hill, and eventually away from the riverside altogether, their old house had passed to various landlords. First of all it had been rented to a single family and then, over the years, had been divided up into apartments and then single rooms.

Mrs Collins, the live-in caretaker, kept it clean enough and preferred respectable tenants. The idea of letting the largest room to the newly formed reading class appealed to her. She had gone out of her way to find tables and chairs and make the room as comfortable as possible.

So far there were two different groups that each met twice a week. One group was for women and one for men. It was the men who had objected to being taught with the women. A matter of pride, Edwin thought. The charitable trust that Edwin had applied to for the money also sponsored classes on cooking and domestic hygiene but Irene was not involved with those, although Edwin had suggested that she might be.

When the evening classes began, just after Christmas, Edwin had done all the teaching and let her observe him, although he saw to it that she was paid for her time. Now, he often let her take the class on her own and he had suggested that he might not always need to be there. Irene was pleased that he thought her competent but she would be disappointed not to have his company.

Mrs Collins came to collect the tray and Irene took her coat from the cupboard. Soon she and Edwin were walking up Byker Bank. 'Are you happy about leaving Ruth with Mrs Flanagan?' Edwin asked.

Irene glanced at him sharply. Was he trying to make her feel guilty? But, no, the expression she saw in his face was one of kindly concern. 'Yes. I was hesitant at first because of her son-in-law. But it's marvellous what a little money will do.'

'You mean you pay her?'

'Not very much and I know fine well that Seth MacAndrew takes it from her the moment she goes home, but she doesn't do it for the money. She does it to get away from her family for a while.'

'And to sit by your fire and no doubt get a bite to eat?' Edwin added.

Irene smiled. 'That's right. And on nights like tonight I'll probably be bringing a few treats home. On these occasions, if the cook's pleased with you, she'll give you a few leftovers. Mrs Flanagan and I will sit and eat together and, sometimes, she stays the night with me and sleeps in the armchair.'

'You make it sound reassuring but I still wish you weren't going to be out late at night.'

'Do you?'

'Of course. They still haven't caught this man – the man who murders . . .'

'Prostitutes. Don't worry. I've too much sense to cut home through the park, even though it would be quicker. I'll stick to the main roads.'

'Good. Ah, here we are.'

'Good night, Mr Randall,' Irene said as they stopped outside her door.

'Edwin,' he said. 'I think it's time you started calling me Edwin, don't you?'

'Oh, but—'

'After all, we are working together, aren't we?' He smiled at her.

'Yes, we are. Good night, Edwin.'

She stood by the door and watched him walk away up the bank, wondering why his smile, although warm enough, had not quite reached his eyes.

Mrs Flanagan had already got Ruth to bed and she lay sleeping peacefully in the cot Irene had found in the second-hand shop. Irene was disappointed to have missed bedtime but pleased that she would be able to get ready without interruption. She would be provided with a white pinafore, cap, and cuffs, but she had to wear her own respectable black dress.

When she was ready to go the old lady was knitting by the fire and the room was warm and peaceful. Irene regretted having to leave such a domestic scene but she knew she had to. She needed the money that tonight's work would bring.

As she walked up the bank she allowed herself to dream of a life for herself and Ruth that didn't involve such hardship. A life of comfort in a well-ordered household with perhaps a servant or two to cook and clean. She, Irene, would be responsible for the running of the house, and for seeing that her husband had good hot meals ready on the table when he came home from his work in the hospital . . .

'And where are you off to, Lady Muck?'

Irene's dreams vanished swiftly at the sound of the harsh voice. She turned and peered behind her, and two figures stepped into the circle of light cast by the nearest streetlamp. 'Oh, hello, Jess.'

'Aoh, hellooo,' Jess Green mimicked, and succeeded in sounding ridiculous. 'Aren't we getting posh!' Jess turned to her sister, Sarah, and they burst into ill-natured laughter.

Irene stared at them. The tightly fitting coat Jess wore emphasized the fact that she was getting stout. She was tidy enough, but her features were coarsening and Irene judged that it wouldn't be long before she would have to accept only the roughest of back-lane trade.

Her younger sister, on the other hand, was slim and attractive, with delicate features. Irene wondered, uneasily, if her childlike looks appealed to a certain type of man. Although Sarah certainly didn't dress like a little girl. Her clothes aped the latest fashions and, in a poor light, she might even pass for a much better class of person than she really was.

135

'Where are you off to, then?' Jess asked, when she had done laughing.

'None of your business. Haddaway and fester!' Irene said.

Jess grinned. 'That's more like it,' she said. 'I like you better when you don't forget where you came from.'

'And where's that?'

'Bottom of the heap, like the rest of us.'

Irene wanted to say that she certainly hadn't come from the bottom of the heap. That her mother had been a respectable working woman, unlike the Green sisters' lazy trollop of a mother, and that her father had earned good money at sea, and that the Lawsons had once owned most of the land round here. But she knew that that would only provoke further scorn.

'Listen, I've got to get to work,' she said.

'Another dishwashing job?'

'Not dishwashing. Waiting on, at a party.'

'Ooh, la-de-da!' Jess said, and Irene was vexed with herself for bothering to try and impress.

'Hawway, our Jess,' Sarah suddenly said. 'Let's gan on, I'm getting cold standing here.'

Jess turned to her young sister and her expression changed entirely. 'Are you, pet? Divven't fret. We'll not stay out too long the night. As soon as we've got enough money to keep Mr Brady sweet, we'll get some fish and chips and a jug of porter and gan yem and sup by the fire.'

They seemed to have forgotten about Irene so she began to walk away from them up Shields Road. She was dismayed when Jess called out, 'Hey, Lady Muck, wait for us! We're all working lasses so's we might as well walk up the road together!'

Irene didn't want an argument so she held her peace. She only hoped that no one she knew would see her. She was glad when Jess said, 'Tarra then,' and the Green sisters cut away along a side street towards Reilly's, a notorious public house.

Once back in Newcastle in good time, Lorna got a cab outside the station. She was back in Heaton within twenty minutes. Violet must have been waiting in the hall, listening for the cab to stop outside the house, for Lorna had barely closed the gate behind her when her grandmother's maid opened the front door.

'Come in, miss,' Violet said quietly. She looked troubled.

The train had been in good time so Lorna now regretted having made the phone call. It would be an hour at least before her grandmother and Rose came home so she would have plenty of time to dispose of the letter herself. Now she had to try to explain her actions to Violet as well as decide on the awkward matter of some kind of 'reward', as Maurice had put it.

She put down her travelling bag and began to unbutton her coat. She was still deciding what to say when Violet spoke first. 'I'm sorry, Miss Lorna,' she said, 'but I gave her the letter. I had no choice. She told me to send you up to her room the minute you walked through the door.'

Lorna stared at the young woman in consternation. 'What are you saying? My grandmother has come home and you have given her my letter? Is that it?'

'Yes, miss.'

'But why? I told you to destroy it!'

'I know – and I would have done. But you see she was here when I took your telephone call.' Violet took Lorna's coat and hat and stood holding them miserably.

'Here? But I thought she and my cousin had gone to the theatre. And then on to supper with Mrs Haldane.'

'They did go to the theatre. And Miss Rose is going to stay the night at the Haldanes'. But, you see, your grandmother was poorly again. She took a funny turn, couldn't breathe properly. They sent her home in their motorcar with Mrs Haldane's maid to look after her and a message to call the doctor. Dr Gibson has just left.'

'But I still don't understand. Why did you give her the letter?'

'She heard the phone ring, when I was settling her in bed – waiting for the doctor. Naturally she wanted to know who it was.'

'But you could have just told her that I had phoned to say I was on my way home!'

'Miss Lorna.' Violet suddenly looked mulish. 'You asked me to do something and I agreed. You didn't explain and I didn't ask. But I knew something wasn't right. And when your grandmother asked me I . . . I just couldn't lie to her.'

'But it wouldn't have been a lie. You could simply not have mentioned the letter!'

The look Violet gave her was cold. 'That's playing with words, Miss Lorna, and, remember, it's Mrs Cunningham that pays my wages. I'd be grateful if you'd go up and see her now while I take your things to your room.'

Violet started up the stairs ahead of her and then turned suddenly to say, 'And try not to upset her.'

137

Lorna was totally taken aback by the maid's manner. I suppose I deserve it, she thought. I shouldn't have involved Violet, tested her loyalty. For, of course, her loyalty lies with my grandmother. When Maurice asked me whether I had a friend in the house I should have said no.

She had reached the first landing and she hesitated outside her grandmother's door. She realized that Violet had not actually said that her grandmother had read the letter. Was it too much to hope that she was too ill to care at the moment and the envelope would lie unopened on her bedside table? She knocked and entered when she was summoned.

Mildred Cunningham lay in the bed that she had shared with her late husband, propped up amongst a mound of pillows. She was a handsome, imposing woman so Lorna was shocked to see now how frail she looked, and how colourless in her white nightdress and against the starched white bed linen. Her white hair, which in certain lights passed for blonde, now looked a dull grey and it hung around her face like witch's locks.

She looks old suddenly, Lorna thought, and she was overtaken by a rush of sympathy. But those feelings died when her grandmother turned to look at her and Lorna saw the anger glittering in her eyes. It was then that she noticed the letter clutched in her grandmother's hand, and the hope died that what she had done would remain undiscovered.

'What on earth made you think that he would marry you?' her grandmother rasped.

Lorna noticed that she sounded breathless but stung by the note of scorn, she forgot Violet's admonition and replied, 'What makes you think that he will not?'

Her grandmother looked at her pityingly. 'Because you're here. Because you've run back home the minute you discovered what his true intentions were, that's why.'

'And what can you know of his true intentions?'

'Nothing. But I can guess. A man like that isn't going to marry you. Violet told me you were on the way home before I'd even opened this pitiful missive but I think, even if I hadn't read it, that I would have guessed that he'd led you up the garden path.'

The words and the certain way in which they were spoken hurt so much that Lorna gasped with pain. 'Don't speak like that!' she said.

'Isn't that what he did? Led you on, said that he loved you, that he wanted to marry you—'

'No!'

138

'He didn't say that he loved you?'

'Yes, constantly, but he didn't – he didn't . . .'

'He didn't say he wanted to marry you? Is that what you're trying to say? Then I must admit I'd thought better of you.'

'But I thought that's what he meant,' Lorna said quietly and she was suddenly overcome with weariness. She dropped her head into her hands.

'Sit down, Lorna,' he grandmother said, and the anger had gone from her voice. 'No, not so far away, bring the chair nearer to me. That's better. Now we must talk.'

Lorna sighed. 'What is there to say?'

'Much. First of all I believe you when you say that you thought he meant to marry you. It proves you are gullible but not immoral.'

'Thank you.'

'Don't look at me like that, miss, or I might change my mind about being pleased to see you.'

'Are you pleased to see me?' Lorna was surprised.

'I wouldn't have wanted you to make such a terrible mistake. As I say, I knew he would never marry you and I would have hated the idea of you living as his mistress, especially as he's going to marry Rose.'

'You would have allowed the marriage to go ahead?' Lorna was astonished.

'Of course. And made every effort to make sure that Rose never discovered Maurice's other arrangement.'

'But that would have been truly immoral!'

'Maybe. But Rose must be protected from scandal, whether the scandal of being jilted at the altar or the scandal of word getting out that the other woman was her cousin.'

'And it wouldn't be too nice for you either, would it?'

Her grandmother ignored the sarcasm. 'No, it wouldn't. I had enough to put up with when your mother ran off and married that – that sailor.'

'That's not what you were going to say,' Lorna said softly.

'No, but, Lorna, let's not quarrel. Reassure me that you decided to come home the moment you realized that he wasn't going to marry you.'

'Of course I did, why do you doubt it?'

'Because I suspect that Maurice did not intend you to leave the letter for me. That's right, isn't it?'

'Yes.'

'And when he discovered that you had, he got you to telephone Violet and ask her to destroy it. Then he sent you packing.'

'You can put it like that.'

'If I sound cruel it's because that's the way it looks. But it is Maurice Haldane who has treated you cruelly, not I.'

'And yet you will still allow Rose to marry him.'

'Try stopping her.'

Lorna looked at her grandmother in surprise. She was actually smiling, a dry, cynical little smile and yet, nevertheless, there was warmth in her eyes at last. 'You believe me, don't you?' Lorna asked.

'About what?'

'That I would have come home anyway – it wasn't just because Maurice sent me packing?'

'Yes, I believe you. And now I must trust you.'

'Trust me?'

'Never to tell Rose what has happened. She wasn't supposed to stay at the Haldanes' tonight. It was only because I was unwell. But now I'm glad it happened because you and I can talk. We can agree to forget what you did today and make sure that it is never mentioned again.'

'Is that what we're going to do?'

'We must.' Her grandmother paused and looked at her searchingly. 'It's for your sake as well as Rose's, you know. A matter of pride.'

Lorna closed her eyes. Both Maurice and her grandmother were relying on the fact that she would be too proud to admit how foolish she'd been. So Rose would gain her heart's desire and marry Maurice Haldane. The only comfort Lorna could find was that she doubted very much whether they would be happy ever after.

Her grandmother left her to her thoughts for a while and then she said, 'Lorna?' She sounded slightly out of breath.

'Yes?'

Lorna opened her eyes and found her grandmother pressing one hand flat against her chest. Her breast was rising and falling visibly as if she had just been running.

'I'm tired now,' her grandmother said. 'Dr Gibson told me to get a good night's sleep.'

'And will you sleep any easier knowing that I'm home?'

Mildred Cunningham frowned. 'Of course I will. Now we can look forward to the wedding – and getting Rose settled.'

Lorna was too upset to wonder about the last part of her grandmother's answer. In spite of all the years of feeling that she was merely tolerated in this house she had been hoping for some sign of affection. Particularly now when she had been forced to acknowledge that the love Maurice had professed was not the sort of love she had been looking for.

In fact you couldn't really call it love at all.

Irene had expected to be finished by eleven thirty but by the time she was ready to leave the dancing school it was nearer midnight. The work hadn't been hard and she had really enjoyed herself listening to the chatter of the guests and observing the clothes they wore.

She could see why Mr and Mrs Parker had wanted a buffet; it was so much friendlier than a formal dinner. The rooms to the left of the front door, on the ground floor of the house, had been knocked into one large room where Mr Parker obviously held his dancing classes. There was a piano at one end and chairs all round the walls. And, she guessed, for this occasion only, long tables had been set up down one side on strips of carpet to protect the sprung floor.

Two decorative gasoliers illuminated the room from above and, spaced out along the tables, there were brass oil lamps combined with containers for fresh flowers. All the flowers were white, and dark green leaves and ivy trailed attractively across the white damask cloths.

The food was set out on silver platters with lace doilies. Not even at the Commercial had Irene seen such fancy savouries and cakes. She stared, fascinated, at the little flags rising from the middle of each dish: 'Anchovy Croûtes' 'Croûtes à l'Indienne', 'Angels on Horseback', 'Cheese d'Artois', 'Cheese Fritters', 'Mayonnaise of Eggs'.

Then the cakes, hardly more than one bite in each one of them – there were Genoese pastries, cherry and gooseberry tarts and baskets made of spun sugar containing tiny apples, oranges, bananas and strawberries made from almond paste and coloured just like the real thing.

The host, Mr Parker, looking handsome and dapper in his evening suit, moved from group to group, making sure everyone was enjoying themselves. Mrs Parker, plump and excitable, never stopped talking. Their daughter, Ellie, looked about sixteen or seventeen, and Irene had never seen anyone so lovely. She should probably have envied someone who was obviously so pampered and cosseted but, instead, she found herself speculating about the girl's future, and hoping that she would always be so happy and carefree.

When it was time to go, the cook, as Irene had hoped, gave her a parcel to take home with her. 'I've put some of the marzipan fruits in a little tin. You said you'd love your baby sister to see them,' she said.

'Thank you,' Irene said. 'You're very kind.

141

'No, not kind, grateful,' the cook said. 'We're not usually as posh as this in this house, you know, but Mrs Parker reads too many ladies' magazines and gets these high-falutin ideas about "How to give parties everyone will talk about!" ' The woman laughed and Irene could see that she was really quite fond of her mistress.

'And you've done very well tonight, pet,' she continued. 'Moving amongst the guests quietly and without making a fuss and keeping your eye open for whose plate needed filling up. I owe Mrs Hepburn a favour for recommending you.' She paused to take breath at last and then she asked, 'Now, how are you going to get home? Is anyone meeting you?'

'No, no one's meeting me, but I don't have far to go.'

'Well, then keep to the main roads where there's plenty light. But I'm sure I don't have to tell you that. You're a sensible lass. And, for a start, you can slip out the front door, there's no gaslamps in the back lane.'

The hallway was empty and the double doors that led into the dancing studio were closed but Irene paused and listened for a moment. Someone in there was playing the piano, a gentle sentimental tune, and the chatter and laughter had died down. The guests would be leaving soon; soothed by good food and drink, the gossip of friends and pleasant music to send them on their way.

They would get into hansom cabs and motor-taxis, some of them would walk home, but only a short distance to one of the other big comfortable houses nearby, whereas Irene had a long cold walk through deserted streets to her meagre room down near the Ouseburn, one of the worst areas in Newcastle.

She remembered her daydreaming the night of Wilkinson's Christmas party at the Commercial. She had thought how pleasant it would be to have a job at the wholesale draper's, handling the bonny fabrics. How she might meet a respectable young man there, one of the other employees, how they would marry and make a nice little home together.

But since then she had had other daydreams. She had begun to hope for someone better than a mere salesman. The dream had again involved a nice home, but this time with servants to order and a clever doctor husband who needed a sensible, hard-working wife.

But there was something not quite right with that dream. Oh, there was no doubt that she still wanted Edwin Randall, but she wondered if the kind of doctor he wanted to be, working amongst the dregs of society, would ever be able to live in a house like this, or would think it proper to spend so much money on a mere party.

Irene sighed. If she had to choose, the man was more important to her than a life of ease and comfort. She knew that. But did Edwin Randall even guess that she was prepared to face a life of good works and sacrifice with him – if he would only ask her?

For the first time Irene found that she didn't want to hurry home. She wanted to linger in the atmosphere of warmth and gaiety. She almost went back to the kitchen to offer to stay later and help to clear up and wash up after the guests had gone but, guiltily, she remembered that she had told Mrs Flanagan that she would be home before midnight.

Not that the old woman would mind if she was late, Irene mused. Eventually, her guilt at realizing that, for once, she hadn't been longing to get home to see her baby sister made her open the door and step out into the rain.

The night was cold and the damp struck up through the thin soles of Irene's shoes. She had never felt so wretched. She knew very well that she could have a much better life if she didn't have to look after Ruth. She loved her baby sister with all her heart, she would never do anything to harm her, and it wasn't her poor mother's fault that she had died leaving Irene with the responsibility of bringing Ruth up.

But it wasn't fair. Life wasn't fair. She knew she was attractive and she knew she was intelligent, and yet, here she was, living from hand-to-mouth and forced only to daydream of a better life instead of going out and finding one.

She was so taken up with the turmoil within her that, at first, she didn't hear the dreadful screeching. Gradually it impinged on her consciousness and drove her uneasy thoughts away.

'Sarah! Sarah, where the hell are you?' someone was wailing.

Irene stared at the figure running backwards and forwards along the pavement at the other side of the road near the gates of Heaton Park. A big, ungainly lump of a girl, Jess Green.

Suddenly Jess stopped running and peered across the road. 'Sarah? Is that you, lass?'

'No, Jess, it's me, Irene.'

'Ee, Irene, will you come over here and help me? Me sister was supposed to meet me a while back. I'm near frantic.'

Irene waited as a tram, probably the last, rattled past her along Heaton Road. It was full of people, mostly men, coming home from town, and the lighted interior looked warm and cheerful. The cobbles on the road were wet and slippery and Irene carefully and unwillingly crossed over to join Jess Green.

'Has she kept you waiting like this, before?' Irene asked, practically.

'Nivver. She's a good lass. She knows I worry about her. We've been on wor own since Mam died, yer know. And I promised to look after the bairn . . . our Sarah.'

Irene stared at Jess and fleetingly experienced a faint fellow feeling for her. They had both been left to look after a younger sister but, apart from that, their lives were very different. Irene wondered what the late Mrs Green would think of the way her daughters were earning a living. But then, their mam had been on the game herself and if there had ever been a Mr Green nobody had ever met him.

So she refrained from saying that encouraging Sarah to be a prostitute was a funny way of caring for her. 'Tell me where you arranged to meet your sister,' she said.

'Along there,' Jess looked over her shoulder and nodded towards the distant row of shops, 'at the fish-and-chip shop near the corner of Shields Road. She's never been late before. I've got our supper – look.'

The girl held a grubby knitted bag out towards her and Irene saw the newspaper-wrapped bundle stuffed inside it. Jess stared down at it as if the very fact of its existence made it impossible for Sarah not to turn up and share it with her.

'It'll be cold now,' Jess said, and then she began to cry. 'I told her not to go in the park,' she said between sobs, 'even if there was no other business.'

Irene suppressed a spasm of irritation. The rain was falling faster and she wanted to go home. 'But you think she went in the park in spite of what you said?' she asked.

'One of the other lasses came into the chip shop. Said she saw her there, with a tall fellow, walking past the bandstand. But that was more than an hour ago.'

'Have you been to have a look?'

'No sign of her. But it's dark once you get off the paths. I wandered round for a bit, shouting me head off but she didn't answer. Irene, I don't suppose you'd come back into the park with us, would you? Two of us together might hev more chance of finding her.'

'Wait a minute, Jess. Have you thought she might have gone on somewhere else? If she found another . . . another customer.'

'I've telt you, she wouldn't do that. If I telt her to meet me at a certain time she would. She's a good lass, our Sarah.'

Irene sighed. She wished with all her heart that she had never crossed the road, that she had just gone on walking when she'd realized that the person making all the noise was Jess Green.

'Look, Jess,' she said. 'It's pitch-black in there once you get away from the streetlamps. And what if we do find her, and she's with a – with someone. He would be annoyed.'

'I divven't care. I just want to find Sarah and take her back yem.'

Irene could see that the girl was seriously rattled and she was just about to agree to go with her when a man's voice said, 'Now, what are you two lasses doing making all this commotion in a respectable street at this time of night.' They turned to see a policeman had approached them. 'Oh, it's you, Jess,' he said. 'And who's this?' he asked staring down at Irene. 'I've never seen you before.'

She felt herself flush with anger and embarrassment. 'I'm not—' she began before Jess interrupted.

'Leave her alone, Sergeant Eckford,' the girl said. 'It's just a lass I was at school with. She's been working in one of them big houses over there and she was gannin' yem when I asked her to help me.'

'I see. And what's the matter?'

'It's our Sarah . . .'

Irene listened as Jess repeated the whole story to the big police sergeant. At first she thought he might think as she did, that Sarah had gone on somewhere with another customer. But, as the tale unfolded, she could see that he began to look very grave.

'All right,' he said when Jess had sobbed herself to a stop. 'If this friend of yours wouldn't mind staying here with you, by the gates, I'll take a look around the park.'

Jess drew nearer to Irene when Sergeant Eckford left them. Irene's instinct was to move away. The greasy aroma of the cold fish supper mingling with the girl's own body odour was almost more than she could bear. But when Jess reached for her hand and held on to it tightly, she didn't have the heart to reject her.

They watched as the large caped figure of the policeman, a black silhouette against the mist, progressed along the paths, swinging his torch slowly from left to right in a large arc, and stopping now and then to examine a group of bushes. The fact that he did so brought it home to Irene what exactly he might be looking for.

Then he vanished as he made towards the ruin – an old castle, some people said. Minutes passed, Irene didn't know how many, before the figure of Sergeant Eckford reappeared and seemed to walk towards them reluctantly. When he reached them he put a large hand on Jess's shoulder and looked down sadly into her worried face.

'Now bear up, lass,' he said.

'Why . . . what is it?' The girl's voice cracked with fear.

'I've got bad news.'

145

Chapter Twelve

April

Lorna stopped to look at the 'Chippendale' dining-room set displayed in Haldane's window. Everything was arranged as though it were a proper room in a grand house. The sideboard, table and chairs were placed on a Turkey carpet in front of a mock window draped with red velvet curtains. Beyond the window there was a painted backdrop depicting a formal garden with impossibly bright flowers and foliage under a blue sky dotted with fluffy clouds.

The table, covered with a white damask cloth, was set up for a meal with silver cutlery, crystal glassware and a china dinner service with a green dragon pattern and gilt rim. On the sideboard there were silver entrée dishes and a crystal decanter. Plant stands at each side supported Benares brass pots containing waxy, broad-leafed houseplants.

Discreet cards showed the make and the price of each item. A small easel in front of the table supported a larger card extolling the virtues of the carpet and declaring that Haldane's imported oriental carpets in all sizes, and that real Turkey carpets had never been so low in price.

Another easel announced that inside the shop there was a selection of display rooms similar to those to be found in the home of clients – library, billiards room, drawing room, dining room, bedrooms and even a garden room. Haldane's would not only supply the furniture and furnishings but would also carry out any work required to make the house into a home. In fact Haldane's was a perfect place for the couple about to be married, and their families, to come to browse.

The couple about to be married. Rose and Maurice. Lorna knew that Rose had already begun to draw up a comprehensive list of things she must absolutely have for her new home in Gosforth. The house, a large villa overlooking the Town Moor, was to be completely refurbished for the young couple. Mildred Cunningham's property company would be responsible for the building and renovation work, and Maurice's father would supply everything that was needed to furnish it.

Rose spent hours greedily poring over catalogues of household goods: furniture and soft furnishings, tableware, bed linens, ornaments both for the house and for the garden. The choice of kitchen equipment and the maids' uniforms she was content to leave to her grandmother.

Time and again she had tried to persuade Lorna to help her. 'You have such good taste,' she would say, 'and I want to impress Maurice's mother. She is so cultivated, so discerning.'

Lorna wondered that Rose couldn't see how second-rate it would be to pass off someone else's judgement as her own. When Lorna refused, Rose accused her of being jealous. She had no idea, of course, that Lorna might have had good reason to be jealous.

Am I jealous? Lorna mused as she stared at a silver photograph frame on a small side table. The frame contained a photograph of a radiant bride and groom. The card beside it announced that Haldane's supplied everything needed for the fashionable wedding and could even engage the staff for the wedding breakfast.

Do I still love him? The familiar feelings of shame and loss surged through her. Shame because she had been so mistaken about his intentions and a desperate longing that it could have been different.

So what am I to do with myself now? In the weeks since she had returned from the aborted elopement she had escaped the house as often as she could in order to get away from Rose's relentless planning of every last detail to do with the wedding. Rose, always used to getting her own way, was now in a stronger position than ever because their grandmother had never really recovered from her latest indisposition.

Mildred Cunningham refused to allow that she might be seriously ill. She insisted that it was only the fact that she was getting old. But Lorna did not believe this, and, furthermore, she was convinced that her grandmother was putting up a pretence for Rose's sake – who had her wedding to think about.

But their grandmother rested more often than she used to and Dr Gibson called regularly. She had had the morning room converted into an office and she ran her property business entirely from home now, never visiting the offices on Shields Road. Mr Pearson, her general manager, called every week day to make his report and receive her instructions.

Lorna remembered what Maurice had said about her grandmother's property empire being much larger than she had imagined. It would all belong to Rose one day and, as her cousin had never shown the slightest

147

interest in matters of business, Lorna wondered if Maurice was hoping to add it to his own commercial empire. Probably.

She wondered what Rose would think if she guessed that that was why Maurice was marrying her. Not because he loved her – he had told Lorna that he didn't – but because of her future inheritance.

Do I care? Lorna wondered. She sighed and turned away from the shop window. Although the pavements were wet from a recent shower, the clouds had blown away and the flower stall at the entrance to the Grainger Market seemed to have caught the sunshine in the bunches of daffodils and narcissi. Lorna paused to smile at them before hurrying inside the market and making her way to her place of refuge: the second-hand bookstalls.

For a while she managed to lose herself as she gazed at the shelves inside one of the stalls. She took down a book now and then to inspect it more closely. Some of the books were very old, and there was a faint damp mustiness about them that suggested they had come from old houses where they had once been treasured, then neglected and, finally, cleared out when their owners had died.

She was examining one such volume, a diary of a journey on the old Silk Road, and wondering if she would have the patience to persevere with the old, gothic print, when she sensed someone behind her.

The pressure of the air changed. A primitive instinct told her that this person was standing close, too close. Her nerves jangled, not with fear but with excitement. Whoever it was remained quite still and she felt an invisible and soundless communication so strong that the hairs on the back of her neck rose and a deep thrill jolted her senses. Maurice – it must be Maurice!

He knew this was where she would be and he had come for her. He had been cruel – she had not known he could behave like that – but he had come to say sorry, that he knew now how wrong he had been and he would change . . . that he couldn't go through with the marriage to Rose . . . that—

She turned to find Edwin Randall smiling at her.

'Oh!' She was shocked that she could have been so wrong. Puzzled that she could have reacted in such a way, and keenly embarrassed to see Edwin's expression when he saw the disappointment on her face.

He chose not to mention it. 'I'm sorry,' he said. 'You were so absorbed in that book that I didn't want to startle you. I was waiting for the right moment to speak.'

Only when he took the book from her hands did she realize that she was trembling.

'I really did startle you, didn't I? Do you want to purchase this book?'

'No, I don't think so.' She was relieved to find that her voice was steady.

'Then let me put it back.' When he had done so he turned to look at her. 'Are you well, Lorna?' he asked.

'Yes, why do you ask?'

'You look pale, perhaps a little tired. And, also, you haven't been to my uncle's shop for ages. Not this year, in fact.'

'No . . . I'm fine. There's nothing the matter.'

'It's not because I asked you to help me, is it?'

'I don't understand.'

'I thought perhaps you'd been avoiding me because I'd asked you to help with the reading classes.'

'But why should I do that?'

'You didn't seem sure so I asked you to think about it. Remember?'

Lorna frowned. In fact she had been so sure that she would be married by now that she had not given Edwin's request another thought. 'And, I'm sorry, but—'

'But you've decided you don't want to. I thought that was the case and you were embarrassed to come and tell me.'

'No . . . it's just . . .'

As she stared at him, not knowing how to explain, the old gentleman who owned the bookstall came towards them, looking vexed. 'Sir, madam,' he said, 'if you do not intend to buy, I would ask you to make way for other customers. This space is limited and, although I do not mind you looking at the books and perhaps not making a purchase, I cannot allow you to use my stall as a lovers' trysting place.'

Instead of being offended Edwin laughed and took Lorna's arm as he guided her out into the market. 'Don't take any notice of him,' he said when he saw her expression. 'The old rogue knows me well and I guess he knows you too – as a good customer. He was simply being mischievous. But, as I was saying, you don't have to explain about not wanting to help. I shouldn't have asked.'

'No . . . you had very right. But I—'

'Lorna. There's no need to say anything. But I hope you won't avoid my poor uncle's shop because of this. And, even more important, I hope this won't spoil our friendship.'

'Of course not.'

'Because, if it makes you feel any easier, I found someone to help.'

'Irene Lawson.'

Edwin looked surprised and pleased. 'You remembered? Yes, Irene, and she's very good. In fact, I believe that if she had been given the chance she could have benefited from a proper education. She might even have become a teacher.'

'Good.' Lorna was puzzled by her own lacklustre response. She ought to have been happy that the girl had found a champion.

All the while they had been talking they had been walking through the market. Lorna was still shaken by her response to Edwin's presence and disturbed that he should have thought she would avoid him because she hadn't wanted to help with his reading classes.

'I feel guilty,' he said suddenly.

'Why?' She looked at him in surprise.

'For creeping up on you like that. I gave you a bad shock. You still look perturbed.'

'No, really—'

'I think you need a hot, sweet drink. Shall we go in here and order a pot of tea?'

'Where?'

'The tearooms – look – behind you.'

Only then did Lorna realize where they were. She stared at the familiar café aghast. She couldn't go in there – the place where she used to meet Maurice.

'Come along, there's a table free by the window,' Edwin said, and he took her arm and began to steer her towards the door.

She pulled away from him sharply. 'Oh, no, no, really. I couldn't! I'm sorry . . . I must go.'

She glimpsed his expression of hurt and surprise but it didn't stop her turning and hurrying away.

Edwin watched her go. It wasn't long before the crowd swallowed her and he was left with only a trace of her perfume, an elusive scent of ferns and woodland. He remembered the moment in the bookstall when his senses had leaped as he caught sight of her.

She had stood so still as she examined the old book. Her head bent, her neck revealed above the collar of her coat. He had gazed at the flawless honey-coloured skin and suppressed a wild urge to lean forward and press his lips there. At first she hadn't realized he was there and he stood, breathing in her perfume, longing to take her in his arms, pull off her ridiculous hat with its trembling feathers and take the pins from her glorious dark hair so that it would tumble down on to her shoulders.

He had seen the moment that she sensed his presence. He had seen her shudder and turn, her eyes full of hope. And then, before she could

150

disguise it, the dreadful disappointment. He, Edwin, was not the person she had been hoping to see.

The old man had joked about a lovers' tryst. Had Lorna been waiting in the bookstall for a lover? Is that why she had stopped coming to his uncle's bookshop? Was she engaged in some delirious love affair? If she was, it certainly wasn't making her happy. In spite of her beauty there was no disguising the anguish in her eyes, and she had become a shadow of what she used to be.

Edwin found himself hating the unknown man – he was sure that there was one – who had made Lorna so unhappy. And he hated him on his own behalf too. Hated him for snatching away from him the chance to win the woman whom he loved more than anyone in the world.

The sky had clouded over and the afternoon was dark, but Irene didn't light the lamps. Ruth had fallen asleep on her knee and, rather than disturb her little sister, she settled back amongst the cushions and, with her feet up on the cracket, she tried to rest. The picture book they had been looking at together had fallen on to the rug. It lay open, showing a picture of three kittens playing round a saucer of milk.

The cats who lived round here don't look like that, Irene mused. And they would be very lucky if they ever tasted milk once they were weaned from their thin half-starved mothers. Folk tolerated them, threw them scraps, and even encouraged them to come indoors now and then, because they were useful to keep down the rats. The rats that Edwin said were responsible for spreading disease.

Edwin was so clever, with his charts and maps and graphs, as he called them. He had explained to her that, apart from malnutrition – that meant not eating enough or not eating the right kind of food – so much could be done to make folk healthier if only the landlords would make improvements to the dwellings.

Irene thanked God that her mother had been a clean, decent woman who had brought her up to be scrupulous about hygiene – one of Edwin's words – no matter how hard it was with one tap in the shared scullery and one outside privy for the whole house.

She remembered one day when she was little, listening to one of the neighbours arguing in the street with some charity worker who had come round giving out food parcels. The woman had made some remark about the children being dirty, and drew the retort that if she had to choose between a bit soap and a bit rice and milk for pudding, what would she do?

And what choices do I have to make? wondered Irene. Just like my mother before me I have to choose, not so much between food or soap, but between clothes for Ruth and a new dress for myself. Feeling guilty about the direction her thoughts were taking, she hugged Ruth all the tighter.

At least we are here alone together, she thought. I don't have to live like poor Mrs Flanagan, with a daughter and son-in-law who don't want me and a pack of unruly children who tease the life out of me. She could hear them now, their voices whining and quarrelsome. Occasionally their mother would raise her voice and scream at them but it had little effect.

It was only when Seth MacAndrew came home that they would be quiet. The threat of their father's belt was the only discipline they understood. And Irene suspected that he used it on his wife too, and perhaps even on his mother-in-law.

Lost in her gloomy thoughts she had not heard the knocking at the front door, so when there was a rap at the door of her room she was startled. She held Ruth close and was just about to rise when the door opened and Mr Brady walked in. He was carrying something wrapped in brown paper.

'How did—' she began, but he put his finger to his lips.

'Whisht,' he said, and, nodding at the sleeping child, he closed the door quietly behind him.

'But—'

'Put her in her cot,' he said quietly, with a nod in that direction. 'I want to talk to you. To thank you.'

'Thank me?'

Irene was intrigued enough to do as she was told. She covered Ruth with a blanket and turned to find her visitor standing at the table. He moved quietly for a big man, she thought. On the table there now stood a bottle of stout and a pork pie.

'I need glasses, a couple of plates and a knife,' he said, and without waiting for her directions, he found his way to the cupboard and got everything he required. 'One of the bairns from upstairs let me in,' he went on to explain. 'Now, shall we sit at the table or by the fire?'

'The table,' Irene said. She thought the fireside would be too cosy – too intimate.

'Why thank me?' she asked when she had pulled up a chair and sat down.

He didn't answer immediately. She watched as he cut the pie and put a generous slice on her plate. A smaller one for himself. Then he poured them each a glass of stout. 'Drink up – it'll do you good.'

He waited until she had taken a bite of the pie and a sup of stout. 'Jess is all right. I thought you'd want to know.'

Irene shrugged.

'Divven't pretend you divven't care.'

'I don't.'

Brady put his glass down on the table and looked at her speculatively. 'You stayed with her that night. You brought her back here. You saw that she was all right.'

'What else could I do?'

'You could have walked away.'

'Sergeant Eckford said I had to go to the police station with her. They had to get a statement.'

'Then you could have gone home.'

'I know. I could have left her sobbing her heart out and hardly being able to string two words together. I could have come home to my own warm cosy room instead of sitting in that draughty corridor up at Headlam Street, holding on to her and trying to stop her slipping off the bench on to the floor.'

'You've a way with words,' Brady said, and he smiled. 'Must be all the books you read.' He glanced over to the small table under the window where she kept the books she needed for the reading classes, along with some that she'd borrowed from the library. 'But what you say shows that you must have felt something for the lass.'

'Her sister had just been murdered. No one else seemed to care.' Irene stared across the table at him, meeting his eyes and holding his gaze.

'Jess and Sarah had no family,' he said.

'I know.'

He seemed to know what she was thinking. 'They would have starved if I hadn't found them work.'

'Work that sent one of them to her death.'

She saw his fists clench on the table top. 'If the police don't catch him, I will. Sooner or later, you can be sure of that.'

Irene knew whom he meant: the man that was murdering the poor stupid women who put themselves in danger every time they went out on a dark night to prostitute themselves.

She looked at Brady now, assessing him. He was something of a dandy. His coat had a velvet collar and a white silk scarf was tucked into the neckline. His dark hair was sleeked back with some kind of perfumed brilliantine.

He was big, well made, and his broad florid features could even be

153

called handsome. But his looks wouldn't last. He must be in his thirties, Irene supposed, perhaps nearer forty, and yet there was already a network of broken veins tracing red patterns across his nose and cheeks, and his features were becoming puffy, with only his blue eyes hinting at his undoubted intelligence.

'Why do you do it?' she asked, and was amazed at her own daring. Before the night Sarah Green had been murdered, she would have been too frightened of this man to question him like this.

'Do what?'

'You know what I mean. You live off . . . you profit from prostitution.'

'The girls don't do so badly out of it. Some of them would starve otherwise.'

She shook her head. Edwin had told her what she had already observed – that many of these women died young, riddled with disease. If they weren't murdered.

'And I look after them,' he went on.

'Look after them!' Irene said angrily.

'I've told you. I'll put a stop to that. And as far as Sarah Green is concerned, I came as soon as I heard, didn't I?'

'Yes.'

He'd been waiting outside the police station. He had walked down the bank with them and persuaded Irene to let Jess come home with her. He'd given Jess something to make her sleep and she'd spent the rest of the night snoring in the armchair near the fire. Mrs Flanagan had insisted on staying too. She'd told Irene to get to bed and she would sit up and see to things.

The next morning a woman Irene had never seen before had come, very early, to take Jess away. Irene had not seen her since.

'She's working in one of my houses,' Brady answered her as if he'd read her mind again. 'No, not what you think,' he added when he saw her raised eyebrows. 'She cleans the rooms, changes the beds, makes cups of tea for the girls. That sort of thing.'

'I don't want to hear this. And you still haven't really told me why you've come here today.'

'Like I said, to thank you for looking after Jess that night.'

'And that's all?'

'Not quite. That other matter . . .'

In spite of all the time that had passed since the night Billy Potts fell – was pushed – from the bridge, Irene felt a knot of tension tightening inside her. Before he could speak she said, 'They think it was an accident; you must know that.'

154

He put his glass down and sat back in his chair until his face was in shadow. She couldn't see his expression when he said. 'And so it was, wasn't it?'

'If you say so.'

'I do say so. Remember that when you're out and about with that fine young medical student.'

'Edwin? How do you know about—?'

'I make it my business to know about things which might concern me. Now word is that the police hev decided that, even if it wasn't an accident, they would never be able to prove owt. I divven't want you forgetting yourself and confiding things you shouldn't in your sweetheart.'

'He's not my sweetheart!'

'No?' Brady sounded surprised both by the denial and the vehement way she had made it. 'Well, your friend, then.'

'I would never tell him what happened! How could I?'

The man opposite her seemed to relax a little. 'Whist,' he said. 'Divven't raise your voice. Remember the bairn. But you're right, of course. Edwin Randall would be shocked to know what you did.'

'I didn't do anything. It was you.'

'But you kept quiet about it. You were only too pleased to keep our little secret.'

Irene hated the way he seemed to draw her in with those words. She didn't want to share a secret with Mr Brady; somehow it made her part of his world. A world she despised. 'Only because you said no one would ever believe me,' she said. 'That you would simply deny that you were even there.'

'That's right. So if you value your neck, remember that.'

She stared at him aghast and then at the food and drink on the table before her. Whatever had possessed her to sit and eat and drink with this man? Had she been taken in by his quiet manner? She should have remembered the danger underneath the surface.

Or had she been swayed by how genuinely he seemed to be concerned about Jess the night her sister had been murdered? Perhaps he did care in his twisted way for the women who worked for him. Perhaps he meant it when he said that if the police didn't catch the murderer he would.

Irene closed her eyes and tried to drive all thoughts of him away from her mind. She didn't want even to try to understand him or his motives. She heard his chair scrape across the floor and opened her eyes again to see him looking down at her.

155

'I'm going. Enjoy the rest of the pie. It's from me brother's shop on Shields Road. I'll see that you get one delivered now and then. Every week, if you like.'

'No. I don't want anything from you.'

'Nevertheless, you'll get one, and it would be a sin to waste good food. And you might like to know that I've arranged for the old woman to get something every week. A pie, some boiled ham, pease pudding, Scotch eggs, that kind of thing. She doesn't know it's from me, of course.'

'Of course not.'

Irene knew which old woman he meant. Poor Mrs Potts whose son, Billy, she and Brady had killed between them.

'So you don't hev to worry about her,' he added. 'She's better off than she ever was.'

She stared at him, wondering whether he really believed that. 'Please go,' she said.

He made no move to go. 'You don't hev to stay here, you know,' he said.

'What do you mean?'

'This house. Oh, you've got your room nice enough, but hev you thought what it will be like when the bairn grows up a bit?' He glanced up at the ceiling. 'Do you want her playing with that lot upstairs?'

'She won't. I won't allow it.'

'Who will she play with, then? Will you let her out in the street to make her own friends?'

'Of course not.'

'Why?'

'You know why. The streets round here – they're dirty – not safe – she could catch something.'

'Yes, I'm sure you know all about that from Mr Randall. So what, then? Are you going to keep her prisoner in this room?'

'She'll go to school.'

'Which school? The one nearby, where she'll be sitting with all the children you don't want her to play with?'

'No. I'll be away by then.'

'Away? Where? Hev you got something lined up?'

'No, not exactly.' She looked down at the table. 'But I have plans.'

'I see.' His eyes narrowed. 'You don't sound so sure. So remember this, if those plans come to nothing, I can take you away from here. In fact, I'll take you right now if you want.'

'Why on earth would I go with you?'

'Because I'll give you a job. A good one.'

'Get out. Get out now!'

She had risen to her feet in fury. She looked at him, eyes blazing. He made calming movements with his hands. He smiled. 'You've leaped to conclusions. The job I'm offering is quite respectable. I've bought meself a house at the coast. Somewhere I can go to now and then to breathe the clean air, walk on the beach, hev meself some grand fish suppers.'

'You want me to be a cook?' She shrugged dismissively. 'I can't cook. Never had much to practise with, bar the basics.'

'No, not a cook. I'll hev a cook and a maid and a skivvy, whatever it takes. You can decide.'

'Me?'

'Yes. I need a clever, respectable lass to run the house, keep it in order, like a housekeeper. I won't be there all the time so I need someone the staff would respect. Like you. Just think what it would be like for little Ruth – playing on the beach, good food every day for both of you.'

Irene stared at him. It was as if he were the devil, tempting her with all the things she wanted in life . . . except one thing. A decent man to share it with.

'No,' she said quietly. 'I couldn't. The money you paid me with – I would still know where it came from.'

'All right. But remember, the offer's there.'

Instead of replying she simply shook her head and he left as quietly as he had come.

Outside a chill, damp wind blew up from the river. Brady paused in the doorway of the old house and pulled up his collar. Then, bending his head, he cupped a box of matches, struck one and, shielding it from the wind, lit a small cheroot.

He stood in the doorway for a moment, trying to think if there was anything else he could have said to persuade her. He'd heard how much time she spent with Edwin Randall, teaching at the reading classes, and sometimes going with him to visit the people he helped. Gossip said that she was sweet on the medical student. That she had started trying to improve herself.

He'd noticed straight away that her way of speaking was changing. Was it simply because she was doing a bit of teaching or was she trying to get herself a better class of husband? She'd said she had plans. Did those plans include Edwin Randall?

157

The same gossip had said nothing about Edwin Randall being sweet on Irene. In fact, when he'd asked a few questions, Brady had been told that Randall hadn't seemed to notice how much the lass admired him and treated her the same as everyone else – with kindness and good manners. So their mutual work hadn't drawn them any closer personally. They hadn't become more than friends.

Was she likely to tell Randall what had happened on the bridge that night? Brady didn't think so. Apart from the fact that Brady himself had put the fear of God into her about the outcome if she did, Irene wouldn't want the man she admired to think badly of her. She wasn't the type to confess and take the consequences.

For all she worked so hard to look after her baby sister, when many a lass would have handed the bairn over to the Parish, Brady nevertheless sensed she had a strong streak of self-interest. And that attracted him to her all the more. For that was the truth of it. Ever since the night he'd thrown Billy into eternity, he'd been thinking of the bonny little lass who'd been less than grateful to be rescued.

Bonny? She could be beautiful, given good food, fine clothes and an easier life. And that's what he was prepared to offer her. Not just a job looking after his new house; although it could start that way.

Brady left the doorway of Irene's house regretfully and began to walk up the bank. He'd have to leave it for a while. He couldn't see Edwin Randall proposing marriage – and that's what she wanted, no doubt of that. No, she'd be let down eventually and that's when he would try again.

That daft lad had no idea what he would be missing out on. Brady had. And that's why he wanted to marry her.

Chapter Thirteen

August

Edwin gagged at the smell. It was low tide and stinking black mud revealed the assorted junk that had been thrown into the water: an old handcart, broken crockery, part of an iron bedstead, and unidentifiable animal carcasses. Probably cats and dogs, although one could have been a sheep washed down from some farm in the Northumbrian hills.

Fearful of what he was going to find once he had broken into the boathouse, he had paused to gaze riverwards to where the big old doors had long since dropped off their hinges. It must be bitterly cold here in winter, he thought. But that was irrelevant now.

After gathering his courage, he made his way to Jane Potts' packing case house at the landward end of the building; Bella Charlton followed. There they were met with a more disturbing stench.

He held his handkerchief over his nose and mouth and, in the light of the candle Bella held aloft, he gazed in despair at the body of the old woman. How wrong he had been. He had thought she would survive here until her horde of stolen coal ran out, probably in the autumn of this year. He had been preparing himself to face her reluctance to go into the workhouse. But instead of the harsh weather and the cold it was the heat of summer that had killed her.

'Ee, Mr Randall, I'm sorry,' Bella murmured. She pulled up her pinafore with her free hand and buried her head in it. He voice was muffled and broken with sobs.

'Why, sorry, Bella? This isn't your fault.'

'I feel that it is. I was keeping an eye on her, you know. But I was sick meself. A bit of bad meat, probably. Too bad to leave the house for nearly a week. But when I was on me feet again I came straight over and found a crowd of bairns outside the door holding their noses and

159

going on about the smell. I think I knew what we'd find, so I sent for you. I'm sorry.'

'No, you did right. And don't blame yourself. We are all at fault to have allowed an old woman to live like this.'

The pity of it was, Edwin thought, that he had been concerned ever since Billy had died so tragically. Jane Potts had been avoiding him. He knew why; it was because she was convinced he was going to drag her off to the workhouse at the first opportunity. So he had asked Irene Lawson to make discreet enquiries. When Irene had told him, some weeks ago, that a benefactor, she didn't know who, was sending food parcels to Mrs Potts every week, he had relaxed a little.

He shouldn't have done. He looked at the bounty now: half-eaten pies, a dish of cut meats, and a cooked chicken, left mouldering on the table. There had been nowhere to store them in the spell of hot weather and Jane's unknown benefactor had probably caused her death.

A sudden movement made him look at the mess on the table more closely. A rat was gnawing at the chicken carcass. Edwin reached for the nearest weapon, a dirty enamel pail, and flung it with all his might. The rat fled but, now, as the smoky candle flame dispersed the shadows and he peered down at the body lying on a makeshift bed of old blankets, Edwin realized that he and his fellows had been enjoying a richer feast.

'Don't look, Bella,' he said. 'There's nothing we can do here. I'll bar the door somehow, and we'll tell the authorities.'

Edwin pulled the broken door shut behind them. It had been easy enough to break in; the timber was old and the frame was rotting. Although bolted from the inside, all it had taken was one hefty kick and the door had splintered and burst inwards.

Now he had to rearrange the broken panels as best he could so that the door looked as it had before. He hoped that the police, once he'd informed them, wouldn't take too long to get here. He didn't want any children wandering in and finding the horror inside.

He turned, blinking in the bright sunlight to find that Bella looked far from well, although her pallor was probably caused by what they had just seen as much as her recent illness.

Edwin glanced at the usual crowd of barefoot ragamuffins playing by the bank of the Ouseburn. 'Is there any one of those that you trust?' he asked. 'One of the older lads who would take a note up to Headlam Street without opening it and reading it?'

Bella's mouth twisted into a wry smile. 'Aye, Davy's a good lad,' she said. 'He'll gan to the polis, for yer. If ever I need an errand done, I send him. He's bright enough to carry long sentences in his head, but the pity of it is that he's never at school long enough to learn to read. So your message'll be safe on both counts.'

The walls of the old dwelling were thick and the windows small, so Bella's kitchen was cool enough, in spite of the fact that she had a fire going. The fire was the only means of cooking and also of providing hot water, so there was no option but to keep it burning. If you had coal.

Bella must have been more shaken than she would admit, because, after she'd given Edwin's hastily written note to Davy, she sat quietly at the table allowing Edwin to make a pot of tea.

'Poor old Jane gave me a plate pie,' she said as Edwin placed her cup on the table in front of her. 'She said she hadn't been able to eat everything and it was a shame to see it wasted.'

'You think that's what made you ill?' Edwin asked.

'Mebbes. She said it had just been delivered, although I should hev questioned that. Just lately she didn't seem to know what time of the day or even what day of the week it was. Anyways, it was still wrapped up in a bit greaseproof paper or – God forgive me – I wouldn't hev taken it from Jane Potts' hands. You know what her place is like.'

'Yes.' Edwin nodded and sat quietly while she supped her tea.

Then, still worrying, Bella said, 'It looked and smelled all right or I wouldn't hev given some to Albert.'

'And was your husband ill?'

'No. And he had more than me. But then he's got a constitution like an ox. Could that be possible, Mr Randall? If the meat was bad could it make me ill and not him?'

'It's possible; if your husband is a fit, strong man his body could deal with the ill effects. But as for Jane, there'll have to be a post— The doctors will have to find out what killed her – and I wouldn't be surprised if it were food poisoning. Not necessarily because the meat was bad in the first place but because of the way she kept it.'

'She wasn't used to heving so much. Her and Billy used to live from day to day.'

'Bella, do you know where the food came from?'

'I divven't. You can get the likes of this at Brady's or any of the butcher's or pie shops round here.'

That was true, Edwin thought. In fact he'd seen plate pies like the one Bella had described on Irene Lawson's table.

Bella Charlton continued, 'All she telt me was that a young man, little more than a lad, that she'd nivver seen before, started calling by, very early in the morning, or last thing at night, when nobody much was around, and leaving her the pies and such.'

161

'Didn't she ask him who was sending them?'

'She did but he just telt her it didn't matter, and some nonsense about not looking a gift horse in the mouth.'

'I suppose it could have been one of the local shopkeepers who'd heard what happened to her son and felt sorry for her,' Edwin said.

'Could be. The story got round, you know. In fact it was in the newspapers. Ee, what a dreadful way to die, falling off the bridge like that.'

Or being pushed, Edwin thought, although he didn't say so. He still had doubts about that night, and now it looked as if there might be someone who knew something. Someone who had been expiating guilt by making sure that the old woman didn't die without her son to look after her – and had ended up killing the mother as well as the son.

Or was that being too fanciful? Perhaps, after all, the food had been sent by some good-hearted local tradesman who kept quiet about it because he didn't want the rest of the poor folk around here to think he was an easy touch. Edwin had come across people like that. If that were the case Jane Potts' benefactor would be as horrified as he was at what had happened.

'I'm all right now,' Bella Charlton said. 'You needn't sit here any longer.'

Edwin looked at her and was satisfied that a little colour had come back to her cheeks. He glanced at the scrubbed table top, the clean swept earth floor and the shining grate. 'You keep your house spick and span, Bella,' he said.

'Aye, it's easy enough when there's just me and Albert. And I only had the one lad, not like some of the folk round here. And Albert may only be a labourer but he works hard and brings home good money – so long as he hasn't met the bookie's runner on the way!' She smiled. 'So I can afford to keep clean and tidy – and we were lucky to get this place, you know, even if we hev to pay more rent than most.'

'Lucky?'

'Oh, aye, it's an old building, but long ago, longer than anyone can remember, it used to be a farmhouse. So it's solid-built, and when it was divided into three there were enough outbuildings to give each house its own earth closet out back. Now mebbes it lacks proper wooden floors but at least the fire has a back boiler so, as long as we've got coal, we can hev hot water.'

'That's a great advantage.'

'Aye, and so's the nice cool pantry with stone shelves – ee, if only I'd thought on, poor old Jane could have stored her bit pies here with me!'

'You were ill, Bella, or I'm sure you would have thought of it.'

'Do you think so?'

'I'm sure of it. Now I'll have to go up to the police station. Don't worry if the police want to speak to you. They'll only want to ask you questions about why we broke in and – and what we found. They won't be blaming you.'

'I'm sorry, she just wasn't hungry.'

Lorna had taken her grandmother's tray to the kitchen herself. She put it on the table and looked up into the reproachful face of Mrs Hobson.

'It was only a bit beef tea and bread and butter, couldn't you hev made her sup a little?'

In spite of the gravity of the situation, Lorna smiled. 'Me? Make my grandmother do something?'

Mrs Hobson laughed and, with a wave of a large, capable hand, she indicated that Molly should take the tray and deal with it. When the young skivvy had vanished into the scullery, the cook turned to Lorna and said, 'Sit down, Miss Lorna. You look fair done in. How about a glass of lemonade and a slice of raisin cake?'

'I'd like that.'

Lorna sat down and closed her eyes. She heard Mrs Hobson moving about the kitchen fetching plates and glasses from the dresser and a cake tin from the pantry. She placed these on the table and then Lorna heard her go through to the scullery.

'You can sit in the yard with the others for a while,' Lorna heard her say to Molly. 'But take my advice and keep to the shade under the wall.'

A clink of ice in the lemonade jug announced that she had come back into the kitchen. Lorna opened her eyes and watched as the cook poured them each a glass.

'Thank goodness for the ice chest,' she said as she sank down on to a chair with a sigh. 'We couldn't do without the ice man in this weather.'

She pushed one of the glasses across the table to Lorna and then raised hers and smiled widely. 'Chin-chin!' she said, and raised her glass before they both began to drink.

'Mm,' Lorna said. 'That's good.'

'Fresh made.'

For a while neither spoke as they ate their slices of raisin cake. Lorna found that she was hungry. The late nights sitting with her grandmother until she fell asleep, and the constant running up and downstairs in order to save the servants had taken their toll on her physically. She felt worn out most of the time, but at least her appetite hadn't suffered.

'That's right,' Mrs Hobson said. 'It's good to see you enjoying that. You're a young healthy lass, after all.' Mrs Hobson mopped her perspiring face with a large clean handkerchief. 'Do you think Mrs Cunningham will eat something later?' she asked.

'I just don't know.' Lorna suppressed a yawn. 'She's sleeping now. The heat makes her so tired.'

'Yes, well, it's not just the heat, is it? I mean, her poor heart's struggling to keep her alive at all, in my opinion. Ee, Miss Lorna, I'm sorry. I shouldn't talk to you like that.'

Lorna shook her head. 'Don't worry. I know you speak from concern.' Lorna was almost sure that Violet must have relayed to Mrs Hobson anything she learned during Dr Gibson's visits. Perhaps Violet had known long before Lorna that her grandmother had a weak heart.

Apparently Mildred Cunningham had suspected as much for some time but had gone on working just as hard as ever. She only called the doctor when, at last, the breathlessness and the pain she sometimes felt became unbearable.

For months she seemed to have been living on her nerves and sheer willpower but, once Rose had been married in June, she had declined rapidly. Dr Gibson called every day. Apart from the usual advice about rest and a careful diet, he had said there wasn't very much he could do. He warned Lorna that, if she loved her grandmother, she must shield her from anything vexatious or any sudden shocks and surprises.

Do I love my grandmother? Lorna wondered, now. She looked across the kitchen table at the cook, who was cutting two more generous slices of the rich dark cake. Mrs Hobson thinks I do. And Violet must think so too, the way I've been devoting myself to Grandmamma's comfort ever since she took to her bed.

But what else could I have done? It surely has been my duty to care for the woman who took me in when my mother died. Duty? That's it. I have done my duty. I have been driven by a sense of obligation when it could have been so much more.

'You'll be glad that Mrs Cunningham has agreed to hev a nurse in at last,' Mrs Hobson said suddenly.

'I am.'

'She should have had one weeks ago. It's not right, a young lass like you having to wash her and see to her – her comfort the way you have.'

'You mean the bedpans?'

'Yes. It's not as if you were brought up to it.'

And what have I been brought up to? Lorna wondered. I went to a good school. I have not had to seek employment, and yet it's obvious that my grandmother never expected me to marry.

Good works, then? Is that my future? Fleetingly Lorna thought of Edwin Randall and his request that she should help him with the reading classes. But Irene Lawson had taken that role.

Irene. Lorna thought of her now. She had liked her. She had felt as though they had something in common. Both their fathers had sailed away and seemingly vanished, both their mothers had died.

But here the similarities ended. Lorna had been taken in and kept in comfort, no matter how grudgingly, by her grandmother. Irene had no one except herself to rely on, and she also had a baby sister to take care of.

But she had also won Edwin Randall's friendship.

Only this morning, when her grandmother had agreed that Dr Gibson should appoint a sick-bed nurse and that the woman should begin work tomorrow, had her grandmother broached the subject of what would happen when she died.

At first Lorna didn't know what she meant when she said. 'I've left instructions. Worked out every detail.'

'What for?'

Her grandmother closed her eyes for a moment and Lorna instinctively dipped a clean cloth into the bowl of iced water, wrung it out, and mopped her brow. The heat was making Mildred Cunningham's last illness even harder to bear.

'Thank you,' she murmured. 'For my funeral, of course. Rose and Maurice might not be back from their travels . . .'

She paused as if wanting Lorna to protest, to say that of course, she wasn't going to die yet, but Lorna remained silent. Why should there be anything but the truth between them?

'So it will be up to you, I'm afraid, to see that my last wishes –' she gave a wry smile, 'sounds like something from a novel, doesn't it? – that my last wishes are carried out.'

Lorna warmed to her grandmother at that moment. She had always been formidable and now she was facing death with dignity – at least as much dignity as the sick bed allowed – and humour.

'I'll do everything that's required of me,' Lorna said.

Her grandmother didn't speak for a while. She clutched a lavender-scented handkerchief to her breast and turned her head to gaze out of the window. Earlier she had requested that the lace curtains be tied up so that she could look out over the park. Although, even with her mountain of pillows, she could only see the tops of the trees.

Lorna watched her breast rising and falling. She was obviously having difficulty with her breathing, and every now and then a look of pure fright widened her eyes. Eventually she said, 'You'll be taken care of.'

'I beg your pardon?'

'You must have wondered what would happen to you.'

'No, I haven't.' And that was the truth. Not until this very moment had Lorna wondered what would happen to her when her grandmother died.

'You can't live here – everything goes to Rose. But you'll be all right. You'll see.'

The last word was more like a long sigh. Mildred Cunningham had fallen asleep. Lorna had picked up the tray with the uneaten food and brought it down to the kitchen.

Everything was to go to Rose. That was no more than she expected. And if this house was to be left to Rose she couldn't imagine what her cousin would do with it except sell it. She certainly wouldn't need it.

So where am I to go? she wondered. My grandmother owns many houses. Decent little houses that she rents out to working people. Am I to be given one of those? And would I mind? Lorna decided that she would not mind. In fact she would relish her independence; she would like living alone. But that did not solve the problem of what on earth she was going to do to fill her days.

'Miss Lorna?'

'Mm?' She looked up to find Mrs Hobson looking at her with concern.

'Why don't you go and lie down for a while?' the cook asked her. 'Violet will listen for Mrs Cunningham's bell.'

'Yes, I think I will.'

'I'll send you something up on a tray later. Something nourishing. I suppose you'll be sitting up with her again tonight?'

'Yes.'

'Well, come tomorrow, I hope you'll leave that to the nurse. And about time too.'

Unexpectedly Lorna felt a rush of tears and she hurried from the kitchen, blinking them back. It wasn't the fact that her grandmother was dying that had caused her to cry, it was because of the cook's genuine concern for her wellbeing.

Angrily she hurried upstairs to her room. She was angry because she was very near to giving way to self-pity, and she had learned, years ago, when she had first come to this house, that self-pity served no purpose except to leave her dangerously exposed.

If she had ever felt loved and wanted she might never have been so eager to search for love elsewhere. That search had led to Maurice Haldane.

The morning sun began to make striped patterns on the cool marble floor. Rose was still asleep but Maurice left her lying, pulled his robe round his naked body, and raised the shutters which he'd left half closed the night before. He pushed the doors open and walked out on to the balcony. The warmth met him, making him narrow his eyes for a moment as he acknowledged a slight headache.

He reached in his pocket for his cigarettes, lit one, and threw the spent match down beside an empty wine bottle. Then he leaned on the stone balustrade and gazed at the streets that twisted down through the small town to the harbour far below. It was early. There was no one about save on the beach where a few fishermen, tiny figures, clustered round their boats.

This part of the town almost seemed to be suspended on the cliffs and, from here, you looked down on layer after layer of rooftops and terraces full of pots of brightly coloured flowers. The older houses round the harbour were slightly shabbier, with peeling paint, but all were equally clean and well kept.

The little town was set in a deep gorge. Behind the hotel the cliffs rose steeply into a perfect summer sky. The aromatic plants on the mountainside filled the air with fragrance. Below, beyond the harbour, the Tyrrhenian Sea shimmered in the morning light.

They had travelled leisurely through France and Italy to spend their honeymoon here, on the Amalfi Coast. Rose should have been enchanted but, instead, she had grown bored and was already fretting to go home to their new house.

Suddenly Maurice's attention was caught by a movement in one of the streets below him. A figure, a woman, was hurrying up the steep incline towards the hotel. One of the maids, Maurice wondered, coming to start work?

Something about her bearing made him linger and watch her. She was dressed in black, like a widow, but her upright bearing and the way she hurried, told him that she was young. When she looked up briefly he saw her face and discovered that she had beauty to match the graceful proportions of her figure.

He was intrigued. Who could she be? For a wild moment she reminded him of someone he knew. He gripped the stone parapet of the balcony as he dismissed from his mind any hope that it could be Lorna.

Lorna . . . who would not have been lying indolently in bed for the best part of every day . . . who surely would have accompanied him on his walks through the orange groves and his visits to the ruined temples. Pagan temples . . .

Lorna, whose luminous intelligence would have engaged his mind as well as his body. Who could have taught him how to respect her sex. Who might have helped him to change . . .

And Lorna would not have lain submissively while he made love to her night after night, accepting satisfaction as her due. He had sensed a passion in her that would have matched his own. He would have had to awaken it, of course, but then she would have moved with him, ridden him, been a willing pupil, eager to learn all that he could teach her.

With Lorna in his bed he might have been satisfied and he would never have had to seek his pleasures elsewhere. Pleasures that left him spent but angry. Angry enough to be driven to desperation.

The woman had stopped short of the hotel. Maurice leaned out to watch more openly. She stood at the bottom of a flight of wide stone steps that led to a church. Her hands were raised to press against her breast, one hand on top of the other. Her head was bowed.

Why is she going to church alone at this time of the morning? What is she going to do there? Pray for her husband – some fisherman who is just about to venture out in waters so calm that they were like a painted backdrop? Or had she come to light a candle for a child? A desperately sick child or parent? No, if that were the case would she leave the sick bed even for an instant?

And why does she hesitate? Then, her decision made, she looked quickly, furtively, all round her and hurried up the steps, pushed the door open and vanished inside the church.

Maurice knew then why she had come. She had come to confess. He was sure of it. When no one else could see her she had come to confess to the sleepy priest some crime that would have brought shame on her head in this small community.

What will happen then after she is absolved? he wondered. And what has she done? Which commandment has she broken? Maurice could think of only one transgression that might send a young, beautiful woman hurrying to confession so furtively. He wondered if she would find it difficult to sin no more.

Behind him Rose stirred. He stayed a moment longer in the sun, finishing his cigarette. Only when he heard her murmur his name did he turn and walk into the shadowy room.

The sunlight lay across the tiled floor but fell short of the bed. Blinking as his eyes adjusted to the dimness, he observed his wife only as a pale mound under the white bedclothes.

She pulled herself up and seemed to be staring up at him. 'Oh, do come and sit down, Maurice. I can't see you properly if you stand against the light like that.'

He did as he was told. 'Shall I order breakfast now?' he asked her.

'That would be nice.' Rose reached over and turned the brass handle set into the wall near the bed that would set a bell ringing on a numbered board downstairs in the kitchen.

'When they come, tell them to set up the table on the balcony,' Maurice told her. 'I have a slight headache and I'm going to see if a cool shower will help.'

Rose did not dress before breakfast. She had tied her hair back and slipped on a pale blue silk robe over her white nightgown. She sat in the shade of the table parasol enjoying her second pastry.

'More coffee?' Maurice asked.

'Mm, please. These little honey cakes are delicious. What a lovely idea, having cake for breakfast. Shall we do this at home?'

'As well as the usual English fare or instead of?'

'Oh, as well!'

Maurice smiled. He wouldn't spoil her enjoyment, not yet. But once they were home he would have to ask his mother to have a word with his new wife. At first he had been delighted with the way Rose had been willing to sample foods she had never eaten before. She was not completely the provincial girl she might have been.

She tasted and enjoyed *mortadella*, *pancetta*, and even the *capitone*; the fried eels that had at first made her shudder at the sight of them, and then shiver with delight when she tasted a tiny forkful.

And as for the pastries and the desserts, she had declared herself in heaven. She adored the honey-flavoured *struffoli* and the *zeppole* but her absolute favourite was the peaches stuffed with crushed amaretti biscuits, soaked in amaretto liqueur, and then drenched with cream.

It pleased him to indulge her, to watch her eat like a greedy child. This, in some way, eased his guilt. He had married her without loving her. If it had been possible, it would have been her cousin sitting here with him on the terrace overlooking the sea. He was not sure how deep Rose's own feelings were for him. But in any case she must never suspect his previous involvement with Lorna. That would not make for an easy life.

No, Rose should have anything she wanted, within reason. But she must not grow fat. She must remain beautiful and elegant. He would rely on his mother to take her in hand when they got home.

Rose dabbed at her lips with the clean white napkin, threw it down on the table, and sat back and frowned slightly. 'Maurice . . .' she began.

'What is it?'

'Did you go out last night?'

'We both did. Don't you remember?' He laughed. 'After dinner, when you had drunk at least two glasses of wine, perhaps three, I suggested that we should walk to get some fresh air. We strolled down to the harbour.'

'Of course I remember. And the air wasn't exactly fresh. It is so warm here even after dark! But the lights on the fishing boats in the harbour were so pretty. And we saw Lucia.'

'Lucia?' Maurice sipped his coffee and looked at her through narrowed eyes.

'Yes, Lucia, the chambermaid, the one who's been helping me with my wardrobe. Now don't say *you* don't remember!'

'Lucia. Ah yes.'

'She was quarrelling with someone, a fierce young man. I think it was the English artist. So wild-looking – so bohemian! Anyway, then she flounced off along the promenade and left him. You went after to her to ask if she was all right and apparently she told you that she was. You see, I remember everything.'

'And do you remember that shortly after that we came back to the hotel together?' Maurice asked.

'Of course I do, don't tease.'

'And then, my darling, we went to bed. Now don't tell me you've forgotten what happened then?'

Rose smiled. 'How could I?'

She was trying to be flirtatious. It sickened him. He turned away and kept his tone light when he said, 'But now it's time to get ready and go out.'

Rose made a *moue* of discontent. 'Another long walk, no doubt, while I wait here all alone!'

'No, my darling. I shall not leave you alone. You are coming with me.'

'But, Maurice, I don't really want to.'

170

'Don't worry, I'm not planning another walk. I'm going to take you on a sea trip. In an hour's time the boat leaves the harbour for an excursion to Capri. Can you be dressed in time?'

'Oh . . . yes . . . I think so.'

'Well, just to make sure I shall go down and ask them to send up Lucia to help you. And while you're getting ready I'll go to the kitchen and ask them to organize a hamper with all your favourite things in it.'

'Oh, good. And, Maurice?'

'Yes?'

'Ask them to put in some *pastiera*, those lovely soft cakes with the little lumps inside!'

He rose, kissed her lightly, and left her to finish the dish of pastries.

The girl who came to the door a few minutes later was not Lucia. She spoke enough English to inform Rose that her name was Elena and that Lucia was late for work and would be in trouble when she arrived.

Rose was perfectly capable of dressing herself but she enjoyed the luxury of having a maid to help and she fully intended to choose a suitable girl to be her own lady's maid when she got home.

Elena pleased her by exclaiming over her clothes, whereas Lucia had simply been efficient. And, on reflection, probably a little too pretty. Maurice had certainly found excuses to linger when Lucia was in the room.

Soon Rose was ready in a dress of white muslin; the floating layers of which were trimmed with ribbon and flowers of the palest blue. Her shawl, with its deep silk fringe, had been made to match the dress, and so had her parasol. Her hat, a ridiculously large affair decorated with cream silk cabbage roses, was held in place by a filmy veil. Going by the generous admiration in Elena's eyes, she knew she looked sensational.

When Maurice returned he informed her the hamper had been sent to the harbour and that they should set off themselves.

'Maurice,' she panted at last as she tried to keep up with his long stride, 'it's too hot to hurry like this. And if our hamper has been loaded on to the boat, surely they will wait for us.'

He slowed his pace immediately and apologized. 'Of course, they will. I'm sorry. It's just that I'm keen to get away for the day, I suppose. To visit somewhere new.'

'But what exactly are we going to do there?' Rose asked him.

'We are going to act like tourists,' Maurice said.

'Oh.'

171

'We shall visit a Roman villa, some beautiful gardens where we shall sit and explore the contents of the hamper, and then I shall buy you some jewellery.'

'Oh?'

'I thought that would please you. You shall have a cameo necklace and earrings – a brooch as well, if you like. Do you know this kind of jewellery has been carved from shell in this part of the world since Roman times?'

The further they got down the hill towards the harbour, the busier the streets became. Rose held on to Maurice's arm and could not help being pleased that people stopped to look at them as they went by. They were both so fair and Maurice was so tall. She was sure that in their fashionable, expensive clothes – Maurice wore a cream linen suit – they must make a striking couple.

She almost wished that they had set off on this trip later in the day and then they would have had a larger audience. For she had noticed that the people from the more humble houses went up the hill to Mass in the afternoon. Then, afterwards, they would return and put their chairs out into the streets and sit and chat to one another.

In her mind she was imagining herself and Maurice disembarking from the boat and walking back up the hill. The poor people they passed would raise their hands and say, *'Bella, bellissima!'*

And then she heard the words, *'Correte! Correte!'* She frowned. This wasn't part of her pleasant daydream. The shouting was real, and urgent, and she didn't know what it meant.

She could also hear the sound of people running. 'What is it, Maurice? What's happening?' she asked just as he took hold of her and pulled her into the opening of a narrow alleyway.

'They're telling us to run,' he said, and he held her close. They stood here and watched as the street where they had just been walking filled with people all making for the harbour. Above the sound of the cries and the running feet Rose heard the sound of horses' hoofs coming down the steep street behind the people.

She was just about to peer out when Maurice pulled her back. 'Be careful!' he said.

He had pulled her back just in time. First one horse and then another galloped down towards the harbour. The riders were men, dressed in black with swords at their belts and cloaks flying out behind them. Each wore a black hat with a white cockade.

'The *carabinieri*,' Maurice said. 'The local police officers.'

After a moment, when all they could hear was the sound of the

172

horses receding in the distance, they peered out. The street was empty and the town was strangely quiet.

Rose held Maurice's hand as they began to walk down to the harbour again. There was no question of them going back to their hotel. Apart from the fact that they were supposed to be going on an excursion to Capri, they both wanted to know what had caused such a commotion.

'Do you think it's some kind of revolution?' Rose whispered.

Maurice smiled as he gripped her hand more tightly. He shook his head but he didn't say anything. Rose thought he looked strained; the smile hadn't reached his eyes. But she was confident that he wouldn't take her into danger.

When they reached the harbour they saw that the crowd had gathered at the far end of the promenade where the stone walkway gave way to a rough path that led to a rocky outcrop with a tiny bay beyond. Maurice had taken her there the first day but she had not enjoyed sitting on the shingly beach. They had not gone there again.

Now everyone had fallen silent. As they approached they saw that the two police officers had dismounted and their horses stood patiently, the reins of each held by a small boy.

And then the crowd moved, at first surging forward and then parting. At the same time there was a cry of horror and then a dreadful wailing.

'What is it?' Rose asked. 'What are they carrying?'

At that moment Elena burst from the crowd and came running towards them. 'Ah, *signor*, *signora*,' she cried. 'They have found Lucia. *E morta!*'

'What are you saying?' Rose cried. 'Wait!'

But Elena had gone running past them and back up the hill towards the hotel. Rose turned to Maurice and gripped his arm. 'What did she mean?'

'She said that Lucia was dead.'

'No! But how? An accident? Maurice, please go and ask someone what has happened.'

'Very well.' He seemed reluctant but he walked over to the crowd and she saw him in conversation with one of the *carabinieri*.

When he came back to her his expression was grave. 'Some children were playing in that little cove,' he said. 'They found Lucia lying there. It seems she was murdered.'

Chapter Fourteen

Dear Lorna,

We will be coming home soon. By the time you read this we may have begun our journey. I'm not sure how long it will take, as Maurice wants to make several business calls on the way. For example, he wants to arrange to import gentlemen's silk neck ties from Naples and ladies' hats from Paris. I must say, Lorna, I had not realized our honeymoon was to be combined with a business trip.

Lorna smiled as she read this last sentence. She could imagine Rose's petulant expression as she wrote those words. The letter had arrived as part of a small package this morning but Lorna had not had the chance to read it until now. It was afternoon and, leaving her grandmother in the capable hands of Miss Gillespie, the trained nurse, she had come up to her room to rest.

The weather was still warm and she had opened her windows, only to close them a short while later because of the rising stench of horse manure from the busy road below.

Eventually she took off her dress, sponged her face and neck with cool water and pulled on a loose cotton robe. Then she had propped herself up amongst the pillows on her bed and sipped the ice-cold freshly made lemonade that Molly had brought up for her before opening the package and starting to read the letter.

Now she laid the letter aside for a moment and opened the intriguing little parcel that had come with it. A piece of parchment-like paper with Italian printing on it was neatly wrapped around a small box. The paper was secured with a fine brown satin ribbon.

Lorna untied the ribbon and opened up the paper. The box was dark brown with gold printing on the top. Again, the words were in Italian.

She lifted off the lid to reveal a cameo brooch set on a card of tan velvet.

The brooch was oval in shape with a raised female head in profile. The background was dull orange and the figure, who looked like a goddess from ancient myths, had flesh of a delicate peach colour and a garment of cream. The roses in her hair were shades of cream and orange. It was truly beautiful.

Lorna picked up the letter again and read:

Even our trip to Capri yesterday was partly business. It seems that brooches like the one I've sent you have been made here since Roman times. And necklaces and earrings, too. They are carved by local craftsmen from conch shells.

Anyway, Maurice lured me to Capri on the pretence that we were to behave just like tourists, and, in fact, we did visit a couple of old castles and some more ancient ruins as well as a beautiful garden. But after we had eaten *al fresco* we went shopping for souvenirs.

I was left to browse alone for nearly an hour while Maurice talked business; but he made it up to me by buying me the most beautiful set of jewellery. A pendant necklace, earrings and a brooch. Maurice was very taken with the brooch. He said it depicted Flora, the Italian goddess of flowers and spring, and that she had been painted by many famous painters such as Titian and Rembrandt. He said I should buy another one to send to you.

Well, of course I had fully intended to choose something for you, some little souvenir, perhaps a pair of dainty earrings, but, seeing that Maurice was obviously feeling generous, I was delighted to get you the brooch. Except, of course, I said yours should be set in silver, not gold like mine, as I didn't think you would want us to be exactly the same.

Lorna put down the letter again and picked up the jewellery box. She examined the brooch and saw that it was indeed set in a delicate twisted silver frame. The silver shone palely and somehow enhanced the delicacy of the carved portrait.

She closed her eyes and imagined a sky full of stars above the white columns of an ancient temple, the temple itself on an island surrounded by a moon-silvered sea . . .

She could imagine the brooch set in gold that Rose had preferred

175

and she was glad that her cousin, no matter what her true motive might have been, had chosen the silver for her gift.

But it was Maurice who had prompted her to buy it. What was she to make of that? Maurice had thought of her even though he was on his honeymoon. Had he wanted Rose to tell Lorna that the gift was his idea? Did he want her to know that he was thinking of her? Suddenly she knew, with great conviction, that he did, and the knowledge made her confused and unhappy.

She remembered the day she had thought they were eloping and her shock and dismay when he had told her that he would never be able to marry her. She had felt betrayed and cheapened by his assumption that he would be able to persuade her to live with him as his mistress. She had thought he didn't love her enough to stand up to his parents and tell them that she was his chosen bride, not Rose.

And yet . . . what had he said?

'. . . *I love you so much that I cannot imagine life without you. We have to be together. I had to find a way. Don't you understand? . . .*'

No, she hadn't understood. In spite of his promised gift of the house and everything she would ever want or need, she had not been able to accept the solution he had found. She had refused him.

Had she made a mistake? Surely she should have been able to accept that their love for one another was more important than convention. Her own mother had defied society when she married an Arab seaman. She had lived apart from her family from the moment of her marriage until she died.

But that was it, of course. She had been married. Shouldn't Maurice have been prepared to give up everything in order to marry the woman he loved? Lorna sighed. Maurice had so much to give up. She had to acknowledge that it was different for a man.

Lorna had always lived apart from the world her cousin inhabited; as a child of mixed race she had never been accepted. What difference would it have made if she had become a mistress instead of a wife? She was used to a life apart.

Was it pride that made me spurn his plans for us? she wondered. Was I using Maurice to try to force people to accept me?

She closed her eyes while she thought of the last few months: miserable and restless, tied to her sick grandmother by duty and not knowing what on earth she was going to do with her life.

'. . . *married or not, I want you to be mine. I want to be able to come to you whenever I can . . .*'

Maurice had urged her to think of the life she had had until now.

176

'. . . she hasn't loved you . . . you have not been happy . . . I love you and we will be happy together . . .'

Maurice had said they would travel – had he sent the brooch to remind her that they could have seen such places together; could have escaped to a world where no one knew them where they could have been accepted as a man and woman who belonged together? No one would have known that they didn't have a marriage certificate.

What have I done? she wondered. Because I asked too much of Maurice I have ended up with nothing. I misjudged him. I was so much in love that I didn't realize how bound he was by the conventions of his class. When I refused to live with him as his mistress his disappointment made him cruel.

But he still thinks of me . . . he still loves me. If I had been able to control my own hurt and anger might I have found a way to make him change his mind . . .?

Wearily she picked up Rose's letter. As she read it she tried not to think of Maurice. She learned that Rose had quite enjoyed her excursion to Capri and that the sea air had made her pleasantly tired. But that when they had returned to the little town on the Amalfi coast where they were staying: 'The place was still in uproar about the murder!'

Murder? Lorna, intrigued in spite of her emotional state, leafed back through the letter but could find no mention of a murder. She read on and, in Rose's muddled composition she learned that Lucia, one of the chambermaids from the hotel where Rose and Maurice were staying, had been discovered lying in a little cove to the west of the harbour. Murdered, it seemed. Rose wrote:

According to Elena, another chambermaid, the poor girl must have lain there all night. And, do you know, we may have been among the last to see her alive? Maurice and I saw her arguing with a young man. A young Englishman, actually. He's an artist, or so he claims. I think it's just an excuse to get young women to pose for him. When I learned what had happened I wondered if he was the culprit but it seems he has an alibi. The old couple with whom he lodges claim he came home early and never left the house again. But the old man's nearly blind and the old woman's as deaf as a post. It would be easy enough to bamboozle them.

There are rumours of some kind of love triangle. A young fisherman who was jealous of the attention the Englishman paid to Lucia. But I doubt that we will ever know what happened. For, now, with Elena's help, I must begin to pack our belongings. Maurice is suddenly keen to begin our journey home.

And, to tell you the truth, so am I. Lorna, I am so looking forward to being mistress of my own house! There is still so much to do there and I so wish I could ask you to come and help me organize things, but Maurice's mother is quite adamant that she and I will arrange everything between us. I am not even to call on Grandmamma.

How is Grandmamma, by the way? I thought she looked quite poorly when she waved us off, but then she had been working so very hard to organize the wedding, hadn't she? And she was so quiet during the wedding breakfast, wasn't she?

Oh, I forgot, you weren't there. Well, take my word for it, she hardly said a word. Between you and me I suspected that she was a little overawed by her social superiors. You know what I mean, the sort of people the Haldanes consort with are far removed from Grandmamma's provincial worthies.

Please tell her that I will come to see her the moment we get home. I have bought her the most beautiful silk shawl, but don't say anything; I want it to be a surprise.

Help! I have run out of notepaper. I could send Elena for more but it is time to start my packing. I have no idea how long it will take us to travel home, what with Maurice wanting to make business calls, so tell Grandmamma that I love her and I will see her soon.

Love,
Rose Haldane

Lorna stared at the signature for a moment and then crumpled the letter and threw it into the waste basket. She knew that she shouldn't be surprised that Rose wanted to show off her new married name and, also, that Rose would have no idea that by doing so she would cause hurt.

No, it wasn't just the signature, it was the knowledge that Maurice still thought of her and that Rose had no idea of what had happened. And then there was the shawl.

Somehow, the thought of the silk shawl was more disturbing than the rest of it. Because it was a more urgent problem. She was surprised to find her eyes had filled with tears. Bitter scalding tears. Inasmuch as Rose was capable of loving, she loved her grandmother. But her grandmother loved Rose deeply; she had devoted herself to making life pleasant and easy for Rose whereas Lorna she had simply tolerated.

Lorna believed that Mildred Cunningham had kept herself going long after she should have taken to her bed. She had done so in order to see Rose safely married and not to cast a shadow on the wedding. And now, she was keeping herself alive only so that she could see her favourite granddaughter once more. Lorna was convinced of that.

She was also convinced that willpower alone would not be sufficient in this case. Dr Gibson had warned her that the end was near. Rose had asked her not to mention the shawl, and yet, if she didn't, their grandmother would never know that Rose had thought of her, had bought her a present and would be bringing it to her soon.

But it wouldn't be soon enough.

Should Lorna disregard Rose's request and tell their grandmother about the shawl? Give her something sweet to think about in her dying days? If Rose knew the truth she would want her to.

Why am I agonizing like this? Lorna asked herself. Why should I care so much about people who care so little for me?

Then, angry with herself for sinking into self-pity again, she rose abruptly from her bed and rang for Molly. She would ask the girl to bring up a jug of fresh water. She would wash and dress and go into town. I need distraction, she thought. I need books, magazines, nothing serious, anything that will help me to escape for a while.

Soon, in an afternoon dress of pale green muslin and a straw hat with a wide brim, she went downstairs. The house was dark and quiet. The heat seemed to rise up and greet her, bringing with it the lingering odours of countless meals eaten in the sombre dining room, combined with the scent of layer after layer of furniture polish. The atmosphere of her grandmother's house was suffocating her, making it all the more urgent that she should escape.

She encountered no one. The domestic staff had been creeping around the house with long faces for weeks; as if their employer were already dead and they were in mourning. Violet had hardly spoken. Lorna knew that she was fond of her mistress, and loyal, but she suspected that her grandmother's personal maid was also worrying about her next position, wondering where she would go next.

Lorna paused on the landing outside her grandmother's room. All was quiet. Dr Gibson would be calling later and now Mildred Cunningham would be resting. If you could call it rest, that tortured half-alive state when every breath was laboured. She might be sleeping.

Should I go in? Lorna wondered. Should I risk disturbing her and tell her about the shawl Rose is bringing? No, let her rest. And, anyway,

179

why should I bother? Why should I worry for a moment whether she learns of the shawl or not?

Swiftly Lorna turned away and hurried down into the hallway. When she opened the front door the heat almost seemed to come to claim her. She closed the door behind her, leaving her worries inside, and gave herself up to the busy scene outside.

'Bigamy, arson and murder! Is that sensational enough?' Edwin smiled as he handed Lorna the book. '*Lady Audley's Secret* has hardly been out of print since it was published more than forty years ago,' he said. 'It's very popular.'

'Let me see.' Lorna took the book from him and glanced at it briefly. She bent her head so that the brim of her hat obscured her face. Edwin was left staring at the confection of white silk flowers and pale green ribbons that encircled the crown. 'Yes, this will do,' she said. 'And have you more novels by Mrs Braddon?'

'I think so.' Edwin scanned the shelves behind him. 'Ah, yes, *The Doctor's Wife.*'

Suddenly he felt awkward. Don't be foolish, he told himself. Lorna is far too indifferent to my feelings to read any significance in the title. He took the book down and handed it to her. He watched her look at it before she placed it on top of the first one.

'I'll take it,' she said. 'And anything else you can recommend. Any book that would not require me to think too deeply. I want to be entertained, to escape from this world. There's nothing wrong with that, is there?' she asked when she saw the way he looked at her.

'No, of course not. I believe that literature should entertain you as well as make you think. And I think I know why you want to escape.'

'Do you?'

She looked startled, frightened, almost, and he didn't understand. 'Well, you've been looking after your grandmother, haven't you? It can't have been easy.'

'No,' she said quickly. 'It isn't easy. Do you mind if I sit down and just let you choose another two or three books for me? Love stories, detective stories, anything, so long as they have a happy ending.'

'Detective stories with a happy ending?' Edwin smiled.

'Of course. And don't smile like that. You know what I mean. No matter how dreadful the crime or how gruesome the murder, the story must end with everything being put right again. Order restored, justice served.'

For a moment, while she spoke, Lorna became animated. It was the old Lorna, the Lorna he understood, not the sad distracted creature she seemed to have become. But then she sighed and sat down on the chair that was kept at the other side of the counter.

There were no other customers. The town centre was hot and dusty and it seemed that no one had the energy to shop. Edwin had been sitting with his medical books spread out on the counter, doing some revision, when Lorna had entered.

The tinkle of the bell above the door had alerted him and he had looked up from his book reluctantly, smothering a yawn.

'Forgive me,' he said when he saw who it was. He stood up and reached for his jacket from the shelf beneath the counter.

'No, you don't have to put that on on my account,' Lorna said. 'It's too hot for formality.'

She stood in a shaft of sunlight, surrounded by dancing motes of dust, looking like a pagan goddess with her honey-coloured skin set off to perfection by the cool green fabric of her gown. She was a vision of the verdant countryside; she seemed out of place in the hot barren air of the city.

I wonder if she knows how lovely she is? Edwin wondered. Or what effect she has on me? I don't think so.

He had pushed his hair back from his brow and put on his jacket regardless of her words. Vanity, he thought, and decided to forgive himself. He knew he was not conventionally handsome so why shouldn't he make the effort to present his homely self in the best possible light?

When he had chosen another four books he put them on the counter with the others. Lorna was staring into the mid-distance. It seemed to take her a while to turn and smile at him.

'Two romances and two detective stories,' he said. 'But you may have already borrowed this one from the library.'

'What's that?'

'*The Hound of the Baskervilles*. Do you like the Sherlock Holmes stories?'

'Yes I do, and I haven't read it. Thank you.' She made no effort to get up. Instead she indicated two stacks of books at the end of the counter near the window. 'Those don't look like new books,' she said. 'I didn't know you sold second-hand volumes.'

'Well, as a matter of fact we do. The medical and engineering students bring their books back when they have finished with them and we sell them to the following year's students for a small commission.'

Lorna got up and went to examine the books more closely. 'But these aren't textbooks,' she said. 'They're novels and children's books and even cookery books.'

'I know. They're donations.'

'Donations?'

'From our customers and their families and friends. They're for my reading pupils. Irene and I are setting up a small library.'

'Irene.'

'Yes, and as a matter of fact I was going to ask you if you had any books you could give me.'

'Probably.'

Edwin had thought Lorna would be enthusiastic about his library. Being such an avid reader herself he'd been sure that she would think it a good idea. But, instead he watched as she looked at the books on the counter listlessly. Then suddenly she became more animated.

'*Lorna Doone*,' she said. 'Oh, Edwin, I love this book!'

He smiled. 'It's a swashbuckling story, I suppose. And there's definitely a happy ending.'

'Of course, but it's more than that. Do you know that's how I got my name? From this very novel.'

'Why? Let me guess – your mother read the story as a girl and was enchanted?'

'Yes, but it's even better than that. She used it when she was teaching my father to read and write English. At the end of every lesson they would read some of it together.'

'And your father fell in love with the characters too.'

'Of course. So, naturally, when I was born, they had to call me Lorna.'

She clasped the book to her breast; her eyes were shining. Edwin started to smile in response and then he realized that the shine was the glitter of tears: They began to overflow and stream down her face. He vaulted over the counter and reached out and took her in his arms.

'What is it?' he murmured, but she only shook her head. Edwin drew her close and discovered that she was trembling. 'Hush,' he said. He spoke softly as if to a distressed child.

'Don't tell me not to cry,' she said.

'Of course I won't. Cry if you want to.'

She laid her head sideways on his chest so that all he could see was the crown of her ridiculous hat. But as he held her trembling form in his arms, Edwin had to fight to control a wild surge of emotion. She

182

had come to him for comfort and he sensed that if he offered more than that he would drive her away.

In the warm dusty stillness of his uncle's bookshop Edwin learned how easy it would be for her to break his heart.

As Irene got off the tram the woman behind her stood on the hem of her dress. She turned round and glared but, rather than apologize, the woman scowled at her.

'Look what you've done,' Irene shouted over the noise of the departing tram.

The woman, who had already begun to hurry away, turned and shouted, 'Are you talking to me?'

She was large and angry-looking. Fleetingly Irene wondered if it was wise to go on but exasperation drove her to say, 'Can you see anybody else in the vicinity?'

'Vicinity!' The woman's eyes widened sarcastically. 'That's a fine big word for a little lass like you. Hev you got a gob full of dictionary pudding?'

Irene controlled the urge to snap back. The woman made a show of looking behind her and all around.

'Na,' she said, and then turned to look at Irene challengingly. 'I canna see anybody else.'

'Then it's you I'm talking to,' Irene said, 'and look what you've done to my dress.'

As she said this she twisted round and took hold of a handful of fabric, bringing it forward to show the woman the dirty toe print on the pale blue linen and the ragged tear.

'Divven't blame me. You should hev taken more care. You were standing there on the platform daydreaming instead of getting a move on.'

Irene sighed. She was hot and tired and she obviously wasn't going to get an apology from the woman so there was no point in continuing the conversation.

She was just about to move away when the woman said: 'Lissen, pet. I'm sorry.'

'What?' Irene stared at her opponent in astonishment.

'Divven't yer mean, "I beg yer pardon"? It's rude to say "what".' The woman's broad, none-too-clean face had creased into a smile. 'Well, anyways, I didn't mean to stand on your bonny frock. New, is it?'

'Yes. I sat up till all hours finishing it off.' Irene surprised herself by her admission but the woman who had seemed to be an enemy had suddenly turned into a sympathetic friend.

'And very nice it is too. Off to meet your lad, are you?'

'My lad?'

The woman grinned. 'Your sweetheart.'

'No. I haven't got a sweetheart.'

'Hevn't yer? Well, perhaps you'd like to hev. Perhaps that's why you're dressed up so bonny, like.'

'No, you're wrong, and I have to go.'

'Wait a minute. Hev you got a pin or two in that bag of yours? If yer hev, I'll pin the tear so's he won't notice.'

'I've told you, there isn't any "he"!'

'Whatever you say. But gan on, look in yer bag. But let's step into the arcade – get out of the way.'

It was a relief to move from the hot bright sunshine into the lofty shade of the arcade. The mosaic-tiled floor was cooler and cleaner than the pavements outside, and fresh green foliage trailed down from containers along the railings of the balconies at first-floor level. The plants must have been watered recently because they were still dripping water into gathering pools below them.

'Watch yersel.' Her new friend took her arm and guided her away from one of the pools. 'Yer divven't want to land on yer behind. That would make a mess of yer bonny new frock.'

Irene flinched at the coarseness but managed a smile of thanks. Then, as she opened her bag, she had a moment of doubt. Had the woman dragged her in here to rob her? Had the whole incident been a trick right from the moment she had trod on her dress on the platform of the tram?

She looked up to find the woman looking at her innocently enough. 'Gan on, hinny,' she said. 'Divven't take all day.'

If she was going to rob me she'd have taken the bag and be gone by now, Irene reasoned, and she reached into her bag for her purse companion. It was made from leather and lined with satin. It contained a tiny pair of scissors, a button hook, cards of different coloured threads, a needle case containing both pins and needles. There was also a tiny penknife.

When Irene had first been given the case as a child she had been more fascinated with the knife than with the sewing implements. There were two tiny blades, one at each end, which folded over into the handle. She would play with it constantly, opening out first one blade then the other.

184

Her mother had been constantly anxious that she would cut off one of her fingers and she had scolded her father for giving it to her, for the purse companion had been brought home from one of his voyages. He said it had come from Morocco and he had shown Irene where Morocco was on one of the big maps on the wall of the shipping office.

Each time he came home he had brought gifts for her mother and herself. And he had taught her about the sea routes of the world on those old maps.

'Here you are,' she said as she opened up the needle case. 'There should be enough pins there.'

'Well, there's no need to bubble. I'll do me best.'

Irene wiped the tears from her eyes. 'Just a speck of dust,' she said.

'If you say so. Ee, me knees!' The last was said as she kneeled down. 'Now, hold the pins so's I can reach them. That's right.'

Irene watched as the woman turned the bottom of her dress over and made a neat enough job of pinning the tear together. She felt a momentary misgiving when she saw how dirty her hands were but it was too late to stop her now and, anyway, it was the wrong side she was touching.

'There. There's enough material in this skirt to hide the pinned bit. And when you take your leave, back away until the last minute and then scarper quick. He'll nivver notice.'

'I've told you, there's no particular he.'

'Yes, pet. Now I must be on me way. And I am sorry. I didn't mean to stand on your skirt like that.'

'I know. I should have got down more quickly, but I'm tired, I suppose.'

'Aye, you said. You were up until all hours finishing your dress. And you've done a good job – you look very bonny.'

'Do I?'

'Pretty as a picture. The blue matches your eyes and the ribbon round your hat's an exact match. He won't be able to resist a lass as bonny as you are!'

The woman started to laugh when she saw Irene's discomfiture and she turned to go. 'I've gotta gan, off to the market. If I don't get yem soon me man'll think I've got lost.'

As she walked away she started burst out laughing and then she started to sing, ' "Lost stolen or strayed . . . a beeootiful blue-eyed maid . . ." '

Irene smiled in spite of herself. She walked to the other end of the arcade and turned to continue down through town towards the bookshop.

She was pleased with the rough woman's compliment. She wanted to believe what she'd said.

He won't be able to resist a lass as bonny as you are!

Over the last few months Irene had made tremendous efforts to improve the way she spoke. She had always kept herself clean and she knew that she had a good brain. And she knew also that she was attractive. There had been a moment when she'd thought that Edwin thought her so. But there seemed to be something holding him back.

She knew she had to change his perception of her. Instead of a poor but respectable charity case she must appear as a suitable partner for him. One way would be to wear the kind of clothes that people in his social circle wore. She had saved up until she was able to afford a decent length of material from Parrish's and the latest paper pattern. She'd had to sew it all by hand – and she hated sewing.

Old Mrs Flanagan had proved an unexpected ally. To Irene's surprise she told her that long ago, before she was married, she'd worked in a big house in Jesmond as a laundry maid and that part of her duties had been to do basic mending.

She had no idea of style but she was good at plain sewing and she was content to sit for hours and help Irene work on her new dress. She'd even made the ribbons to trim the plain boater from the leftover scraps of material. Hopefully she would be able to make a proper mend to the tear in her skirt when Irene got home.

When she reached the top of the Bigg Market Irene paused nervously. Edwin wasn't expecting her. Her excuse was that she wanted to collect some of the books which had been donated for the library they were going to set up. Her real reason was to let Edwin see her in her new outfit – and possibly in a new light.

She began to walk downhill past the open-air stalls that lined the way. The market traders shouted their usual calls and Irene had to be careful not to slip on any of the discarded fruit and vegetables.

And then she reached the place where the road divided and the right fork became the Groat Market. The tall buildings rose steeply at either side of the cobbled road, making it like a canyon.

Canyon . . . A canyon was a deep gorge, usually with a river running through it.

Irene knew that because she had first come across the word in a novel she had read about the American West. She always looked up any word she didn't know in a dictionary. Teaching at the reading group had made her want to learn even more herself.

This canyon didn't have a river running through it; instead, a small stream of water flowed past her from the fish stall where the ice was melting. It carried with it bits of debris from the vegetable stalls.

She had reached the bookshop. She had never been here before and she hadn't really rehearsed what she would say to Edwin. She paused, going over in her mind what her exact words would be.

As she did so she glanced in the window cautiously. Edwin might be busy with a customer; he might not be able to talk to her straight away. The bright sunlight made it difficult at first to make out what she saw in the dimmer interior of the shop.

Then, when what was happening just a few feet away from her became quite clear, the shock was almost unbearable. Edwin was holding a woman in his arms, pressing her close, and even though his eyes were closed, his face betrayed his emotion.

Irene couldn't see the woman's face but the dark coppery curls revealed under the brim of her hat was enough to identify her.

'No . . .' Irene whispered, and she began to back away.

The pavement was narrow and she stumbled into the gutter. The water running down from the market stained the hem of her new dress. The dress she had sat up half the night to finish.

But that hardly mattered now.

Chapter Fifteen

On the way home in the tram Lorna took every opportunity to press the damp handkerchief Edwin had given her to her face. When she'd said she must leave he had taken one look at her and told her to sit and wait. Then he'd hurried away into the room at the back of the shop.

While she waited she'd taken her mirror from her handbag and looked into it to see what had made him look so concerned. She'd discovered that her eyelids were swollen and the skin transparent so that they looked like blisters. She'd been glad to accept the cold damp handkerchief but had felt too embarrassed to stay for much longer so she'd taken it with her.

Nobody in the tram took much notice. They probably thought she was suffering from the heat like those who were wiping their brows with their own handkerchiefs or fanning themselves with newspapers.

By the time the tram reached her stop and she stepped down on to a pavement that was so hot that she could feel it through the soles of her shoes, she had an intense headache and her eyes were still smarting. She found it painful to keep them open. It was as if she had a fever.

Dr Gibson's motor car was parked at the kerb outside her grand-mother's house. She had been out so long that she thought his usual visit might be over by now and she paused anxiously before opening the gate, wondering why he was still here and looking at the vehicle as if it could answer her question.

But it was the house that gave her the answer. After closing the gate behind her she glanced up at her grandmother's window instinctively. The curtains were closed. That might not have been unusual – her grandmother might have asked for them to be closed so that the bright sun didn't disturb her rest – but it wasn't just her window that was shrouded against the daylight. Every window from the ground floor to the attics had its curtains drawn too. There could be only one explanation. Of all the complex emotions that began to surface immediately and would haunt her for months, if not years, to come there was one that would never leave her.

Lorna knew that for the rest of her life she would feel guilty about one thing she had done. Or rather hadn't done.

I didn't tell her about the shawl, she thought, and now it's too late.

Then, dry-eyed, for hadn't she cried enough today, she went into the house to learn what she already knew. Mildred Cunningham was dead.

Mary Flanagan was tired and hot. Tired because she had sat up half the night helping Irene to finish her bonny new dress, and hot because of the weather. Even with the top half of the window wide open, the room felt like an oven. Today there didn't seem to be even the slightest breeze blowing up the bank from the river.

Still, she was glad to be here minding Irene's little sister rather than upstairs with her own grandbairns. The summer heat seemed to bring out the devil in them. They never stopped screaming and tormenting one another. Their mother, Mary's own poor daughter, had no life at all.

This weather could make even an angel lose his wings. Ruth, normally a little cherub, sat on a blanket on the floor, grizzling miserably. She clutched her rag doll to her body with one hand and sucked the thumb of the other. She was flushed and sticky with sweat, and her fair hair hung about her red face in damp curls. Mary had stripped the child down to her petticoat but she was still too warm.

'Poor bairn,' the old lady said, and she got down on her knees on the rug beside her and started to sponge her down with a clean rag wrung out in a bowl of cool water.

'No!' Ruth said angrily and pushed Mary's hand away. Then she began to scream in earnest.

Mary fell back against the enamel bowl and tipped it over, spilling the water across the rug.

'Oh, no,' she breathed as the water drenched the screaming child.

But at least the novelty of it had the effect of stopping the screaming. Ruth began to laugh as she splashed her doll up and down in the puddle that had collected in the folds of the rug.

I'd better hang that out in the back yard to dry, Mary thought. Her smile was strained as she got to her feet unsteadily. Her bad ankle was still hurting her and making it difficult to walk properly. Wearily she went to the chest of drawers for clean dry clothes and a towel.

'Hawway, me bonny bairn,' she said as she lifted Ruth up and then sat down with her in the armchair. 'It's too hot to stay indoors on a scorcher like this. We'll put you some clean clothes on and gan for a walk.'

A short while later Mary left Ruth in her cot as she went to hang the rug in the yard and get the pram out from under the stairs. Irene kept it covered with a big old blanket to stop the cats getting into it. But even so, Mary knew that the lass was always washing it inside and out with carbolic soap. She was determined that nothing would harm the little sister she so doted on.

As Mary lifted Ruth into the old pram she knew she would not be able to help Irene out for much longer. At least not while the bairn was awake. Ruth was growing much too strong and sturdy for her old bones to manage.

Once out in the street Mary didn't know which way to turn. Up the bank to Shields Road or down to the river? Whichever route she chose she would face an uphill push either on the way or on the way back. But she would take her time and she wouldn't go far. She wouldn't have to, by the looks of it. The bairn was already less fractious and, with any luck, she might drop off and sleep and stay that way until Irene came home.

At the moment Ruth was laughing and pointing at the children, ragged and barefoot every one of them, who whooped with delight as they followed the water cart coming down the hill towards Mary and the pram.

As water gushed from the outlets along the side of the cart and spilled into the road, the bairns ran alongside, pushing each other into the spray and paddling in the cool stream as it flowed down the gutter, washing the collected grime down into the drains.

Mary made up her mind. She would walk downhill so that Ruth could watch the fun as it passed by. She heard the bairns screaming with laughter as they ran down the bank behind her.

As soon as she rounded the corner Irene saw the crowd on the bank. They were gathered outside someone's front door and, for so many people, they were strangely quiet. She glimpsed a uniform, a police uniform, but she couldn't make out what was happening. But she could hear someone sobbing. She thought she recognized the voice.

It wasn't unusual to see the police call at someone's house round here. There were fights between neighbours, children caught stealing, men who got drunk and beat their wives. And usually a crowd would gather to see the fun. But this time no one was gossiping or laughing and, as she got nearer, she could see how grave the faces were. Particularly those of the women.

And then she saw it was her door they were gathered at. Her first thought was that Seth MacAndrew had finally murdered his poor wife and the police had come to arrest him. That would make sense because now she realized that it was Mary Flanagan that was sobbing.

Irene began to hurry. She took care where she trod because she noticed the pavement was wet. It hadn't been raining so the water cart must have been by. Now she saw faces turning to look at her. Heads drew together and she heard someone say, 'It's her.'

She started to run and when she reached them the people at her door drew apart. She recognized Sergeant Eckford; he stood at the centre of the crowd. He held something in his arms; the limp body of a small child. A beautiful child with golden ringlets and wide blue eyes staring up at the sky. But Irene knew that those eyes could no longer see the sky. And there was a dreadful red mark on her face and down her white dress. Blood.

It seemed as though everyone held their breath as Irene stared at the child, not wanting to believe what she saw. The sobbing grew louder and Irene glanced distractedly at where Mary Flanagan stood, supported by her daughter.

'I couldn't help it, Irene,' she said, and her words didn't make sense.

'Couldn't help what?' Irene's throat was dry.

'The bairns knocked me as they went by – not on purpose, they didn't do it on purpose. I stumbled – went over on me ankle – me bad one. I just didn't think – I tried to stop meself from gannin' down and I let go of the pram. Ee, Irene, I couldn't stop it—'

'No . . . no . . . no . . .' someone began to keen.

Irene looked all around and saw the shuttered faces. She realized that the sounds were coming from her own throat.

'The pram just went careering down – the bairn was screaming—'

'You're lying!' Irene screamed, and Mary Flanagan stopped with her mouth open.

'What?' she said.

'You're lying. It didn't happen. It can't be true!'

'Irene.' Mary's daughter, Ann, let go of her mother and stepped forward. 'Irene, pet, come inside,'

Irene stared at her worried face. And then she looked at the stupid old woman who'd been making up such stories, trying to frighten her. And then, her eyes were drawn to Sergeant Eckford and that dreadful thing he was holding in his arms. It looked like a broken doll. It couldn't be Ruth, could it? It couldn't be her little sister?

Ruth was safe in their room where she'd left her just a few hours ago. She'd left her with the old woman from upstairs while she went in to town, to the bookshop to see Edwin Randall.

Irene looked around her wildly. She looked at the decaying houses, at the tired and shabby people who lived in those houses, at the dirty ragged children who played in the festering lanes that led down to the river.

She was going to take Ruth away from all this, wasn't she? She was going to work hard, get a better job, improve herself, perhaps marry a good man— No – wait – that plan had come to nothing. And now it seemed that all of it had come to nothing.

The thing in the policeman's arms wasn't a broken doll, it was Ruth. And Ruth was dead; she would never escape from this dreadful place.

Irene clenched her fists as she drew breath and then she launched herself forward. 'You stupid, stupid old woman!' she screamed.

Someone grabbed her arms from behind but she took no notice. She carried on screaming, 'Why did you bring her out? She was all right as long as she stayed inside our room. She was safe in there. Look what you've done! No, don't turn your head away – look at her – look . . .'

Mary Flanagan's daughter took hold of her mother's shoulders and pushed her towards the front door.

'No! I haven't finished! Come baaaa . . .' She was aware of her voice fading, of the world spinning.

'Go to your homes,' she heard Sergeant Eckford say, and carried Ruth into the house. He turned his head and said over his shoulder, 'Bring her in, will you?'

She couldn't see anything. Her eyes were open but everything was as grey as a winter sky. She felt herself falling towards the pavement but the person who was holding her from behind let go of her arms and swiftly gathered her up like a child.

'You heard the sergeant,' she heard the person say. 'Haddaway, the lot of you. I'll deal with this.'

'Mr Brady?' she murmured, and she tried to look up at his face.

'Aye, pet, Jack Brady.' He carried her in and kicked the door shut behind him.

Edwin Randall sat at the table in the MacAndrews' crowded upstairs apartment. The family had two rooms. Seth, his wife, Ann, and the three younger children, two girls and a baby boy, slept in the smaller of

192

the rooms and the two older children, twin boys, had to sleep in the larger room, which also served as a living room. And, since she had come to live with them, Ann's mother, Mary Flanagan, had slept in this room too.

Today all the children save the baby were out in the streets. Those who were old enough might even have been at school; only the baby was here with his mother. But Edwin could imagine the noise and the lack of privacy and he truly pitied the old woman. No wonder she had escaped downstairs to Irene's room whenever she could.

Now she sat by the meagre fire, kept burning in spite of the heat because that was where the cooking was done, and stirred the stew pot wordlessly, acting as though there was no one else in the room. She certainly hadn't responded to anything Edwin had said to her.

Her daughter, holding the sleeping baby to her body with one arm, placed a cup of tea on the table before Edwin. He looked down at the cracked and stained cup and steeled himself to at least sip it. He didn't want to offend her. At least he had seen the water boil before Mary poured it into the pot.

'She's like that all the time,' Mary said, indicating her mother with a weary nod in her direction. 'She helps me with the washing and the cooking but she won't speak, not even if she's spoken to. It drives Seth mad. I'm frightened he'll do her harm. I wish there was somewhere else for her to go and sleep before he gets back from work.'

The woman sat opposite Edwin and, still holding the baby, she sipped from her own cup. 'Ee, I needed that,' she said. 'I'm glad you called by, Mr Randall; it gives me an excuse to sit down for a minute. A break from me housework.'

Edwin saw Mrs Flanagan look up at those words and her eyes widen. For a moment there was a flash of her old self and Edwin, looking round the chaotic room, knew why. If Ann MacAndrew did any housework it was hard to see what it might be.

'Well, don't worry,' Edwin told the younger woman. 'I don't think your mother is physically ill.'

'How do you mean?'

'There's nothing wrong with her body – apart from the fact she's getting old.'

'And her ankle's not really mended.'

At those words the older woman seemed to flinch.

'No,' Edwin said, 'and maybe it won't ever be the same as it was. But your mother's problem is not in her body, it's in her mind.'

'That's just what me man says.'

193

'Is it?' Edwin was surprised.

'Aye, Seth says she's a complete loony.'

'That's not quite what I meant.'

'He says they should take her away and put her in the mad house.'

Edwin glanced at Mrs Flanagan quickly and saw her eyes flash with fear. But still she didn't say anything. 'No, your mother isn't mad,' he said quickly. 'She's shocked – and that's natural after... after what happened.'

'After she killed the bairn, you mean?'

A low moan came from the woman at the fire and Edwin said angrily, 'She didn't kill the child. It was an accident. There were plenty of people in the street, including the water cart man, and they all saw what happened. Those children didn't just bump into her, they pushed her over, although they didn't mean to. The police were quite satisfied that it wasn't her fault.'

'She should never hev taken the bairn out. Irene didn't like her going out.'

'It was hot. The child was miserable. Your mother thought she was acting for the best.'

'She never took my bairn out – or any of them. Her own grandbairns.'

And that was the reason for the animosity, Edwin thought. Ann MacAndrew, knocked about by her husband and not able to control her own children, must have resented her mother helping the downstairs neighbour.

'And yet it was better for her to gan downstairs,' Ann said as if she had read his thoughts. 'My bairns run rings round her and, once Irene started paying her a bit money, Seth liked to get her out of our way.'

And no doubt he would like to find some way of getting rid of his mother-in-law now, Edwin thought. If ever she became a real burden instead of a limited help to them, then God help her.

'Well, if it's in her mind will she ever pull herself round?' the younger woman asked.

Edwin looked again at Mary Flanagan and he saw silent tears coursing down her cheeks. He shook his head. 'I don't know,' he said. 'Let's pray that she does.'

But he doubted very much if those prayers would be answered. He knew that until her dying day Mary Flanagan would blame herself for Ruth's death and for driving away the only true friend that she had in the world.

'Have you heard from Miss Lawson?' he asked quietly.

'From Irene? That's likely. After the funeral she couldn't get out of this place quick enough.'

'She didn't tell me, you know. I didn't find out until it was all over. In fact I haven't seen her since . . . since . . .' Edwin frowned.

'Since the day it happened.'

'I beg your pardon? As I said, she never told me.'

'No, I mean before the accident. Irene had gone into town to see you, hadn't she? That's why me mam was minding Ruth.'

'To see me?' Edwin was astonished.

'Aye, her and me mam had sat up half the night making a bonny new frock for her. I hev to say she looked grand when she set off that day.'

'She came into town?'

'Aye, to the bookshop. Do you not remember?'

'No, I don't.'

He couldn't remember because she hadn't come to the shop. She'd never been there. This was a puzzle that wouldn't be solved until he spoke to Irene. If he ever found her.

'Anyways,' Ann continued, 'if anyone knows where she is it'll be Jack Brady.'

'Jack Brady?'

'Aye, you know who I mean. That big smart fellow who—'

'I know who Jack Brady is. And what he does. Why on earth would Irene have anything to do with Jack Brady?'

'I divven't know. I just know he turned up that day and took charge. Paid for the bairn's funeral, so the gossip goes, and the next thing we knew Irene had gone. The place as clean and empty as if it had never been lived in. There's new tenants now, a newly married couple.'

'Yes, I saw the wife when I knocked.'

'She's a canny lass, isn't she?' Ann smiled sadly. 'Poor little beggar. She doesn't know what lies ahead of her. Not the half of it.'

'It's all happened so quickly,' Edwin said.

'Oh, rooms gan quick, even on the bank.'

'I didn't mean that. I meant it was only a few days since I last saw Irene and now . . .'

'And now you can't find her. Well, if she hasn't left word for you, perhaps she doesn't want you to know where she is. Hev you thought of that? But, anyways, I shouldn't worry. That lass can take care of herself if anyone can.'

Edwin didn't say anything. He'd finished his tea so he thanked Ann MacAndrew and rose to leave. He had thought that he knew Irene. He had admired her spirit and her determination to better herself and care for her baby sister. But now he realized that he hadn't known her at all.

More worrying still was the nagging feeling that he was in some way responsible for what had happened to her.

Chapter Sixteen

September

Lorna watched her cousin, pale and attractive in mourning black, place an elaborate wreath of lilies on their grandmother's grave. Before doing so she had asked Lorna to help her remove those put there on the day of the funeral. The flowers had long since died, the petals brown and sickly, the leaves withered.

'Haven't you been here, since?' Rose had asked.

'No.' She hadn't explained and Rose, sensing her anger but perhaps not wanting to acknowledge it, hadn't asked why.

'Where are you going?' Rose asked in surprise as Lorna began to walk away.

'I saw a small wheelbarrow near that outbuilding, a gardener's shed, I think. I don't suppose anyone would mind if I borrowed it.'

'But why?'

Rose's eyes widened and Lorna smiled. 'It's all right, I haven't been driven mad by grief,' she said. 'I simply want to dispose of those dead flowers.'

Rose shook her head. 'I can't understand you, Lorna. You don't seem to be taking this seriously. To be . . . to be grieving properly.'

'Here I am, in black from head to toe.'

'Lorna! You sound . . . you sound so uncaring.'

'Oh, I care, believe me. Look, I want to help, that's why I'll take the old wreaths away and leave you to have a few quiet moments with her. If you believe there's anything left of her to commune with.'

'Right . . . well . . .'

Lorna could tell Rose wasn't sure what to make of her attitude, but that was too bad. She moved the discarded wreaths across to the other side of the path and then set off to get the wheelbarrow.

It had been raining all the night before and, although the sun was shining now, the leaves were still dripping from the overhanging branches of the trees, and puddles had collected here and there along the gently steaming paths. There was a sharp smell of damp vegetation, some of it just beginning to die. Recent winds had already brought down a scatter of yellowing leaves.

September . . . the weather was breaking and soon there would be more fallen leaves lying in drifts behind the headstones and all the monuments to the dead. The stone torches, the lilies, the wreaths, the pedestals bearing urns and angels and open books – the dying leaves would whisper past all of them before collecting inside the railings of the grander family plots.

Mildred Cunningham had been laid to rest in such a plot.

Lorna found the wheelbarrow and began to walk back towards Rose. The rusty handles were wet, and she felt the damp spreading through her gloves. They'll probably be ruined, she thought.

She hadn't gone far when she realized that the wheel was making a squeaking noise. It was the only noise to break the almost unnatural hush of the place. She controlled a wild urge to apologize to the respectable city worthies enjoying their final sleep at each side of her.

Rose heard her coming and turned round and glared. 'Really, Lorna,' she said. 'What do you look like!'

'Look like?'

'Don't you care if people laugh at you, pushing that ridiculous old wheelbarrow? Dressed as you are in mourning it's quite inappropriate.'

'There's no one here to laugh at me except you. And you're not laughing, are you?'

Rose's eyes filled with tears. 'I don't know why you're doing this, Lorna.'

'Doing what?'

'You seem determined to quarrel, and I just can't face it. Not now. Not in a place like this.'

'I don't want to quarrel with you, Rose.'

Although there is good reason, Lorna thought, as she began putting the dead wreaths in the wheelbarrow. It hadn't been Rose's fault that she had been the favoured child, but she had never failed to take advantage of her position. Often at Lorna's expense. Would I have acted any differently if it had been me our grandmother had loved and spoiled, and Rose that she hated? I hope I would have.

'I won't be long,' she told Rose when she had picked up all the flowers. 'There's a sort of compost heap behind that building. I'll leave the wheelbarrow there and then we'll go home.'

She left Rose staring at the recently turned earth of the family grave. She wondered if her cousin would even notice that there was one member of the family whose name was not carved on the arched marble headstone.

The inscription told that Mildred Cunningham had been laid to rest alongside her husband, William. A tall sad-faced angel carved in relief held an open book with a further inscription.

Here were the names of three more departed family members who had been buried in a foreign land: William and Mildred's only son, Roger; Roger's wife, Emily; and Roger and Emily's baby son, James. It was stated confidently that they would all be together in heaven.

And will my mother be with them in heaven? Lorna thought.

It had shocked her profoundly when she had discovered, only on the day of her grandmother's funeral, that her mother was not buried in the family plot, nor even mentioned on the headstone. After defying her parents to marry the man she loved, a man of another race, she had not even been allowed to rejoin her family in death.

Lorna had come back alone the day after the funeral, and searched the cemetery until she found her mother's grave. And there she received another shock. Esther Cunningham was buried here, she read. Not Esther Hassan, which was her rightful name.

The headstone was respectable enough but the grave was uncared for. Did my grandmother even come to the funeral? Lorna had wondered. As a child I didn't question that the funeral arrangements were never mentioned. Why should I? And over the years, my grandmother never brought me here although she must have visited the other grave.

For, after all, a grave is as much for the living as it is for the dead, she thought. We need a place of remembrance where we can stand apart from the world and recall everything we knew and loved about the person that we've lost.

Did my grandmother want to banish my mother from her thoughts for ever? Did she walk by the place where her only daughter was lying without a single tear?

Lorna had visited her mother's grave again on the following day to clear away the brambles and the ivy. She'd brought flowers and a vase, and she'd vowed that she would come again. But, as for the family plot, she would leave that to Rose.

They were both quiet on the way home in Maurice's new motorcar. Rose had arrived at the house in Heaton that morning much earlier than she was expected because she wanted to go to the cemetery and she wanted Lorna to go with her. She'd said Maurice would come along to the house later in order to be with her during the reading of Mildred's will.

The car was open-topped and Lorna glanced at her cousin, who sat very still with a blanket tucked round her knees. She had a naturally pale complexion but, today she looked almost pasty.

'Are you all right?' Lorna asked.

'Mm.' Rose nodded. 'Just a bit fragile. But that's natural in the circumstances, I suppose.'

'You mean because you're grieving?'

'Well, that, but also my condition.'

'Condition? Oh – you mean you're—'

'Hush,' Rose whispered, and inclined her head in the chauffeur's direction. And then after a long pause she said, 'I think you're supposed to be pleased for me.'

'I am, if it's what you want.'

'I'm not sure if I want it, but it's expected, isn't it?'

Not knowing how to take this apparent indifference Lorna said, 'Well Grandmamma would have been pleased.'

'I suppose so,' Rose said. Then she grew more animated. 'You should have written and told me, you know. It was a great shock arriving home and finding that she was dead and buried.'

'I thought about writing, but how would the letter have found you? You were travelling home by then.'

'Grandmamma had our itinerary, the list of hotels.'

'She never showed it to me. I didn't know she had one until Mrs Haldane told me.'

'Mrs Haldane?' Rose looked surprised.

'She wrote to me when she saw the announcement in the newspaper. She asked me what I intended to do about informing you. She had your itinerary too, but she told me that, in her opinion, the post was unreliable, that letters could be chasing you all over Europe and, in any case, it would be unkind to spoil your honeymoon.'

'Oh, I didn't know that.'

Rose fell silent. It was obvious that she had no desire to criticize her mother-in-law. Lorna wondered whether her cousin was fond of Maurice's mother, whether she would take the place of their grandmother.

'Lorna,' Rose said at last, 'I know I asked you not to tell Grandmamma about the present I was bringing for her, about the shawl. But in the circumstances . . .'

'It was already too late,' Lorna said.

'I see.'

For a moment Rose looked so sad, so subdued, that Lorna knew she had been right to lie. She was prepared to carry the guilt.

Mr Adamson, the solicitor, was not due for another hour, and Mrs Hobson had prepared lunch for them. Lorna and Rose sat together at one end of the large dining-table. Lorna barely touched her food but she watched, amused, while Rose enjoyed clear julienne soup, mutton chops in batter with potatoes, carrots, broad beans and peas, and two helpings of ratafia trifle.

'Mrs Hobson will be pleased with you,' Lorna said drily.

Rose put her coffee cup carefully in her saucer and looked at Lorna. 'Are you teasing me? Do you think I've eaten too much?'

'No, poor Mrs Hobson has had no one to cook for – at least not proper meals, as she calls them. I haven't been doing her wonderful recipes justice, so she really will be delighted that you've so obviously enjoyed the meal.'

'But you still think I've been greedy. I can tell by that superior look in your eye.'

'Rose, I'm not criticizing you, really I'm not. I'm glad you can enjoy your food like this. I believe other women are too sickly to eat properly when they are in your condition.'

'Yes, well, I don't find it so.'

'Good.'

'Lorna,' Rose dabbed at her mouth with her napkin, 'as you don't seem to appreciate Mrs Hobson, I think I shall ask her to come and work for me. As you know, we are still with Maurice's parents but we'll be moving in to our new house soon and I shall want my own staff.'

'That's probably a good idea,' Lorna said, 'but now we must go to the drawing room and see if everything is ready for the reading of the will.'

Mr Adamson looked like a schoolmaster, with his spectacles halfway down his nose and his papers spread out across the table Lorna had arranged for him. The fireplace was behind him but the fire had been kept deliberately low in order not to roast the poor man and his threadbare young clerk.

The young man's job seemed to be mainly to hand papers over to Mr Adamson each time he stretched a hand in his direction. Mr Adamson never took his eyes from the documents he was arranging in a neat pile but the clerk seemed to know exactly which paper was required.

The fireplace was large, and above it hung a gilt-framed mirror that was as wide as the mantelpiece and reached almost to the ceiling. From her position near a curtained alcove and behind everyone else, Lorna was able to see not only Mr Adamson's balding pate, but also the expressions on the faces of the people assembled before him.

There were not many. Mr Adamson had come to see Lorna on the eve of Mildred Cunningham's funeral and courteously explained that, as her cousin Rose, now Mrs Haldane, was the main beneficiary, he would prefer to read the will when Rose returned. Lorna had agreed. Why shouldn't she? Before she had died her grandmother had told her that everything was to go to Rose but that she was not to worry; she, Lorna, would be provided for.

So gathered here today were Rose and Maurice; Violet, their grandmother's personal maid; and Mrs Hobson, the cook. From outside the household was Mr Pearson, Mildred's works' manager, and Hannah Bates, Mildred's cousin. Lorna had met Mrs Bates for the first time at the funeral.

Mr Adamson had helped her to arrange everything. He explained that his formidable client had itemized everything about the day of her interment to the last detail. There was nothing much to do except carry out her instructions and send notice to the business associates, friends and family that she had listed.

Mildred's cousin, Mrs Bates, was one of the guests to be invited. Lorna discovered that she was a pleasant countrywoman who had seemed overawed by the grand people who came to bid farewell to her town-bred cousin. She remained uneasy when she returned to the house for the baked meats and, when Lorna had asked her if she wished to stay the night, she had told her that she must get back to her husband and the bairn.

Lorna had been surprised at the mention of the bairn. Hannah Bates looked a little old to still have a dependent child at home. Today Mrs Bates had sat herself beside Mrs Hobson and Violet as if she felt more at home in the company of the servants of the household rather than with her relatives.

Rose and Maurice sat slightly apart from the others, with Rose at the end of the row of seats. Lorna noticed that Rose made no move to make Hannah Bates welcome. She imagined that her cousin acted this way because, according to her, she'd had a thoroughly disagreeable time when she'd been forced to stay with her in the country.

However, Lorna also noticed that Rose seemed nervous and she could not think why. Surely her cousin could not imagine that their grandmother had had a change of heart when she was at death's door and had decided to leave everything to the granddaughter who had stayed at home to nurse her?

No, she would never believe that. So what was it that was prompting her to drop her head and glance sideways in the direction of the others every now and then? And gradually to shuffle her seat back so that she was shielded from view by Maurice?

If anyone had looked up into the mirror over the hearth, as Lorna was doing, they would have seen the way the new Mrs Haldane was fiddling with one of the black satin ribbons of her mourning gown, twisting it round one of her fingers and then untwisting it to begin all over again.

Eventually Maurice noticed and reached for his wife's hand. He bent his head towards her and whispered something in her ear. No doubt it was meant to comfort her but Lorna saw that Rose remained uneasy.

Maurice. Lorna looked at his reflection as he sat watching the proceedings through half-closed eyes. He and Lorna had not spoken. She had merely nodded politely when he was shown into the room. He had seemed relieved that she had withdrawn as quickly as possible to sit behind everyone else.

A stream of sunlight filtered through the lace curtains, spotlighting the tabletop as if this were a melodrama on the stage at the Theatre Royal. In spite of the solemn occasion Lorna smiled. The reading of the will was a scene that featured large in many of these melodramas and the more sensational novels that she allowed herself to read for light relief.

At the moment the only sound that could be heard was the muted sound of the horse traffic outside on the main road. The solicitor paused to sip from a glass of water. Then he put down the glass and cleared his throat.

His voice was as dry as the papers he rustled; Lorna soon found her attention wandering as he began to read the last will and testament of Mildred Cunningham. After all the preparation and the dramatic build up it really didn't take long. Lorna wondered if Mr Adamson actually enjoyed these occasions. Perhaps he had once had ambitions to be an actor and, failing that, he now enjoyed the drama of situations such as this and made the most of them.

In any case everyone in the room soon learned why they had been called there. Mrs Hobson and Violet had been left relatively generous bequests; Mr Pearson had been treated more generously and had been given greater powers to deal with the business on Rose's behalf, although he was only to advise and must defer to her instructions.

Mildred's cousin, Mrs Bates, had been provided with a small annuity. Mysteriously there was a provision that Mr Adamson, or the firm he represented, was to administer this annuity not only during Mrs Bates's lifetime but also after she died.

And Lorna herself? Just before he dismissed everyone, Mr Adamson said that the deceased had been aware that Miss Lorna Hassan should be provided for and had laid aside sufficient funds, but he would prefer to discuss this matter with Miss Hassan in confidence.

Mrs Hobson didn't know who to come to and, seeing that Rose was still hanging back beside her husband, eventually she came to Lorna and asked permission to go back to the kitchen. Lorna asked if she would send some refreshments in for the guests and was told that that had already been seen to and a light repast waited in the dining room. She would get Molly to take tea and coffee there straight away, but, if Miss Hassan didn't mind, Mrs Bates had expressed a desire to have something in the kitchen with the staff.

So, Mr Adamson's young clerk, Maurice and Mr Pearson set off for the dining room, leaving Mr Adamson to have a final word with Rose. Inexplicably Rose seemed agitated and she kept glancing towards the door. At one point Mr Adamson took her hand and shook his head.

'Please trust me, Mrs Haldane,' Lorna heard him murmur. Then he added that he would call at the Haldanes' house in a few days' time to see if, after she'd had time to reflect, Rose had any questions about the business side of the will.

Then, as he sat down again to sort out his papers, Rose, looking a little more at ease, came over to speak to her.

'So, it seems you'll be leaving here, Lorna?'

Lorna rose to her feet. 'Shall I?'

'Well, Mr Adamson said that Grandmamma had made some sort of arrangements for you and, in any case, this house will be far too big for just you. And besides . . . besides . . .'

'It belongs to you now.'

Lorna said that without any rancour and Rose relaxed a little more and smiled at her. 'Yes, but to tell the truth, I shan't be setting foot in here again. We shall probably rent it out.'

'We?'

'Maurice and I. Oh, don't look surprised. My grandmother has been very clever. She's tied everything up in such a way that the business remains mine, but Maurice and I are man and wife and should share everything, don't you think?'

'Of course. Particularly as Maurice has so much more to share with you.'

Rose's smile vanished and she tutted with exasperation. 'Really, Lorna! Why do you have to be so unpleasant? It seems Grandmamma has left adequate provision for you – although she didn't have to.'

'Didn't have to? Why do you say that?'

Rose was genuinely puzzled. 'Well, why should she? I mean you – er, your mother . . .'

'What about my mother?'

'She ran off and married an Arab, that's what! She broke Grandmamma's heart. She deserved to be cut off without a penny!'

'And me too? The sins of the fathers? I suppose that's what you're getting at?'

Rose drew herself up. 'I haven't the remotest idea what you're talking about. And I'm thoroughly sick of the way you've always acted so superior when you really shouldn't. You should have been grateful that Grandmamma took you in at all.'

Lorna was so angry that she couldn't speak. She felt hot rage boiling up inside her. She must have looked fierce because Rose's eyes widened and she took a step back and stumbled into the assembled chairs behind her.

'Well . . . I'll be going now,' she said. 'I'll send for anything I want from this house in the next day or two, but, er, don't worry, I shan't ask you to leave until you've found somewhere suitable to live.'

'How kind of you.'

Rose flushed. 'Well . . . look, Mr Adamson is waiting to talk to you. I'll go and join Maurice in the dining room but we'll probably be going straight home.'

'Right. Good. Goodbye.'

Rose retreated as gracefully as she could and Lorna was left wondering whether she would ever see her cousin again. Or if she wanted to.

Mr Adamson was still seated at the table seemingly reading certain documents but Lorna guessed it was an act. He must have heard every word of the exchange and was tactfully pretending that he hadn't. Lorna decided not to be embarrassed. She imagined that, as a solicitor, he must have been subjected to much worse on such occasions.

He rose to his feet as she approached and smiled at her. 'Miss Hassan,' he said. 'Will you sit here, beside me? This may take some while.'

'Some while?'

Lorna couldn't imagine why. Surely she was just about to be dealt with in the usual manner for the poor relation. A small annuity and a promise from her not to be a nuisance. That wouldn't take long.

'Yes,' Mr Adamson said, 'and I've taken the liberty of asking your cook to send in some tea and sandwiches. I hope you don't mind?'

'Of course I don't.'

Lorna took her place beside him and thought what a nice man he was. There was absolutely no need for him to be so polite to somebody so unimportant in the scheme of things, and yet he was treating her with as much courtesy as he had treated Rose.

Perhaps he feels sorry for me, she mused.

At that moment they were interrupted by Molly and Mrs Hobson herself, who hovered anxiously while the young maid put a tray on the table.

'Cold roast beef sandwiches and a bit of Madeira cake,' Mrs Hobson said. 'I hope that will do.' Mr Adamson smiled and nodded as if dismissing her but the cook lingered until Molly had left the room. Then she said, 'Mrs Bates is going to wait and have a word with Miss Lorna before she goes, like you asked.'

'Ah, yes. Thank you, Mrs Hobson,' Mr Adamson said, and the cook left the room, shutting the door behind her.

Lorna busied herself pouring the tea. She wasn't quite ready to face Mr Adamson yet. Now, in addition to the solicitor's manner, there was more to puzzle over. Why had he given instructions for Mrs Bates to wait and talk to her? It was to the Bateses' smallholding in the Tyne Valley that Rose had been sent in order to get over her unsuitable attachment to the actor Harry Desmond.

Perhaps now I am going to be banished, Lorna thought. Perhaps Mr Adamson thinks the best thing for me is to live out of sight and out of mind in the country where I can be conveniently forgotten about.

She watched as the solicitor helped himself to milk and sugar. After stirring his cup he looked up and said, 'Perhaps before we discuss business we should eat something and drink this tea. If you don't mind my saying so, you look a little tired. Of course, that's understandable.'

Unexpectedly Lorna found herself blinking back tears. The idea that Mr Adamson should care about her wellbeing was touching.

'Very well,' she said.

So while she nibbled at a sandwich, and then a piece of cake, the solicitor talked to her as if this were a social visit. He talked about the weather and the programme of concerts in the park – although, of course, he knew she wouldn't be attending any of them because she was in mourning.

Lorna smiled at that. 'I attend them whether I want to or not,' she said.

'And how is that?'

'On summer evenings, with my bedroom window open, I can hear the music quite clearly.'

'I'm sorry. That must be upsetting.'

Lorna didn't respond. In fact she liked to lie on her bed with her eyes closed and give herself up to the music. It was another form of escape.

Mr Adamson, she noticed, had made light work of the rest of the sandwiches and the Madeira cake. He dabbed at his mouth with the napkin Mrs Hobson had provided and carefully removed the tray to the far end of the table.

'And now,' he said, 'I have something to show you.'

Lorna watched, intrigued, as he took a piece of card out of his briefcase. He laid it on the table in front of her. She saw that it was a photograph of a beautiful child – still quite a baby, really, with an angelic smile and a mass of fair curls.

'Why, it's Rose,' she said as she picked the photograph up. 'Why are you showing me an old photograph of my cousin Rose?'

'It's not Mrs Haldane and the photograph is not old. In fact it's quite recent.'

'But then, who . . .?' Lorna looked up to find Mr Adamson looking at her keenly.

'You really don't know? You've never guessed?' He paused while she continued to stare at him in puzzlement. 'That's Louise Cunningham,' he said at last. 'Your cousin's illegitimate daughter.'

Chapter Seventeen

Maurice watched Harold Pearson and the young solicitor's clerk paying court to Rose. Pearson because Rose was now his employer, and the young clerk because he was obviously smitten.

Even in severe black, unadorned by any jewellery, Rose was beautiful. She had obviously been dismayed when his mother had told her that strict observance of mourning dictated the wearing of black for a year and that also meant no frivolous adornment of any kind.

Rose, overawed by Mrs Haldane senior, as well she might be, had timidly suggested that the tiny holes in her ears might close up if she stopped wearing earrings and his mother, still very taken with her new daughter-in-law, had smiled and told her that perhaps she could wear some tiny pearl drops. The pearls were a lustrous smoky grey and they seemed to shine against her fair skin.

His mother had also seen to it that Rose had the best mourning clothes that were available in the ready-to-wear department of Haldane's, and had set the shop's senior seamstress to work on making more. The new gowns would be skilfully designed to conceal his wife's condition for as long as possible.

Then his mother had brought grateful smiles to Rose's face by suggesting that, this being the twentieth century, perhaps they would be able to relax the rules in a few months' time for a young mother-to-be.

Both his parents had been pleased that they had come back from their honeymoon as prospective parents. His father, having secured an heir himself, would not be happy until Maurice had gone on to provide an heir of the next generation. He was most anxious that neither of his sons-in-law, chosen for their position in society rather than their intelligence, would ever get their hands on the Haldane commercial empire.

And what had Rose brought to this empire, apart from her apparent fecundity? Much more than she imagined. Maurice's father had had several long discussions with Mildred Cunningham before the match was struck and he was satisfied that Rose's contribution was more than satisfactory.

Adamson hadn't spelled it out in detail just now, he hadn't needed to, and in fact it was better not to do so. It wouldn't do if it became common knowledge that Rose now owned, not just whole streets of respectable artisans' dwellings, but also a large proportion of the filthiest, most decaying slum dwelling in Newcastle. No, with the current opinion amongst certain of the middle classes in favour of social reform, it was much better to keep that secret.

Now Rose sat at a small table with a glass of Maderia wine and a plateful of savoury pastries, managing to look graceful and fastidious as she devoured far more than she should do. Every time her plate was empty, either Pearson or the solicitor's clerk rushed to fill it. He watched her now as she raised her head to eye the cake stand loaded with iced fancies.

Blast! The young pup had seen that look too, and he was already dashing to the table. I'll have to intervene, Maurice thought. I know she's with child, but she really shouldn't be eating as much as this.

Too late. Her shabby suitor had brought the entire cake stand over to her and she had already taken three small cakes.

'Pink, yellow and white icing,' he heard her say. 'How can I choose? I know, I'll have to have one of each!'

The young man laughed as if she had said something very witty and even the stocky, tough-looking Pearson smiled indulgently. Maurice sighed. Well, at least she has the sense to restrict the amount of alcohol she's drinking, he thought. She had only taken small sips of the wine and he had heard her ask the young maid to bring a cup of very weak tea.

He had asked his mother to talk to Rose about her appetite but, once she knew that Rose was pregnant, the senior Mrs Haldane had been prepared to indulge her. 'She will have some strange desires at first,' she told her son. 'And remember, she's eating for two.'

But Maurice remembered that neither of his sisters had indulged themselves like this. Both Charlotte and Geraldine had been so concerned about keeping their fashionable hourglass figures that they had almost gone the other way and hardly eaten enough for one, never mind two.

Once when their mother had reprimanded Charlotte and told her she was neglecting herself, Maurice's elder sister had rounded on her and told her that 'eating for two' was just an old wives' tale.

Well, perhaps he would get his sisters to advise Rose. He knew that she admired them. Yes, that was it. But whatever they told her now would not stop her body changing and thickening over the next few months. And he didn't relish the thought of what she would become. An overblown rose, he thought, and the image drew a rueful smile.

At first it had been pleasant enough to make love to her. She was soft and compliant and her rounded body was at least shapely. Suddenly he had an image of her soft white belly and he felt sickened.

Lorna . . .

Strangely, for all the obvious differences of hair colour and skin, Lorna and Rose looked somewhat alike. Rose was slightly taller and heavier but they had the same bone structure. But Rose's delicate features were already being obscured by too much flesh. She had already begun to walk more sedately like an older woman.

Lorna was quick and graceful and lithe. She looked like a girl. But a girl with all the passions of a woman. It was almost more than he could bear to be in the same house with her and not to be able to take her in his arms.

'Come, Rose,' he said suddenly, and he strode over to where she was sitting. Something in his tone made her look up in alarm. He forced himself to smile. 'I don't want you to tire yourself,' he said.

For the benefit of Pearson and the clerk he acted the devoted husband. 'My dear, I noticed how distressed you were before.'

'Did you?'

Maurice frowned. Why on earth had such a simple statement panicked her? 'Yes, and that's quite natural in the circumstances. Coming back to your former home for such a sad occasion.'

'Oh, of course. And Lorna and I had been to Grandmamma's grave this morning.'

Why on earth is she trying to convince me – and perhaps herself – that her behaviour is natural? Her condition must have addled her brain. Maurice controlled his irritation and smiled as fondly as he could. 'You've been marvellous,' he said.

'Have I?' Rose looked surprised but pleased.

'Yes, I'm proud of you.'

Rose flushed happily, and remained smiling as she rang for Molly and asked for their coats.

210

How easy it is to deceive her, Maurice thought. She has no idea how boring I find her. As they said goodbye and left together he wondered how on earth he was going to survive the long years ahead.

Rose was surprised and gratified at the attention Maurice paid her as he escorted her to his motorcar and tucked the rug around her knees. Molly had informed their chauffeur that they were about to leave and he hurried from the kitchen where, no doubt, he had been sampling Mrs Hobson's delicious baking.

It seemed Hannah Bates had chosen to eat in the kitchen too.

Rose shivered with unease when she remembered her horror at seeing her grandmother's cousin here today. She should have expected it, she supposed. The stupid old woman would want to know if she'd been left anything in recognition of what she'd done. But at least she'd had the sense to keep her mouth shut.

Oh, no!

What if she'd gossiped, said anything she shouldn't to Mrs Hobson in the kitchen? Maurice's chauffeur had been sitting there. The gossip would get back to the Haldanes.

But no, Hannah Bates would know that her nice little pension would depend on her keeping her part of the bargain. And Mr Adamson had assured her that her grandmother had thought of everything. He'd told her not to worry.

'Are you all right, Rose?' Maurice was looking at her and frowning again. 'You're shivering.'

'I'm fine, really. Just a little tired.'

'Of course. When we get back to my parents' house I think you should go to bed and perhaps stay there for the rest of the day. I shall supervise a tray to send up to you at dinnertime.'

'Oh, but . . .'

Rose was about to protest. She would feel like a child if she were sent up to her room when she wasn't feeling ill. In fact there was nothing the matter with her physically. She'd simply had a bad fright when Hannah Bates had turned up. But she couldn't tell him so.

Maurice was everything she'd ever wanted in a husband. Tall and handsome and rich. He could give her anything she wanted: fashionable clothes, jewellery, and a way of life far above that which she'd been brought up to. And so far it seemed that he was prepared to indulge her.

She would have to make sure it stayed that way. Nothing must spoil things now. Maurice must never discover her past and she must do everything in her power to keep him sweet.

211

'You may be right, Maurice,' she said, and she feigned a yawn. 'I'll go to bed and stay there, so long as you promise me you won't miss me too much and you won't be bored with having to dine alone with your parents.'

'I won't be bored,' Maurice said. 'In fact, I shall probably go out tonight.'

'Oh.'

Rose looked up to find he had turned away from her. She thought of asking him where he would go but decided not to. She didn't want to become the sort of wife who demanded to know where he went every time he left her side.

But all the same, she knew she would be happier if Maurice were the kind of husband who would tell her such things without being asked.

Lorna heard the motorcar start up and drive away. Then Molly came in to clear away the tray and Lorna placed the photograph of the child face down on the table. She sat silently, waiting for the young maid to leave the room; irritated with herself for having so instinctively protected Rose.

'Would you like to ask for more tea?' Mr Adamson said, and Molly paused at the door, waiting for her answer.

'Do I look as though I need some?' Lorna managed a smile.

'Perhaps.'

'No, I won't have more tea. I think I shall have something stronger. Molly, would you bring the Madeira and two glasses? You'll join me, won't you, Mr Adamson?' He nodded. 'Good.'

Mr Adamson poured the wine when it came and he smiled as he handed her her glass.

'So why have you shown me this photograph?' Lorna asked after she had taken a sip of the wine.

'Because I wanted you to see what an enchanting child Louise is.'

'Why? Why do I need to know about her?'

The solicitor didn't answer straight away. He looked at her gravely as though he were assessing her. 'Because—' he began, but Lorna interrupted before he could finish what he was going to say.

'You're going to ask something of me, aren't you?'

'Yes, I am. But it's not me who is asking, it's your grandmother. Or rather she left explicit instructions.'

'Why should I?'

'I beg your pardon? Why should you do what?'

'You're going to ask me to live in a cottage somewhere and bring up Rose's daughter. Well, why should I?'

'No, Miss Hassan, that's not quite what your grandmother wanted. Hannah Bates is devoted to Louise and the child is happy.'

'Then what?'

'Your cousin – Mrs Haldane – wants nothing to do with her daughter. And, to be fair, your grandmother never intended that she should. When Rose confessed to her that she was with child your grandmother was heartbroken. She had such plans for her, and those did not include her marrying a second-rate actor.'

'Harry. Harry Desmond. Of course. Poor Harry, do you consider him second rate, then? I wonder, would it have made any difference if he had been a first-rate actor?'

Mr Adamson looked at her reprovingly. 'Miss Hassan, I know you must be upset, not to say shocked, but please let us discuss this sensibly.'

'Of course. By all means. We must be sensible. Does Harry know?'

The solicitor looked startled by this sudden change of tack. 'I beg your pardon?'

'Does Mr Desmond know that he has a daughter?'

Mr Adamson frowned. 'I'd be very surprised if he did. Mrs Cunningham whisked your cousin off to the country the moment she discovered that – er – there were the usual physical signs.'

'I see. But if my grandmother went to such lengths to keep this matter secret, why should she have wanted me to know now?'

'Mrs Cunningham thought it best that your cousin should put the episode behind her.'

'The episode. Giving birth to her daughter, you mean?'

'Miss Hassan, please.'

Mr Adamson looked shocked and Lorna relented a little. 'I'm sorry,' she said. 'None of this is your fault and I know that you are simply carrying out my grandmother's instructions.'

'Is that what you think? That I simply carry out instructions. Do you think that I have no feelings of common decency?'

Lorna looked at him in surprise. He was angry and paradoxically this made her like him better. 'Of course you have. Please tell me how I am to be involved. I'll try not to interrupt again.' She smiled and was pleased to see that he responded.

'The child's future is secure,' he said. 'Your grandmother has set aside sufficient money and I have invested it. But please don't think the arrangement was ever just a business transaction. Mrs Cunningham wanted Louise to be cared for by a member of the family and she –' he paused as if surprised at what he was going to say – 'she actually grew quite fond of the little girl.'

'I suppose that's why she took to visiting her cousin more often.'

'Very likely. And every time she went she noticed how like her mother the child was.'

Lorna picked up the photograph and looked at it again. 'Yes, I thought she *was* Rose,' she said. 'So, if Louise's future is taken care of, again I ask why I have to be involved.'

'Mrs Bates is old and so am I. Should either or both of us pass away before the child is settled in life, your grandmother didn't want her to go to strangers.'

'I see.'

'And we thought it best that you should know straight away rather than have the knowledge thrust upon you in years to come. And there's also the fact that . . . I don't know how to put it . . . well, one day the child might want to seek out her mother. And you must make every effort to prevent that. Rose must be protected.'

'Oh, of course!'

'Miss Hassan—'

'No, tell me. What right had she to do this? To ask me to look after the interests of this child?'

Mr Adamson didn't answer at once but he looked at her over the rims of his spectacles.

'Oh, I think I understand,' Lorna said. 'It's because she took me in when my mother – when my mother was dying.'

'She did. In spite of her disapproval of your parents' marriage – her extreme disapproval. But it's not just that. As I said, your grandmother had grown fond of this child.'

'Because she looks like Rose?'

'Maybe. But she knows that Rose will never acknowledge her daughter – cannot acknowledge her – and Mrs Cunningham found that hard to bear. She hated the idea that she could not oversee the child's welfare after her death.'

'She wants to exert control from the grave.'

Mr Adamson smiled. 'Miss Hassan, if you had dealt with as many last wills and testaments as I have you would realize that that is not at all unusual! However, your grandmother wanted there to be some family contact after she had gone. Obviously, you were the best—'

'The only!'

'Very well, the only person to entrust with the task.'

'What made her think I would do it? Gratitude?'

'She thought you would feel sympathy for a motherless child and that your integrity would prompt you to do the right thing.'

'My integrity.'

'Your grandmother admired your good qualities.'

'But she didn't love me as she loved Rose.'

Mr Adamson looked embarrassed and Lorna wished she hadn't said that. She fought a wave of self-pity and said, 'I'm sorry. I'm making things very difficult for you.'

'Don't worry, Miss Hassan. I'm paid very well.'

She realized that he was trying to lighten the atmosphere and she liked him even more. But his next words spoiled everything.

'Remember, for as long as Mrs Bates is fit and well, you won't have the day-to-day care of Louise, although your grandmother did think it might be better if you should take a small house in the country, not far away from the Bateses' smallholding.'

'And how am I supposed to do that?'

Mr Adamson looked as though he were going to say something, stopped himself, and, after a moment's thought, he said, 'You will be paid a small allowance for as long as you agree to act as Louise's guardian. It will be quite sufficient to pay the rent of a decent house and provide a pleasant way of life.'

'And if I don't agree?'

'You don't get the allowance.'

'Nothing at all?'

'Your grandmother has made no provision for you in her will. This is a separate arrangement for, as you may know, wills are public documents and it would not do for Maurice Haldane to discover the existence of the child.'

Lorna stared at him, hardly taking in his words. 'But my grandmother said . . . what did she say exactly? She told me that I would be taken care of. She also told me that it would be up to me to carry out her last wishes. She didn't tell me that one was dependent on the other!'

Mr Adamson said nothing. He made a business of arranging some papers on the table before him. At last he looked up and said, 'So, will you agree to become Louise's guardian once either Mrs Bates or I are no longer here to fulfil that role? Will you sign these papers accepting the allowance?'

'No.'

'I beg your pardon.'

'I won't sign anything. I won't be blackmailed. And, as that means I shan't be provided for, then I shall have to seek employment.'

215

She expected some kind of protest. She expected him to try to persuade her as much for her own sake as for the child's, who was at least financially secure, but he merely shrugged and reached for his document case.

'You don't seem surprised,' Lorna said at last.

'I'm not,' he said. 'I was carrying out your grandmother's instructions. I promised her that I would tell you of this matter first. She seemed to think it would secure your co-operation. I suspected it would not.'

All the time he spoke he had been making a show of putting his papers away. Once more Lorna was reminded of an actor. Now he looked up at her as he laid a hand on top of a sheaf of papers still lying on the table.

'Understand it was not because I thought you heartless,' he said.

'Heartless?'

'I didn't think you the kind of person to ignore the interests of the child.' Lorna felt a twinge of conscience at his words. 'It was simply that I was pretty sure that you would not be bribed. Blackmailed, as you put it. I believed you would feel insulted by the way your grandmother has tried to make you do what she wanted and I was right. It seems she didn't know you well enough. But she and I did agree about one thing.'

'And what was that?'

'That it was safe to trust you with this secret, whatever you decide.'

Lorna bowed her head. She knew he was right. No matter how angry she was now, no matter how hurt that her grandmother could make provision for another child and not for her, she was not the sort of person to carry tales or deliberately ruin another woman's life.

'I'll do whatever has to be done for Louise,' she said.

Mr Adamson didn't say anything. He reached for the papers he had just put away.

Lorna raised a hand to stop him. 'No, I'm still not signing anything. I don't want Mildred Cunningham's money. I shall seek employment, as I told you. You say Louise has been provided for financially, so she won't need anything from me except my promise to do whatever else is required.'

'Are you sure?'

'Absolutely.'

She looked up to find Mr Adamson beaming at her. Beaming, that was the only way to describe it. She was surprised and more than a little taken aback. After all, she had just made herself penniless, hadn't she?

Before the solicitor could respond she said, 'She must have hated me.'

'Why do you say that?'

'Her will. Everything to Rose.'

'It wasn't you she hated. You must understand. She never got over what she saw as your mother's betrayal.'

'Betrayal?'

'Her marriage to a man who belonged to the same race of people who were responsible for Roger's death.'

'I know. My uncle was a soldier. He served with General Gordon in the Sudan. At school we learned all about the Mahdi and his uprising against Egyptian rule. My uncle was killed during the siege of Khartoum. His wife and baby son died too. Only Rose survived.'

'Your cousin came to live here, a bereaved and sad little girl. It's perfectly understandable that your grandmother should have become devoted to her.'

Lorna was silent for a moment, and then she said quietly, 'I was a bereaved child too, you know. My mother died and my father . . . my father sailed away to seek his fortune and never returned for me.'

'And your grandmother took you in, as was her duty.'

'Duty. That's all it was.'

'Of course. She was shocked by your mother's choice of husband. Like many other people still do, she thought it wrong for the races to intermarry. But worse than that, your father was an Arab.'

'But my father was from Aden – that's at the other side of the Red Sea. He had nothing to do with the fighting in the Sudan.'

'Nevertheless, he spoke the same language and he had the same religion as the men who, in your grandmother's eyes, had murdered her only son. And have you ever thought of this? Having you here was a constant reminder.'

Lorna was silent. She tried to imagine her grandmother's pain and how it had influenced her actions over the years. Mildred Cunningham had been a young widow with a business to run. She had lost both her children in harrowing circumstances. In her eyes she had lost her daughter even before she had died of consumption.

Then she had been left to care for her grandchildren. One the child of the son she adored, and the other the child of the daughter she thought had betrayed her. Of course it had been difficult.

But I was only a child . . . I shouldn't have been made to suffer for things that other people did. For things that happened before I was born . . .

217

Did I suffer? Lorna wondered. Not in a material sense. I was clothed, fed, and educated as well as Rose. But I was always made to feel somehow different and made aware that I must live a life apart.

And to make it worse I have always remembered what a loving home *should* be like. My home with my mother and father . . .

But at least I've had my books. And I would not have been able to buy so many if I had not been given such a generous allowance. Lorna frowned.

'What is it, Miss Hassan?'

She became aware that Mr Adamson was observing her thoughtfully. 'I was thinking that, in spite of her animosity towards my parents, my grandmother had at least been generous in other ways.'

'How exactly?'

'I've never lacked for anything. I've been to a good school, I've had a generous allowance.'

'Of course. You can afford it.'

'I can afford it? What do you mean? I have nothing. I have lived off my grandmother's charity.'

Mr Adamson sighed. 'I'm truly sorry that you've been made to feel that was the case. But I was instructed not to tell you. Although, of course, you would have discovered your true situation on your twenty-first birthday.'

'My true situation?'

'Yes, Miss Hassan. You have no need to feel grateful any longer. Apart from the first two or three years, your grandmother did not have to spend a penny of her own money on your upkeep. She had no need to.'

'No need? I don't understand.'

Mr Adamson's hand was still resting on the other pile of documents. He pushed them across the table so that they lay between them. Lorna remembered something he had just said, what was it?

'*I promised her I would tell you of this matter first . . .*'

There was something else he had to tell her.

'And you will not have to seek employment. I am delighted to inform you that you have a fortune of your own.'

Chapter Eighteen

'Excuse me, Miss Lorna, but Mrs Bates says she has a train to catch.'

Lorna looked up at the young maid and frowned. 'Mrs Bates? Oh, yes. Goodness, is she still waiting in the kitchen?'

'Yes, miss. But she says she's got to go soon.'

Lorna gazed at Mr Adamson. He had just been going to explain his last startling statement when Molly had knocked and entered.

'Apologize to Mrs Bates and send her in,' Mr Adamson told the young maid. 'And tell her not to worry. We won't keep her long and I'll order a cab to take her to the Central Station. In fact you can run along to the cab stand and get the cab now. Ride back to the house in it, if you wish.'

'Ooh, yes, sir!'

Molly curtsied clumsily before she left the room. The child was obviously unsure of how to conduct herself and, really, it should have been Violet acting as parlourmaid.

But Violet had not been able to meet Lorna's eyes for a long time. Not since the night she had given Grandmamma Cunningham the letter and, lately, she had taken advantage of the turmoil in the house to get slacker and slacker about her duties. Lorna guessed that now she knew of her inheritance, Violet would be giving her notice.

Mr Adamson saw her glancing at the documents on the table and smiled encouragingly. 'Be patient, Miss Hassan. I will explain everything to you as soon as I have dealt with Hannah Bates.'

Mildred Cunningham's cousin was pleasant but almost speechless. She sat and nodded as the solicitor assured her that everything would be as before. Louise would stay with her and Mr Bates, and they would all receive the usual allowance.

219

He also explained that Miss Hassan had agreed to act as Louise's guardian should the need arise.

At these words Hannah Bates glanced at Lorna. They had never met before the day of the funeral and now, Lorna guessed, she was assessing her.

'I knew your mam,' she said at last. 'Yer grandma used to bring the bairns to the farm for holidays. Roger and Esther. Such bonny little mites, they were. They got on so well too, not like some brothers and sisters. Who would've thought yer mam would've married where she did.'

Lorna flushed. She was about to retort angrily but Mr Adamson intervened. 'That's not what we're here to discuss, Mrs Bates. In fact I think we've covered everything we have to today, and you can go. I've ordered a cab for you and here's a half a crown. That's more than enough to pay for it.'

'Thank you, sir. I'll be going, then.'

'Wait. Before you go, I wonder if there's anything Miss Hassan would like to ask you?' He smiled at Lorna and nodded encouragingly.

She knew what he was doing. He was telling her that this simple country woman had not meant to offend her. And he was giving her the chance to assert her authority.

'I'm sure Louise is well looked after,' Lorna said, and she knew she sounded haughty. She'd intended to.

Hannah Bates bristled slightly. 'Of course she is. You can come and see her any time you like – and you needn't give warning.'

Lorna softened. 'Thank you. But if I do come, I'd do you the courtesy of writing first.'

Mrs Bates looked at her suspiciously, probably trying to decide whether Lorna was still acting superior. Eventually she said, 'Is that it? Can I gan yem, now?'

'One more question,' Lorna said. 'Where will Louise go to school?'

Mrs Bates smiled. 'Divven't worry. We're not in the middle of nowhere. It's not over far to walk to the village school.'

'Oh, that's good. At first, I mean. But when she's older?'

Mr Adamson cleared his throat. 'That's all been planned for. Louise will go as a weekly boarder to the school you and Rose attended in Jesmond.'

'I see.'

Lorna hadn't really been interested in Louise's education. She had simply been looking for something, some question, with which to assert her authority. But, now that she had the answer, she found herself wondering about the child. Whether, after a country upbringing with unsophisticated people, the little girl would fit in with the rather snobbish element at her old school.

But why should I worry? Lorna thought. She's Rose's daughter, not mine.

Molly came in to announce that the cab was waiting and Mrs Bates took her leave.

'Now,' Lorna said to Mr Adamson, 'please explain your extraordinary statement about my having a fortune. I suppose you mean that my grandmother has provided for me after all. All that went before was some kind of a test, like in "The Princess and the Pea".'

' "The Princess and the Pea"?' Mr Adamson frowned.

'Oh, you know, the fairy story about the poor girl who had to prove she was a real princess. Did I have to prove something before you told me about my allowance?'

'No. Nothing so convoluted. I am not talking about a mere allowance. It's obvious that you have no inkling that your father had been providing for you all these years.'

'My father?'

Lorna was glad that she was already seated. Nevertheless she put the palms of her hands flat on the table top and pressed hard to stop the sensation of the room going round.

'Your father. I always wondered how much your grandmother had told you.'

'Nothing! She told me nothing! I had no idea that my father was providing for me. I even thought him dead.'

'Why was that?'

'Because my mother promised that he would come back for me. He didn't, so the only possible reason could be that he was lost or dead.'

'Perhaps that's what your grandmother wanted you to think. She never told me what she did with his letters.'

'Letters? What are you saying? My father has been writing to me?'

'Not for some time. Perhaps because he received no answers.'

'But this is dreadful – it's wicked. Why did she do this?'

'I'm not sure. She would never speak of it. Perhaps she didn't want him to take you away – she didn't want to lose you.'

'Huh!'

'Or perhaps she didn't want him to claim his daughter.'

'Revenge.'

Mr Adamson looked at her for a long time. 'I wish I could say that was impossible,' he said at last.

221

'But you can't. My father . . . alive . . . writing to me . . . and I never knew.' She stopped when the ache of misery in her throat wouldn't allow her to go on. Her eyes brimmed with tears that spilled over and scalded her cheeks. 'I'm sorry,' she said when she could. 'I'm sorry. But what can I do?'

Mr Adamson smiled. 'You can write to him.'

'You have his address?'

'Yes, of course.'

'Where . . . where does he live? Did he come back? Is he at our old home?'

'No, Miss Hassan. He doesn't live in England.' Mr Adamson frowned. 'Although he did come back once, but that was a long time ago.'

'Tell me – tell me what happened.'

'I don't know. You must ask him. But now he lives in Egypt. In Cairo, to be precise.'

'Cairo? I've been looking at the wrong maps!' Half laughing, half crying, Lorna explained about her obsession with books and maps of Arabia and the Middle East.

'He has an office in Paris but he is based in Cairo.'

'Egypt . . . Cairo . . . Paris . . .' Lorna stared at Mr Adamson without seeing him. 'My father has a business based in Cairo? What exactly are you telling me?'

'I'm telling you that you're a very rich young woman. And now that your grandmother is dead and can no longer control your affairs, I am going to see to it that you receive the money that is owing to you.'

Mr Adamson picked up the sheaf of papers and began to lay them out on the table before them.

'Now,' he said, 'I cannot possibly explain everything to you today, but let me begin by showing you exactly how your father has built up his fortune . . .'

The tide was out and Irene stood on the glistening wave-ribbed sand and stared out to sea. The day had been sunny but there was a fair breeze ruffling the waves and they broke on the shore in a froth of sandy foam. The only sounds were the harsh cries of the gulls and the splash of waves breaking, and then the long drag back across the pebbles.

The only other people on the beach were the fishermen getting their Cobles ready for the night's fishing. Cobles, that's what their fishing

222

boats were called. Irene had learned that in the short time she'd been living here.

She'd watched them on the beach below their cliff-top cottages as they mended their nets, baited their hooks and auctioned the catch when they returned. The women worked as hard as the men; and the women had the added stress of waiting, when the weather was bad, for their husbands' safe return.

Irene had never spoken to any of them. And if they were curious about the young woman in unrelieved black who had suddenly appeared in the village, they didn't betray it.

Theirs was a hard life, Irene had decided. Even if she had been able to make friends with any of the women, they surely wouldn't have wanted to hear her troubles. What was the death of a child, even a beloved young sister, compared with the tragedy they faced constantly, when fathers, husbands, brothers and sweethearts, whole families sometimes, could be lost in one night's fishing?

The breeze strengthened and Irene pulled her shawl around her body and began to walk back up the slope to the cliff top. Mrs Campbell would have the evening meal ready. And Jack was coming this evening so it would be something special.

Mrs Campbell was the cook-housekeeper and it was obvious that she liked Jack Brady. But why shouldn't she? He was a good master. He had high standards but he paid her well and didn't object when she said she needed extra help with the cleaning and the laundry.

Irene sometimes wondered how he lived at home. And where exactly was home? For although he had furnished this house at the coast with the very best Haldane's had to offer, making it both comfortable and elegant, he had never spent the night here. Not yet.

Even before Irene had reached the top of the slope, she saw him striding along the cliff towards her. He stood out against the skyline in his russet checked tweed jacket with matching waistcoat and trousers. Irene guessed it would be good quality, and, on anyone else it would have been the garb of a country gentleman but poor Jack, with his broad features and slicked-back hair, only managed to look like a bookmaker at the races.

Poor Jack? Is that how I think of him now? Irene wondered. Have I become arrogant because he has been so good to me? Because he has made it so plain that he wants much more than friendship and yet is prepared to be patient?

Whenever I think this way I should remind myself of how this man makes a living, of how he can afford such a fine house at the coast, and

I should remember that I am being looked after at the expense of other women.

If only he didn't look so pleased to see me . . .

'Irene!'

They met at the top of the bank and Jack took her by the shoulders. She knew he would have reached for her hands but she had purposely kept them inside the folds of her shawl. She stood within his grasp for only a few seconds before she hunched her shoulders slightly and stepped backwards.

He let his hands fall awkwardly. 'You look better.'

'Do I?'

'Not so pale. The sea air is doing you good. I knew it would.'

She smiled at him. What could she say? He said this every time, as if willing it to be true. Did she look better? She didn't think so. Every morning when she combed her hair the same pale face looked back at her from the mirror.

'But I wish you wouldn't wear black,' he said suddenly.

It was the first time he'd mentioned it and she was surprised. 'But I'm in mourning.'

'I know. But Ruth was just— No listen to me – Ruth was just a bairn. And not your bairn.'

'My sister. And she might as well have been mine. I was the only one to care for her after our mother died.'

'Irene, you've never told me. What happened to your father?'

She shook her head. 'I don't know. He was a sailor. He sailed away one day and never came home.'

'What do you think happened? Jumped ship somewhere?'

She turned her head away for a moment and looked down at the beach, at the fishermen and their craft which, sturdy though they were, hardly seemed protection enough from the ever-hungry sea.

Her father had ventured afar in a much larger craft. Had crossed deeper oceans. But he had always returned. And she knew that he had loved her mother and the one daughter he knew about.

'I think he's lost,' she said. 'Drowned at sea. Otherwise I know he would have come back to us.'

Jack looked at her gravely for a moment and then he said, 'Well, then, time to go home.'

Home, she wondered. Is this house by the sea my home now?

'Will you take my arm?'

Jack raised his elbow and she slipped one hand in the crook of his arm as they set off along the promenade. They had hardly gone a few steps when he covered her hand with his. She had to exercise the greatest restraint not to withdraw her hand immediately. His hand was large and his skin was rough. But it wasn't that. She simply didn't know what it was that made her flesh crawl at his touch.

'Mrs Campbell has a fine meal ready and waiting for us,' he said.

'Does she?'

'Mm. Gravy soup, roast pork and apple sauce, with riced potatoes and boiled artichokes. Followed by apple flan and cream. And I've brought down a nice bit of Stilton and a bottle of port wine.'

'Oh, no!'

'What do you mean, "Oh, no!"? Don't you approve of the menu?'

'Of course I do. But, remember I'm not used to such rich living.'

'I know and I intend to change that.'

'I don't know why you bother.'

Jack stopped walking and turned to look at her. 'Don't you?'

No, she thought, please don't look at me like that. 'No, I don't,' she said firmly. 'But shouldn't we hurry, or this fine meal will get cold waiting for us and Mrs Campbell will scold us?'

Jack laughed. 'As if she would.'

And as he said that Irene glimpsed the other Jack Brady. The Jack Brady who lived in town and made his money in ways that decent people wouldn't even want to think about.

The Jack Brady who had tossed poor Billy over Byker Bridge . . .

Edwin locked up the shop and retreated to the room at the back to eat the supper that his aunt had prepared for him, and to spend an hour or two with his books before returning to his uncle's friendly, comfortable and chaotic home in Spital Fields.

He pushed the hob over the small fire in the hearth to boil the kettle for his tea, then he opened up the hamper and carried the assorted sandwiches and cuts of cold pie over to the table where his books were spread out waiting for him.

He began to read.

No age group or class is immune to typhoid, or what is known in the slums as putrid fever, but it chiefly affects children and adolescents. Overcrowding, poor sanitation, defective sewers, inadequate washing facilities encourage the disease.

All the conditions to be found barely a mile from where he was now sitting, he acknowledged. And if even the highest in the land, such as

225

the Prince Consort, could succumb to typhoid because of a fractured and overflowing sewer at Windsor castle, what hope was there for the people who live in the poorest parts of this city where untreated sewerage sometimes flows and festers in the streets?

Edwin pushed his food away from him. Suddenly he'd lost his appetite. He began to read again: 'At the beginning there is little to distinguish typhoid from influenza, a temperature, a cough, a sore throat, a severe headache.' Edwin realized that his head was aching but he knew the cause to be tension rather than physical illness. He tried to concentrate. '. . . after about a week the patient displays the first of the classic signs – a rose-pink rash on the chest and the abdomen . . .'

Edwin turned the page. Wait a minute – where was the rash? Realizing that he couldn't remember a word of what he'd just read, he turned back and began again. Soon he knew it to be hopeless. I need something stronger than tea, he thought. He sat back and contemplated leaving the shop for a while and slipping up the road to the wine cellar.

No doubt, if he went there, he would find people he knew. It was a favourite meeting place for some of his fellow medical students and he got on well with most of them. He knew that he was well liked and he was even hopeful of involving one or two of them in his work in the slum dwellings.

Slum dwellings such as there were in the Ouseburn valley.

Where had she gone . . .?

Edwin slammed his books shut. The wine cellar beckoned. He would seek distraction in the convivial atmosphere of old-fashioned swinging lanterns, wine-barrel tables, and sawdust-covered floor. Perhaps after a drink or two he would be able to relax and return to his studies in an easier frame of mind.

All too often these days the thought of Irene Lawson was coming between him and his studies. He didn't know why but he had this nagging feeling that he'd failed her. That somehow he was responsible for her going off with Jack Brady.

Jack Brady!

Surely Irene couldn't know what sort of man he was? He hoped to God she wasn't involved in the way Brady made his living.

Edwin locked the shop door behind him and stepped out into the Groat Market. There'd been a light shower and the pavements were damp . . . just as they'd been the last time he'd seen Lorna.

Lorna!

Edwin groaned. If Irene was haunting his conscience than Lorna was haunting his mind, his soul and every particle of his being. Anything, everything, reminded him of her.

That summer day, in the shop, when he'd taken her in his arms to comfort her, he had been so shaken by the powerful surge of attraction that he had hardly known how to prevent himself from stopping her tears with kisses.

He would never be able to forget how much he had wanted to kiss her, hold her, make her his own there on the shop floor, surrounded by the dusty volumes that had drawn them together in the first place. He was ashamed of his own thoughts, and yet not ashamed, for he knew that he loved her.

He wondered when he would see her again. He knew she was in mourning for her grandmother, and he supposed her life would be changed. Presumably Mildred Cunningham would have made some sort of provision for her granddaughter, but now that her cousin Rose was married, Lorna would be all alone in that big house in Heaton.

He would have to be patient. He was sure that the lure of the bookshop would draw her eventually. If not, after a decent time had passed, he would call at the house. Why shouldn't he? It was time he made his intentions clear.

Maurice adjusted his homburg so that the brim threw a shadow over his face before paying off the hansom cab at the top of the Bigg Market and making his way down to the alleyway that led to the wine bar. The wine bar had once been the cellar of a priory. But that was long ago. The monks had moved on centuries before, when the district had become commercial.

Tonight it was noisy with students. They weren't the worse for drink. Most of them could only afford to sit nursing one glass or tankard for the whole evening – or until the landlord wearied of them and asked them to leave.

Maurice stood just inside the entrance and looked over the heads of the crowd. He saw one of his drinking companions sitting at the back of the long, low room beyond the overhang of a stone archway, and he began to make his way towards him.

He didn't push his way through the crowd, although he could have done. His shoulders were wide enough and, in any case, the drinkers were good-natured. Instead he edged around the wall as unobtrusively as possible. He was almost there when his friend looked up and saw him.

'Haldane!' he cried. 'Over here!'

Maurice grimaced with annoyance. 'Keep your voice down, can't you? No need to tell the whole town that I'm here.'

Bertram grinned. 'Instead of with your beautiful bride, you mean?'

'No, I didn't mean that. I may be married but I can still come and go as I please.'

'Compliant little woman, is she?' Bertram smiled up at him.

'She knows how to behave. She knows the rules.'

'Clever girl.' Bertram raised his glass. 'I drink to Rose Haldane!'

'For God's sake, be quiet.'

There was real anger in his tone and Bertram looked abashed. 'Sorry,' he muttered.

Maurice sat next to him on the stone bench that ran along the back wall. 'God, this cold stone punishes your backside,' he said. He rose again and took a discarded newspaper from the next table, folded it, placed it on the bench and sat down again.

'Look, I really am sorry. It's the drink talking,' Bertram said. 'I know that you like to be discreet about your – your trips to town.'

'Of course I do,' Maurice said. 'Why should a fellow wish to have his drinking habits – and the places he visits – observed and recorded by hoi polloi?'

Bertram frowned. 'Is that why you're wearing that hat?'

'You've lost me.'

'Well, as I've remarked before, you're hardly built to slip about the town anonymously. I mean your height – and that bright hair. It's so distinctive. No doubt you want to cover it up.' Bertram grinned foolishly.

'I merely thought I'd try the new style. Top hats are only for certain occasions now, and as for bowlers – well, even tram drivers are wearing them.'

'Get your point. Well, anyway, you look very modern. Very twentieth century. Now, do you want to share this bottle of claret? It's so good that I've had two already. You can buy the next one. Waiter, bring another glass!'

As Maurice sipped his wine he stared down at the table top moodily. It was true that he was conspicuous, no matter that he had never been a showy dresser. He knew instinctively that expensively tailored conservative clothes were flattering to his figure. And he favoured dark colours.

But his hair – if he wanted to be inconspicuous, that would always be a problem. So he'd have to cover it up. But, in fact, he hated hats and, if the truth were known, he thought the homburg he was wearing made him look like some sort of greasy businessman.

228

Well, of course, that's what he was. A businessman. But thanks to his father he was a very grand businessman who was fast aspiring to join the ranks of the landed gentry. If that family of butchers could do it, and get a title to boot, he didn't see why the Haldanes shouldn't follow in their footsteps.

Maurice sipped his wine and resigned himself to a couple of hours of idle chatter with Bertram. But, when it was his time to buy the next bottle, he would order something better than this watered-down gut rot that Bertram had been fobbed off with.

Eventually, and as Maurice knew he would, Bertram passed out and slumped across the beer barrel that had been converted into a table. Maurice left him there and edged round the room until he reached the door. Then he slipped out into the alleyway.

He felt no twinge of conscience over his old friend. The landlord would take care of him, as he did of other good customers. He would sweep him up with the spit and the vomit in the sawdust and take him outside and put him in a hansom cab and send him home.

The cabby would take the exact fare from his pockets, adding a tip, and then carry him down the stairs to the servants' entrance in the semi-basement of his parents' home on Rye Hill. His father's man-servant would clean him up and put him to bed. And, in the morning, he would have only a hazy recollection of who he had been drinking with the night before.

But Maurice wasn't ready to go home yet. He thought of his wife, slumbering complacently in his parents' home. Then of Lorna, more beautiful than ever, and who had barely glanced at him when he had gone with Rose to hear the reading of Mildred Cunningham's will.

He thought of how nearly he had made Lorna his and how she had spurned his offer. Apart from doing his conjugal duty in order to produce an heir and a spare on two, he would have been true to her. With Lorna in his bed he would never have had to resort to the kind of woman he would be seeking out tonight. At least that's what he believed.

But in one respect Lorna had proved no different from any other woman. She'd wanted a wedding ring. All women, it seemed, wanted payment for their favours. Society ladies, such as his mother aspired to be, were no different from the backstreet sluts, but instead of coppers, they bartered their compliant bodies for marriage, a house and servants, and domestic power.

Incredible as it seemed, his intelligent, good-natured father was completely enslaved by his cold, autocratic mother, even now. If

Maurice had been her husband, he pushed down a wave of nausea at the thought, he would have beaten her into submission long ago.

The idea excited him and he acknowledged the rising tide of anger that was even stronger than the desire for sexual release. He hurried away down the twisting alleys that led to a part of the city where he would be able to vent that anger.

Chapter Nineteen

December

Bella Charlton placed the tin Edwin had just given her on her scrubbed table top and opened it. 'Ee, that's kind of you, Mr Randall,' she said as she gazed at the iced Christmas cake. 'Did you say your aunt made it?'

'My aunt and all the ladies she could persuade to help her. They've been baking for weeks now and I've only just started delivering the cakes they've produced.'

Edwin smiled as he gestured towards the large double-lidded grocery delivery basket on the floor at his feet.

'Well, the folk round here will be grateful, I'm sure. And it might be the only bit of Christmas cheer some of us will get.'

'Why do you say that?'

'A lot of us hev had the rent put up, didn't you know?'

'No, I didn't. But why? Has the landlord carried out any improvements?'

Bella's laugh was cynical. 'Now, that's likely, isn't it? No, there's a new landlord. I think the old one died – I divven't know for sure – we've never dealt direct. But the gossip is that whoever came in for the business decided they weren't getting enough for these rat runs and wanted to bring the rents in line with the twentieth century. In line with the twentieth century indeed! It would be more to the point if they brought the property in line, wouldn't it, Mr Randall?'

'Yes it would.'

'Ee, but don't just stand there. Would you like a cup of tea? Don't worry, I can still afford me groceries.'

'Yes, I would, thank you.'

'Sit down then, Mr Randall, hinny. I'll brew us up a pot.'

Edwin sat at the table while Bella busied herself fetching cups and

231

saucers and milk and sugar. This was one of the few dwellings where he felt at ease with the standards of hygiene. Bella was a strong-willed, intelligent woman who had enough about her to deal with most adversities that fate sent her way, and was even making heroic efforts to stop her husband wasting his pay on gambling.

A few weeks earlier she'd told Edwin what had prompted her to take complete charge of the pay packet, no matter what this might do to her man's pride.

One day the rent man had called demanding his money straight away. Now, Edwin wondered whether this had coincided with the new landlord taking over. Anyway, Bella had told the man that if he wanted his money he would have to come with her to get it.

She'd pulled her shawl around her shoulders and set off for the small shipyard where Albert worked. Albert was up in the riggings but Bella had buttonholed his foreman and explained her predicament. She'd said that as it was payday anyway, how about handing over Albert's pay packet right now.

Albert, looking down, had seen Bella and smiled and waved. But a moment later, when he saw his foreman leading Bella to the hut that served as accounts office, he began to worry. Then, when he saw the pay packet in Bella's hand, he nearly dropped out of the rigging with shock.

'And why do you think that was?' Bella had asked Edwin. 'Because the rascal was earning a canny bit more than he'd admitted to, and he'd been keeping the difference back for his gambling!'

Bella had laughed when she told Edwin the story and she'd gone on to say that, ever since, she'd met Albert at the gates on payday and demanded that his pay packet be handed over unopened.

'And now, he plays fair with me and I play fair with him. I always make sure he gets a bit money for himself, a bit drinking money. After all, he works hard. He deserves it,' Bella said when she'd finished her tale.

Edwin watched her now moving about her spotless, welcoming home, and thought Albert Charlton a lucky man.

'Bella,' he said as he sipped his tea, 'could I see your rent book?'

'Of course you can. But why's that?'

'I'd like to know who your landlord is.'

Bella rose from the table and went over to the fireplace. She took the rent book from its place behind the clock on the mantelpiece and gave it to him. 'Well, you won't find out by looking at this,' she said. 'There's just the name of some company with an office on Shields Road.'

'That will do for a start,' Edwin said, and he made a note his diary before handing her back the book.

A little later, when he rose to go, Bella said, 'Well, you hevn't asked but there's still no word of her.'

Edwin was startled. 'Of who?'

'Divven't pretend, Mr Randall, hinny. I know fine well you've been asking about for Irene Lawson.'

'Ah.'

'Look, I might as well come right out with it. Are you sweet on the lass?'

'No.'

She raised her eyebrows before she said, 'Well, you should know, I suppose. But she was sweet on you.'

Edwin knew what novelists meant when they used the expression 'his heart sank'. His present feeling of dismay was definitely physical. It was all the worse because he had suspected as much and hadn't wanted to admit it.

'Oh, I don't think so,' he said.

'Stop kidding yersel. Why do you think the poor lass started helping you at the reading classes?'

'Because she thought the classes were important.'

'Well, mebbes she did. But why do you think she started speaking posh?'

'Because she was teaching.'

Bella grinned. 'You've an answer for everything, hevn't you? So why did she start dressing herself all bonny, then?'

'She always dressed neatly.'

'You know what I mean. She started to take extra care with her appearance. A lass usually does that when she wants to catch someone's eye. And you might as well know what folk round here are saying, Mr Randall. They're saying that she succeeded – that she caught your eye – but you realized too late and now you're kicking yourself for not getting in before Jack Brady.'

Edwin shook his head. 'Listen, Bella, the truth is that I am concerned about Irene. All the more so because she might be with Jack Brady. But it's not because I'm sweet on her, as you put it, although I like her and respect her. It's because of the sort of man Jack Brady is. Do you know what I mean?'

Bella stopped smiling. 'Aye, I do. And you're right to be worried. If I hear anything useful I'll tell you, I promise. That's the best I can do.'

In the last house he called at Ann MacAndrew was equally pleased to accept a Christmas cake and Edwin heard the same story about the rent being higher since the new landlord took over. The only good to come out of it, Ann told him, was that Seth no longer grumbled so much about her mother living with them because she was proving useful.

Mary Flanagan now spent her days sitting by the window to catch the winter light as she worked on the mending jobs that she'd started taking in. After dusk it seemed she worked by lamplight, and Edwin guessed that she probably gave herself headaches straining over the fine stitching.

It had been Ann's idea to tout for mending work and she'd told Edwin that she wondered why she hadn't thought of it before. That night her mother had sat up helping Irene with her new dress had first of all made her resentful and then made her realize that she could turn her mother's skills to advantage.

Edwin didn't mention Irene or his concern for her. He knew that if Ann had heard anything she would follow him to the door and tell him quietly so that her mother wouldn't hear. Mary Flanagan was still grieving over what had happened.

But when he took his leave Ann MacAndrew simply thanked him once more and wished him well for Christmas.

The trams into town were full. Edwin saw how unpopular he would be if he tried to get on with the large basket so he decided to walk home. If he didn't dawdle it should take only about half an hour.

As he walked over Byker Bridge he glanced down at the houses nestled crowded along the banks of the Ouseburn. From this distance, with smoke pluming up from the chimneys and rays of winter sun catching on the windows, the place didn't look so bad. The roofs were sparkling with a sheen of frost. If you narrowed your eyes and didn't focus too clearly it looked almost picturesque.

But the wind was blowing cold off the river and it wasn't a day to linger. Edwin found that he was keen to get back to his uncle's house. He needed the warmth and the love that was so unselfishly given there, and even the cheerful bedlam provided by his girl cousins.

He was looking forward to Christmas with his family. For they were his family since his parents had died. Some weeks ago he had decided to ask Lorna to join him there for Christmas. He had told his aunt about her and she agreed that she must be invited.

So, yesterday he'd called at the house in Heaton. But he'd been told by a young maid, little more than a child, that Miss Hassan was out. In fact she was out most days and no one was sure when she'd be in. And furthermore, she'd given everyone permission to go home to their families at Christmas and to stay until the New Year.

So that probably meant she'd be going away herself.

Lorna sat at the table in Hannah Bates's comfortable kitchen and watched Rose's daughter roll pastry with a toy rolling pin. She was a beautiful child, with Rose's fair complexion and blue eyes and a mass of silky blonde curls that Hannah had coaxed into ringlets and tied with ribbons into two bunches.

Lorna had arrived that morning with the Christmas presents. Isaac Bates had met her at the station. He hadn't said much, and as soon as they reached the small farmhouse he had mumbled something about errands to run, and vanished.

Hannah, wrapped in a large pinafore with her sleeves rolled up, was baking. Louise sat at the table, watching her with wide eyes. Lorna had not been able to resist giving the child one of her presents straight away. A toy baking set.

'You'll stay for a bite to eat, of course,' Hannah said. 'There's a rabbit stew cooking. I'll just pop this pie crust on top and we'll eat as soon as Bates gets yem.'

Lorna had not intended to stay any longer than necessary but the cooking smells were enticing. She agreed to share their meal.

Hannah glanced at the brightly wrapped parcels that her husband had placed in the corner of the room and said, 'I didn't expect anything this year. We've got nowt for you.'

'I didn't expect anything. But I thought that Louise might wonder if the usual presents didn't arrive.'

'She's too young to notice,' Hannah said briskly. 'She's not yet three. A doll made from an old sock means as much to her as an expensive toy.'

'Oh.'

Lorna looked down at the table top, aware that she had brought some very expensive toys indeed, and she wondered if they would be spurned. She was beginning to wish she hadn't come. She needn't have come. Nothing she had signed had laid down that she must continue with her grandmother's Christmas visits but, perhaps thinking of her own childhood, she had wanted to.

That first December she had spent in her grandmother's house in Heaton all those years ago had been the first Christmas she had ever

235

been apart from her parents. And she had never seen either of them again.

On Christmas morning there had been parcels under the tree – but none for her. There was no explanation or apology; it simply wasn't mentioned.

The next year Christmas Day was different. There were as many presents for Lorna as there had been for Rose. She knew now that they had probably been bought with money sent by her father, but at the time she had hoped that her grandmother had begun to love her.

She had never forgotten that first Christmas, however, and perhaps that was what had prompted her to make this visit. She knew very well that Rose would not send gifts for her daughter.

'You shouldn't hev gone to so much trouble.'

Lorna looked up to find that Hannah Bates had gone over to examine the parcels. 'It was no bother. I wanted to do it.'

'But there's presents here for Isaac and me as well.'

'It would have seemed churlish not to include you.' Lorna knew that she sounded stiff.

'What's the matter?' Hannah asked.

'Matter?'

'You're sitting there with a face as long as a fiddle and you're talking like a schoolteacher. All long words and nice manners.'

'I'm sorry,' Lorna said, 'but I feel awkward. I don't think I should have come here.'

Hannah sighed and her manner softened when she said, 'Of course you should hev come. But if you think I've been a bit unwelcoming, it's because I don't want any interference.'

'Interference.'

'I've had Louise since she was a baby and I love her as if she was me own. Isaac and me never had any bairns, you know.'

'Oh, I would never interfere, believe me!'

Hannah smiled. 'That's all right, then. Now, would you like to take Louise over to the sink and clean her up a bit while I clear up and set the table?'

'Of course I would!'

Isaac appeared and sniffed appreciatively as Hannah brought the pie out of the oven. He left his boots at the door and Lorna saw with satisfaction that the slippers he put on were showing signs of wear. She hoped he was not too attached to them, for one of his presents, along with a half-pound tin of Victoria Cut Plug pipe tobacco, was a new pair of slippers.

236

When she had cleared out her grandmother's writing desk, she had learned from old receipts not only that Mildred Cunningham regularly bought slippers and tobacco for Isaac Bates, but also what size the slippers were and what brands of tobacco he favoured.

Hannah, she learned, liked rose-scented cold cream and either floral bath salts or Parma violet bath powder. All these items, and many more, Mildred Cunningham had ordered from famous London stores. Lorna had spent a wonderful afternoon leafing through the latest catalogues sent to her grandmother from Harrods, Gamages and the Army & Navy Stores, knowing that she could afford to buy anything she liked.

In the end, not knowing Hannah and Isaac Bates personally, she had been guided by her grandmother's previous choices. But for Louise she had let her imagination run wild and ended up with toys she would have loved to have owned when she was a child herself.

As well as the baking set she chose a set of wooden building blocks decorated with letters of the alphabet and nursery rhyme pictures, because she thought they would be educational. But then she found she couldn't resist a plush lion on wheels with a beautifully curly mane and magnificent tail.

And then, a doll, with a handsome celluloid head and curly wig and a jointed kid body; the doll was advertised in Gamages' catalogue as being almost indestructible. The problem was that the illustration showed it wearing nothing except socks and shoes, so, of course Lorna had to order a complete set of the prettiest little clothes which came in their own cardboard travelling trunk.

When she had sent off her order she realized that she had rarely had so much fun. In Christmases past she had dutifully saved part of her allowance to buy gifts for her grandmother and Rose. She had long ago given up hope of receiving any but the most perfunctory of thanks. But just to imagine Louise's face – a child she had never seen – gave her so much pleasure.

Rose . . . Should she buy a present for Rose? Of course she should. But what on earth do you buy for a girl who has married the heir to Haldane's?

Lorna opened the catalogues again and began to leaf through. Eventually she decided that all she could do was to choose something she would like herself, that would make the present personal. So she had chosen a delicate little brooch in the form of a spray of lilies of the valley.

Yesterday she had wrapped it carefully and posted it to Rose's new home in Gosforth.

She did not imagine she would be visiting her cousin over Christmas.

Now, at the Bateses' home the atmosphere round the table was decidedly easier. She enjoyed her meal of rabbit pie followed by suet pudding and custard. Louise, she noticed, ate everything on her plate and, when the meal was over, she yawned and almost fell forward on the table.

Hannah caught her and then lifted her up. 'She'll rest for a while now,' she said. 'Do you want to give her a kiss before I take her up?'

Lorna was surprised and pleased by the question. She rose from the table and bent to kiss the child's soft cheek. She noticed that she smelled of soap, and freshly ironed clothes, and custard. Louise half smiled at Lorna and then put a thumb in her mouth before her eyes closed. Isaac already had the door open and Hannah carried her out of the kitchen.

'You'll come again, then?' Hannah said before Lorna took her leave.

'If I may.'

'Of course you can. Whenever you like. You'll be welcome.'

Then, as Lorna prepared to leave, Hannah surprised her by asking, 'Would you like to come and spend Christmas with us? It would be nice for Louise . . . and me too. I'd like a bit of female company. You can see Isaac doesn't hev much to say for himself and I like a bit gossip now and then.'

'Oh! I would have loved that, but the Adamsons have invited me.'

'The Adamsons? Oh, yer grandma's solicitor. Are they friends of yours, then?'

'I suppose they are. Mr Adamson has been very kind.'

'Poor lass, you make me feel ashamed.'

'Why's that?'

'I should hev thought of it. You and me's related, you know. You shouldn't hev to go to strangers.'

'No, it's all right, really. I wasn't sure whether I would accept his invitation. I didn't like the idea of anyone feeling sorry for me. But he explained that since his son-in-law took their daughter and their grandchildren off to Australia, Mrs Adamson dreads Christmas – just the two of them on their own. He said it would be good for his wife to have some company. I'm sure he meant it.'

'Aye,' Hannah said, 'he's always been straight with me about Louise. He wouldn't kid you on. Well, I'm glad you won't be staying in that gloomy old house on yer own for Christmas. Too many memories, I should think.'

Lorna wondered what Hannah meant. Did she imagine that she'd been happy there? Perhaps she did. Mildred Cunningham was her cousin, after all, and she had been warm and loving towards Rose and Louise.

'Yes, too many memories,' was all she said. 'And, in fact, I won't be on my own there much longer. After Christmas I'll be moving out. I've bought . . . I mean, I've taken a house at Tynemouth. Oh, and I've just thought. In the summer you will have to come and stay with me. We can take Louise to the beach. She'll love it!'

'Aye, pet, we will. The bairn may not hev a mother who cares tuppence for her, but she's lucky she's got you.'

Rose, now mistress of her own home, had ordered breakfast in bed. It wasn't that she felt poorly, far from it. Now in the fifth month of her pregnancy, her hair shone, her skin glowed with health and her eyes sparkled. When she looked in the mirror, she knew that she was still beautiful, so it was hurtful that Maurice hadn't been as attentive as she would have liked lately.

In fact it had been weeks, oh, she couldn't remember how long, since he had last spent the night with her. She supposed it was because she had put a little weight on. Although she was carrying the baby well, she couldn't deny the fact that her breasts were full and her waistline had thickened.

She covered the last piece of toast with honey and sipped her second cup of tea. When she had finished she wiped her hands on the napkin, picked up the small package that lay on the breakfast tray. She recognised the writing as Lorna's and she knew very well that, arriving now, just a few days before Christmas, it must be intended as a present, but she might as well open it now.

After all, nothing would spoil. Poor Lorna wouldn't have been able to afford anything very special. It was sweet of her, really, to buy anything. Yes, Rose decided, she would open it and then decide what she would buy for Lorna in return.

Inside the layer of brown paper there was a small gift card which confirmed that Lorna was the sender and a velvet-covered box, and, inside the box, a silver brooch in the form of a spray of lilies of the valley. Each little flower was made from a paste gem. It was charming. She would never wear it, of course – she had some much better pieces now – but it was a nice gesture.

'Maurice!' She looked up and smiled with pleasure as her husband entered the room.

'Rose.'

He came over to the bed and leaned down to kiss her brow. He was fresh from the bathroom and the smell of his aftershave was refreshing and also enticing. Rose felt her senses stir but, when he sat down on the bed, he moved back so that he was out of reach. Was it deliberate?

'Are you well?' he asked.

'Mm. Just feeling lazy.'

'What's this?' He picked up the empty wrapping paper.

'A Christmas present.'

'Then why have you opened it?' He smiled as if she were a naughty child.

'Oh, it's only from Lorna.'

'Ah, only from Lorna.' His smile faded.

Rose was puzzled. 'Why do you look so disapproving? You know what I mean.'

'I'm not sure that I do.'

'Well . . . you know . . . Lorna will not be able to afford . . . I mean, it will simply be a token.'

'And therefore not worth waiting until Christmas Day to open.'

Rose glanced at Maurice nervously but she relaxed when she saw that he was smiling. 'And have you thought that you might invite your impoverished cousin to spend Christmas with us?' he asked.

Rose was astonished. 'No, I haven't. Remember we're going to your parents' house for Christmas and staying until the New Year. And your mother has made it quite plain that Lorna would not . . . would not fit in.'

Maurice looked away. 'Of course.'

Rose felt uneasy. 'Look, Maurice, it's kind of you to suggest it.'

'Kind?'

'Well, you must have thought I would worry about my cousin being on her own – and that's thoughtful of you – but there's no need to worry about Lorna. She's always been independent. She'll be perfectly happy, wherever she is.'

'And do you know where that will be?'

Maurice kept his head turned away and Rose began to feel more and more uneasy. Did he think she was uncaring? Selfish? But why should he suddenly care about Lorna?

'No, I don't know where she'll be,' Rose said, and she had trouble disguising her irritation. 'But Mr Adamson said that she would be moving into a house of her own very soon and then I could decide what to do with my grandmother's house.'

'And what will you do with it, your grandmother's house?' At last he turned towards her.

She smiled. 'Oh, I don't know. Sell it? Let it to some respectable family. I shouldn't like it to be converted into apartments like some of the big houses. You don't get such a good class of tenant, do you?'

'And what does my little wife know of such matters?' Maurice was amused and she was encouraged to flirt.

'Well, I may not know very much at the moment. But I'm always willing to learn.'

She tried to inject another meaning into the last sentence and, for a moment, she thought he was responding. He leaned closer, his eyes widening, but then, disappointingly, he pulled away.

'So, where is Lorna moving to? Do you know?'

'I have no idea.'

Rose pulled at the eiderdown in exasperation and the box with the brooch in it and the letter slithered on to the floor.

'And have you not wondered, Rose, how your cousin can afford a house of her own?'

'No, I haven't. My grandmother must have made some arrangements – an allowance, I suppose.'

'And yet there was nothing in the will. It wasn't just that Adamson didn't read it out. I asked to see it.'

'Did you?' Rose was genuinely surprised. 'Why?'

'Well, I have to protect your interests, don't I?'

'Oh, of course. But are you sure there was no mention of Lorna?'

'Absolutely. I can only imagine that a separate arrangement was made. In fact, Adamson said as much in a roundabout way.'

'But what could that arrangement be?'

'Well, presumably, like most young ladies of her class, she had an allowance?'

'Yes, we both did.'

'That's it then. Whatever provision was made for her predates the will.'

'Predates?'

'Was made some time ago.'

'Yes, I suppose that must be it.'

Rose sighed. She was bored with this conversation. She was beginning to think that Maurice had only come into her room this morning to talk about Lorna, and she couldn't imagine why.

'Don't frown, sweetheart.'

Maurice's voice was teasing, softer. She looked up to find him

241

smiling at her tenderly. He took her hand and raised it to his mouth, and then he turned it over and brushed his lips across her palm. She couldn't stop herself shivering with delight.

'I'm only concerned about your interests, you know, that's why I've been asking such bothersome questions.'

'Is it?'

'Of course. Now, what are you going to do today?'

'I haven't decided yet.'

'Well, would you like to come with me down to the store?'

'To Haldane's? Why?'

'A new consignment of oriental carpets has arrived. The best yet. You know you said you wanted some. My father says you must have your pick.'

'Oh, I'd love to come!'

'Good. There's no need to hurry. We'll have an early lunch together and go this afternoon. My father is going to meet us there; you know he likes to spoil you.'

Maurice rose to go but then he stooped swiftly and picked something off the floor. 'Ah, your Christmas present from Lorna.' Rose held out her hand but Maurice opened the box and looked inside. He raised his eyebrows. 'Why, it's charming!'

'Yes, isn't it? The little paste flowers seem quite real.'

'Real?' Maurice smiled. 'You mean like real flower petals?'

'Don't tease. You know what I mean. They sparkle like real diamonds.'

'But my dear Rose, they are real diamonds.'

Rose stared at him. 'But they can't be. I mean, how could Lorna . . .? I mean, she couldn't afford . . . could she?'

'I shouldn't have thought so.' Maurice closed the box and handed it to her. 'But take my word for it, these gems are real.'

Irene held up the silver chain and gazed at the heart-shaped pendant. It was set with tiny diamonds that sparkled in the glow from the lamplight.

'It's beautiful,' she whispered.

'Put it on,' Brady said.

'No . . . I can't accept it.'

'Why not?'

'You know why.'

'It's just a gift. For Christmas. I divven't want owt in return.'

Irene knew he didn't mean that he didn't expect a gift from her. 'But you've given me so much already. You've brought me here, you've fed and clothed me.'

242

'You're looking after the house for me.'

'That's nonsense. Mrs Campbell looks after the house.'

'She's the housekeeper. You're—'

'I'm what?'

'For God's sake, Irene. You know I want to marry you.'

She stared at him aghast. He'd said it at last. All this time she'd known that one day he would. Whatever it was that had started between them the night Jack Brady followed her across Byker Bridge had led to this moment.

She had been in genuine terror of her life that night. Tired after the hours spent working at the hotel, responsible for the welfare of her baby sister, cold and wanting to get home, she had not recognized Billy Potts as a harmless drunk. When he had started running towards her and shouting at the top of his voice she had been terrified.

And Jack had saved her. But what devil had prompted him to throw the poor wretch over the bridge instead of simply laying him flat as he so easily could have done?

Irene knew it was because of the world he lived in. A world where a man wouldn't think twice of murder. The world from which he was trying so hard to keep her separate in this respectable house on the bay at Cullercoats. With its mahogany furniture, its oriental carpets from Haldane's, its oil paintings of the sea and the fisher lasses bought from the famous local artist, this was a gentleman's house.

And that's what Jack Brady wanted to be. A gentleman. The more he prospered from his criminal activities, the more he craved respectability. The more shameful his working life, the more he wanted another life, and a place to come to where, for a few hours, he could pretend he was a decent man.

Suddenly Jack reached for the necklace. 'Turn round,' he said. Irene did so and she held her breath while he fastened the delicate chain round her neck. 'There,' he said. It seemed she had accepted it.

He took hold of her shoulders and turned her to face him. This time she didn't flinch at his touch or move away. She stayed quite still, feeling the warmth of his large hands on her upper arms through the fabric of her sleeves. She looked up into his face, saw the question in his eyes and tried to answer it with a smile.

He had done so much for her. He had been there when she needed him. When she had been out of her mind with grief he had dealt with the horror of the aftermath of Ruth's death, then taken her away from that dreadful place, given her peace and rest as well as fine new clothes and nourishing food.

Had she been dishonest to accept such bounty, when in her heart she doubted she could ever repay him?

Could she repay him?

Through a blur of tears she saw his face come closer. She parted her lips in anticipation of his kiss and when it came she marvelled at its gentleness. He moved his mouth across hers softly, tenderly and she felt tremors deep within her.

She felt his arms go round her, pulling her in close to his body, and as the feelings inside her began to coil into a knot of what she knew to be desire, she raised her arms and placed them round his neck.

It was then that he pulled away. 'Not now, Irene,' he said, 'not yet,' and she saw that he was smiling. 'That was only a beginning.'

After he had gone she put on her warmest coat and went walking by the shore. The recent high tides had dragged the sand away and exposed some rocks that had lain hidden far below the surface for many years. They glistened, black and menacing in the moonlight.

She stood looking out to sea, a dark, heaving, restless mass of water under the cold sky. Eventually she turned and started to walk back to the slope that hugged the cliff face. The streetlights on the promenade marked the curve of the bay. The houses facing the sea looked solid and cheerful. At one house there seemed to be a party in progress. Every window blazed with light and she could hear music.

Irene remembered the night she had worked at the party at the dancing school on Heaton Road. She hadn't wanted to leave the warmth and the gaiety and go home. She had wondered if she could ever live in a house like that. Well, now she could. If she would accept Jack Brady.

But she remembered that until that night she had dreamed of another kind of life. Comfortable but not luxurious, warmed by the love of an entirely different sort of man. Edwin Randall.

She almost cried out aloud when that other memory came flooding back. The memory of Edwin holding that girl in his arms – Lorna Hassan. So beautiful and so clever. That was the woman Edwin wanted to share his life with, no matter if her father was a dark-skinned heathen, who had probably planned to jump ship as soon as he got to an English port.

Lorna would not have accepted help from a man such as Jack Brady. Irene knew that and the certainty made her bitter. But Lorna, for all her mixed blood, had never known poverty. She had lived in a nice house, gone to a good school and had never had to sit up half the night sewing so that she could have just one decent dress.

Her father might have vamoosed just as Irene's had done, and her mother might have died young, again just like her own, but Lorna had not been left with sole responsibility of a helpless baby. She'd never had to go out cleaning and scrub her poor hands to the bone just to keep herself and her sister out of the workhouse.

And now, what do I do? Irene wondered. Will my conscience let me stay here or do I thank Jack for everything he's done for me and walk out? And, if I do, where would I go? Could I ever get used again to living the way I used to?

There was another question that Irene suppressed almost as soon as it formed in her mind . . .

And, even if I wanted to, would Jack let me go . . .?

She had reached the top of the path and here, high on the cliff, the wind seemed keener than ever. Irene pulled up the collar of her coat and hurried across the road towards the house.

Chapter Twenty

January 1905

'Look, Lorna, I've caught one – I've caught a leaf!'

Lorna remembered her mother's voice calling to her. They had been standing here in the park. Lorna looked up into the branches now. They were bare and black against the sky. It was January and the winter was more advanced than it had been that day her mother had brought her to her grandmother's house for the first time.

Now only one or two shrivelled brown leaves clung to the branches but there was a mist shrouding the trees just as there had been that day in November all those years ago when Lorna was a child.

Shrouding . . . shroud . . . is that why her mother had shivered when she looked up and saw the enveloping vapour? Because she knew she was dying and imagined her own winding sheet, her grave clothes?

Lorna remembered how beautiful her mother had been that day, with the fur of her hat trembling as she breathed, and her pearl earrings luminescent in the winter light. Lorna still had one of those earrings; the one she had found on the floor of her grandmother's porch after her mother had gone. Today she had tucked it into her glove and she felt it warm against the palm of her hand. She wondered what had happened to the other earring. Had her mother taken it with her to the grave?

As she walked towards the ruined castle there were other voices. Voices she had never heard in life but could imagine. Those of her mother and her Uncle Roger playing there as children.

'I'm sure you will come and play here with Roger's little girl, your cousin Rose . . .' her mother had said.

Lorna remembered her feeling of rebellion, of rage almost, because she was going to be left with strangers. She had blamed her poor mother for forsaking her. And she had never played in the park with Rose. Her cousin was not the sort of child to enjoy climbing trees or clambering over old ruins. She had preferred to stay inside, even on the warmest of summer days, and play with her dolls and her dolls' house.

Had they ever been friends? Lorna didn't think so. And yet they might have been if it hadn't been for the way their grandmother had treated them. She had made it obvious in so many ways which was the granddaughter she preferred.

Lorna made her way towards the pavilion. The tea stall was closed but she sat at one of the tables anyway. She felt in her pocket for the bread roll she had brought to feed the birds. Just one roll wrapped in a clean handkerchief. She crumbled it up and scattered the crumbs. It wasn't long before a sparrow, and then another, came to peck them up.

As she watched them hopping around the chair and table legs she remembered reaching out across the table – this table – and taking the second leaf from her mother's hat, and her mother putting it in her pocket.

. . . *it doesn't matter that you gave your luck to me because you will have some too . . .*

She remembered the stains that the hot chocolate had made on her mother's white glove . . .

Mr Adamson had tried to explain to Lorna how shocked her grandmother had been at her parents' marriage. Many people believed that it was actually against God's will that the races should intermarry.

'And what do you believe?' Lorna had asked.

'We're all human,' had been his reply.

She sensed his evasion and said, 'But if your daughter had announced that she wanted to marry a man of a different colour, how would you have felt about that?'

'I would have been deeply troubled,' Mr Adamson had had the honesty to reply. 'Not because I would have believed the man inferior in any way, but because of the disapprobation of society and the difficulties my beloved Susan would have faced. Not to mention the problems facing any children.'

'Problems?'

'Of acceptance.'

'By society?'

'Of course.'

Lorna had thanked him for being honest with her.

The sparrows had finished all the crumbs. Lorna got up and tipped the chair against the table, leaving it the way she'd found it. She walked to the gates of the park and stooped to gaze across at her grandmother's house.

The road was always busy with horse traffic and now there was a growing number of motorcars. Lorna, distracted by a smart two-seater, wondered whether she should buy herself one.

Then she looked up towards the window of the room that had been hers. She'd made the room a refuge, filled with books and maps and dreams. Dreams of how happy she would be when her father came for her at last.

Above the noise of the horses' hoofs and the motor traffic she heard her own voice echoing across the years.

'*How long will I have to stay here?*'

'*Until your father comes home.*'

'*Will he know I'm here? Will he find me?*'

'*Don't worry, sweetheart, I'll make sure he knows where to find you . . .*'

But her father had never come to take her away from this hateful place. She had worried for years that her mother had never told him where she was. Then she thought he had forgotten her. That he didn't want her. That he must be dead.

But now she knew there was another explanation. Somehow her grandmother had interfered, had stopped her father coming to claim her. Mr Adamson had told her that she could write to her father but, strangely she hadn't been able to. Not at first. After all these years she simply hadn't known what to say.

If she had still been a child it would have been easy. She could have written to the father she knew as a child, using the words of a child. But, now she was a grown woman. A woman her father didn't know. And she didn't know him, now, did she?

It was only when she remembered how much she had loved him, still loved him, that she had been able to write a simple letter and send it to his office in Paris. Mr Adamson did not have his home address in Cairo. She had written,

My Dear Father,
My grandmother, Mildred Cunningham, has died and I have only just learned that you have continued to care and provide for me. I do not know why she kept all knowledge of you from me but I would dearly like to hear from you.
    Your loving daughter,
    Lorna

Now she awaited his answer.

248

Lorna waited until there was a lull in the traffic and crossed the road, remembering as she did, how her mother and she had run across together. The front door of her grandmother's house was closed but she didn't open it. She took the keys out of her pocket and slipped them through the letter box. Mrs Hobson would give them to Rose.

She stooped to pick up the small suitcase she had left on the step and hurried away down the path. She didn't look back.

'Of course, we've developed the designs to suit Western tastes,' Raoul Baudet said.

Maurice and his visitor faced each other across the polished surface of the desk in his father's office at Haldane's. He had been entrusted with dealing with the representative of Orientale, the trading company that supplied Haldane's with oriental carpets.

'The latest designs are proving very popular with our customers,' Maurice said. 'Tell me, how've you done it?'

The winter sun streamed in through the window behind him and Maurice was able to examine the Frenchman closely; whereas his visitor had to half close his eyes against the light. The business card he had proffered announced that he was a partner in the company.

Monsieur Baudet was middle-aged, elegantly dressed and confident. As well he might be considering how successful his company was. He smiled and gestured expansively.

'By employing designers who've been working in the English carpet industry,' he said. 'Combining their knowledge of what looks pleasing in an English home with the age-old weaving skills to be found in Persia could not fail to produce something of great value.'

'And who decided to do this?'

'The founder of our firm, of course.'

'The founder?'

'Yes, as you may know, he was a trader of spices, brassware, leather goods, rugs, tapestries, wall hangings – anything to satisfy the growing demand for luxuries. He had already grown wealthy. But when he saw how popular the carpets were, he decided to make that his main concern.'

'So now, as well as continuing to trade in other goods, he now manufactures carpets?' Maurice asked.

'He opened a workshop in Sultanabad, employed weavers with traditional skills, using hand-spun yarn and traditional dyes. And, as I told you, the combination of Eastern weavers and Western designers has proved to be an inspiration.'

249

'And who is this intuitive entrepreneur?'

Monsieur Baudet smiled. 'He is my brother-in-law. Now, Monsieur Haldane, perhaps I could direct your attention to the order book?'

After the man had taken his leave, Maurice realized that he still didn't know the name of the founder and director of Orientale. He made a note to ask his secretary to pull out the file containing all the correspondence with that firm. The names of the directors should be somewhere – perhaps on a letterhead.

In fact, that's where he thought he'd seen the name, some time ago, without then realizing its significance.

Lorna and Mr Adamson stood in a large, empty room on the first floor of her new home in Tynemouth.

'What do you think?' she asked him.

'You've made an excellent choice,' he replied.

'I must thank you for finding a list of suitable properties and guiding me through the purchase of this one. And also for persuading Captain and Mrs Carr to leave some basic items of furniture.'

'They didn't need as much for their new home. Now that the captain has retired, Mrs Carr wants a simpler décor.'

Lorna's footsteps echoed on the bare floorboards as she walked over to the window. 'I wonder how many times she stood here watching for his ship to come home,' she said. 'Look, you can see the mouth of the river, ships coming and going with the tides.'

'When it's not foggy like it is today,' Mr Adamson said as he came up behind her.

Lorna smiled and they both leaned forward and peered out of the window. Immediately in front of this row of grand terraced houses, at the other side of the road, there was a short expanse of grass-covered headland before low cliffs dropped steeply down to a narrow strip of beach at the mouth of the River Tyne. From here, on a clear day, Lorna could see the north and south piers and also the town at the other side, South Shields, where she had been born.

'It's eerie at nights in weather like this, you know,' Lorna said. 'When I lie in bed I can hear the foghorns on the ships and the clanging of the bell on the buoy marking the Black Midden rocks.'

'Aren't you lonely?'

'No, I've been too busy. And, when I do have time to sit down, I've got my books.'

'But, nevertheless, I don't like the idea of your being alone here.'

'But I'm not alone. I have a cook-housekeeper, a parlour maid and a

250

maid of all work as well as a visiting laundrywoman and a gardener. Which seems excessive for one young woman, don't you think?'

'There's no need to feel guilty about that, Miss Hassan. You are providing honest employment. How else would some of these respectable women live if they could not find work in big houses such as yours? And I warrant you probably spend more on provisions for their table than you do for you own.'

Lorna smiled in acknowledgement and then she said, 'But I know what you meant about my being alone. You're worried that by moving to the coast I've cut myself off from family and friends. Well, I don't imagine I'll be seeing much of Rose, and as for the one good friend I have, it's easy enough to get into town on the train, isn't it?'

'And may I ask who that friend is? Forgive me, if these questions seem intrusive but, since you stayed with my wife and me at Christmas, we have grown fond of you.'

'I know. And I'm grateful. The friend I meant is Edwin Randall, whose uncle owns the bookshop in the Groat Market. And I have to admit that, over the last few months, I've neglected that friendship shamefully. Very soon I must make the excuse of buying some new books to see whether he'll understand and forgive me.'

'If he's a true friend he will. But, meanwhile – and I assure you you don't have to agree to this – my wife said I must tell you that it would give her great pleasure if you would allow her to help you choose the furnishings for this house.'

'Oh, but I'd love that. You must bring her here to visit me as soon as she likes. I'll make sure all the fires are lit and we shall go from room to room and she will give me her advice. Then, if she wishes, we will go to Bainbridge's and Fenwick's together – I shan't be going to Haldane's.'

'No, I understand.' Mr Adamson looked at her and, for a moment, it seemed as though his eyes had filled with tears. 'Thank you, Miss Hassan, you're very kind.'

'I think by now you should call me Lorna,' she said. 'And I don't know why you call me kind for accepting help.'

'Because you have visited us and you know as well as I do that my dear wife has no idea of fashion, or colour or style, and that she has made the offer because, lacking the company of our own darling Susan, she has come to regard you almost as a daughter.'

'Almost a daughter,' Lorna said. 'I like that.' She sighed. 'And now, the question that I've been avoiding. Have you heard from my father, yet?'

251

'No. I imagine your letter will have reached him in Egypt by now and his reply should be on its way. As soon as it arrives at my office I shall bring it to you, don't worry. And now I must get back to town. Perhaps you'd like to come with me and visit your friend in the bookshop?'

'No, not today. There's another visit I have to make first. Something I've been promising myself for some time.'

Lorna was glad of the deep fur collar of her coat, which could be pulled up on to her head like a hood. The wind was keen and the water choppy. The ferry boat rose and dipped down again crazily as it made its way across the river from north to south.

There was also a fine drizzle and the warmly lit passenger saloon was full of cold wet people, so Lorna sat almost alone on one of the slatted benches on the upper deck. Underneath the benches, a notice told her, were the stacked lifebelts in case there should be a mishap. The only other passengers on the deck were a young couple, sitting close, and an older man with a small, shivering black and white dog on his knee.

The air smelled cold. But there was also the underlying odour of oil and fish and brine. Lorna closed her eyes and felt the fine pinpricks of moisture on her face. She could hear the chug of the engines and the slap of the waves against the side, and also the unchanging call of the herring gulls. They sounded exactly the same as they had that day when she and her mother had made the crossing together, going the other way. Only her mother had returned.

Lorna felt the moisture running down her cheeks and knew it to be tears as she imagined her mother's lonely passage back across the river. What must it have been like for her, still a young woman, to have had to leave the daughter she loved with a woman who had become a stranger, and return to die alone?

Had she hoped that her husband, a man she had loved so much that she had defied convention to marry him, would come home in time to hold her in his arms before she died? In time to tell her that he loved her and that he would always care for their beloved child?

Her mother had trusted Said Hassan. She had believed that he would never desert her, abandon her. He could not have known how gravely ill she was when he had sailed away. How swiftly she would succumb to the consumption that was rife in the poorer parts of town.

There was a jolt as the ferry bumped into the landing dock and Lorna opened her eyes. She could hear the engines working overtime as the skipper manoeuvred his craft into the exact position required to lower the ramp. She lingered on the upper deck and watched as the other passengers disembarked and streamed up the slope towards the market square.

As Lorna followed the crowd she realized that she was looking for someone. Someone who should have been standing waiting for her.

'*I'll hev yer supper ready when you get back.*'

Who had said that?

Hilda . . .

Lorna remembered the tall thin woman who had worked for them. But she had been more than a servant. She had been a friend. Hilda would have been waiting for her mother; she would have looked after her until . . . until . . .

Lorna stumbled slightly and she heard a dog yelp. Oh, no, she had trodden on the little black and white dog. She looked down to see him holding up a paw.

'I'm sorry,' she said. 'I didn't mean to hurt you.'

'That's all right, lass.' The dog's owner bent down and scooped the dog up. 'It was his own fault. Always getting under people's feet.'

Lorna watched as the man tucked the dog inside his coat and walked away. But he'd only taken a few steps when he turned and said, 'You look a bit lost, pet. Do you know where yer gannin'? Can I help you?'

'No, it's all right. I think I can remember the way.'

It didn't take long for Lorna to find the streets she had known as a child, but try as she might she could not find the house she used to live in; her old home. I should have come long before now, she thought, while my memories were fresh, while I could have turned the right corner without thinking and walked the right number of steps along the pavement to stop instinctively at the right front door.

She was aware that she attracted curious looks from passers-by. Not only was she a stranger but she was a young, well-dressed woman walking here alone. And yet she did not feel afraid.

The people she saw were mostly men. She knew them to be sailors of many nationalities: Arab, Indian, Malay, West Indian and West African as well as Chinese. They sought lodgings in this area near the river, each group staying mainly with their own kind to talk their own language, eat foods that were familiar to them and also to seek comfort and friendship. A few of them had made permanent homes here. As her father had done.

Some of the doors she passed were open and she could look straight into communal rooms where groups of men sat cross-legged on the clean-swept floorboards. In one house she passed they were playing dominoes. In another house she saw a group sitting round one man who was reading the newspaper to them.

In another, a similar group seemed to be listening to a storyteller. Lorna stopped to listen. She couldn't understand a word and yet the rhythms of the man's speech, the cadences, suggested he was reciting poetry.

Lorna lingered and, when he had finished, another man took up an instrument that looked like a flute. When he began to play the music was melancholy; different from anything she'd heard for many years. And it reached straight into her heart and her soul.

All the men she saw were clothed in respectable jackets and trousers of European cut. Only the language in which they conversed, their dark complexions and the easy way in which they moved revealed that they came from far away.

And then, when she had searched the streets for nearly an hour, she came to the end of a road where she could go no further. A high brick wall blocked the way, and at the other side of the wall Lorna could glimpse the roofs of riverside warehouses.

She had already turned to retrace her steps when she saw it: the narrow lane squeezed in between the gable wall of the end terraced house and the brick wall. Without thinking she walked over to it. She began to hurry along the cracked paving where weeds sprouted. And she didn't need to count the steps before she stopped at the front door of her old home.

She looked up. The windows were clean. The net curtains that hung there looked freshly washed. The door brasses were polished and the doorstep soapstoned. Everything looked as it had when she had lived here.

Without thinking she raised her hand to knock at the door and then fell back, hesitantly. What would she say if anyone answered? She contemplated turning to run like a child playing knockie-nine-doors, but it was too late. The door opened and a tall, thin woman stood there looking at her questioningly.

The questioning look turned into a frown, and then the woman's eyes widened with shock.

'Lorna?' she gasped. 'Is it you?'

'Hilda . . . you're here . . . I can't believe it!'

They stared at each other for a moment, and then the older woman stepped back and gestured for her to enter. 'Hawway inside, pet,' she said. 'It's too cold to stand talking here.'

Chapter Twenty-One

Hilda led the way along a narrow passage to the kitchen at the back of the house. A fire burned in the range and a clean oilcloth covered the table. Lorna removed her coat and sat by the fire while Hilda made them a simple meal of tea and bread and jam.

'I'd hev made a few scones if I'd known . . .' Hilda began, and they looked at each other, not knowing what to say.

But when the fire and the hot sweet tea had warmed Lorna, her mother's old friend began to talk without being prompted.

'I stayed with yer ma until the end.'

'I seem to remember my grandmother saying something about my mother going into hospital,' Lorna said.

'Aye, Mrs Cunningham made it clear that she was prepared to pay whatever was necessary when the . . . when the end was near. I was supposed to write and tell her. But yer ma didn't want to spend her last days among strangers. She wanted to stay here with me. And I believe she hoped against hope that she might last out until yer dad came home.'

'But she didn't.'

'No. She didn't live much beyond Christmas. In fact, after she came home from yer grandma's house that day she seemed to fade fast.'

'I remember your coming to my grandmother's house to tell me. I don't suppose I really understood what it meant. I thought you would be able to take me back with you.'

'I know, pet. I wished I could hev done.'

'Why did she leave me there? We could have been together for just a little longer.'

'You know why, Lorna, pet. She didn't want you to see her getting weaker and weaker. Didn't want you to be frightened by the coughing fits. To be here when she died.'

'She said my father would come for me.'

'He did.'

'What?'

'By the time yer dad came home the poor lass was long buried. Lorna, he was heartbroken. I've never seen a man take on so. I thought he was going to throw himself in the river. But, of course, he wouldn't hev done, not when he had you.

'He blamed himself for leaving her. He said he loved her so much he should hev known that she was poorly. Well, I telt him that wasn't his fault. Not his fault at all. Yer mam had guessed something was wrong but she didn't want to worry him. Not when he was starting out on his new venture, as they called it.'

Hilda paused and turned to gaze out of the window. The sky was growing dark but, instead of lighting the lamps, she rose from the table to heap more coal on the fire. Lorna moved back a little and sat with her face in the shadows.

Hilda sighed as she sat down again. She remained silent. Eventually Lorna prompted her, 'You said my father came for me.'

'He did. He wrote to your grandmother and she arranged to meet him. She said that on no account was he to come to her house. She would come here.'

'My grandmother came here?' Lorna was astonished.

'Aye. Yer dad had me cleaning the place for days, and baking too. The poor man was convinced that yer grandma would bring you with her.'

'She didn't even tell me!'

'I know, pet. Ee, Lorna, the poor man stood at the ferry landing all morning waiting to meet you. I'm glad I never saw his face when he realized you weren't with her. By the time they arrived here, he could hardly speak.'

'But if she didn't bring me home why did she come at all?'

'She said it was because she wanted to hev a look at the place where her granddaughter was going to be fetched up. But you could see she'd already made up her mind; she was just tormenting him.'

'She hated him.'

'Aye, for heving the gall to marry her daughter,' Hilda said. 'She sat in this very room and telt yer father that it would be criminal to hev you living in poverty here instead of her fine house in Heaton. She showed him photographs of you and your cousin Rose in yer bonny frocks, the like of which he couldn't provide. She told him that she intended to send you to a good school and bring you up an English lady, and that he didn't even know the meaning of the word.'

256

'Why did she care?'

'What do you mean, pet?'

'Why did she care what happened to me?'

'You were her granddaughter. She must hev loved you.'

'No, she didn't.'

'Are you sure?'

Lorna didn't answer and Hilda shook her head. 'Oh, I know she said she'd never forgive yer ma for what she'd done, but it wasn't your fault, and she must hev had some feeling for you. But, anyways, she said that what her daughter had done was bad enough and she couldn't hev the scandal of a granddaughter of hers being fetched up a little heathen.'

'Pride, then.'

'Mebbes.'

'And revenge.'

'Mebbes that as well. Poor bairn. You were caught in the middle. Anyways, yer dad said he had no intention of fetching you up in poverty and that he had every intention of making good. So then yer grandma pointed out that if he was going to make his fortune trading he'd hev to gan back to sea and leave you here on your own. Huh! The cheek of it, she knew fine well yer da intended to keep me on, but I wasn't good enough.

'She wore him down. In the end he agreed that the best place for you was with her.'

'Oh no,' Lorna groaned softly.

'And she telt him it would be too unsettling for you to see him. She said he must wait until you'd settled in with her. The poor man was persuaded it was for the best. He agreed with everything she said.'

'But she never told me any of this.'

'What about the letters yer da wrote you?'

'I never knew about them.'

'That explains it. It broke his heart all over again when you didn't answer them. He'd asked yer grandma to send them here and, each time he came home he would look for them. And I had to tell him there was none. Eventually he got a letter from yer grandma saying that you'd forgotten all about your old life and that you were perfectly happy.'

'What a lie!'

'And that the kindest thing to do would be to leave you in peace.'

'How wicked!'

'So that's when yer da stopped coming back to Shields at all. He made his home elsewheres. He gave this house to me and said I could take in a lodger or two to make me living. He said yer mam would hev wanted that.'

'But he writes to you?'

'Now and then. He always mentions you.'

'I've written to him. Explained that I didn't know.' Lorna brought her hands up to her face.

'Don't cry, hinny,' Hilda said.

'I'm not crying. I'm just thinking of all those wasted years. All the years when I thought my father had forgotten about me. I didn't even know that he was sending money for my keep. More than that, he has set up a trust so that I shall be provided for for life.'

'She must hev known you'd find out one day.'

Lorna dropped her hands and shook her head. 'She probably didn't think it would be as soon as this. She did not consider her own death. Her cousin Hannah is nearly seventy. My grandmother probably assumed that she would live to be much older. By which time she would have made sure that my life had been ruined.'

Hilda smiled gently. 'Hardly ruined, pet. You were comfortable enough, surely. You didn't lack owt.'

'Except my independence!' Lorna saw Hilda's expression and she laughed. 'I know, I'm being dramatic. And anyway, I can put all that behind me now. Hilda, I'm so glad I came today.'

'And you'll come again?'

'Of course. And maybe by the time I do, I'll have had an answer from my father.'

Mrs Campbell looked uneasy. She was a middle-aged widow who enjoyed her work as cook-housekeeper. Irene and she got along well together but they had never become intimate. Irene sensed that Mrs Campbell would not have thought that proper. In order to retain respect on both sides, their stations in life had to be observed.

Irene had been reading the morning paper when the older woman had knocked and entered. She stood in the doorway, a frown marring her usually pleasant features.

'There's a young woman to see you,' she said.

Irene was surprised. She knew no one in Cullercoats. 'Who is it?'

'She wouldn't give her name. Just said she was an old friend.' Jack's housekeeper paused. 'Shall I tell her to go?'

'Yes – I mean, I don't know.'

Irene was intrigued. No one from her old life even knew she was here. And, as for the girl being an old friend, Irene wasn't sure that

258

there had ever been anyone to fit that description. But perhaps because she suddenly realized how isolated she had become, she allowed her curiosity to overcome any doubts she had.

'Show her in,' she told Mrs Campbell.

A moment later, as the housekeeper ushered the unexpected visitor into the room, Irene stood up so quickly that the newspaper fell to the floor and lay there unregarded.

'Jess Green,' she said, 'what are you doing here?'

Jess hadn't changed. The coat and hat she wore were respectable enough and she looked a lot cleaner than she used to, but she had the same slightly belligerent expression on her plain face.

Mrs Campbell remained in the doorway, watching the scene with troubled eyes. 'Is it all right, Miss Lawson?' she asked. 'Shall I show the young woman out again?'

'No . . . it's all right. Leave us.'

Jess grinned. 'But how about bringing us a nice pot of tea?' she said. 'I've nearly froze to death just walking along from the station.'

'Is that all right, Miss Lawson?' the housekeeper asked.

'Yes, thank you, Mrs Campbell. And some of your homemade shortbread.'

The housekeeper left them and Jess stared at Irene for moment. 'I wish you could hear yersel',' she said. 'Talking as if you'd never even heard of Byker Bank. But I suppose yer life has changed a lot since you took up with Jack Brady.'

'Perhaps you should go right now,' Irene told her and she walked towards the bell pull.

'No, divven't call the woman back. I can find me own way out if you want me to leave, but I didn't come here to quarrel with you, really I didn't. I'm sorry if I spoke out of turn.'

Irene stared at her coldly. The silence lengthened.

Jess sighed. 'You must admit you've changed, Irene. And I'm pleased for you, really I am. You were always bonny, but, now, with those stylish clothes and your hair done nice and the way you talk – why, you're just like a proper lady.'

Irene smiled in spite of herself. 'A proper lady? Well, at least you don't call me an improper lady, whatever you might be think-ing.'

Jess scowled. 'I divven't know what you're talking about. And that's one thing that hasn't changed about you, isn't it?'

'What's that?'

'You were always too damn clever. Sharp as a knife, you were at school, and you thought yersel' much better than the rest of us poor bairns.'

'Now I wish *you* could hear yourself. Screeching like a fishwife. Although why they say that I don't really know. If you met the fisher lasses who live round here, you'd see that they were real ladies compared to the likes of you.'

They glared at each other and as Jess's scowl deepened, Irene caught sight of the two of them in the big mirror over the mantelpiece. Like bairns in the schoolyard, she thought. Not like grown women. She found herself wanting to laugh.

'What are you grinning at?' Jess said.

'At us. At the pair of us. Look.'

Irene gestured towards the mirror and Jess glanced up and saw the way they stood at either side of the hearth. Jess's shoulders were hunched, her arms tensed as if she were going to take a swipe at her opponent. Her eyes widened, and then she too saw how funny it was.

'I thought you said you hadn't come here to quarrel?' Irene said.

Jess grinned. 'No, I didn't. But we never got on well as bairns, did we? It seems as if we'll always be at loggerheads.'

They were interrupted as Mrs Campbell came back with the tray of tea and shortbread. Irene lifted a small table forward so that they could sit nearer to the fire. When the housekeeper had gone she kneeled down to put some more coal on.

'Doesn't that wife do that kind of thing for you?' Jess asked.

'She would, but I don't like to ask her. I suppose I haven't got used to being a lady, proper or improper.'

Jess shook her head but she let the words go by. She watched as Irene poured the tea and then helped herself to milk and sugar. 'Very nice,' she said as she began to eat a piece of shortbread.

'Now, why did you come here?' Irene asked.

Jess looked solemn. 'Well, I know you'll find this hard to believe, but I felt sorry for you.'

'Sorry for me?'

'When I heard about your sister.'

Irene began to shake her head, the familiar lump of misery growing in her throat. 'Don't, Jess. I don't want to talk about it.'

'It's all right, I won't go on about it. I just wanted you to know that I felt real sorry for you. I know exactly what you must hev gone through.'

'You?'

260

'Well, divven't look so surprised.' Jess looked hurt. 'I may be stupid, according to your lights, but I've got feelings just like anyone else. And I lost a sister too, you know.'

Irene stared at her. 'Of course you did. I'm sorry.'

'And it was partly because you were so good to me that night. Helping me look for her when I could see all you wanted was to get home and get to bed. And then staying with me at the police station until things were sorted. And then taking me home with you.'

'Anybody would have done what I did, Jess.'

'No they wouldn't. Most folk couldn't give a toss what happens to a pair of street lasses. They think they deserve anything that happens to them. And you probably thought that, too. But you still did the right thing that night. I began to think you were human after all.'

Jess grinned and Irene felt the misery begin to subside. 'They've never caught him, you know,' she said, 'the villain that murdered poor little Sarah – and some other lasses beside.'

'I know.'

'Rumour is, amongst the other lasses, that he's a toff. But he keeps to the shadows. All they know for sure about him is that he's tall. And vicious.'

'I'm truly sorry. I know you loved her.'

Jess sighed. 'Aye, well anyways, I hevn't seen you since the morning after it happened, when Mr Brady came to take me away. He gave me a job, you know, just cleaning, really. I'm not posh enough to be one of the maids in the new house. And I hevn't got the looks either, if the truth were known.'

'Looks? To be a housemaid?'

'Depends what sort of house it is, doesn't it?'

'I don't understand.'

'Yes you do, if you just think about it. Brady's moved his business upmarket. No more poor little tarts like me sister and me. Too many of his girls came to grief at the hands of that maniac. Mr Brady didn't like that. He does care what happens to the girls, you know.'

'Does he?' Irene wished Jess would stop talking about the way Jack made his living. Every day she stayed here she tried to put it to the very back of her mind.

'Of course he does. He may be a villain but he's not a murderer!'

'Isn't he?'

'Of course he isn't. Why are you staring like that? Oh, I can see you've heard the old story about why he had to give up boxing. You've heard that he killed a man in the ring. Well, what if he did? It wasn't murder, was it? Them fellows know what they're letting themselves in for it they want to make their living that way, don't they?'

Irene watched Jess's mouth moving, her homely face animated as she defended her employer. In fact she had never heard that story about Jack; she hadn't known that he'd been a boxer, although she remembered that first night she saw him on Byker Bridge, squaring his shoulders as he attacked poor Billy, she'd thought then that he looked like the pictures of the boxers on the posters outside St James's Hall.

So that wasn't murder, was it, not if a man died in the boxing ring? But what if you threw someone off a bridge when a hearty shove or a punch would have done instead? Wasn't that murder?

'. . . so it's only indoor trade now.'

Irene realized she had lost the thread of what Jess was talking about. 'Indoor trade?'

'For goodness' sake, Irene, don't act as if you're ignorant of what goes on! Mr Brady doesn't hev any of his girls walking the streets now. Of course, a lot of the poor old tarts, the ones who were past it, were put out to grass, or he found them cleaning jobs, like mine.'

'Good of him.'

Jess gave her a funny look. 'I'm surprised at you. Talking in that tone of voice. You're doing nicely out of it, after all.'

'Yes, I suppose I am.'

'There's no suppose about it.'

'And this . . . this house. Where is it?'

'Hasn't he told you?'

'He doesn't talk to me about his – his business.'

'Huh! Too much of a lady are you, now?' Jess's grin took the edge off her words. 'Bottom of Westgate Road. He calls it a gentlemen's dining club and, mind, you should see the prices on the menu! What some of the fellows spend on one meal would keep a poor family for a month or more! There's a bit of gambling goes on there too. But to tell the truth, Irene, it's nowt but a glorified brothel, and Mr Brady's doing very well out of it.'

Irene remained silent and Jess grew uneasy. 'You know, I'm not sure if I should hev come here, after all,' she said.

'Why not?'

'Well, mebbes I've talked too much.'

'That's all right. I won't say anything.'

'You must promise me you won't. Because there's another thing. I'm not supposed to be here.'

'What do you mean?'

262

'Mr Brady thinks nobody knows where this house is. And nobody else does. Only me.'

'How did you find out?'

'Well, I telt you. I've been thinking about you. I was real sorry about your little sister and I wanted to see if you was all right. Everybody knew you'd gone off with Jack Brady and it was a fair guess that he was keeping you somewhere nice. So, one day, when I saw him gannin' into the Central Station, all dressed smart like, I guessed he might be coming to see you. And I followed him.'

Suddenly Jess's eyes widened as though she had only just realized how dangerous her actions had been. 'Ee, Irene, you won't tell him, will you? I mean, I hevn't bothered you, hev I? I hevn't made you mad at me?'

'No, I'm not angry. I'm glad you came.'

'Really?'

Jess sounded as if she could hardly believe that and Irene smiled. She was glad that Jess Green had come to see her but not for the reason the poor girl might think.

'Really. And I won't tell Jack you've been.'

'What about that wife that answered the door? Will she say anything?'

'Not if I tell her some story.'

'Such as?'

'Oh, I'll say you were just a poor girl who I used to know who came begging, something like that—'

'Huh!'

'And that I don't want to bother Mr Brady with such matters. Don't worry, she's a kind woman and I think she likes me. She'll agree.'

'That's all right, then. I'd hate to lose me job.'

'Is that what you think would happen?'

'If Mr Brady found out I knew one of his secrets? Of course I would.'

When Jess had gone Irene kneeled down to pick up and straighten the newspaper which had lain forgotten on the floor. The girl was right to be frightened, she thought. She wondered if Jess realized that people who angered Jack Brady could lose much, much more than their employment.

Maurice faced Rose across the dining table. In the sixth month of her pregnancy her face was beginning to look puffy. Nevertheless, she'd made every effort to look her best.

Since she had begun to put on weight she had found it easier to wear loosely cut tea gowns for most of the day. Tonight she was wearing one of cloud-grey silk, with voluminous matching chiffon sleeves and a high neck trimmed with smoky lace. His mother had decided that, although Rose was still officially in mourning for her grandmother and, strictly speaking, should be wearing black, grey was not too startling an alternative.

Maurice noticed that she had also started wearing jewellery again. Tonight she wore the cameo pendant and earrings that he had bought for her on their honeymoon. He wondered if Lorna ever wore her cameo brooch.

But what of his wife? Rose certainly saw to it that he came home to a good meal every night. She was even learning to choose the wines to accompany the meal, although, at the moment, she drank very little herself.

'Thank you, my dear, that was delicious,' he said, and he thought how like his father he was beginning to sound. He brought his napkin to his lips to hide the cynical smile the thought prompted.

Rose looked pathetically pleased at the compliment. 'Don't you think it was a good idea of mine to persuade Mrs Hobson to come and work for us?'

'I do. Now, shall we sit by the fire in the drawing room for a while? I'll forego my cigar and bring my coffee in there with you.'

He noticed how clumsy she was as she pushed herself up from the table. And how badly she was walking. She tried her best to hold herself well and to remain dignified but she looked like a galumphing country girl who had just fallen from her horse. He looked away in distaste as she waddled ahead of him into the drawing room.

The room was large but the area near the fireplace was welcoming. The lamps shone and the fire crackled. In front of the hearth was one of the Persian rugs that Rose had chosen. Its subtle colours, glowing in the firelight, added to the attractive ambience. Outside the wind howled across the town moor and hurled rain at the windows. It was a night for staying in.

If only he could be satisfied with what he had.

'Oh, Maurice, you shouldn't have!' Rose exclaimed with delight when she saw the box of Turkish delight waiting for her on a small table near the sofa. She had barely sat down before she had taken off the circular lid and pushed aside the waxed paper. At least she remembered to offer him the box first.

'No, thank you,' he said. 'It will spoil the taste of this cognac.'

264

He stood to one side of the fire, resting one arm along the marble mantelshelf, and nursing his brandy glass with the other as he watched her choose a piece of Turkish delight.

'Shall I have the lemon or the rose flavour?' she asked.

'Why don't you have one of each?'

'Shall I? Oh, yes, I will. And then I shall put the lid back on and make myself wait until tomorrow.'

He knew that she wouldn't but he had long ago given up any hope of controlling her appetite. Perhaps it would be different once she had delivered their child, he thought. He hoped so. Already he couldn't bear to go near her. If she didn't recover her former figure quickly he doubted if he would have the will to father any more children.

Rose put the first piece of Turkish delight into her mouth and then licked her fingers clean of the powdered sugar. 'You spoil me,' she said.

'It's the least I can do.'

She frowned. 'What do you mean?'

'I mean you are carrying my child and yet you still make every effort to make yourself look lovely and to create a comfortable home for me.'

Poor Rose, he thought, when he saw her flush with pleasure. It was so easy to say the things she wanted to hear. Sometimes he wondered where he found this ability to pass himself off as the perfect husband – well, not perfect – he knew that she would have been even happier if he could only bring himself to make love to her.

But he had always found it easy to please people. As a very young child he had found it better never to defy his parents. He had learned that by appearing to agree with everything they said, everything they asked of him, it was then much easier to do exactly as he pleased. And to make sure that they never found out. Over the years he had become a master of deception. His parents and his sisters thought him a model son and brother – intelligent, easy-going and well mannered. Not one of them had guessed at the turbulent emotions that lay behind the placid façade.

His life of deception had begun one night when he was a small child, still young enough to find comfort in his mother's arms. He had woken from a bad dream. The nursemaid was snoring gently so he'd slipped out of bed and left the nursery to run along the shadowy corridor.

At the top of the stairs that led down to the floor where his parents' bedrooms lay, he paused and listened to the strange sound echoing through the quiet house. His mother was laughing. But small as he was, he sensed there was no joy in that laughter. Nevertheless, with the hot tears still on his cheeks, he went downstairs and ran to his mother's room.

When he opened the door his mother was still laughing. The room was dark save for a shaft of moonlight striking between a gap in the heavy curtains. It fell across the bed where both his parents sat amongst a mound of pillows. Neither noticed him. His mother was turned towards his father who had his head sunk in his hands. Now Maurice could hear another sound. His father was sobbing.

Maurice stood there, hesitantly, a small figure in white with his pale gold hair falling cross his flushed face in baby fine ringlets. He had almost made up his mind to cross the shadows on the carpet when his mother shrilled, 'For God's sake, stop that crying. That won't change anything. In fact I don't know why you bother to come to my bed these days. You're useless!'

His father groaned and began to get out of bed. Maurice fled.

At the time he hadn't understood the full significance of what he'd heard. Only that his mother had been angry and that, somehow, she thought it was his father's fault. But, as he'd grown into understanding, he'd realized that he must become adept at concealing his knowledge of what went on between his parents. His kindly father must never know that his baby son had witnessed his humiliation, and therefore, his mother must never guess how much he hated her.

No one ever suspected that there was another Maurice, almost another person living within the same body. And this other man, seeking relief from the role he played, craved excitement in ways that were best kept secret. He was well aware of the dangers of his addiction.

It is an addiction, he mused. Some poor wretches, like Bertram, crave alcohol; he knew of others who had become slaves to opium. And me? He closed his eyes momentarily to shut out the sight of the foolish, self-indulgent woman he had tied himself to for life. She would never satisfy him. She would never be able to help him resist the darker side of his nature. In fact, very soon after marrying her, he had found it had made matters worse.

He opened his eyes to find her taking another piece of Turkish delight. 'Have you heard from Lorna since she moved?' he asked abruptly.

She looked up, irritation flashing momentarily in her eyes. 'No. Why do you always ask about Lorna?'

'Do I?' He would have to be careful. He smiled. 'I just wondered if, perhaps, she was neglecting to keep in touch with you now that she seems to have come into some kind of fortune.'

'Fortune? Lorna? Don't be ridiculous! She's as poor as a church mouse. When she came to live with us she had nothing. She's lived on my grandmother's charity all these years.'

'Am I being ridiculous? You know that she's moved to Tynemouth?'

'Well?'

'Whatever you might think, I've discovered that your impoverished cousin has bought a house in Collingwood Terrace.'

'Collingwood Terrace?'

'Perhaps you don't know it. The terrace is part of a development built on a promontory near the mouth of the river. The houses are much sought after and very grand.'

'Well, then, she can't have bought it. She must have found some sort of employment there. A companion to an old lady or governess to a child, perhaps. Being a governess would suit her very well.'

'And why do you say that?'

'Because she's irritatingly clever. I'm sure she'd just love to torture some poor child with multiplication tables and French verbs!'

'Do you hate her so much?'

He spoke quietly and Rose was taken aback. She frowned. 'No, I don't hate her,' she said. 'I think we could have been friends if only . . .'

'If only what?'

'If only my grandmother had loved her as much as she loved me.'

'Why should that have made any difference?'

'Because I was a little beast,' Rose said with a rare flash of honesty. 'It's very hard for a child not to take advantage of being the favourite, you know.'

Without seeming to know what she was doing Rose took out two pieces of Turkish delight and put them into her mouth at the same time. She left a dusty trail of sugar on her chin.

'Well, my little spoiled child,' Maurice said, 'whatever you may think, I have heard that Lorna has bought that house and is living there in some degree of comfort. Furnishing it with goods from Haldane's rival establishments, I hear.'

'Maurice, you must be wrong.'

'I don't think so. Could your grandmother have made some separate arrangement for your cousin? Is there something we don't know about perhaps?'

'No! I mean – what could there be?'

Something has occurred to her, Maurice thought, and she doesn't want to tell me. Now that's interesting because, in fact, I'm pretty sure I've guessed where Lorna's money is coming from and, if I'm right, it has nothing to do with Mildred Cunningham. So what remembered secret has suddenly made my wife appear so flustered?

'Oh, dear, I'm so-oo tired.' Rose raised a hand to her mouth and yawned exaggeratedly. 'Do you know, I think I'll have an early night. Are you . . . will you be going to bed soon?'

'I might go out.'

'Oh, Maurice, not again.'

'It's still early. I don't much fancy sitting here by myself.'

'Shall I stay down? We could talk . . . I could read a magazine . . . You could catch up with the papers . . .'

'No, you said you're tired and in your condition I think that means you should rest.'

'But where will you go?'

Maurice was surprised. She had never questioned his movements before. 'Oh, nowhere special,' he said. 'I might try to find a card game. There's a club on Westgate Road.'

'But . . .' Rose saw him raise his eyebrows and she bit her lip. 'All right, Maurice. I'll say good night, then.'

Clutching her box of Turkish delight she left the room without looking at him again or coming to him for a kiss. He could see by the set of his shoulders that she was angry and disappointed. As he watched her, he felt the familiar rage begin to grow inside him. And there would be no release tonight. The weather was foul enough to keep the whores off the streets.

He'd have to find a game of cards just as he'd said he would. But if he did decide to visit a brothel he would have to exercise restraint.

Chapter Twenty-Two

February

'If you and Miss Hassan would like to sit at the table, Mr Randall, I'll brew us a cup of tea.'

Mrs Charlton smiled and Lorna realized that the woman held him in genuine affection. And as for Edwin, he looked completely at ease here in this sparsely furnished dwelling in the Ouseburn Valley. But Lorna had seen enough during this morning's visits to appreciate that Mrs Charlton was a different sort of housekeeper from most of her neighbours.

Lorna guessed that her husband must be in work, and also that they must be childless – or their sons and daughters had grown and left them. For she could see it was much easier to keep good standards of hygiene when there was only the two of you, and all day to follow some kind of routine.

Mrs Charlton put a cup of tea on the table before her and Edwin nodded slightly as if to reassure her. There were other houses where tea had been offered and he had made some polite excuse when he refused it.

Lorna was content to sit and listen to Edwin and their hostess talking. She learned that Albert Charlton had the chance of a job at a boat builders downriver at North Shields and they were seriously considering moving. They would be paying the same kind of rent for any place they found but the property would be that bit better.

'We went to Shields to hev a look round,' Bella said. 'If we could find a place near Clive Street, there's all those shops. I wouldn't hev to carry me basket up and down Byker Bank any more. And then, on a Sunday afternoon, we could gan to the beach at Cullercoats or Tynemouth.'

'And, uhm, what about Albert's . . .?'

269

'Fondness for his four-legged friends? His gambling, is that what you mean?'

'Yes.'

'Divven't worry, Mr Randall, he's beginning to see that he'll never get the better of the bookies. And for all his studying the form in the sporting papers, he's still a poor judge of horse flesh. The rag-and-bone man's old nag is faster than some of the horses my Albert's put his money on! No, these days, Albert hands his pay packet over to me unopened and I give him as much for himself as we can afford. The man works damn hard. It's not up to me to spoil his bit fun – even though all it brings him is grief and bewilderment.'

'Albert's a lucky man,' Edwin said.

'Lucky? It's the bookie's runner that's lucky when he sees him coming!'

'I didn't mean with his bets, I meant because he has a wife like you, Bella. You know the old saying about gamblers? Well, Albert's lucky in love.'

Bella Charlton's raw-boned face flushed with pleasure. 'Get away with you, Mr Randall,' she said. 'Save your fancy talk for the bonny young lass there, not an old besom like me.'

Edwin began to talk to Mrs Charlton about some of her neighbours and the problems they were having with the new landlord. They didn't involve Lorna, and her attention wandered. She was pleased to be here with him today. She had been hesitant about contacting him.

She remembered how she must have disappointed him by her lack of enthusiasm when he had asked her if she would like to help at the reading classes he had organized. She also remembered her mixed feelings about his arranging for Irene Lawson to take the classes instead.

And, then, it had been so long since she'd been to the bookshop; not since the day her grandmother had died, in fact. She worried that he might think she'd been avoiding him. She had thought of writing to him. But what could she say? Too much had happened in her life to be explained in a simple letter. She had decided it would be better to go and see him.

She had purposely waited until it would be time for his uncle's bookshop to close. It was a damp, raw evening and the streetlamps were lit. She'd watched from a shadowed doorway at the other side of the street until what she thought to be the last customer came out. Then she hurried across the narrow cobbled road and grasped the handle of the door just as Edwin appeared there to turn the card over to read

'Closed'. His eyes widened when he saw her and he opened the door at once.

'Lorna,' he said. 'Come in.'

She entered and he closed the door. She stood there, smiling for a minute in the confines of the shop, and as her eyes adjusted to the dim light she saw that he was smiling too. Neither of them spoke. Eventually it was Lorna who turned to adjust the card in the window.

This seemed to rouse him. 'I was just about to make myself some coffee,' he said. 'I need to keep awake while I go over some work. Would you like a cup?'

She nodded and he led the way past the shelves of books as though it had been only yesterday that they had seen each other last.

The little room at the back looked just the same, with a fire burning in the hearth and a kettle gently steaming by the grate. The table at the back of the room was covered with books and papers. Lorna went over to have a look at them while Edwin busied himself measuring coffee grounds into a small pan, filling it with water, and placing it on the hob.

He glanced round and saw what she was looking at. 'That's some work of my own,' he said.

'Your own?'

'A private project which isn't directly connected to my medical studies.'

'How do you find the time?'

'With great difficulty!'

When the water boiled, Edwin gave the pan a stir and then drew the flat of the spoon across the top before straining the liquor into a jug. 'I take it black,' he said. 'How about you?'

'Oh, I like it black, Turkish style.'

Edwin laughed. 'That's just as well because I haven't any milk left.'

Lorna marvelled at how readily they had fallen into their old habit of easy companionship. Edwin hadn't asked her why she had stayed away for so long, so as they sat at each side of the hearth, she told him as much as she wanted him to know of her grandmother's death and how she had discovered that her father had been providing for her after all.

She told him that her father was living in Cairo but she didn't mention that she'd written to him. She couldn't talk about that to anyone. Not even to Edwin.

He listened solemnly and she liked him all the better because he didn't offer any criticism of Mildred Cunningham. Lorna did not tell him of the existence of Rose's daughter. That was not her secret to divulge; nor did she tell him how greatly her circumstances had

271

changed. She simply implied that she was comfortably off and well able to look after herself.

As well as the coffee, they shared some bread rolls with cheese and slices of rich dark fruit cake from the usual overgenerous hamper that Edwin's aunt had provided. When they had finished, Lorna asked him about his private project. Immediately he grew serious.

'It's about public health,' he said. 'Even though we have known since the middle of the last century that large towns are desperately unhealthy, not enough has been to done improve living conditions.'

'But who is responsible? Who should do this?'

'The city council and the landlords must work together,' he told her. 'Otherwise every summer will bring outbreaks of food poisoning and epidemics of cholera and typhoid fever. And in the winter poorly nourished people living in poorly heated houses will succumb to influenza. You've seen what it's like. Remember when you came with me to visit old Mrs Potts?'

'I do. I was shocked. And yet she would rather stay there than go into the workhouse.'

'Poor old Jane. That's not a problem now.'

Lorna realized what he meant. 'Oh, I'm sorry.'

'But hers was an extreme case, living in the abandoned boathouse like that. However, some of the houses are hardly any better.'

'But apart from the help you give already, what can you do?'

'If I can present my findings and my projections to people of influence, if I can publish these papers and have them recognized, it's to be hoped the right people will take notice and do something about it. It will only be a beginning, you know. But we must start somewhere.'

'Is there any way I could help you?'

'Do you mean that?'

'Of course, I do. Oh, but how could I? I have no medical knowledge.'

'That doesn't matter,' Edwin said. 'You see all those papers? For months now I've been collecting facts and figures –' he grinned enthusiastically – 'information about one particular area, the dwellings clustered round the Ouseburn, in order to use as a model. Information about the overcrowding, the washing facilities – or lack of them – the defective sewers, the number of families that share one privy. I'm sorry, does this offend you?'

'No, go on.'

'But the trouble is I can't devote as much time to this work as I'd like to. I still have to go on with my medical studies, you know. If I don't

272

qualify as a doctor then I won't be any use to anyone. So I need someone who is capable of helping me pull all this information together. Someone to organize it. Would you at least give it a try?'

Of course she had agreed. And she was here as a result.

Suddenly she realized that while she had been thinking about what had happened the previous day, Edwin and Mrs Charlton had dropped their voices and were talking more quietly. She heard a name that she recognized: Irene Lawson. She began to pay attention to the conversation.

'Don't take this as gospel,' she heard Bella Charlton say quietly, 'but word is that Irene's living at the coast. Jack Brady's set her up in a bonny fine house at Cullercoats.'

'How do you know this?'

'Well, I'm not supposed to say, but someone who used to know her is supposed to hev visited her there.'

'Is Irene . . .? Are they . . .?'

'Living together? Well, I'm telt he doesn't stay there overnight. But that could mean owt or nowt with a man like that. I'm surprised at her!'

Lorna saw that Edwin was troubled. He looked across at her as if suddenly aware that she was listening. She felt uncomfortable; it was as if she'd been eavesdropping, and she recognized his concern.

Then he seemed to make a conscious effort to smile at her. He rose to his feet. 'We'd better go,' he said. 'We've taken too much of Bella's time.'

On the way back up the bank he asked her if she still wanted to help him.

'Of course I do. When shall I begin?'

'Well, the problem will be the sheer amount of paperwork. I already have too much for the little room at the back of the shop and there's never enough peace and quiet at my uncle's home for us to work there. Not that my aunt wouldn't welcome you.'

'But that problem can be solved easily,' Lorna said. 'I have a house of my own and rooms to spare. I'll make one of them into a study for you. I'll get a desk – some bookshelves, whatever you need. You can safely leave your work with me. Just tell me what I must do and come and check up on my progress whenever you wish.'

Edwin stopped walking and turned towards her. 'Lorna, I don't know how to thank you.'

'I haven't done anything yet.'

They smiled at each other and then began to walk again. 'Do you like living at the coast?' he asked.

'Very much. I needed to find somewhere new. The weather can be miserable, sometimes, but the air is fresh and clean.'

'Not like it is here.'

'No.' Lorna wrinkled her nose at the ever-present stench of the polluted river, the industrial waste and the filth in the streets. 'It must be terrible to have to live in these conditions. And I heard you talking to Mrs Charlton about increased rents.'

'The rent on some of the properties was increased when a new landlord took over.'

'A new landlord?'

'The previous one died.'

'Oh.'

'It wouldn't be so bad if the properties had been renovated, but they haven't. It's simple greed.'

'Can anything be done about it?'

'I've made a list of basic improvements. We can always ask.'

'Do you know who owns the properties?'

'No, I only know who collects the rents. I've been to the rent office, as a matter of fact, but I am never allowed to see anyone in authority. I'm always put off by young clerks. But at least one day I heard the name of some kind of manager mentioned. I shall endeavour to trap him in his lair.'

'And where is that?'

'Not far from here. In an office block on Shields Road.'

'And the name of this man?'

'Mr Pearson.' He looked at her and laughed.

'What is it?'

'You're not thinking of confronting him, are you?'

'Why do you say that?'

'Because you suddenly looked so serious – and so fierce.'

'No.' She tried to smile. 'I shall leave that to you. But I would like to see the list you've made. Is that possible?'

'Of course. If you come back to the shop with me I can give you a copy today.'

Lorna was about to ask him if he would like to come home with her, they could have a meal at her house and start discussing his work straight away, but he said suddenly, 'You heard me talking to Mrs Charlton about Irene Lawson?'

'I did. You're worried about her?'

'Yes.'

Edwin told Lorna what had happened. How Irene's baby sister had

274

died in a tragic accident and how Irene had packed up and left her home. He didn't mention that Irene had gone away with another man and that she might be living with him, but Lorna sensed he was embarrassed. And he was obviously deeply anxious.

But was it more than that? Could he be in love with Irene? Lorna realized with surprise that that troubled her. Also she was forced to acknowledge that the horror at what had happened and the sympathy she felt for Irene Lawson were tempered by another emotion. Jealousy.

'What is this all this nonsense, Lorna?'

The weather was cold and damp, and beyond the window the garden looked dismal in the grey winter light. Inside the morning room Rose sat propped up amongst a nest of velvet cushions on a day bed near the fire. Every now and then she dabbed her face with a handkerchief sprinkled with cologne. The aroma hung heavily in the close atmosphere.

She was still attractive, Lorna thought, but her cheeks had filled out – maybe because of her pregnancy but also perhaps because of the treats she indulged herself with. A half-empty box of luxury Swiss chocolates was within reach on a small table. At the moment Rose was flushed with irritation as well as heat.

The papers Lorna had just given her were spread out across the cashmere shawl she had draped across her thickening body. She moved angrily and one sheet fell to the floor.

Lorna picked it up and gave it back to her. 'I've told you. It's a list of improvements that you're going to make to some of your properties. And, by the way, I suppose I may sit down? If you're going to be a society hostess you really should ask your guests to sit down, you know.'

'Sit if you like. But you're not a guest, you're my cousin. And, in any case, you weren't invited here; you just marched in.'

'Marched in? Hardly. I heard your maid announce me in the proper manner and you didn't tell her to send me away.'

'You didn't give me a chance. You just followed her into the room.

'Would you have sent me away?'

Rose suddenly looked unsure of herself. 'Well . . . no . . .'

'There you are then. But you keep it like a hot house in here so I'll take my coat off, if you don't mind, although not my hat. It took too long to arrange the ridiculous thing on top of my hair.'

Rose looked up at her and then said grudgingly, 'It's not ridiculous. It's the height of fashion.'

275

'Why do you sound so surprised?' Lorna placed her coat over a chair back and pulled up another chair so that she could sit beside her cousin.

'Well, it must have cost – I mean, it's obviously expensive.'

'Wicked, I know. But I have developed a weakness for hats. Actually, I think I always had it but the difference is that now I can indulge it.'

Rose scowled. 'I don't understand you, Lorna. You never used to be like this.'

'Like what, exactly?'

'So . . .' she searched for a word, 'so . . . flippant.'

'Is that the impression I give? I don't mean to. Perhaps you mistake my new mood of confidence for flippancy. Well, you shouldn't. Now, go on, look at those lists.'

'I won't.' She glowered while Lorna looked at her steadily. 'Why should I?'

'I've told you. Because they itemize improvements that you are going to make to certain properties that you own.'

'Improvements . . . I'm going to make . . . I've never heard such nonsense!'

'Believe me, you wouldn't think it nonsense if you had to live there. Have you no concern at all for the welfare of your tenants?'

'Why should I have?'

'I can't believe you said that.'

Rose looked genuinely puzzled. 'I don't understand this at all. Mr Pearson runs the business for me. I have nothing to do with it.'

'Except to live very comfortably off the proceeds.'

'Well, yes. I don't deny that our grandmother built up a profitable property empire, and it all began with our grandfather's jobbing builder's yard. But they both worked very hard. Why shouldn't I benefit now?'

Lorna leaned forward slightly. 'Look, it may be true that when Grandfather started building houses instead of just carrying out repair work, he provided some very fine homes for working people. Some of the best in the North East, in fact. But it seems that after he died, Grandmother began to buy up other property, property that Grandfather hadn't built in the first place. And all she was interested in was collecting the rents.'

'That can't be right. What about all the plumbers and joiners and labourers she employed to carry out repairs?'

'Perhaps she thought some of the property wasn't worth repairing. Perhaps it would have cost too much, so she was content to profit from it as long as she could. And to leave a substantial fortune for you.'

276

'But if it's going to cost so much why should you expect me to order the work to be done now?'

'Because you must.'

'I must?'

'Rose, if only you would come with me and see for yourself. I'm sure you wouldn't be able to sleep easy in this lovely home of yours if you saw the way some of those people have to live.'

'I'd rather just take your word for it.'

'Then you'll do as I ask? Look.' Lorna took the top sheet of paper from Rose. 'Look, it's all listed here. As well as some general maintenance work, basically what is needed is better washing facilities and more privies – and perhaps some proper flooring in some of the properties. The other pages will make it easy for you to explain things to Mr Pearson. And don't worry. If he does things the way we've suggested it won't cost so very much after all.'

'We? Oh, I see. Someone has put you up to this!'

'No, nobody has put me up to it. It was all my own idea to come to you. But I needed someone to explain what was to be done.'

This was true enough, she thought. And she didn't want to waste time telling Rose about her involvement with Edwin.

Rose frowned as she studied the papers for a while and then she looked up and said, 'It's no use, Lorna. I won't do it.'

'For heaven's sake, why?'

'Well, Maurice will want to know why, for a start. I've never taken any interest in the business up until now.'

'Yes, I suppose that is a problem. Couldn't you simply say that with all this resting you're doing you had to find something to occupy your mind and you asked Mr Pearson to tell you more about your properties?'

'Maurice wouldn't believe that. And, in any case, it would be too easy for him to check up with Mr Pearson.'

Lorna stared at her cousin perplexed. Rose began to gather the papers together, smiling smugly.

'You'll just have to blame me, then,' Lorna said.

'What do you mean?'

'Tell Maurice the truth. Tell him that I came to visit you today and made you aware of how some of your tenants are living, and that you want to do what you can to put things right.'

'He wouldn't believe either.'

'Wouldn't believe what part of it?'

'That I want to put things right.'

'Whyever not?'

'You know me. Have I ever been concerned about anyone but myself?'

Lorna was so astounded that she only half caught the underlying edge to her cousin's tone. 'Well, at least that's honest,' she said.

They stared at each other speechlessly for a while and Lorna began to see that Rose, selfish and self-indulgent though she may be, was certainly not happy.

'What is it?' she asked. 'What's the matter?'

Rose seemed to make an effort to pull herself together. 'Oh, nothing,' she sighed. 'It's just the way I am, I suppose. Things will get better once the baby is born.'

'What things? Your health?'

'No, not my health. I'm fine. The confinement should be trouble free. That's what Dr Gibson says.'

'Then are there problems with your new family?'

Rose shook her head.

'With Maurice?'

She took a long time to reply. 'Not really.'

'You'd better explain.'

'Well, he's never actually said anything but he's not as – as attentive as he used to be.'

'He neglects you?'

'Oh, no. I have everything I could possibly want – Maurice sees to that. He's always kind and polite.'

'Polite?'

To Lorna that hardly seemed a satisfactory description for the behaviour of such a new husband, but then Maurice had admitted that he didn't really love Rose. Suddenly she couldn't meet her cousin's eyes. She felt warmth creeping up to colour her neck and face. Fortunately Rose was too preoccupied with her own thoughts to notice.

'Yes,' she sighed, 'always perfectly polite.' She stared into the fire. Lorna thought she looked bewildered. And then she said, 'But sometimes when he looks at me, I seem to see something in his eyes . . . oh, I don't know . . . something so deep, but it's an emotion I can't describe.'

'Try.'

Rose's glance was uneasy, as if she were embarrassed to be so fanciful. But then she said, 'It's as if he's hiding something.'

Lorna heard her own voice falter. 'What do you mean?'

'As if he's hiding his real feelings. Lorna, I think he's bored with me.'

'Oh, poor Rose.'

278

Lorna's own guilty feelings perhaps made her response a little too vehemently and Rose looked surprised.

'Oh, it's good of you, but there's no need for you to be upset on my behalf. At least I don't think so. It may be just what happens to all marriages when the wife is expecting a baby. I mean, in bed, I must look—'

'Rose!'

'Sorry. Have I embarrassed you?'

'No, but I don't want to hear . . . I mean, Maurice might not like it if he thought you were discussing such intimate—'

'Perhaps you're right. But I have no one else to talk to, you know.' Rose dropped her head and she was barely audible when she said, 'Lorna . . . I've thought about it a lot lately. We both lost our parents . . . we were alone in the world apart from Grandmamma and each other . . . two little girls . . .'

'What are you trying to say?'

'We should have become friends, shouldn't we?'

'Yes.'

'Do you think we still could be?'

'I'm not sure. There may be too many unhappy memories.'

For a moment Rose couldn't meet her eyes. 'But that life is past,' she said.

'And now our lives are so very different.'

They looked at each other candidly for a moment, neither wishing to explore too deeply the gulf that lay between them. Then Lorna smiled and said, 'We'll see. Now, these improvements . . .'

Lorna gestured towards the papers still resting on her cousin's lap but Rose moved her hand impatiently.

'In a minute,' she said. 'But first there's something else I've just remembered. Maurice seems to think you've come into a fortune. I told him that can't be true. But he insists that you've bought the house you're living in, not just renting it or working there or whatever.'

Rose was smiling as if the idea of Lorna buying a house was a joke. Lorna was prompted to tell her the truth about her new circumstances, but she decided not to. She saw no reason to broadcast the fact that she was now a wealthy woman.

'I have bought it,' she said. She saw her cousin's eyes widen and her mouth shape a surprised 'Oh!' but before Rose could say anything, Lorna hurried on, 'It seems that Grandmamma was good at keeping secrets.'

279

'Secrets?' Rose took a fold of her shawl into her hand and began to play with it nervously.

'Yes. You can imagine how surprised I was to learn that my father's business venture proved successful. He has provided for me after all. There was sufficient money to buy a house and furnish it.'

'Sufficient?'

'Mm.'

Rose relaxed a little. 'Oh, is that all?'

Lorna noticed wryly that her cousin showed no interest in learning any more about Lorna's father, whether he was dead or alive, but that suited her very well; she didn't want to be distracted.

'So that's the secret you meant?' Rose said.

'What else could there be?'

'Oh, I don't know. But, anyway,' her cousin gathered up the pages of the document Lorna had given her and held them out to her, 'I won't be needing these. I've thought about it and it just wouldn't work. Nothing I could say would make Maurice believe that I am the least bit interested in the lives of slum dwellers.'

Anger at Rose's uncaring attitude surged through Lorna. She made no move to take the papers from her. 'I'm sorry,' she said, 'but you'll have to find a way.'

Rose looked startled. 'Or?' she said. 'It sounded as if there was an "or" at the end of that sentence. Oh, was it an "or else!" '

'Perhaps there was.' Lorna got up and started to put on her coat.

'Where are you going?'

'Home. Where else?'

'But these papers – and you haven't explained—'

'Do you know,' Lorna said, 'the house I've bought seems too big just for me. I rattle around in there all on my own.'

'What are you talking about now?'

'I've been thinking of inviting Louise to come and live with me.'

Even in the rosy light of the fire it seemed that Rose's face drained of colour. The papers fell to the floor and now she clutched her shawl with both hands. 'Louise,' she whispered. 'How do you know about Louise?'

'I'm one of her guardians.'

'You! But why?'

'Does it matter why? Grandmamma wanted to arrange things so that you would never have to worry about her. Do you ever worry about your daughter, Rose?'

'Be quiet!' Rose looked round wildly. 'Don't ever talk like that in this house.'

'I'm sorry. I won't. I'll never mention her again, to you or anyone you know.' Rose calmed down a little. 'But I'm still considering inviting her to live with me.'

'So?' Rose scowled uneasily. 'There's no harm in inviting an – an orphaned child to share your home.'

'Have you ever seen a picture of your – of the *orphan*?'

'No.'

'Look.' Lorna took the photograph that Mr Adamson had given her from her handbag. 'Isn't she lovely? You can see why Grandmamma was so taken with her, can't you? The child is the image of her mother.'

Rose looked at the photograph without taking it from Lorna's hand. Her eyes widened and then she shook her head as if denying what she saw. 'Put it away,' she said at last.

When Lorna had done so Rose clutched her shawl and leaned over to pick up the papers. When she righted herself she was breathing heavily. 'I suppose I could find a way to do what you want,' she said. 'As you suggested, I could blame you. Maurice seems to be fond of you.'

'Does he?' Lorna was startled.

'Yes,' Rose said waspishly, 'he's always asking about you. He'd probably be quite indulgent to any suggestion that came from my dear cousin.'

'Do you know,' Lorna said, 'that child we were talking about is very happy living in the country, and the woman who cares for her really loves her. It mightn't be such a good idea to uproot her, after all.'

She wanted to say so much more. She wanted to say: Rose, your daughter is enchanting. And she would have liked to ask her cousin how she could bear to be living apart from her own child, never to see her, never to hold her in her arms.

But she held her peace. Rose could barely meet her eyes. She had not offered tea or coffee and she did not invite her to stay for lunch. Lorna left almost immediately.

When the heavy front door closed behind her she found that the sun was trying to break through the grey clouds. The garden smelled fresh and clean.

Have I been guilty of blackmail? Lorna thought, as she hurried down the curved driveway, avoiding the drips from the overhanging branches of the trees. Well, if I have, I don't feel guilty.

But I could never have betrayed Rose, that's the irony of it. Apart from the fact that I could not destroy another woman's life, I could never have used an innocent child as a pawn.

281

Once she reached Gosforth High Street she hailed a cab to take her to the Central Station in town. Edwin was coming to have dinner with her tonight. On the train on the way home she would have to concoct an edited version of what had just happened.

But whatever she said, she could already imagine the pleasure it would give him to learn that work would soon begin on improving the homes and therefore the lives of the people he cared for.

Chapter Twenty-Three

It was much easier than she had imagined. She realized that she didn't have to lie to Edwin. All she had to do was tell him slightly less than the truth. And she started by saying that she had realized who the landlord was as soon as he mentioned Mr Pearson's name and had decided to go and see Rose.

'And your cousin agreed to carry out the improvements to her properties?'

'Yes. She had no idea the conditions were so bad. She's only just inherited the business, you know.'

Edwin shook his head. 'I don't know how to thank you.'

'You don't have to.'

'Perhaps some of the other landlords will be inspired to follow suit!'

In that moment Lorna saw how much this work meant to Edwin. And how anyone who became close to him would do better to share the same enthusiasms. And also how rewarding that might be.

'Well,' she said, 'right now I would like to inspire you to come to the dining room. You are my first proper dinner guest.'

Edwin laughed, his whole demeanour lightening, and she saw how attractive his intelligent features were. Her smiling response was tinged with regret that she had not seen this more clearly long ago.

The meal began with tomato soup. Lorna broke one of the crusty rolls nervously, scattering crumbs. She was slightly in awe of the cook Mrs Adamson had found for her. Mrs Capstaff had worked in some very grand households and Lorna suspected that she thought her talents were being wasted cooking for a young women who kept a relatively modest household.

Lorna had told her that the guest tonight was a man who was used to

283

being spoiled at the table by an indulgent aunt. Mrs Capstaff had taken that as a challenge.

The soup was followed by beefsteak pie with Savoy cabbage and creamed potatoes, and then steamed Russian pudding with chocolate sauce. Edwin accepted every course with enthusiasm and Lorna relaxed and began to enjoy herself.

'I had no idea what wine to serve,' she said at one point, 'so I asked Mrs Capstaff to choose that too. I was afraid she would think less of me but she was delighted.'

When they had finished they took their coffee to the first-floor sitting room. Edwin carried the tray himself as neither of them wished to pull the bell cord and summon Pamela, the young maid.

'It's strange,' Lorna said. 'When my grandmother was ill, I took over the running of her household. It was easy because everyone just carried on as before. They knew what to do – what she preferred. But now that I have my own establishment, I find I'm hesitant to give orders. I suppose I don't really believe that this all belongs to me. Perhaps I'll wake up one morning and find it's all vanished, like in a fairy tale.'

'What has happened to you does sound like a fairy tale, you know,' Edwin said. 'Like something from the Arabian Nights.'

'Yes.'

Lorna put down her cup and went over to the window. She had not drawn the curtains and she pushed aside the nets to gaze out at the river mouth and the sea. The moon rode high above scudding clouds and glinted on the water. The wind was strong enough to dash the waves across the top of the piers and keep the buoy bell clanging as it rode the swell.

'I've written to my father,' she said. She saw Edwin's reflection as he got up and came over to join her. 'So far I haven't had an answer.'

He didn't say anything. He simply stood very close and they looked out together. They could see lights of several ships sitting out beyond the bar, waiting for the tide to turn.

'Is that why you've moved here?' he said at last. 'Does it make you feel nearer to him?'

Lorna nodded. She didn't trust herself to speak.

Edwin had stayed late. She'd shown him which room she would furnish as a study for him and they arranged what their working plan would be. Eventually he'd had to leave in a hurry; to run for the last train to town.

She'd lain awake for hours, thinking about the time they would be spending together and wondering if it would be awkward working so closely with a man who was in love with another woman.

He hadn't said as much, but she was sure that he was in love with Irene Lawson. When Lorna had brought up the subject of the reading classes, asking him whether he would like her to take over now that Irene had gone, he'd become subdued. He had thanked her for the offer and changed the subject.

Was he hoping to find Irene and win her back from this man called Brady?

The next morning Lorna began to read through some of the papers Edwin had left, but she couldn't settle. After lunch she decided to go for a walk and she ventured as far as the ruined priory. Beside the priory there was a later building, a ruined castle keep where it was said Black Bothwell had once been imprisoned after he had dared to marry the Queen of Scotland.

The ruins looked forbidding against the winter sky, and soon a heavy sea fret that was more like rain drove her homewards. Maurice Haldane was waiting for her on the front doorstep.

'What are you doing here?' she asked.

He smiled. 'That's not very gracious. Aren't you pleased to see me?'

Was she? Lorna examined her feelings carefully and was dismayed to find that, in spite of the anger, she still felt a certain attraction. She looked up into his eyes and was disturbed to feel a familiar tug at her senses.

'No, I'm not pleased to see you,' she said.

He looked at her as though he didn't believe her. 'Well, I'm pleased to see you.'

'Why have you come here?'

'Do I have to have a reason?'

'Of course you do.'

'Aren't you going to invite me in? We shouldn't stand here on the doorstep. People will wonder.'

Lorna glanced up and down the deserted street. The sea fret had turned to rain. She raised her eyebrows. 'What people?'

Maurice smiled. 'I'm sure I saw the lace curtains twitching in the house next door.'

'Oh, come in,' she said.

She left him shedding his coat in the hallway and went along to the kitchen to ask for coffee for two.

When she returned she found that he had wandered into the dining room. She stood in the doorway and watched as he looked at her new furniture. She couldn't help thinking that he was calculating how much it had cost her.

As they climbed the stairs he said, 'You've chosen well.'

'Meaning the house?'

'Yes, and everything in it.'

In the sitting room the first thing Maurice commented on was the carpet. 'It's beautiful,' he said. 'But you didn't buy it at Haldane's.'

'No.'

'Do you know where it came from?'

'Of course. Bainbridge's.'

Maurice laughed. 'You know very well that I wasn't asking where you bought it.'

'It's a Turkish carpet,' she said.

'I know that, and supplied by a company called Orientale, I think.'

'So?'

'What made you choose it?'

'It's beautiful.'

He looked at her for a moment and then seemed to dismiss the subject. Before he could say anything else their coffee arrived and he waited until the maid had gone before he asked, 'What have you been saying to Rose?'

The change was so sudden that she was taken aback. She looked at him and found that he was frowning.

'I'm not sure what you mean.'

'Of course you know. You two haven't seen each other since your grandmother died and suddenly you call, and then I find my wife is interested in improving the conditions of her tenants.'

'Well, surely Rose told you. When I pointed out how bad things were . . . I mean . . .' She saw it was hopeless. Her cousin had been right. Maurice would never believe that his wife would undertake such a project willingly. 'I bullied her, I suppose,' she finished lamely.

'Or blackmailed her.'

'What?'

'Blackmailed her.'

'How could I do that?'

'I don't know. But there is something I don't know about. I've thought so ever since the day your grandmother's will was read. Rose was agitated that day, do you remember?

'Surely that was natural.'

'Perhaps. But there was another puzzle. Why did your grandmother

286

make no provision for you? Or did she – was there some other arrangement?'

Lorna shook her head.

'What exactly are you denying?'

'Maurice, this is pointless.'

He shrugged. 'Perhaps it is. For, in any case, I don't care. Rose can do whatever she wants with her properties – and if it pleases you, that's all the better.' Suddenly Maurice dropped his head in his hands and groaned. 'Lorna,' he said, 'what a dreadful mistake I made.'

'Mistake?'

'In marrying Rose. I should have been stronger, I should have told my parents that I loved you, I should have been prepared to brook no opposition.'

'Why didn't you?' Lorna whispered.

'Because I was weak. I was frightened my father would disinherit me. If only I'd known your true circumstances.'

'My circumstances?'

Instead of answering, he leaped to his feet and reached for her hands. He pulled her up into his arms. Lorna tried to step back but he held her all the closer.

'Lorna, don't fight me,' he said. 'Perhaps it's not too late. Divorce from Rose is not impossible . . . I'm sure there's something she's concealing from me. And if I tell my father what I've discovered . . .'

'And what have you discovered?'

His answer was not what she was expecting. 'That you are a wealthy woman in your own right; that, in fact, your fortune greatly exceeds that of your cousin.'

'How do you know this?'

'I have guessed who your father is. His business empire far exceeds our own. Once my father knows this he would soon overcome any misgivings about your racial heritage.'

'How dare you!' She tried to break free.

'Don't fight me, Lorna. You love me, you know you do.'

'No, I don't.' She twisted out of his arms and stepped back. 'Thank God I have realized at last that I don't love you, Maurice. I imagined I did because I was lonely, and you – God forgive me – you were courting Rose.'

'What has that to do with it?'

'I'm ashamed to admit it, but I think part of the reason I wanted you so much was because my cousin did too. I hope she never discovers how I betrayed her.'

'Lorna . . . please. Rose means nothing to me. I can't stand the idea of being tied to her for the rest of our lives. Just think what life would be like if we were together. How happy we would be!'

'No, stop it. I wouldn't be happy. Not with you. Now please go. And don't come here again. I don't want to see you again. Ever.'

He made to take her in his arms but, swiftly, she reached for the bell pull and tugged it to summon the parlourmaid. He stared at her wildly and then turned and left the room.

When her maid appeared Lorna asked her to follow Mr Haldane down and see him out. Then she crossed over to the window and looked out into the street. After a moment she saw Maurice striding away through the rain.

Maurice turned up his collar and hunched his shoulders against the weather. The rain was turning to sleet, and the wind blowing in from the North Sea was bitterly cold. But he was burning with anger.

How dare she refuse him? He'd offered marriage this time, hadn't she understood that? Oh, divorce was unsavoury, but it was becoming more accepted and Rose would go quietly if the settlement was large enough. And, even if she didn't, he was pretty sure now that there was something she was hiding. Something that could be used against her.

Surely Lorna wasn't holding out because of any loyalty she might feel to Rose. No, he couldn't believe that. She'd been happy enough to deceive her at first. Sneaking out to meet him in the park like any shop girl.

They were all the same. No matter how virtuous they pretended to be. Even that little Italian chambermaid – what was her name? Lucia? Even Lucia, who attended Mass twice a day, even she had succumbed to a big enough purse. Although she pretended she needed the money for her sick mother. No, in the end they could all be bought. Whether for a few coins in a back alley or a wedding ring on their finger, it was a financial transaction, that was all.

It was the money. That was it! Now that Lorna had money of her own she was hoping for a grand match. Didn't she know what sort of man she would attract once it got around that she was some sort of heiress?

But how sly the old woman had been! She must have known all along that her other granddaughter was a better match financially. That's why she kept Lorna in ignorance of her true situation – so that she could marry off her precious Rose first! She made fools of us all.

It was late afternoon. Should he go home and spend a boring hour or two with his wife before dinner or should he go straight into town? Town, he decided. He could have a bite to eat and find a game of cards. Or perhaps some other distraction.

There was only one other passenger in the carriage when he caught the train back to Newcastle. A young woman. From force of habit Maurice looked at her, pulling down the brim of his hat to shield his gaze.

The lamps were lit in the carriage, making it appear darker outside, so instead of looking at her directly, he stared at her reflection in the window. She was well dressed, with a good coat of astrakhan trimmed with a white fur collar. Her hat, also of white fur, was Russian style. It sat on her piled-up hair at a jaunty angle. And yet her air was not jaunty. She looked tired and sad.

The young woman appeared not to notice him at all. She had her head turned away from him, as if she was looking out at the passing scene, but Maurice doubted if she saw anything. Her attitude was one of distraction.

She had a fair complexion, perhaps a little too pale, but that could be because of her mood, and she'd be attractive if only she would stop frowning, he thought. It crossed his mind to strike up some sort of conversation – you never knew where that might lead – but at that moment, she turned round and looked directly at him.

She pulled up the fur collar of her coat to shield her face and turned away again. Her glance had been so unwelcoming that Maurice gave up any idea of talking to her. Just as well, he thought. We're alone now, but you never know who might get on to the train at one of the stops and remember me.

When Irene got off the train at the Central Station she hung back and let the other passenger leave well ahead of her. At first she hadn't been aware that he was looking at her, she had been too lost in her own thoughts, but then she had gradually become aware of his reflection in the window.

She'd stared at the reflection, idly for a moment, noting that the man was tall, well dressed and good looking so far as she could see. He had the brim of his homburg pulled down and well forward.

But she was alerted to the fact that something was not quite as it should be when she realized that he was sitting very still. He hadn't moved for some time and his head was turned in her direction.

He's watching me, she thought. And that made her nervous. It was the fact that he was tall . . .

What had Jess said? Something about the man who had murdered her sister and the other girls being tall . . . and being a toff. That's all they knew about him.

She'd turned suddenly to glare at him, at the same time adjusting the collar of her coat, and he had looked away. That was all that had happened. But it had unnerved her.

The café in the main concourse of the station was busy. People waiting for trains home after a day's work in town read newspapers; women who'd been on shopping trips sat surrounded by bags and parcels as they gossiped. There were hardly any seats to spare.

Irene found a table with a group of schoolgirls and ordered a pot of tea. The three girls hardly glanced at her. They were talking excitedly about the play rehearsal they had just attended after school. Their eyes shone and their young voices were cheerful and confident. They looked bonny in their green school uniforms, Irene thought. She judged them to be about fifteen. By their age she had been working for three years. She wasn't that much older than they were now, but her life had been so different from theirs. Could she go back to that life now?

Ever since Jess Green had come to see her she had known that she would have to make that decision. But what could she do? She could never go back to Byker. Apart from the fact that there was no work there for her, there were too many memories . . . bad memories.

What then? Find a job where she could live in? But she didn't want to go into service. She acknowledged that she thought herself too good for that, so what did that leave? Some of the big department stores had hostels for the shop assistants. That might do. She remembered how she had once thought it marvellous if she could get a job in Wilkinson's.

She knew herself well enough to know that she yearned not just for comfort but also for a certain amount of luxury. She thought of the way the house at Cullercoats was furnished and how she'd enjoyed living there. But if she decided she couldn't live there any longer, would she be able to gain a sort of second-hand satisfaction from working with the fine fabrics that Wilkinson's sold? The silks, the satins, the velvets . . . choosing and advising those who could afford them?

The schoolgirls had gone; she hadn't noticed them leaving. She looked around. There weren't so many people now and the waitresses were taking the opportunity to fill up the sugar bowls and place more sandwiches and cakes in the glass counter.

Two of them were looking at her, heads together. Without appearing to, she listened to what they were saying.

'. . . been there a while . . .'

'. . . just one pot of tea.'

'. . . thought she was with the girls at first. One of the teachers.'

'No, she's too well dressed.'

'What do you think?'

'She looks respectable enough.'

'Some of them do. But it's just about time for the evening trade to begin.'

'Has she paid her bill?'

'Yes, and a tip.'

'Better ask her to leave. Say we need the table. Be polite.'

The girl started to make her way between the white-clothed tables but, long before she reached her, Irene got up and walked towards the exit, trying to look as dignified as possible.

She knew very well what the two waitresses had been trying to decide: whether she was one of the street girls who plied for trade in the station. The rougher sort hung about in the portico outside, but the more expensive girls would sneak into the buffet if they could and try to look like respectable customers. Their clients were businessmen and commercial travellers.

And how respectable am I? she wondered. I have allowed Jack Brady to feed and clothe me, to keep me in comfort, and I have given him nothing in return. And to do him justice, he wants to marry me. If I agree I would never want again. Life would be easy.

But would my mind be easy? Could I ever get used to the idea that my comfort and respectability had been bought by other women?

Jess Green had told her that Jack Brady looked after the girls who worked for him. She knew that he believed he was helping some make a living who otherwise would have lived in poverty. But even Jess admitted that the old and the ugly had been relegated to cleaning or work in the kitchens.

Irene walked out through the grand portico of the station. It was still raining and the streetlamps shone on the pavements and illuminated the flakes of sleet. She felt her fur hat get heavier as it collected moisture.

The roads were busy with the usual horse traffic, motorcars and trams. Irene walked past the cab stand. She wouldn't take a cab. She wasn't going far and she still had to nerve herself for what she was going to do.

Jack had kept her distanced from the way he made his living. It seemed that he wanted to put her in a separate compartment. But that wouldn't do. If she decided to marry him she could not do so without

291

facing up to what that would make her. A woman who was prepared to prosper and take her ease from the proceeds of prostitution. The prostitution of other women.

In spite of the hardship she would face if she left him, she didn't think she could do it. But she knew how much she owed him and she wanted to be fair. It was no good trying to discuss the matter with him in the comfortable haven of his house in Cullercoats.

She would have to face him in his other world – his real world – in the house on Westgate Road.

'Mr Brady, sir, there's some trouble upstairs.' Mulligan looked uneasy.

Jack was eating from a tray in his private room. He had furnished it like a gentleman's study with a mahogany desk and filing cabinet, but he often took his meals there, away from the public dining room where he was always on show.

He was enjoying cold roast beef sandwiches and a pint of brown ale. Not the sort of thing he served to the punters, who paid top prices for menus thought up by the chef he'd brought in from Paris.

'What kind of trouble? Someone won't pay?'

'No, not that, Mr Brady.'

Mulligan's huge frame looked impressive in the formal evening clothes that Brady insisted he wore. But his face and ears could have belonged to no one except an ex-boxer. Brady kept him here at the house on Westgate Road as a precaution. Up until now he had only had to ease a few high-spirited young sparks out into the night when they got overboisterous. There had been nothing he couldn't handle.

Jack sighed, pulled the napkin from his collar and threw it down on the desk. 'What then?'

'One of the girls is screaming. It doesn't sound good.'

'Why don't you go in and stop whatever's happening?'

'I would, Mr Brady, sir, but it's Mr Haldane in there. He's a toff – important. He could cause trouble. I thought I'd better tell you.'

Brady crossed to the door swiftly and began to race up the stairs. As he ascended he heard the screams. They were muffled as though someone was trying to stop them. On the top landing he found two of the other girls, wrapped in silk robes, hovering uneasily, clutching each other's arms.

'Go back to your rooms,' Brady told them. 'I'm going in. Mulligan, wait here.' He opened the door, entered the room, and then closed it behind him.

'What the hell . . .?'

292

The man turned round and glared at him furiously. He was kneeling on the bed with both his hands around the girl's throat. She was naked. He had on only his shirt. Brady hurled himself across the room and got an arm around his neck, tightening his grip and pulling him backwards at the same time. The girl fell free and began to sob. Brady threw her attacker to the floor, where he lay gasping for breath.

'Are you all right?' Brady asked the girl.

She nodded, unable to speak. She began to rub her throat with one hand and Brady noticed there were red marks on her wrists and a weal round her neck. There was a trickle of blood at the corner of her mouth and her lips and eyelids were beginning to swell.

Brady picked up her robe and put it round her shoulders. 'I'm sorry,' he said. 'He won't be allowed in here again. Go to the other girls. They'll look after you.'

When she'd gone he turned his attention to the man who was beginning to pick himself up. 'You could have killed me,' he complained.

'Pity I didn't.'

'It was just a bit of horseplay. Some of them like it, you know.'

'That wasn't horseplay. That was brutal.'

'I paid her well. She agreed.'

'She would never agree to be marked.'

Brady walked over to the dressing table and picked up the china dish full of coins. 'How much did you pay her?' he asked, and, without waiting for an answer, he tossed the entire contents of the dish across the floor. Some of the coins clinked against the empty wine bottles lying near the bed. 'Take your money and go, Mr Haldane,' he said. 'And never come back here again.'

Haldane began to pull his clothes on. Brady noticed that he was unsteady and his eyes were wild. He started to laugh. 'They're all the same,' he said, 'all the same.'

'What are you talking about?'

'Women. They all have a price. Perhaps I just didn't pay enough.'

'Don't you know you could have killed her?'

'So? Would that have been a great loss to the world?'

In that instant Brady knew who he was dealing with. He'd never be able to prove it, but he could put the word around. This man must be stopped one way or another.

Mulligan and Brady escorted Haldane down the stairs, taking an arm each. When they got to the entrance hall Brady smiled at him and said politely, 'Shall we get you a cab, sir?'

293

This was for the benefit of a group of gentlemen who had just entered.

Haldane laughed. 'No, I think I'll walk home. Never know what I might pick up on the way.'

Brady was just about to signal Mulligan to follow him when the front door opened again and, to his astonishment, Irene came in.

'What are you doing here?' he asked.

Irene stared at him mutely. Raindrops glistened in her pale hair and in the white fur of her hat. The surprise of seeing her made him forget Haldane, so he was taken by surprise when the man lurched forward.

'Why, it's you,' he said to Irene.

Irene looked up into his face and her eyes widened.

'Did you follow me here?' he asked.

She shook her head.

'No, of course you didn't – you must work here, that's it.'

Not understanding any of it, Brady was only aware of a mounting fury. 'Do you know this man?' he asked.

'Of course not.'

'Then why is he talking to you like this?'

'He was on the train – the same carriage. He was looking at me . . .'

Haldane began to laugh. 'And you were looking at me, don't deny it.' Suddenly he lurched forward, freeing himself from Mulligan's grip. 'I'm going,' he said. 'I'm not wanted here.'

He opened the door and, at the same time, he seized hold of Irene's arm. 'Do you want to come with me?'

Irene pulled away. He was unsteady and she evaded him easily, but then Brady sprang forward and grabbed him. He propelled him out of the door and down the steps, and at the bottom he hurled him into the road.

The tram driver didn't even see the man before he hit him. But he heard the blood-chilling scream, and it would haunt his dreams for the rest of his life.

Chapter Twenty-Four

'How long has she been here?'

Edwin looked at the forlorn figure huddled in the armchair near the fire.

'Since Albert went to work this morning,' Bella replied. 'But I hev no idea how long she'd been standing outside.'

'Irene?' Edwin said. 'Can you tell me what happened?'

Irene didn't answer him. She didn't even look up. She sat with her hands clasped around the mug of tea that Bella Charlton had given her, making no attempt to drink it. She stared into the flames but, judging by the look of terror in her eyes, she took no comfort from them.

'I've tried to get her to take her coat and hat off,' Bella said. 'The coat's wet through and the hat's sodden. Look at the way the water's dripping down on to her face. She'll catch her death if she stays like that, but she looks terrified if a body gans near her. It was Albert who brought her in – he coaxed her, very gentle like. Just like he was talking to a bairn. We might hev got somewhere with her if he could hev stayed, but he had to gan to work.'

'He did very well,' Edwin said. 'But tell me exactly what happened this morning.'

Edwin sat at the table and Bella joined him there. They drank hot, sweet tea and glanced now and then at Irene as they talked. Irene gave no sign of listening. But Edwin noticed her fingers tightening round the mug as Bella's tale progressed.

'It was still dark when Albert left for work,' she began. 'I always sees him on his way, you know. I know it's daft, but he's as soft as clarts, and he likes to give us a kiss just afore he opens the door. Well, I telt him to be good – like I was sending him to school – and we had a bit laugh and then we nearly died of fright! The moon was still up and she was standing there, on the pavement, like a little ghost, just staring up at the roof of our house.

' "Who the hell are you?" Albert said, and I telt him not swear. Anyways, I pulled meself together and I telt him who she was and we decided we'd better bring her in. Albert coaxed her, like I said, and then I just had to sit here with her until it was light enough to send that lad Davy to your uncle's shop with a note.'

'Poor lad, he walked all the way,' Edwin said.

Bella flushed. 'I didn't think to give him tram fare. Ee, I'm sorry.'

'No, no, I didn't mean it as a criticism. And my uncle made a fuss of him. The three of us had toast and marmalade together in the back shop.'

'And you brought him back safe.'

'Yes. But you did right to send for me.' Edwin frowned. He'd had a chance to read the newspaper this morning before Davy had arrived at the shop but he didn't think Bella would know the news yet. 'Why do you think she came here?' he asked.

'I divven't know.'

'And she was staring up at the roof?'

'Aye, just like I telt you.'

'She said nothing at all?'

'Well, yes, she did. But it didn't explain what she was doing here.'

'So what did she say?'

'Poor Billy.'

'Ah.'

'Well, that's natural, I suppose. I mean, that's where the poor soul landed. Folk round here haven't forgotten. In fact, to tell you the truth, Mr Randall, that's one of the reasons we've decided to move to Shields.'

'So you're going, then?'

'Aye. I'm not a fanciful person, but sometimes, on a dark night, when the wind's blowing and the slates are rattling, I look up and think of that poor soul lying there.'

'No, oh, no . . .' Those were the first words Irene had spoken and they both looked at her. But she said no more; she just continued to stare into the fire.

'Aye, Albert's got the job he was after,' Bella said, 'and there's a bit more pay.'

'I'm glad for you, Bella. But, now . . .'

'I know. What are we going to do with the lass?'

'I'll take her to a friend of mine; I'm sure she'll let her stay for a while.' Edwin took the folded newspaper from the pocket of his overcoat and pushed it across the table. 'Here,' he said. 'I'll leave you my *Daily Journal*.'

'That's all right, hinny, Albert will bring one home. I'll hev a bit read of it afore I gans to bed. And, in any case, Albert'll tell me anything I needs to know.'

Edwin smiled. 'Well, why not be first with the news for change?'

He kept his hand on the newspaper while he looked into Bella's eyes. She frowned and then looked down to where his fingers were pointing. Her eyes widened and Edwin shook his head very slightly.

'Thanks, Mr Randall,' she said. 'I'll sit by the fire and read it while Albert's dinner's cooking.'

Satisfied that she had caught his meaning, Edwin rose and went over to Irene. It seemed to take a moment or two before she became aware of him. Then she looked up.

'Edwin,' she said. She sounded sad.

'Would you come with me?' he asked. 'I'll see that you are safe.'

She gave a great sigh and rose to her feet. 'That's the second time he's done that for me, you know,' she said, confirming what Edwin had long suspected about Jack Brady.

'Don't talk about it now. Just come with me.'

Bella Charlton didn't know what Irene had been talking about. But she suspected that something had driven the girl out of her wits. When she read the newspaper that Edwin had left for her, she guessed what that was.

HORRIBLE TRAM DEATH IN NEWCASTLE

The son of a prominent Newcastle businessman was killed instantly when he was struck by a tram late last night.

Twenty-five-year-old Mr Maurice Haldane was leaving a gentlemen's club on Westgate Road when witnesses say he was thrown into the path of a tram travelling down Westgate Hill.

Mr Haldane was taken by motor ambulance to the nearby General Hospital where he was pronounced dead.

Sadly, Mr Haldane's beautiful wife, Rose, is expecting their first child. She and Mr Haldane's family are deeply shocked and saddened.

A witness told our reporter that there was some altercation over a well-dressed young woman.

After taking several witness statements, the police are looking for a man.

Mr Jack Brady, a former heavyweight boxer and owner of the gentlemen's club, has not been seen since the incident.

'Are you sure you don't mind?' Edwin said quietly. 'I feel I'm imposing on you but I couldn't think where else to take her.'

He stood with Lorna at the window of her first-floor sitting room and, as he spoke, he glanced over his shoulder to where Irene Lawson sat by the fire. Her hat had slipped forward on to her brow and wet tendrils of hair snaked down to her shoulders. Her eyes were open but she stared into the middle distance unseeingly.

Lorna took so long to reply that Edwin began to have misgivings. She had been standing looking out towards the mouth of the river when the maid had shown Irene and him in, and she had made no attempt to move forward and greet them.

He had taken it upon himself to settle Irene by the fire and, as he did so, he noticed this morning's *Daily Journal* on a small table. The way it was carelessly folded indicated that it had been read.

Lorna barely glanced at them and, even when he walked over to join her, she continued to stare out of the window. He had been so sure that she would agree to shelter Irene. In fact, if Lorna had been with him that morning in Bella Charlton's house, he was sure she would have suggested it herself.

He had thought they were friends and yet she seemed to have put a distance between them. Surely he hadn't been mistaken about her compassionate nature.

'She can stay until you can sort out something more permanent,' Lorna said, at last turning away from the window to look at him directly. 'Presumably you believe Irene is the woman mentioned in the newspaper report.'

'That would be an understandable explanation for her behaviour.'

'But what about the police? Won't they want to see her?'

'I'm sure they will have questioned her last night. But I suppose I'd better call in to the West End police station and let them know where she is.' His eyes widened with concern. 'I never thought of that. You won't want to be involved in any kind of investigation, will you?'

'Involved?'

'I shouldn't imagine you'll want the police calling here.'

'Don't worry. I think I can stand the scandal.'

'You're making me feel worse.'

'How am I doing that?'

298

'By using the word "scandal". It's no use, I'll find somewhere else for her.'

'For goodness' sake, Edwin. You've brought her here so leave her in peace. And perhaps I should persuade her to go to bed for the rest of the day.' She paused. 'All right?'

Edwin realized that she was dismissing him. For the first time since they had known each other there was an awkwardness between them. In fact he believed that they had come very close to quarrelling. Perhaps he had assumed too much when he'd brought Irene here. He acknowledged that even his good-natured aunt might have been hesitant to take such a young woman into her home.

But, no, he didn't think that was the reason for Lorna's displeasure. There was something else. He wished he knew what it was.

Lorna looked at him impatiently. 'I'll have to do something with her fairly quickly because I'll have to go to Rose, you know.'

'Of course. I'm sorry. I just didn't think!' So that was it.

She sighed. 'Look, it's all right your bringing her here. Rose need never know. And I feel no loyalty to Maurice Haldane.'

Edwin was surprised at how bitter she sounded. And more confused than ever.

'Well, I'll go . . . but I'll telephone you later, if I may?'

'I won't be in. I'm going to see my cousin, remember?'

'Oh, yes.'

'Now, I'll summon Pamela, tell her to get a bedroom ready, and then ask her to help me get Irene out of those wet clothes.'

But before Lorna had reached the bell pull by the fireplace, there was a knock at the door and the young maid entered.

'This letter has arrived for you, Miss Hassan.'

'A second post?'

'No, miss. It was delivered by hand. The young man said he worked for Mr Adamson.'

'Is he waiting for an answer?'

'No, miss. He said to tell you that this is something you've been waiting for.'

Edwin watched in astonishment as Lorna seemed to drain of colour. He took a step towards her but she raised a hand to stop him.

'Thank you, Pamela,' she said, and took the letter. Then, strangely, she didn't look at it. She held it close to her body with both hands while she asked the young maid to prepare a bedroom for her guest.

'Oh, and see Mr Randall out, will you?' she added, almost as an afterthought.

299

'Goodbye,' Edwin said. 'And thank you.'

'Mm.'

She didn't even look at him. He glanced back before he left the room and Lorna was standing in the same place, clutching the letter, her eyes were shining, but whether with happiness or with tears Edwin couldn't tell.

It wasn't until Irene was warm and dry and safely sleeping that Lorna gave instructions that she mustn't be disturbed under any circumstances. Then she settled herself by the fire and opened the letter.

My dearest daughter,

My little Lorna Doone. You know why we called you Lorna, don't you? When you were a small child, your mother and I must have told you so many times the romantic tale of how we met at a lecture at the library and how she undertook to teach me to read and write English properly using her favourite childhood story.

That is a happy memory, but there are sad things we have to talk about. I want to tell you how heartbroken I was when I realized that I had lost your mother for ever. She was beautiful, intelligent and kind, and her loving, passionate nature recognized no differences between men and women of different races.

I must also tell you what a painful decision it was to leave you with your grandmother. And, believe me, I would never have done so if she had not convinced me that she would love and cherish you.

At those words Lorna felt hot tears well up and scald the back of her eyes. It was several moments before she could begin to read again.

However, I don't think a letter is the place for what I want to say about that. So we will wait until we are together again. When you can ask all the questions that deserve an answer. And we will be together as soon as I can arrange it.

Once more Lorna had to stop reading. This time excitement made it almost impossible for her to hold the pages steady. She had to wait until her hands stopped shaking before she started to read again.

But there are other things you should know, my daughter. And I want you to know them before we meet. After many years I

300

married again. Does that shock you? I hope not. Your stepmother is a Frenchwoman; I met her in Egypt where I now live. Her family are merchants who settled in Alexandria many years ago.

My wife's name is Amalie and she has made me happy again. I hope that you will love her and that she will love you when you meet. For, of course, you must come and visit your family as often as I can persuade you. I say family because you have a small brother and a sister. Cristophe is eight years old and Fleur is six.

She had a brother and a sister!

I would like to say, come and live with us, but I realize that you may have made a life for yourself in England. Perhaps, my Lorna, you have found your own steadfast John Ridd! If you have, then you are both welcome. It must be for you to decide.

Lorna leaned back into the cushions and closed her eyes. She heard the fire crackling in the hearth and a light rain begin to beat against the window. She tried to imagine her father's house in Egypt.

It would be white, with a flat roof perhaps. Would it have a courtyard and a fountain? There would surely be palm trees. And would there be a shaded garden where Christophe and Fleur played?

Christophe and Fleur . . . her brother and sister!

Did she mind that her father had married again?

No, of course not.

She returned to the letter where her father apologized for taking so long to answer her letter to him. He told her that he had been at the workshops in Sultanabad when the letter had been delivered to his business premises in Paris, and they had sent it on to his home in Egypt. Once he had opened it he'd answered it straight away.

Then Lorna read the last paragraph over and over again:

And now I am arranging to follow the letter in person. It won't be very long before we are together again.

Your loving father.

Have I made a life for myself in England? she wondered. Only because it is all I knew.

Have I found a John Ridd of my own? For a very brief moment I was beginning to believe that I might have.

I would have been happy to live here and help Edwin with his work, but now that he has found Irene again will he want that?

Shall I go to live in Egypt?

Would I fit in there?

Could I make a new and different life for myself?

Lorna knew that she would not be able to decide these matters until she had talked to her father, but now something from her old life called. She must go and see Rose.

Rose was in bed. Her mother-in-law had left strict instructions that she must not be disturbed. No one was to be allowed to see her except close family. Lorna had got as far as the oak-panelled hallway.

'But I am a member of the family,' she told the severe-looking nurse.

The woman was dressed in her professional uniform. Lorna had never seen anyone who looked so scrubbed clean, and when she moved, her starched white pinafore crackled.

'And who exactly are you?' she asked.

'I am Miss Hassan. Mrs Haldane's cousin. Her *first* cousin!' Lorna added when the woman showed no sign of giving way. 'Well, will you at least tell me how she is?'

'Mrs Haldane seems to be well physically, but Dr Gibson thought it best that she should have bed rest in case her grief should start anything untoward.'

'A miscarriage? Oh, poor Rose.'

The nurse looked at Lorna a little more kindly. 'She should be all right,' she said. 'This is, as I said, a precaution. The poor young woman doesn't seem to be able to stop crying.'

'Please let me see her. I really am her cousin, you know. Why don't you go and ask her?'

Unexpectedly the woman smiled. 'I will. And if Mrs Haldane wants to see you, you may be able to do a better job comforting her than her sisters-in-law did this morning.'

A short while later Lorna was shown upstairs to Rose's bedroom by the nurse, whose manner had relaxed considerably. 'She's so pleased you're here,' she whispered at the door. 'Go on in. I'll send up a tray with tea and biscuits.'

Rose's first words, broken by sobs, took Lorna by surprise. 'Lorna,' she said, 'come and sit by me. Tell me it's not all my fault!'

'Why on earth should what's happened be your fault?'

The room was overheated and Lorna took off her coat before sitting on the chair placed by the bed. The tray arrived almost immediately and Lorna sat and listened to Rose's hiccoughing sobs until the maid left the room.

'Rose, please stop that,' Lorna said as soon as they were alone. 'You'll make yourself ill.'

'I deserve to be ill,' her cousin declaimed dramatically. 'If I could have made Maurice love me more, if he had been happy to stay at home with me, he would never have gone to such a place!'

'You can't say that. Many men of Maurice's class go to gambling clubs.'

Rose dropped her head and couldn't meet Lorna's eyes when she said, 'I think it was something more than a gambling club.'

'Rose, I just don't know, and neither do you. And you shouldn't torture yourself like this. Think – think of the baby – Maurice's baby.'

Rose looked sulky. 'That's what his sisters kept saying this morning. Charlotte and Geraldine. They kept going on about the precious babe, their precious brother's mortal inheritance, for goodness' sake. They want me to take care and rest because of the baby – not because of me!'

'Oh, Rose. You haven't changed.'

Rose looked affronted. 'Are you criticising me at a time like this?'

'No, I'm not. It's just that, well, I'm sure you loved Maurice—'

'Desperately!'

Lorna thought it might have been truer to say that Rose had been desperate to be married to Maurice rather than she had loved him deeply but now was not the time to say so. 'Well, in that case you should be concerned about the baby too,' she said.

Rose was silent for a while and then she said, 'Well, of course I am. Very concerned. That's why I've agreed to shut up my lovely home and go and live with Maurice's parents until after my confinement. And maybe for a year or two after that.'

'You won't mind handing over your life to them?'

'Well, no. They've always been very good to me, and this will be their grandchild.'

'They have other grandchildren.'

'You know what I mean. This will be Maurice's child. He will be the – the heir.'

'And what if "he" is a "she"?'

'She will still be Maurice's child. And this is the twentieth century. Women inherit businesses, you know. I did. And as far as business is concerned I'd like you to know that I won't go back on my promise to carry out the improvements on the properties in Byker. But you must keep your part of the bargain.'

'Did we strike a bargain?'

'You know we did!'

'Of course, I'm sorry. But may I ask one question?'

'If you have to.'

'Will you ever want to see her?'

Rose shook her head. 'How could I? The Haldanes must never know.'

'And Harry?'

Rose's eyes widened. 'You said one question! But if you're going to ask what I think you're going to ask, the answer's no. Why should he be told? He took advantage of me, you know!'

'Is that how you see it?'

'Of course he did. I was just an innocent girl and he was much older. He should have behaved better.'

'Yes, he should. But it seems to me that he really loved you – and still does.'

'Does he?' There was a catch in Rose's voice.

'Yes, he does,' Lorna said. 'I'm sure of it.'

Rose lay back amongst the pillows. After a long silence she said sadly, 'It would be impossible.'

Lorna knew what her cousin meant and she also knew that it wasn't the proper time to say any more than, 'Well, it's something to think about, isn't it?'

'Mm,' Rose said. 'I have a lot to think about.' She sat forward again and tried to smile. 'For example, if I were to move back here as soon as possible after my confinement, would you come and see me?'

'You'd really want me to?'

'Yes.'

'Even though I might tell you things you wouldn't want to hear about people you wouldn't want to acknowledge?'

Rose looked at her steadily for a moment and then said, 'Yes. In fact I suspect that may be why I'd want you to visit me.'

'Then I shall come.'

'And, Lorna, do you think we might ever become friends?'

Lorna smiled. 'That's something I shall have to think about. Now, shall I pour this tea?'

Lorna took her leave soon after that. She was relieved that Rose had been too distracted to be curious about her own changed circumstances; for it was not in Lorna's nature to talk about her new wealth.

On the way home she realized that whatever she decided to do with her life, she was going to be responsible for Louise and she accepted that.

304

At home Mrs Capstaff told her that Miss Lawson had slept for an hour or two and then taken a tray in her room. She'd had chicken broth and a milk jelly and managed to eat most of it.

Oh, and a rather rough young woman had called, a Miss Green. She'd asked to see Miss Lawson, and Mrs Capstaff had seen no harm in it. The two of them had talked for a while and then Miss Green had taken her leave. Miss Lawson had still looked strained but perhaps a little more settled after that.

When Pamela looked in on her later she seemed to be sleeping. It would be better to leave her in peace, perhaps. Lorna agreed. Try as she might to summon up her better nature, she knew that she couldn't face Irene Lawson.

She would leave that until the morning.

Chapter Twenty-Five

The room was dark except for a small glow from the hearth. Lorna was already awake when Kate came in quietly to make up the fire.

Lorna didn't stir. Her bed was a comfortable nest formed by the feather mattress, goose-down pillows and quilted silk-covered eider-down. The Irish linen sheets were scented with lavender; that was supposed to induce easeful sleep, but she had not slept well. All night the sound of the foghorns on the ships waiting at the mouth of the river had been an accompaniment to her uneasy thoughts.

They boomed out across the waves, warning each other of danger. In the dark stillness of her room Lorna imagined it was the calls of legendary sea monsters who had awoken in their lairs deep beneath the North Sea.

These monsters stirred the waters with their tails, creating a terrifying whirlpool where even the largest ships could be dragged down into the depths with all their crews. Hadn't the Kraken itself been sighted not far from here, off the coast of Norway?

Lorna was amused by her own imaginings but she acknowledged, nevertheless, how perilous it was to journey out across the oceans of the world. As her father did . . .

Kate rattled the coal scuttle as she put it down and she glanced round nervously. Lorna didn't want to frighten the girl so she stretched and yawned, then sat up slowly.

'Ee, I'm sorry, Miss Hassan, did I waken you?'

'No, Kate, I wasn't asleep. I've been lying listening to the ships.'

'The foghorns, you mean?'

'Mm. It must be pretty thick out there.'

'Aye, Miss Hassan. You can't see a hand in front of yer face. Walking along from the village this morning I was frightened I'd stray off the cliff path and fall on to the rocks below. Me da and me brothers'll be under me ma's feet today.'

'Why's that?'

'There'll be no fishing till this clears.'

'Of course not.'

Lorna's maid-of-all-work came from one of the fishing families in Cullercoats. Kate was the youngest of fourteen children and, like three of her sisters, had been sent into service because there were plenty more at home to help with the fishing.

Kate finished by sweeping the hearth and she stood up. 'Miss Hassan . . .' she began.

'What is it?'

'Seeing you're awake, shall I fetch you up a cup of tea?'

'Thank you. I'd love that.'

Lorna had the impression that the girl had been going to say something else and then had changed her mind. When her tea arrived, it was Pamela who brought it. She put the cup on the night table and stood there hesitantly.

The mystery deepens, Lorna thought. She hoped Pamela wasn't going to tell her that there was some problem with the household, that her newly acquired staff were unhappy. But it wasn't that at all.

'That lass – Miss Lawson – she's gone,' Pamela said.

'Gone?'

'Aye, miss. I mean, yes, Miss Hassan. I told Kate to make up Miss Lawson's fire first and see if she was all right – I hope you don't mind?'

'No, of course not.'

'Well, she's gone. The bed was empty. She'd turned the bedclothes down neatly, mind, but there was no trace of her. We were going to tell Mrs Capstaff but she's not down yet and Kate said you were awake, so . . .'

'That's all right, Pamela. You did right to tell me. Have you and Kate had your breakfast yet?'

'Just a cup of tea. Mrs Capstaff makes a bit of breakfast for all of us when she comes down. That won't be long.'

'Well, would you tell her that I'm getting up now and I'd like my breakfast too?'

'Yes, miss. I'll see to the fire in the dining room straight away.'

'I won't be eating there. Tell Mrs Capstaff that I'd like to join you in the kitchen. I'll have whatever the rest of you are having.'

'Ee, Miss Hassan, I don't know what she'll say!'

307

'Neither do I, Pamela, but you can tell me later!'

They smiled at each other and Kate left the room. While Lorna sipped her tea she thought over what she must do. She hoped Irene hadn't done anything foolish, anything that might put her life in danger. Edwin must be told; but perhaps he would not thank her if she roused his uncle's household at this ungodly hour. She would delay at least until she'd had her breakfast.

The kitchen was warm and everything was spotlessly clean. Lorna sat at the head of the table. Judging by Kate's look of astonishment, Lorna surmised that the white linen tablecloth was not a usual feature of the staff breakfasts, but the meal of porridge, boiled eggs and toast might very well be. She had told Mrs Capstaff from the start that this was not to be a parsimonious household.

Kate and Pamela were quiet but the cook-housekeeper talked to her politely. However, Lorna realized very soon that she had made a mistake. This was Mrs Capstaff's domain. She was the mistress here and Lorna was an intruder. She would not do this again.

Am I destined to sit in my grand dining room and eat all my meals alone? she wondered. I don't know if I will be able to bear that.

After the meal she thanked them all for looking after her unexpected guest and told them not to worry. She would try to find out what had happened to her.

She went through to the morning room and looked in the directory that had arrived with her new telephone. She discovered to her relief that Edwin's uncle had a connection at his house in Spital Tongues.

It must have been one of Edwin's young cousins who answered. When Lorna asked to speak to him there was a surprised silence, a burst of suppressed giggles, then young voices whispering to each other.

'Edwin!' she heard someone call. 'It's for you. The caller gave her name as Miss Hassan.' There was a pause. 'She sounds like a *young lady*.' Another pause, then, 'Oooo, Edwin!'

'I'm sorry about that,' he said when he came to the telephone. 'My cousin Emily can be quite silly at times.' His voice became faint as though he had turned his mouth away from the receiver. 'Emily, Sonia, I would be grateful if you would leave me in peace.'

More giggles and the sound of a door closing. Lorna found the small incident had made her envious. For all it sounded chaotic in that house, Edwin had never had to eat his meals alone. She realized she was feeling sorry for herself, something she detested, and she did her best to bring her mind back to the matter in hand.

308

Edwin was shocked when she told him that Irene had gone. 'And she didn't tell you?' he said.

'No. Not a word.'

'But what can have happened?'

'I haven't said or done anything to make her feel unwelcome, if that's what you're thinking.'

'No, of course not.'

'In fact I haven't spoken to her since just after you left here yesterday.'

'What a puzzle.'

'Oh . . . but . . .'

'What is it?'

'When I got home from my cousin's house yesterday I was told Irene had had a visitor.'

'Who was that?' Edwin sounded alarmed.

'Don't worry, it wasn't Jack Brady. It was a young woman called Jess Green. Does that mean anything to you?'

'Yes, it does.'

But Edwin didn't elaborate. He thanked her for telling him and he said he would phone or call later to tell her what he could discover, if anything.

'Good,' she said, 'you do that.' She replaced the receiver.

She wished she could have sounded as if she cared. She did care inasmuch as she didn't want any harm to come to the girl. For Edwin's sake she hoped nothing terrible had happened. But once this further problem was resolved she really thought she might decide to sell this house and go to Egypt to be with her family.

The fog hadn't lifted and later that day Lorna stood at her customary place by the window, but she couldn't even see the street below, let alone a view of the river. It was as if her house had been cut off from the rest of the world. Outside there was an enveloping rolling greyness that obscured vision and deadened sound.

It played tricks with you, Lorna thought. Now and then the greyness swirled and gave a tantalizing glimpse of – of what? A tree? There were no trees in the street below. A lamppost then? Perhaps. But the shape would very soon merge again with the mist and be gone.

She wondered if the tradesmen, the baker, the butcher, the ice man, had been able to deliver today. Now and then she heard a muffled clopping that could have been a cart horse. Milkmen's horses, it was said, knew their rounds better than the dairymen and would stop at each customer's house of their own accord, even with blinkers on.

When Edwin came, just after lunch, he looked tired. He'd hardly settled himself in the chair at the other side of the hearth when he said, 'I know where Irene is.' He paused as if expecting a question but Lorna remained silent. 'Jess Green told me. Irene is with an old friend of her mother's, Mrs Hepburn, the manageress of a hotel in Newcastle. She's safe.'

'I'm glad,' Lorna said, and found she meant it.

'It took some persuading,' Edwin continued, 'but, eventually, Jess told me what happened that night.'

'And what exactly did happen?' Lorna's curiosity got the better of her.

'I'm told there was a quarrel. Maurice Haldane was leaving Brady's club just as Irene arrived. Although heaven knows why she went there.'

'For goodness' sake, she was living with the man, wasn't she?'

Lorna couldn't control her irritation and Edwin's eyes widened but he didn't comment on her tone. 'Yes,' he said, 'but Jess told me that Irene had never visited the club before. Brady liked to keep her away from his – business ventures.'

'Mm.'

'But, as I said, Irene entered just as Maurice was leaving. The gossip is that he was drunk. He took hold of her arm and—'

'Brady went berserk. Is that it?'

'It seems he was insanely jealous.'

'He loves her.'

'If a man like that can love.'

'Oh, Edwin, of course he can. Love isn't just for the virtuous, you know.'

'I suppose not. But Irene feels responsible for what happened.'

'She told you that?'

'Yes, I went to see her at the hotel.'

'I see. But she mustn't blame herself for what Jack Brady did.'

Edwin frowned. 'Perhaps I shouldn't say this because I have no proof, but I think there was a previous incident. Something that made Irene believe that she was somehow bound to Jack Brady.'

He paused and then seemed to try to shake off some dreadful memory. 'But to get back to Jess,' he said, 'she told me that Brady had sent for her just before he made himself scarce. He gave her a letter and told her to find Irene and give it to her. Irene had fled the scene of the accident and Brady couldn't exactly go and look for her himself.'

'Let me guess what was in the letter,' Lorna said. 'Mr Brady wanted Irene to meet him somewhere.'

Edwin nodded. 'Jess doesn't know that for sure, but she guessed that was the case. However, when Irene had read the letter, she simply shook her head and said, "Tell him I can't." There were tears in her eyes.'

Lorna was uncomfortable with the concerned expression on Edwin's face, and changed the subject. 'Where do you suppose Mr Brady will go?' she asked. 'I mean, he obviously intends to flee.'

'America, probably,' Edwin replied. 'He'll have taken as much money as he could lay his hands on, and a man like that will always find work of some kind. He's clever enough.'

'But Irene didn't want to go with him,' Lorna said. It wasn't a question.

'No, she didn't.'

'Did she tell you why?'

Edwin looked embarrassed. 'I haven't spoken of the matter to Irene herself. I didn't want to upset her further.'

'No, I don't suppose you did. But did she tell you what she intends to do now? For example, I imagine the police will want to talk to her.'

'She's ready to face them. After all, she has committed no crime, and as for her future, she intends to work in the hotel, where she can also have a room, until the time she can find a position in a good department store or a draper's such as Wilkinson's.'

Edwin smiled for the first time since he had arrived. 'Do you know, I'm sure she would make a success of a job like that. It will be a new and better kind of life for her.'

Lorna looked beyond him to the window. She was surprised to see a gull wheel past, shrieking as it lifted higher into the sky. The greyness had lightened and thinned to allow a pale sunlight to filter through. Without speaking she rose and walked across the room.

'And you will be able to offer help and support to Irene,' Lorna said.

'Of course.'

Lorna moved the net aside and gazed out. She could just see the outline of the lighthouse at the end of the north pier. More gulls screamed as they followed the ghostly outline of a boat coming in to the Tyne. Probably a trawler. Lorna wondered whether they'd been marooned at sea all night. They'd be glad to be home.

'I'm pleased for you, Edwin,' Lorna said.

'Pleased for me?' He sounded surprised.

'Well, in helping Irene, you will find happiness yourself in the process.'

'I'm not sure what you mean.'

'Edwin, I know you love her.'

'But I don't! What made you think that?'

She turned to see him coming towards her. 'Your concern for her welfare.'

'But I was her friend, the concern was natural. I felt responsible.'

'Responsible?'

He paused. 'Well, I started by helping her, but there was a time, perhaps . . . I thought I was attracted to her.'

'*Thought* you were attracted?'

Edwin looked abashed. 'Well,' he smiled, 'I was attracted – just a little. She may have guessed and been encouraged to hope for more than friendship. But I didn't take it any further.'

'Why not?'

'How could I once I had realized that I could never love anyone but you?'

Lorna was aware of the sky behind her lightening even further.

'You love me?'

'With all my heart. Isn't it obvious?'

'No, it has been far from obvious.'

'I would have made it so but I believed you to be in love with someone else.'

'Who?'

'I had no idea. But I sensed that some man had made you unhappy. I think I wanted to do him serious harm!'

'Oh, Edwin. There was someone, but—'

'No, there's no need to tell me. Not now. So long as it's over.'

'It is.'

'And now?'

'I would be very pleased if you would make your feelings obvious.'

They looked at each other and began to smile. The smile turned to laughter, but then Edwin caught his breath and he stepped forward and took her in his arms.

'Lorna,' he murmured and he held her so close that she could feel his heart beating. She clung to him, wordlessly. She was aware of a mounting excitement but, when he took her face gently and turned it towards his, she looked at him solemnly for a moment before raising her lips to accept his kiss.

Eventually she pulled away and she turned in his arms so that she was facing the window. Edwin kept his arms around her waist. She could feel his warm breath on her neck. He began to kiss her neck, moving his mouth up and down. She thought she would swoon with pleasure.

Through half-closed eyes she saw the rays of sunlight break through the clouds and begin to play on the water. Now she could make out the south bank of the river.

And nearer, in her own street, two figures emerged from the dispersing mist and walked in the direction of her house. A man and a woman.

'You haven't said you love me,' Edwin breathed.

'I love you.'

The man and woman came nearer and she thought something about the woman was familiar. She was tall and spare, and decently dressed in a warm but unfashionable coat. Hilda.

The man beside her was not as tall as she was. He was dark and slim and elegant, and he moved with a lithe grace. As they drew nearer he looked up towards the window and she saw his dark, intelligent eyes.

She began to breathe more quickly.

'Lorna,' Edwin said, 'will you marry me?'

She turned and put both her hands in his. Her eyes were shining. 'I think you'd better ask my father.'